According to His Purpose

With Patience Wait

By

Donald Bowers

According to His Purpose

Volume One

With Patience Wait

By Donald Bowers

Copyright 2017

ISBN 978-0-9822901-4-9

TMS Press

Galesburg, IL

Acknowledgments

I'd like to thank my oldest friend Marvin Reem, who encouraged me to take up writing in my late fifties. His latest books are available on Amazon, or at his website, www.wardwagher.com

And

http://www.marvinreem.com/

I also want to thank my merciless editor, designer of the cover, and since November, 2015, my wonderful wife, Ellen Anne Eddy Bowers. Her fiber art books and videos are on the web, and her latest novel, due out shortly, may be previewed at: https://sightunseen2016.wordpress.com

(I can't resist plugging these two fine authors' works!)

Finally, I want to thank all my friends who read this book and its six sequels (so far), offering encouragement, suggestions, and the occasional raspberry. You folks kept me writing, always demanding more, and I thank you.

This is a work of fiction. Names, characters, businesses, places, events and incidents are either the products of the author's imagination or used in a fictitious manner. Any resemblance to actual persons, living or dead, or actual events is purely coincidental. So there!

-Don Bowers, August, 2017

July, 2019: This is the very slightly revised edition. I needed to correct a few points of fictional fact to agree with the rest of the series. The real fun still starts with Chapter 21! DB

Table of Contents

This is the first book in a series, telling the story of those two young people, their friends, and their benefactors, as they are changed, molded, and called according to His purpose.

All things work together for good,
Those are the pieces.
To those called according to God's purpose.
That is the picture.
Whether or not we let God assemble the pieces
Determines whether it will be a picture or a puzzle.
God sees the picture from the beginning,
You won't see it till it's finished,
Don't get lost among the pieces.

-Vance Havner

Introduction

June, 1918.

World War One rages across much of the world, and the United States has finally been drawn into it. In France, the Battle of Belleau Wood forges in blood the history of the modern day United States Marine Corps. That battle also changes forever the lives of two young people, thousands of miles apart, and starts them on the road to a fateful Saturday evening seven years later.

At the same time, a unique couple establish a research and development company in little Galesburg, Illinois, and elsewhere. Their calling reaches far beyond the obvious one of introducing new products to the marketplace. They, and their associates, alter the lives of the two young people and their friends in ways none of them can imagine.

Chapter One

Luther: June 13th, 1918. Bois de Belleau, France.

"Oof!"

I landed on my face in the mud as the last explosion echoed around me. I wasn't sure what had happened. In fact, I couldn't remember how I got here.

Then I remembered. I had just charged a German machine gun position, and I was dying.

As the pain started I remembered.

The sounds around me faded, except for the screaming. I was the one screaming.

As I screamed, the pain welled up and volcanoed through my body. I did not know where I had been hit, I couldn't move any body part. The pain was indescribable, and increased by the second.

I didn't know why I was still conscious. I could do nothing at all to change the situation. I was going to die, and I COULDN'T STOP IT!

Then I heard the Voice. Very quiet, very clear.

"Do I have your attention?"

I stopped screaming.

I knew Who spoke. I'd been running from Him all my life— through school, through the Marine Corps, through this war, down to this battle, and here—

"What now, Luther? You can't save yourself."

I had no strength left to argue. I know, I whispered in my mind.

"Who do you say I am, Luther? Will you trust Me? Let Me save you."

Everything I tried to forget from all those years back in Metamora flashed through my mind. I had always thought I could manage my own life. When the Pastor preached about people not being able to save themselves, I thought he was talking about somebody else, not me. Finally, I realized how utterly helpless I was.

"I hurt worse that day than you do, Luther. Let Me save you."

I was lost in every way I could be as I bled out on the floor of that unspeakable forest. I knew it, and He knew it.

"Come unto Me, and I will give you rest. Do not delay."

My last breath. *Now.*

"Lord, I surrender! Save me, and do with me what You want!"

1

My body still screamed—the parts of it I could feel. But the most incredible peace I have ever felt came over me, infused me, and managed the sensations coming from the body.

I was clinging to the Rock; He was holding me… and all was well.

I faded out.

******

July 24th, 1918, the Trimble home, Fremont Road, Knox County, Illinois.

"It's been six weeks since you heard of Hal's death, Sylvia. You can't just stay in the house forever."

Oh? I think I could, I thought to myself, but didn't dare say it out loud. My mother continued.

"I need to go into Galesburg and get some supplies for the classroom. The weather is nice, and you need to get some air."

"But Ma, I'm getting close to term. What about the baby?" *That was true, and a safe excuse.*

"Women have been having babies since the Creation. They have a pretty smooth ride in there, and both of you will be fine. I'll park near the stores, and what I need isn't far inside. You can relax and enjoy the trip."

I won't do either, but I can't say that. She's got me.

"Yes, Ma."

I really didn't have the energy to argue with her. I guess I have to move on with life…for the baby, if nothing else.

I felt better that day than I had in a couple of weeks, except for a slight headache—probably the weather change. The dull, grinding sorrow and grieving never went away, but people said it would diminish over time. I hoped they were right.

Ma and I left the house on the Fremont Road, and walked out to the garage. As we walked I looked over at the low wooden building on the other side of the fence. Ma had taught at the Wagher School for fifteen of my eighteen years, since Pa had retired from the Marine Corps. I always wanted to teach there when I grew up; now I just didn't care.

When he returned to the Marines Pa left strict instructions for the care and feeding of *The Baby*—our 1914 Chevrolet Baby Grand touring car. I minded the controls while Ma cranked it; it started on the first crank. Ma got in as I moved over, and away we went.

The breeze felt good on my face as I stared out over the uneven fields of corn. I remembered the day Hal and I had driven over to Highland Lake for a picnic, when he told me he had enlisted in the

2

Marines, and asked me to marry him in the same breath. I shouldn't have started thinking about that...I set my jaw, and determined I was not going to cry, even while sitting in the car on the Fremont Road.

We drove into Galesburg, up Main Street, and parked in front of *The Big Store*. Ma marched straight in, and I waddled slowly after. My clothing hid the most obvious parts of my pregnancy, but nothing could mask my unwieldy gait.

After the *Big Store* we moved on to the Star Grocery on the Square.

"I have an idea," Ma said as we put the groceries in the car. "Since we're this close, let's go over and see how Bessie Smiley is. I'm sure Helen would like to see you too."

Bessie was Ma's oldest friend; she'd stood up with Ma when she and Pa were married. In turn Helen had become my closest friend. She was three years younger than me, but I always thought she was just as level-headed as me. She supported me during my time of grieving.

We drove over to West South Street, and parked in front of the modest frame house. Bessie saw us pull up and came out on the porch.

"Annette and Sylvia, I am so glad to see you out! Come on in; I just made some lemonade!"

As we walked into the front room, Helen came from the back of the house, saw us, and grinned. Through an open door I could see her brother Lester reading; he looked up, smiled, and waved at us.

While Ma and Bessie caught up on the latest news from town, Helen and I talked about the pregnancy, and things in general. Helen did not mention anything about Hal or the war; much later she told me she had been very worried about how I was coping with his death, and had been praying that the Lord would bring me through it.

I have to report. He did indeed bring me through it, but not in the way anyone would have expected.

The first incredible stab of pain in the abdomen was so unexpected all I did was get a funny look on my face and take in a gasp of air. The second stab, however, produced the more usual response—a tremendous scream! Helen called it *blood-curdling*.

I toppled over in the love seat, and hung onto the arm of it with all my strength as successive waves of pain enveloped my entire body.

Ma and Bessie went into action.

Ma checked me over quickly. "Do you suppose it's labor?"

3

"I don't think so," Bessie replied, "Those pains start small and build. This started at full strength, and got worse."

"Sylvia's never complains of pain, even when I know it's strong."

"Hospital, 'Nett, right now!"

"Right. Can you call the hospital, and Dr. Bohan, and tell them we're coming in?"

"Will do, 'nett. Helen, Lester, help Annette get Sylvia to the car. Helen, you ride with them to the hospital."

"Yes, Ma!" they chorused. Lester had dropped his book and run out to us at the first scream.

Helen and Lester, along with Ma, carried me out to the car. They levered me into the back seat, and Helen got in and held my head as I lay on the seat.

Over many years of teaching at the Wagher School, Ma had developed a dispassionate, direct way of dealing with emergencies. I knew she'd come home when it was all over and cry, shake, and generally lose control; but never during a crisis. Pa said that was about how it was in the Marines too.

So Ma got us to the Cottage Hospital quickly. I screamed and moaned, eyes closed.

A nurse with flame red hair met us at the door—Gloria Hodges, Head Nurse and Ma's friend. She and other nurses picked me up and carried me into a room right off the main entrance.

I passed out, and when I came to a few minutes later Doctor Bohan, our family doctor, was examining me. Through the pain and fog I noticed he was not smiling.

Helen told me later he came out of the room with a grim expression on his face. Ma asked the questions.

"How bad is it?"

"About as bad as it gets, Mrs. Mates. I am pretty sure Sylvia has Preeclampsia, also called Toxemia, and could be developing a general sepsis, or overall infection of the body. We're going to have to operate, and do it now."

"How could this come on so quickly?" Ma asked.

"This could have been building for weeks, even months, with no outward symptoms. Did she complain of anything unusual today?"

"She mentioned she didn't have much energy, but she's been like that since she got the news about Hal."

"Yes, I was so sorry to hear about that."

Ma continued, "Come to think of it, she did complain of a headache this morning. She thought it was the weather changing."

4

"Not this time, I'm afraid. I won't hide it from you, Mrs. Mates; she could die."

"I know she knows the Lord, and she's prepared if He takes her home. That's the best preparation I know of."

Helen said at this point Doctor Bohan bowed his head and made the sign of the cross. I learned later he was Catholic, and did that when under great stress.

He raised his head. "All right, we need to go tell her what must happen, then she needs to be prepared and sent to the operating theatre. We cannot delay a minute!"

Ma and Dr. Bohan, and Helen, entered the room. I was gritting my teeth through the pain, but at least I had stopped screaming.

Ma spoke. "Dear, Dr. Bohan says you have developed a severe infection, and he has to operate immediately. The operation should relieve your pain. Do you understand me?"

I nodded, my eyes barely open to see the group before me. I knew the answer to my one question, but had to ask it anyway.

"The…baby?"

The two shook their heads. "Probably not."

Through my pain I began to weep. I was still weeping when the red-haired nurse put the ether mask over my face, and I faded out.

Chapter Two

Luther: Base Hospital Number Eighteen, Bazoilles-sur-Meuse, France.

Well, this is interesting...

I slowly returned to consciousness, each sense reporting in as my awareness grew. Hearing came first, then gradually I could feel things around my head, and the rest of my body. It felt like I was encased in cloth—bandages!

After a time I seemed to be able to think a little. I determined my eyes were closed, but light seemed to be shining through my eyelids.

Perhaps I should open my eyes....but what would I see?

That question brought to my mind what I had done the last time I was awake. I remembered—I am not my own, now I am bought with a price! *Thank you Lord....*

I could remember nothing else of what had brought me to wherever I was. *Somewhere...but not Heaven yet.*

While I thought I could stay like I was, with that thought, for some time, a voice intruded on my reverie.

"He's moving a bit—I think he's coming around." Again, closer to my ear, "Luther, if you can hear me open your eyes, or move something."

I decided to take the voice up on his invitation, and opened my eyes.

I saw a whitewashed room with a high ceiling. A single light bulb hung from a wire above my bed; others hung over other beds in the room. A middle-aged man with slicked back black hair turning gray, and stubble on his face bent over me; his white coat showed several red stains of varying freshness.

"Well, hello there, Sergeant! We're sure glad to have you back!"

"Hello to you—is it doctor?" I whispered, "If I'm back, where have I been?"

"I'm Doctor Bill Raichart. Where you've been, Sergeant, is as close to the Vale of Death as anyone I've ever seen survive. You still aren't out of danger, but we consider it a major miracle in the literal sense you've made it this far!"

I was falling back asleep, but I wanted to answer. "I agree with your assessment, Doctor. Perhaps the Lord has some use for me other than fertilizer."

"I hope to think so, Sergeant! Anyway, I see you are getting tired. That's going to happen as you continue to heal. Your recovery is going to take a long time."

"That's fine Doc, I have time…now. Ask you later about my…..condition."

"Of course, Sergeant….."

I was already asleep.

******

Sylvia: The Cottage Hospital, Galesburg, Illinois.

I felt like I was swimming in a pool of *something*. Each breath felt like I was sucking in syrup. I could hear sounds, voices, but not clearly. I couldn't open my eyes, but I could feel a bit of wind on my face, maybe from a fan.

As I slowly woke up I remembered more—going shopping, stopping at Smiley's. I winced involuntarily as I remembered the incredible pain that hit me while we were in the Smiley house. I vaguely remembered being carried into a room, and Doctor Bohan examining me. And then...

My eyes snapped open. I lay in a whitewashed room, with two light bulbs on a cord hanging halfway down from the ceiling. I saw an open window, and from the light I knew it was either dusk, or dawn.

I looked down at my body. It seemed much smaller, even covered with a blanket. My skin felt cool, so there was a sheet in there someplace. I felt a dull ache in my lower abdomen, and a funny tickle from time to time somewhere I couldn't place; nothing like the pain I felt when I was brought in.

"Oh, she's awake!" I recognized the voice.

A stocky young woman with dark hair and reddened eyes came into my field of vision. "Helen," was all I could croak out.

"You're back! We've all been praying so hard—"

"Where was I?"

"Do you remember why you're here?"

I started to fall back to sleep. "I got sick?"

"You had an operation. Actually, you've had three operations. Every time they'd get you back in the room to recover, something else would go wrong and they'd have to haul you back to the operating theatre!"

I was glad I didn't remember any of that. I could barely respond.

7

"How long…out?"

"Seven days and an afternoon, all told. You gave us quite a scare!"

I was almost asleep, but had to say one more thing. "Thanks…for staying."

"It wasn't just me, Syl! Somebody has been here around the clock since the first day-they put a day bed in your room for us. Your Ma, my Ma, some of the ladies from your church, your Pastor's wife-about all your friends. I just happened to pull the duty this evening."

Helen told me later what she'd said. I was out from about the third word.

*****

Luther: Base Hospital Number Eighteen, Bazoilles-sur-Meuse, France.

"Okay, Doc, I guess I'm ready to hear how much of me is left."

Even though it was now over a month since I was wounded, I had never asked for an explanation of my injuries. I was content to sleep the days away, only bothered by feeding, bed-baths, and the orderlies attending to my hygiene. So far, I hadn't even had the strength to sit up; I had been assured this was normal for someone with the injuries I had, whatever they were.

Since the sheet seemed to be pretty flat where my right lower leg ought to have been, I figured it had parted company somewhere along the line. Oddly enough, that really didn't concern me—I was beginning to realize the Lord really did have His hand on my life, and the different arrangements were going to be part of that.

Now Dr. Raichart was sitting by the side of my bed, and it was time for an accounting.

"Are you up to hearing this now, Luther? Some men tend to lose it when they hear the extent of their injuries"

"I think so, Doctor. I've already figured out about my leg; if I don't have to look at any of the other wounds just yet, I should be OK."

Doctor Raichart nodded, and looked down at his clipboard.

"All right, here goes. I can tell you your head, face, and mind are in first class shape—you know that already. I can also tell you that you shouldn't have any problem at all becoming a father, if you know what I mean."

I chuckled, then grimaced as a stray pain passed through my chest, heading south.

"Stray pain?"

I nodded.

"Figured. That's going to happen every so often as your internal organs get settled down after all the work we had to do on them. Speaking of that...you took a real load of shrapnel from exploding grenades, all over your body. Some appeared to be from German grenades—we can tell from the fragments—and some from American, probably the ones you threw, especially that last one. Plus five bullets in various and sundry places."

I didn't remember any of it, but said the only thing I could think of. "Wow."

"Wow is right. When you first woke up I said you were closer to death than anyone I've seen here who survived. I meant that. I can't account for your survival in any medical way, but here you are!"

"I think I know why, Doctor...my Savior wanted me to live. Since I'm His now, He makes that call."

"Yes, well, all right, Sergeant," Doctor Raichart said, and fell silent.

With that line of discussion temporarily stopped, another thought came to me.

"If I was so bad off, why did they even try to save me?"

"I asked the Doc at the aid station about that. He said you were still breathing, and had the gentlest expression on your face he'd seen in months at the front, and he just felt compelled to try. And so you're here."

"So I am. Is anything else missing, besides the leg?"

"No, everything is still there. The most amazing thing is the lack of infection in the wounds—just a bit. You'll still be recovering for several months. Later we'll see about a prosthesis. You've still got your knee, which makes a prosthesis much easier to fit and use. People might not even notice you have one."

I was starting to fade again, but I had one more question for the Doctor.

"One last question, Doc. Is this the end of me being a Marine?"

The doctor folded his arms and stared straight at me.

"Son, I'm just a jumped-up bone doctor, but I've learned a few things since I came here. I'm sure you'll be retired with disability after you complete your convalescence and get your prosthesis. You may not be on active duty, but you will always be a Marine. When a Marine says 'Semper Fi', he means it!"

9

"Thanks for telling me, and everything you've done, Doc."

"An honor, and a pleasure, Sergeant."

I wondered why he worded it that way.

Chapter Three

Luther: Base Hospital Number Eighteen, Bazoilles-sur-Meuse, France.

"Lying down on the job, again, I see…"

I opened my eyes to see a familiar face. "Jack!"

"Glad to see you still remember my name, Luther."

I couldn't remember a time when I didn't know Jack Sewell. We went through school together in Metamora, and graduated in 1914. We thought about what we should do after High School—or rather, I thought and he prayed about it—and we both decided to join the Marines. We figured the big war that started in Europe that summer was going to drag us in sooner or later, and we decided we wanted to be prepared before it happened, in the best military organization we knew of.

We managed to survive Marine Boot Camp, and ended up in the Marine detachment of the armored cruiser *Washington* on the China Station for almost three years. We enjoyed Corps life, and thought we might make a career of it. Then the war finally got to us, and over to France we went.

The last time I'd seen Jack was when I picked him up off the battlefield and carried him back to the aid station. He was bleeding heavily, and only about half conscious when I got him to the corpsman at the station. As I turned to go back to the front I heard him croak out, "I'll pray for you Luther." I knew what he meant. I ran back to the front, and away from my best friend's prayers for my salvation.

I looked over at Jack. He looked pretty good, except for sitting in a wheelchair with a big cast on his leg. I knew what I had to tell him, and I didn't know how much time I had before I fell back asleep.

"Jack, I have to tell you something."

"What, Luther?"

"He finally got my attention."

"He? Who—oh." Jack grinned.

"I knew you were a quick study. I should have been dead before I hit the ground, but I wasn't. Then the pain came on, and I wished I were dead, but I really didn't. I couldn't move, couldn't yell for help, couldn't do anything except lie there and die."

"It must have been horrible"

"It was. Then, He spoke…"

Jack nodded.

"And I surrendered. I asked Jesus to save me, and do with me what He would."

Jack said nothing. Tears started to well up in his eyes, and he took a handkerchief out of the pocket of his robe.

I started to cry too. Two tough, battle-hardened Marines, crying like babies. Not a word from anyone else in the ward, though; they knew the score.

Jack handed me a couple of tissues from the box on the bedside table, and eventually we got the waterworks turned off.
"So now what?"

My eyelids started to droop. "Keep healing, I guess…and figure out what the Lord wants to do with the rest of my life."

"Sounds like a good idea. Here's something to help you with that." He reached to the side of his wheelchair and pulled out a book with a green cover. "The American Bible Society came through last week. They usually give out New Testaments, but I talked them into giving me a complete Bible." He handed it to me.

I put it on my chest. "Thanks, Jack. I haven't had much energy to think about this since I got here." I was starting to fade out again.

"I understand, Luther. Went through it myself, but not as bad as you. Get some rest now. I'm in the ward across the main corridor, when you're finally able to get around. I'll be back here, too."

"Much obliged, Jack,"

"I should say that to you, Luther! If you hadn't brought me in I'd have bled to death. I guess the Lord still wants us around for some reason."

"Yeah." And I faded out again.

*****

Sylvia: The Cottage Hospital.

After I woke up and saw Helen, it was another two weeks before I could sit up in bed for more than five minutes at a time. Those few minutes were spent getting food into me; I was usually asleep when the nurses bathed me and tended to other hygiene needs. A word or two to the nurses, or one of my visitors, was all I could manage between bites of soft, easy to swallow food.

About a month after my arrival, Dr. Bohan decided I was strong enough to hear what had happened. With me again that hot

Saturday afternoon in late August were Ma and Helen Smiley. They pulled up chairs around my bed, as did Dr. Bohan. It was a pretty somber group.

Ma spoke first. "Sylvia, I know it's not something you really want to hear about, but you need to know something of what's happened to you this past month. I've asked Dr. Bohan to explain things. Is that OK with you?"

I figured I didn't have a choice, but I put a brave face on it. "Sure, Ma. Please go ahead, Doctor."

"Thank you ladies. Sylvia, when you came here you were suffering from acute Preeclampsia, a severe infection which sometimes happens during or right after pregnancy. It had been gradually getting worse over several weeks, but didn't show any symptoms until that afternoon. We knew you were very sick, and we needed to operate to find out how far the infection had spread, and remove it. Do you remember your mother telling you that?"

"Oh, yes, " I spoke softly. "I also asked a question, even though I knew what the answer was going to be."

"Yes, you did, and unfortunately that is how it turned out. I'm sorry, Sylvia."

"I understand, Doctor. I did my grieving quickly, before I went under. What about the rest?"

"You had three operations. The first one, we went in and cleared out the infected tissue we found. That resulted in a total hysterectomy, as well as removal of connective tissue and small parts of several other organs that were involved."

I spoke quietly. "So I am now unable to have children."

"That is correct. Let me add, if I may be blunt, that your ability to engage in...*conjugal relations*...will be unaffected in any way as a result of this surgery."

Normally Helen and I would have giggled at the euphemism; not that day.

"I understand, Doctor, although that's about the farthest thing from my mind at the moment."
"Of course, but I felt you needed to know."

"So I did. What were the other two surgeries?"

Doctor Bohan took a breath, and continued. "The first one was a bleeding that showed up in the middle of the first night after the surgery. The nurses caught it quickly, and I came back in to fix it. Then, two days later, you started grimacing and writhing, even though you were unconscious. We knew something was wrong, and I suspected it was the gall bladder. I guessed right, and while we were in there I checked your appendix, and it was inflamed too.

13

Those two spots seem to attract any infection that is floating around in the body. Well, they won't any more!"

I nodded. "Thanks, Doctor. I am so sorry to be such a burden."

"You are no burden, Sylvia! You were just about as sick as you could be, but you have survived. You should also know that your friends, and people in several churches, were praying for your recovery. I think I'm a good surgeon, but in cases like yours I'm reminded how little I do, and how much He does."

I didn't know what to say to that, so I kept quiet.

Ma spoke. "So what's next, Doctor?"

Dr. Bohan scratched his head, then looked at me. "I think you need to stay here at least until you can stand and walk to the bathroom by yourself. Your body is still fighting off the remains of the infection, and you will gain strength slowly. I wish we could give you some medication to speed up the process, but I don't have one, not now. When you do go home, I predict you'll be taking naps and reading books as you get your strength back."

I was starting to get tired, but I managed a laugh. "I think I can manage those two activities for a while!"

"Good. Well, ladies, I have to git." Dr. Bohan stood up. "I am confident with your mother and your friends to help you, you will recover completely. So just rest, relax, and let nature take its course."

We all chorused our thank-yous to Dr. Bohan, and he stepped out of the room.

"Syl," Ma said, "I need to take Helen home, and then get over to the school. We start in a week, and I have more things to do than I have time to do them in. I'll be back tomorrow afternoon. Oh, and I brought your Bible; it's in the nightstand drawer."

"OK Ma. See you later. Bye, Helen."

They both waved and left the room.

I closed my eyes and the tears came. Not for the last time, I cried myself to sleep.

Chapter Four

Luther: Base Hospital Number Eighteen, Bazoilles-sur-Meuse, France.

"Okay, on the count of three, up and into the chair. One, two...."

Two strong orderlies had me, one on each side. They were set to help me rise from the bed for the first time in almost three months! Dr. Raichart had finally decreed I could be up in a wheelchair for a little while, and decided I could try standing and pivoting on my left leg to go from bed to chair. Jack Sewell was watching the proceedings from his wheelchair; he had someplace he wanted to take me, and had convinced the orderlies to transfer me to the—

"Three!"

—wheelchair.

I rose from the bed and landed in the wheelchair cushions with one graceful motion—graceful for the orderlies, that is! My foot touched the ground, but I didn't bear any weight on it at all.

"Thank you, gentlemen." I said to the orderlies. They nodded, made sure I was covered with a blanket, and began pushing Jack and me down toward the door of the ward.

"Where are you taking me, Jack?"

"I thought maybe it was time to see a little more of this place than the ceiling and a light bulb."

I thought for a moment. "You know, I've never asked anyone where I am. I figured this was a nice enough place for a hospital, and wasn't Heaven, but hadn't thought any farther."

Jack laughed. "You always did talk about *need to know*! Now you need to know. You are in Base Hospital Number Eighteen, in a place with the unlikely name of *Bazoilles-sur-Meuse*, France. All the doctors and most of the staff volunteered to come over here from Johns Hopkins Hospital in Baltimore."

"I've actually seen that name on a map, Jack. Up to the northeast of Paris. I guess the Huns never quite made it this far."

"Nope. I hear the fighting's still awful, but they are retreating across the board. Nothing we have to worry about, though."

"That's for sure."

We came to a set of double doors. The orderlies pushed us through, then brought us toward a rough stage set up at the front of a large hall. Men and women were on the stage setting up musical instruments.

"An orchestra, Jack?"

"Yep.

"Which one?"

"I figured the *musician* would ask. The *"Orchestre de la concerts du Conservatore"*. That'd be a mouthful even if I could pronounce French words right!"

"I suppose you'd be surprised if I told you I've heard them before."

"Nope. Not from the guy who spent his precious liberty passes going to listen to that organ in Saint Whatever's."

"*Sulpice*, Saint Sulpice church in Paris. You're beginning to sound like a musical Philistine!"

"I didn't think the Philistines had music, just giants."

"Actually, Jack, I think they were also astronomers, and the Israelites were the surgeons."

"I know I'm going to regret asking, but how's that?"

"Simple. Goliath saw stars just before David amputated his head."

Jack groaned loud enough for one of the orderlies in the area to walk over toward us. "Never mind, Private, that wasn't medical— just the reaction to a bad joke!"

The orderly walked away, shaking his head.

"You don't want to upset the orderlies, Jack," I whispered. "They might forget to give you the bedpan."

Jack groaned again, this time quietly.

It had been a very long time since I felt like joking around with Jack, or anyone else. Perhaps I was finally starting to heal.

While we were mangling Biblical history, the orchestra finished setting up, and were starting to tune. They had also wheeled out a tired-looking grand piano. There were no programs, but I figured someone would tell us as it came.

Several hundred men packed the large hall, almost all of them in wheelchairs. Except for Jack, I didn't recognize anyone, nor could I tell what service or even what country they were from. A hospital is a great equalizer, I guess.

A civilian with a baton appeared. I recognized him as the conductor, Andre Messager. With him was an Army Major. The men quieted.

The conductor spoke French, which the Major translated into English. He said the orchestra was headed to the United States for a concert tour the next week, and wanted to play for us before they left. They were going to play two works, both of which I knew and liked—the Schumann Piano Concerto, and Cesar Franck's Symphony in D Minor.

As they spoke, a younger man came out to stand with them. I recognized him as the pianist Alfred Cortot, who I had heard with the orchestra in Paris. He seemed a bit like an overwound pocket watch to me, maybe because of his prominent and staring eyes.

They finished speaking, those of us who could clapped, and the concert began. I have to admit I dozed off during the slow movement of the Schumann, but popped awake for the last movement. I always enjoy keyboard pyrotechnics, and Cortot did not disappoint.

During the break between pieces Jack whispered to me, "How's the Bible reading coming along?"

"You know, it's the most amazing thing. I used to read the Bible, memorized what I had to, and all that, and it was just another book, and a boring one at that. But now, I start reading, and I just don't want to put it down! Things are making sense that never made sense before."

"You know why, don't you Luther?"

"Oh yes, I do. Makes a difference to know the Author."

"You got it, Sarge!"

At that point Andre Messager came back to the platform, and they began the Franck. I've always loved that symphony; in fact, I think it is my favorite. It always seems to turn up at critical points in my life…but that is another story for another time.

The grand last movement ended, and we all clapped as vigorously as we could. The orderlies reappeared to take us back to the wards.

"Hey, Jack, thanks a bunch for bringing me along to this concert." I was beginning to notice how tired I was.

"Glad to do it, Luther. Best afternoon nap I've had in a month." He grinned, but looked like I felt.

"Right."

*****

Sylvia: Saturday, September 21st, 1918, the Cottage Hospital.

I walked back from the bathroom into my room, leaning on Helen's arm. This was the third trip there and back that day. Each time I was exhausted, but it would be a much shorter walk when I got home. After two months, this was heartening progress.

Ma was sitting by my bed. She had a letter in her hand, and a smile on her face.

"Syl, we got a letter from your father today, and I hurried right over to read it to you!"

"Great! Let me sit down before you start."

Helen guided me to the bed, and I sat down heavily.

"I'll leave the room if you'd like—"

"No, no, Helen, stay right here! You're part of this family too," Ma said.

Helen blushed; she really didn't expect to be adopted right then!

"OK Ma, I'm settled now."

Ma unfolded the letter. "Here we go."

"Dear 'Nett and Syl, I finally have a few minutes to write you. I have enjoyed all the news in your letters recently. Syl, I am so thankful to the Lord you survived that illness, even though it carried its own sorrow with it. The Lord definitely preserved your life for some purpose, and I pray He'll show you what it is in His timing. He knows what is best for us, all of us, and if we don't understand now, we surely will when we get Home."

Ma paused a moment to catch her breath, and compose herself.

"I'm having more fun doing this job here than I ever had in my *first* career! I have an opportunity to help make men into Marines, and for some reason I guess I'm doing it like they want. I should've volunteered for Drill Instructor duty back in my active days. These young whipper-snappers think a guy nearing 60 won't be able to out-march them....heh. Marching and drill I can do, just don't ask me to do any running!"

"I'm glad his malaria hasn't relapsed," Ma said, then continued.

"We're getting a pretty good quality of boys in here now. The recruiters have tightened the requirements down to where they should be, and it shows. Some of these boys know the Lord, but many don't. I make it clear I'm available if any of them want to talk about it—and some do. They know more about what they're heading into now, and that makes 'em think."

I saw Ma glance at the next paragraph, and frown.

"We've had people here getting sick with some sort of illness the last couple weeks. Looks to be pretty nasty if you get it. I pray I don't. I'd like to come home when this thing is over...but I have to remember that is up to the Lord. Plenty of times in my career He could have called me Home, especially when I got malaria in the Philippines, but He didn't. So we'll see what He does."

"'Nett, if I remember right, you've been in school about a week already. I hope the young'uns listen up and learn well! Philip

Wagher and the men on the board will support you in whatever you need to do there. Don't be afraid to ask for something if you need it. Young Fred Johnson and his wife look like they'll be first class helpers for Philip—he's not getting any younger!"

"He's moving slower than he used to," Ma remarked, then read on.

"Sounds like my boys are getting a bit rambunctious out in the barracks, so guess it is time to close this, put on my campaign hat, and go have some fun! I love you both very much. Give my love to Bessie, Helen, and Lester-and yes, to L.M. too—the old grump!! Semper Fi, Bill"

"Daddy's not an old grump!" Helen said with a big grin.

Chapter Five

Sylvia: October, 1918, the Cottage Hospital.

The day I thought would never come was here! After three months in the hospital I was finally going home. I felt like I had spent half my life in that hospital room. I had finally proved I could get from the bed to the chair, and from there to the bathroom and back, without assist. I still had to watch out that I didn't run out of strength somewhere in between those three places, but within my limits I was functioning again.

This Saturday a full contingent came to see me off. Ma was there, of course; Bessie and Helen Smiley also stood by to help carry things, including me if needed. And the final member of the cast walked into the room as I was daydreaming.

"Well, are you ready to finally get out of this hospital?" Dr. Bohan asked.

"I think you could safely say that, Doctor." I replied with just a hint of irony.

"Good. You've been a fine patient, but I think we're ready to get rid of you too." He smiled, and turned to Ma. "I want to go down the list of instructions for Sylvia's convalescence with you."

At that moment we heard muffled voices; I recognized the voice of Gloria Hodges, the head nurse.

A tall, thin man entered the room. He was wearing a Marine Dress Blue uniform, and the gold oak leaves of a Major. Four rows of ribbons on his tunic marked him as someone who had been busy.

Ma looked up at the man, and the color drained from her cheeks. I didn't understand why she reacted like that; then I realized a Marine Major in dress uniform did not make social calls in Illinois.

The Major spoke, "Pardon me, but is there a Barbara Annette Mates here?"

Nobody ever called Ma by her first name; she purely hated it. Unless…

"I am she, Major."

"Ma'am, I am Major William Heidner. I am the Commanding Officer of the Marine Recruiting District in this area. I have been asked to deliver this letter to you, and answer any questions I can." He held out an envelope.

Ma took the envelope. Although she looked very pale, she showed no other emotion as she sat down on the bed and opened the letter. She began to read aloud.

"It is with deep regret that I am writing to inform you of the death of your husband, Gunnery Sergeant William P. Mates...."

She trailed off, and just stared out.

Helen began to sob softly; then Bessie began the same. I just sat in the chair, unmoving; Helen told me later I had the most emotionless look on my face she had ever seen. We all seemed frozen where we sat or stood. The Major stood ramrod straight, yet a course of tears ran down his face.

Dr. Bohan stepped over and gently took the paper from Ma's hand. He read it quickly, then turned to the officer.

"Major, were you aware of the contents of this letter?"

"Yes sir, I typed it myself from the telegram I received."

"Cause of death is what appears to be this new type of influenza?"

"So it appears, sir."

"Have you been exposed to this disease yet?"

"No, sir, but frankly I expect to be any time now. Too many men are coming home from Europe either having it, were exposed to those who have it. I have heard the disease is spreading quickly."

"So have I, Major. I have some contacts out east, and they have been keeping me informed as best they can, considering nobody really knows what this disease is capable of, or where it is going to end."

"We're in trouble, Doctor."

"You can say that again, Major. Can you wait outside while I have a few words with the family here? I need to pick your brain a little more, if I may."

"Of course, sir. I'll be right outside."

"Thanks," Doctor Bohan said, and the Major eased out the door.

Doctor Bohan turned back to face us. All of us were reacting in one way or another to the news we had just received. He took a deep breath. Took another breath, and made the sign of the cross. I had forgotten he was Catholic; while I didn't accept the religious basis for that action, I certainly shared the emotion that action represented.

We were in trouble.

"Annette, Sylvia, I am as sorry as I can be for you. I cannot adequately express my grief at your loss...but we need to act for the living, now, right now."

Ma turned her head and looked at the doctor, and sighed once. "Thank you, John, for reminding me. I will go back to grieving later."

All I could do was look at the doctor and nod.

"Thank you, ladies. I know this is difficult, but we have to move on, and this changes what I'm going to tell you."

He looked up and stared out the window at Seminary Street for a moment. A train sounded its whistle on the Santa Fe as it moved through town. "Funny how those little things seem magnified at a time like this," Doctor Bohan said quietly. Then he turned to face us.

"Sylvia, you need to go home today as planned. I can just about guarantee within two weeks we're going to need every bed in this hospital, and then some, to start caring for patients with this influenza. They're coming, sure as I'm standing here, and in carload lots."

We both nodded.

"Next, I want you to take precautions against getting this disease. From what I've read, nobody knows what this disease really is, can't even decide if it is a virus, bacteria, or something new. When we're faced with something this unknown, all we can do is make some educated guesses, and act on them. My *educated guesser*—he grinned fleetingly—tells me this is a virus instead of a bacteria. Not that it matters, since we don't have anything to help the body kill either one."

He definitely had our complete attention.

"I'm also guessing the primary disease is an influenza, and it either kills directly, or sets a body up for invasion by something else, pneumonia or whatever, and that kills. Either way, the less you're exposed to one of these bugs, the better your chances."

Again we all nodded.

"So, Sylvia, once you get home, I want you to stay there. You're going to be doing that anyway, since you've got to get your strength back; this means you resist the temptation to just make a little call somewhere close. And that means no visitors, except the people in this room, and maybe your Pastor—who is that, by the way, I want to talk to him about this influenza and precautions."

"Sylvester Sanford is handling it while our Pastor is away in the Navy."

"Ah, OK, I know him, 'nett. I'll talk to him about this, and how to support you two."

"What about the funeral?" I asked.

"The letter says they are interring Bill there at Parris Island for the time being. It would probably be best if you just had a memorial wake, er, service for him now, and have him buried around here later—the Marines will ship the body when you're ready. And Sylvia," he turned to me, "I wouldn't attend the service, or any services, for the time being. You're too weak, and we need to limit your exposure to the influenza."

"What about me, Doctor?" Ma asked, "I teach school; I get exposed to every little sniffle in a three mile radius. Won't I just bring it all home to her?"

Dr. Bohan stared out the window again for a moment.

"Yes, you will. There's nothing we can do about that exposure. If—no, when—the influenza starts popping up you need to close the school for a while. Individual farms may need to be quarantined; that'll be up to the County Board to decide. I'll talk to my fellow doctors, and start trying to set things up around here. Too much to do, no time I'm afraid."

Ma was back to her usual practical thinking. "Is there anything else we need to do to slow the spread of the disease?"

"Yes. Assuming this is a virus, masks won't do any good; viruses blow right through them if someone sneezes, or even breathes. What will help is *rubber gloves*. If you sterilize them between each use, they'll go a long way to prevent the spread of viruses, and bacteria too. I'll have Gloria give you a few pair, and a bottle of Carbolic Acid to sterilize them with. Read the instructions on the bottle, and be careful; that stuff can kill you if you aren't careful, never mind the influenza!"

I stifled a giggle at that—a good sign. Doctor Bohan continued.

"I suggest you have a couple pair in the classroom, in case you have a student get sick while they're there, or you have to clean up...you know."

Ma quirked a little smile at that, the only smile I was to see for the next week.

"Wash your hands carefully with good soap before and after cooking, giving personal care to someone, and after using the bathroom. You would not believe how much sickness just that one thing will prevent! Contact me anytime with questions, and if one of you gets sick get in here. And ladies—if one of you is away and the other gets sick, do not come to visit! Once they are being treated, stay away until I send word it is safe to come visit. Now, do you understand all this?"

The four of us nodded our heads.

"Very well. Syl, let's get you out of here. I have some other people I need to see, starting with that Major in the hallway."

Chapter Six

Luther: Base Hospital Eighteen, France.

September, 1918 in France reminded me of September in central Illinois—hot, dry and interminable. Not much breeze wafted through the open windows, and what there was smelled like the back end of a horse…on a good day. I gradually became more active as the month progressed. By the end of the month I was close to being able to stand on my leg and put myself where I wanted to sit. I hoped that would get easier when I got my prosthesis.

I was finally able to write and receive letters with only the censor to stand in my way. My Pa was told when I was wounded, of course, and an orderly had written a couple of brief letters for me, but now the floodgate of communication opened—sort of. My Pa wrote many things for his business, but hated to write letters. Since Ma had passed twelve years before, I doubt if he had written more than a dozen letters total until I went overseas, and maybe another four since. That was just his way.

*****

Luther: September 30th, 1918, Base Hospital Eighteen

About 9 o'clock on a brilliantly sunny Monday morning I was sitting in my wheelchair (I spent enough time in it to think of it as mine, anyway) reading my Bible, when two orderlies I did not recognize approached me.

"Pardon me, but are you Sergeant Luther Barlow, United States Marines?"

"Yes, I am, Private. How may I help you today?"

"Sergeant, we have been asked to take you and several others to a meeting with the Commanding Officer of the hospital."

This was interesting. "Of course I'll come with you, Private, but as you see I'm not really dressed for a meeting with the C.O."

"Sergeant, with all due respect I don't think that will be a problem with Colonel Finney. May we take you to the meeting?"

"Of course, Private. Lead on!"

I wanted to add *MacDuff* to the end of that sentence, but I didn't know if these fellows had that kind of a sense of humor. I tucked my Bible into the side of the chair cushion as we moved off.

Four bewildered gentlemen in wheelchairs gathered in the outer office of the Commanding Officer of Base Hospital 18. We introduced around and found we were all Marines, except for a Navy Pharmacist's Mate who had been attached to the Marines. We had all been in that hospital since the battle of June, 1918, now called the Battle of Belleau Wood. Each of us had had a difficult time of recovery, and were going to head back to the States soon for rehabilitation. I appeared to be senior, not that it mattered.

Shortly the Colonel's first, or *top*, sergeant came out of the inner office, and we were wheeled in.

I found out later Colonel John Finney had been head of the Johns Hopkins Department of Surgery since it opened years before. He had offered to come over here with a volunteer staff to run this hospital, and by all accounts had done a masterful job. Why he wanted to see us we had no clue.

He shook our hands. "Thank you, gentlemen, for coming in at such short notice. Don't worry about how you look; this is a hospital, not a parade ground!"

He looked down at a yellow tablet and several file folders on his desk.

"Let's see, we have here Sergeant Barlow, Corporal Steffen, Lance Corporal Dykstra, and Pharmacist's Mate Third Class Folkerts, is that right?"

We all nodded.

"Which one of you is Sergeant Barlow?"

"I am, Sir."

It looks like you're senior in this little band, Sergeant; you're now in charge."

"Yes, Sir." *In charge of what?* I wondered.

"Now that that's out of the way, let me get down to why I asked you four in here. It seems Marine Corps Headquarters in Washington wants you back there ASAP. *There* means Walter Reed, of course. They haven't told me why, but GHQ Marines usually knows what they are doing. In the case of two of you, at least part of it has to be a prosthesis, but I digress."

We four just sat and stared at the Colonel, who continued.

"The Marines have arranged for your passage back to the States in a warship instead of the usual troopship. Considering how fragile you gentlemen are at the moment, I think that is a good idea. Also, you may have heard about the influenza that is sweeping through Europe and starting to affect the States. That disease has me very concerned, and I'm in favor of any way we can lessen your exposure."

The colonel's recitation reminded me of some I'd heard from our company officers, but this time the outcome would be much more pleasant.

"All that is unusual, but doesn't rate a visit to me. What is highly unusual is the method the Navy proposes to get you to Le Havre, where they tell me the cruiser or whatever is going to be. This part of the proposal is completely voluntary on your part. There is some risk involved, but if all goes well you will get to Le Havre in about a fifth the time a hospital train would take, and side-step a lot of pain and discomfort from riding on those awful French railways! It will also be an adventure of the sort you can tell your grandchildren about."

I'm sure we each had different measures of apprehension in our minds, but no one was interested in interrupting a Colonel in mid-performance. Colonel Finney scratched his head, glanced out the window to his right, and continued.

"I guess I'd better spill it. Late this afternoon a British Royal Naval Air Service airship is due to arrive on that parade ground out there," he pointed out the window. "Weather permitting, it will leave tomorrow morning for the channel—and you will be on it, if you want!"

Three of us just stared open-mouthed at Colonel Finney. The fourth frowned and spoke.

"Colonel, with all due respect, Sir, I respectfully request to be excused from this trip. I am terrified of anything having to do with flight, and I have resolved never to go up in any aeroplane or balloon under any circumstances."

"In that case you are certainly excused, er…"

"Lance Corporal Arthur Dykstra, Sir."

"Very well, Lance Corporal, you are dismissed."

"Thank you, Sir!"

Colonel Finney nodded. "TOP!"

The Top Sergeant stuck his head in the door. "Yes, Sir?"

"Please have Lance Corporal Dykstra returned to his ward. Then come back in here. We have to find another victim, er, volunteer."

"Right away, Sir." The First Sergeant's right eyebrow raised slightly before he took charge of Dykstra's wheelchair and maneuvered him out of the room.

When they had gone, Colonel Finney grinned again. "Don't pay any mind to my last statement there; I just couldn't resist pulling Top's chain!" He snorted once, and then composed himself.

"While we're waiting for Top, do any of you know of someone from your unit in the Hospital who might profit from taking this little jaunt?"

I spoke up for Jack. "Sir, one of the Corporals from my squad is here also. His leg is having trouble healing, and it might be good to get him back to the States to have it looked at."

The Colonel nodded. "What's his name?"

"Corporal Andrew Jackson Sewell, Sir. Ward H-7."

"A friend?"

"My oldest friend, Sir. We enlisted together." The First Sergeant stepped back in as I was speaking.

"Hmmm…" Colonel Finney looked on the yellow paper again, then shuffled through the file folders. "Let's see if he's already in the pile here…All right, I see that name, but he's a Sergeant since 01 September." The Colonel looked at me and winked, "If we don't tell him he could have a little surprise come payday."

This officer's sense of humor was almost as dry as Jack's.

"Let me see here…diagnosis is OK….confirmed problems with the leg...All right, looks like he'll do. Top, please have Sergeant Sewell brought here."

"At once, Sir!"

The First Sergeant spun on his heel and strode out of the office.

*****

Luther: October 1ˢᵗ,1918, 0630, the parade ground, Base Hospital Eighteen.

"I told Wilbur, and I told Orville, that contraption would never get off the ground! And you expect me to just climb in it and go flying??"

Jack was in rare form as we were being wheeled toward the very large, very unwieldy-looking craft resting on the parade ground.

"Congratulations, Jack, you just made that ancient joke sound fresh again!"

"Thanks, Luther. Most people who use that line don't have the *actual fact* sitting there on the ground in front of them!"

The *actual fact* in question stretched over half the parade ground, and looked like an elongated, overstuffed sausage. On the tail was a British Roundel, and on the side in huge letters *NS 8*. At least two dozen men held ropes attached to the airship and kept it from floating away. Underneath the sausage, a long narrow boat-shaped hull touched the ground on a single wheel. The front of the hull was full of windows; the back of it was pointed, and another hull behind it sported two engines with large propellers at each end of a braced platform. A man in a strange green uniform stood by an open door in the front of the hull. As we got closer, I saw the man in the green uniform wore a Naval officer's hat.

The four of us were in uniform—sort of—for the first time since June. The hospital quartermaster only stocked Army field green uniforms. He had managed to find Marine buttons and other insignia, which helped. Petty Officer Folkerts wore the same uniform we did, with a sailor's white hat. Gary struck me as a gentle, stolid fellow. Our new uniforms had been altered to fit our collection of casts, bandages, and omissions. I was sure they would be replaced quickly when we got to the States.

Several men stood by the cabin of the airship. Two wore two green uniforms like ours, several others strange blue ones. An officer with a camera emerged from the cabin, and spoke to the other officer. He nodded, and they walked toward us.

As the pair came closer we could see the two and a half rings of a Navy Lieutenant Commander on each officer's sleeve. Our orderlies stopped, and we all snapped off the crispest salutes we could manage from a wheelchair. The officers returned the salute, and moved up to shake our hands.

"Gentlemen, welcome to our little experiment! My name is John Towers, and I am the Officer in Charge of this expedition. The officer about to snap the shutter is Lieutenant Commander Ken Whiting. He's in charge of the Naval Air detachments in France. In the gondola waiting for us are Chief Pharmacist's Mates David Reem and Geoffery Hill. They'll be taking care of your medical needs on this flight. Let's get you gentlemen aboard, then I'll brief you on what we're doing and why."

At the door of the gondola, or *cabin*, we were picked up and levered into wicker chairs covered with blankets in the aft end of the cabin. The Chiefs checked us over, tended to our immediate needs, and pronounced us settled.

The cabin had windows at head level, so we could watch the commotion around the airship as it was prepared for flight. We had absolutely no frame of reference for what we were experiencing, so we just watched and listened carefully. Even Jack was quiet for a change.

Lieutenant Commander Towers came back and took a seat in our midst. Lieutenant Commander Whiting was working with the Royal Navy crew in the front of the cabin.

The officer took a deep breath, and began. "I want to give you as much information as I can before we start the engines, since they make quite a racket. I know this is all strange to you gentlemen, but I thank you very much for agreeing to go through with this experiment. I think it'll be worth your while!"

I spoke up. "Sir, why are we on a Royal Navy airship, instead of an American one?"

Towers laughed. "Short answer, Sergeant, is we don't own any airships! We're evaluating this model of British ship to either buy some of theirs, or build them ourselves. Commander Whiting and I are riding along on this trip to evaluate the ship's performance and utility."

The officer winked, "Mostly. We're also here to get checked out to fly one of these things, and get a little publicity for Naval Aviation. That's why Commander Whiting is taking the photographs."

"How is the ship looking so far, Sir, if I may ask?" Jack picked up the thread.

"It's a mixed bag, Sergeant. We flew over here in it yesterday. This is the most reliable airship the British have, but it still has a few teething problems, mostly due to the lack of practice and unreliable machinery. The good news with one of these is, if we have engine failure, we go down, but slowly and softly. In the aero planes I normally fly, engine failure is a whole lot more interesting."

Commander Towers glanced forward, "Not quite ready to start yet, so I'll go on. What we figured we'd do is set up a practical, useful job for this ship, see how well it works, and what we need to think through before we start using them for real. You, gentlemen, are that job—flying fragile individuals from one place to another would be so much faster and more comfortable than going by train, or those torture-wagons known as ambulances."

We all laughed at that, having had intimate experience with both.

"If all goes well today the flight will take about 8 hours. If we get favorable winds, it'll be less. If we need 'em, we have three landing fields between here and Le Havre that are set up to receive us. We can communicate by radio too—another thing we're testing—and tell them we're coming in. We really don't need this many men to handle the ship on the ground, unless it is windy or, God forbid, we set down in a thunderstorm."

Shouted orders from the front to the ground crew caught Commander Towers' attention for a moment, then he turned back to us.

"So the rules are few. If you need something, get the chief's attention. Especially if you need the bedpan—we don't want to empty those over towns! Don't even think of smoking here; that's hydrogen above us! And enjoy the ride!"

At that first one, then the other, propeller started to turn, and the engines burst into life with a flood of sound and vibration. After a few moments someone in the front of the cabin made a motion with his hand, the ground crew let go the lines, and Commander Whiting called out, "Up Ship!"

The airship rose gently and started to move forward. We were flying!

Chapter Seven

We climbed slowly through the clear morning air of north-eastern France. Commander Whiting was piloting the airship, with a Royal Navy officer at his elbow. We eventually stopped climbing and proceeded slowly along. From the position of the Sun, I figured we were headed West-Southwest, probably to avoid the battle zone.

The four of us gazed out the windows at the scene around and below us. I never imagined such beauty could still exist in ravaged, exhausted France. In a circle off to the north and back to the east a dark haze hung on the horizon over the lines. Under us, and to the west, green fields alternated with small woods. It was hard to tell from our height, but some fields looked cultivated and some looked brown or overgrown. Even with the obvious stains of war on the land, the beauty and majesty of Our Father's World was greater than I'd ever imagined.

Commander Towers came back to sit with us again.

"What do you think, Gentlemen?" He had to speak loudly to be heard.

"Incredible!" I replied.

"Never could have imagined it," Jack added.

"Even in war, God's Creation is truly beautiful!" Petty Officer Folkerts chimed in. He sounded like a Believer; I'd have to ask him when I had the chance.

The fourth person in our little band, Corporal Steffen, continued to stare out the window. He hadn't said more than ten words since we met in Colonel Finney's office. Something seemed to be bothering him...I suspected it might have something to do with the empty uniform sleeve where his left arm should be.

"You gentlemen might be interested to know that we're cruising at four thousand feet, with a speed over the ground of just under fifty miles per hour."

I couldn't resist. "Guess we'd better not get in a race with a duck, Sir."

Commander Towers laughed heartily. "Don't you just know it, Sergeant! In the planes I normally fly, we have to be careful to avoid flocks of birds—one hit can ruin your whole day. In this ship, we have to worry about bird strikes—from behind!"

We all laughed at that one, even Corporal Steffen.

The day stretched on as we crawled our way across France. After a while, the droning of the engines lulled me into a comfortable stupor. It was a bit cool up there, but heat from the engines right outside the hull kept things from getting too cold. We began to fly over areas where the trench lines had taken over the countryside. Even from our height, the land looked blasted, barren, nothing green, seemingly nothing alive down there. We soon tired of looking at that ghastly landscape; we had seen too much of the same, up close and personal.

Lunchtime arrived, and the corpsmen brought out box lunches. The sandwiches were a bit dry, but we were hungry and made do. Since this was a Royal Navy airship, we were offered beer with our sandwiches. Commander Whiting seemed a little put out when only Corporal Steffen took him up on the offer; the rest of us asked for water.

After the Chiefs took care of our hygiene needs, we settled back for the rest of the flight. Again, Commander Towers came back to where we sat.

"I don't want to jinx it, but this is the most trouble-free flight in one of these things I've ever experienced! It's actually been boring."

"Boring is just fine with us, Sir!" Jack said. "I know Luther and I both prayed fervently for a quiet, boring trip."

"Count me in on that one, please!" piped up Petty Officer Folkerts.

Commander Towers' eyebrows raised, but he didn't question us further. Perhaps he had a suspicion what would happen—Jack and I both had carried our Bibles on with us in case we had a chance to read, and to keep them safely with us.

I had a couple of questions for Commander Towers.

"Commander, looking at the size and shape of this airship, I get the impression it wouldn't go very fast regardless of how much horsepower we have pushing us. Am I sensing this correctly?"

"Sergeant, that is a very perceptive question. We're still trying to understand the forces involved in flight through the air, but that's how it seems to me too. There is so much we suspect, but cannot prove, that sometimes it seems every flight and every experiment just poses more questions."

The officer yawned, "equalize air pressure in the ears," he said, then continued.

"All areas of science and engineering have gotten a tremendous boost from this war—the best things happening from the worst situation, I guess. I think the advances we'll see in the next fifty years are beyond our comprehension, and not even writers like Verne and Wells can cipher it out."

Commander Towers stopped and squinted one eye. "How'd I ever get off on a rabbit trail like that? To answer your question, Sergeant, an object like this airship will never go very fast due to wind resistance, and if we just hung more horsepower and propellers on it we'd reach a point where the structure couldn't stand the force of the air it was flying through, and it would just collapse."

"Makes sense, sir," I commented.

The Commander nodded, and continued, "No, these ships will never have more than a limited usefulness. They lift relatively heavy loads, can stay in one place in the sky, and give an airman a chance to come down softly if things go wrong. That's about it. Let's just forget about all that hydrogen for the time being."

I had a thought. "Couldn't we use helium in the airships, sir?"

"Another good thought, Sergeant. We can, and we probably will. It's more expensive and doesn't lift as well, but it surely is safer!"

A stray fact came into my mind. "Sir, if I remember right, helium in practice would give about 88% of the lift hydrogen does, volume for volume."

Commander Towers' jaw dropped. "Sergeant, you are right! Where in the world did you learn that?"

"I had a very good Chemistry and Physics teacher in High School, sir. He was always giving us problems like that and coaching us to find out the answers."

"Did you enjoy that subject, Sergeant?"

"It was my second favorite, sir. My most favorite was learning to play the organ."

"Pipe organ?"

"Yes, sir."

Commander Towers put his index finger to his lips.

"Let's be honest, Sergeant. You will always be a Marine, but my guess is in a few months you'll be a retired Marine. Have you given any thought to what you'll do when that day comes?"

I decided to be honest back. "Sir, I've heard what you just said a few times recently. And I accept it. Honestly, sir, I've been praying about what to do when I'm retired. I've thought about going into the ministry, but the Lord hasn't given me any peace about that. What He has shown me is I seem to be good at fixing things, and figuring out how things work. Not only the physical things, but the physics and math behind them. Am I making any sense here, sir?"

"Sergeant, I really don't understand why you're praying about this, but I do think you're on the right track to be thinking about what you're good at, and going into that area. You sound to me like you have the makings of a pretty good engineer of some sort. I suggest you go to college, if you can afford it, and get some formal training to back up your good sense. I've met engineers, like more than a few pilots, with a whole lot of book learning, but who don't have sense enough to come in out of the rain...or fly an aeroplane!"

"I trust we don't have anyone like that up here with us today, sir!"

Commander Towers smiled. "Not to worry, Sergeant. Ken Whiting is the most sensible and careful aviator I know, and that includes me! And this Royal Navy crew is top notch. I'm just amazed and thankful we haven't had anything to do up here but fly and watch the gauges!"

"Me too, sir. And thank you kindly for the advice. I'll remember it; but I know the Lord will have a thing or two to say about what I do, too."

"You're welcome, Sergeant. And now I have to get up forward; I think it's my turn to drive the omnibus!"

Lieutenant Commander Towers stepped forward to join the others at the controls.

*****

Luther: Le Havre, France

The sun was low on the horizon when we arrived over Le Havre. I had entered France through that port about a lifetime ago; it looked like a toy city from the air. Here and there lights were starting to wink on. I thought it pretty, but the crew seemed to take a more serious view of the time. These ships normally did not fly at night unless in an emergency, Commander Whiting told us. He said we were going to be pushing it to get down before sunset.

We could see what appeared to be another parade ground not far from the waterfront. A large gray warship was tied up to the dock closest to the parade ground, indistinct in the gathering shadows.

We touched down right at sunset. Two military ambulances pulled up to the edge of the parade ground as the propellers swung to a stop. A touring car pulled up behind the ambulances.

Orderlies came from the ambulances to help the Chiefs transfer us to litters, and carry us over to the ambulances. Lieutenant Commander Towers walked with us.

"Commander, we surely thank you and your group for all you've done for us today," I said.

"Glad to do it, Sergeant. That was the most boring flight I've ever been involved with; I'd just love to have more!"

"Will you be staying in Le Havre, sir?"

"Actually, I'm riding the same ship home you are. They're beginning to notice I'm missing from my desk at the Navy Department, and suggested I come back home to do some work," He grinned at that thought.

Lieutenant Commander Whiting walked up alongside us. He was carrying two large cases.

"Here's the film and our reports, Jack. I'm sure they'll make happy reading in Washington!"

"Probably just get filed in the attic, Ken, except for the photos. I think we can get some publicity out of them. Oh—I forgot to ask; did you hear what ship we're riding home on?"

"Yeah, the *New Jersey*."

"That old bucket? Surely you can't be serious!"

"I'm deadly serious...and don't call me Shirley."

Both Commanders guffawed. That must have been some Naval Aviator inside joke. Commander Whiting recovered first.

"Anyway, I gotta scoot. Remember me to our friends back home!"

"Both of 'em?" They stopped and shook hands. "Take care of yourself, Ken. See ya in a few months."

"Will do, Jack. Later!" Lieutenant Commander Whiting walked over to the touring car.

Chapter Eight

Sylvia: October, 1918 and later, the Trimble home, next to the Wagher School, Copley Township, Knox County, Illinois.

I was never so happy to see my room in that small house on the Fremont Road as the day I came home from the hospital. Even with the grief of Pa's death weighing on me, I still felt relief, and a little bit of contentment, coming *back home*.

Helen escorted me in, and Bessie stayed close to Ma, who was still shaken from the letter we'd just received. Bessie offered to stop by Philip Wagher's farm and tell him what had happened; it would spread to the rest of the school board and the church from there. Ma had a good supply of food in the pantry and root cellar, so we were set in case we needed to stay home for a while with the influenza.

I made it to my bed, and pitched into it. I fell asleep right there, in my clothes, for several hours. Ma let me sleep; it gave her time for some private grieving and praying.

We had a succession of visitors over the next few days; however, they stayed on the porch. Ma spoke with them there, and I would occasionally speak and wave out one of the windows. Sylvester Sanford and his wife came over, and had prayer with us from the porch. He said Dr. Bohan had spoken to him at length, and he was ready to suspend church services as soon as the first case of influenza was reported in the church family, both here and at the church in Coleta he was also pastoring. He was a very intense, earnest man with horn-rimmed glasses, but he seemed perpetually tired; I think I understood why!

Other visitors to the 'front porch parlor' included my late husband's Everett and Flora Potter, and their son Jeff. Their older son, Kenneth, had been Hal's best friend; they had enlisted together, and were both killed at Belleau Wood. Ken's brother Jeff almost never spoke, was afraid of odd things, and didn't deal with new situations well. Ken and Jeff were very close, and Ken could understand Jeff better than anyone else; his death had been especially hard on Jeff. I was honored by their visits.

Philip Wagher, and Fred and Violet Johnson stopped by every couple of days to check up on us. Others from the church would come by and drop off meals and raw food from time to time. Even though I wasn't in church for months, the people never forgot us.

37

Ma was back in the classroom the Monday after I came home and we heard about Pa. I was in awe of her inner strength and resiliency. The students were unusually polite and respectful to her (not that they ever were disrespectful), and behavior problems flat vanished for the rest of the school year. I knew she still cried herself to sleep many nights; yet, when she was in the classroom she was *the teacher*, and her effectiveness never suffered.

My routine gradually assumed a rhythm, and a pace I could manage. I grew stronger steadily, but very, very slowly. As I grew stronger I began to try to do some of the chores of the household. I know Ma appreciated that, but she also kept telling me to be careful. She could tell I was exhausted before I'd admit it to myself. After a few episodes of lying on the floor for a while after running out of strength in the middle of something, I learned my lesson. Mostly.

When I ran out of strength I slept, or napped, or just dozed in my chair. After about a month of expending energy being annoyed at my lack of energy, the Lord finally got my attention to remind me I had to let Him work in my body, and also work on my self-will. I am convinced that interminable time as a shut-in was the most valuable time of training I have ever received.

Besides sleeping and trying to help out around the house, I read. I read my Bible, of course, according to a fixed schedule and as a question came up I needed to research. I read everything else in Ma's extensive library. Some fiction, but more often history, science, good literature. Some of them I did not enjoy; Robert Scott's *Kenilworth* (both volumes!) was the dullest book I can ever remember slogging through.

As time went on Ma asked around to borrow things for me to read, and often came home with three or four books from a personal friend or student's parents. I think I also read everything in the library of Deborah Kittridge, our Pastor's wife. All this reading was not only entertaining, but also prepared me for what was to come.

While Ma and I were adjusting to life without Pa, the influenza cut a swath of grief through the entire country. In Knox county 181 persons died from the influenza. The school shut down early in November, and did not reopen until March; this severely affected the children's education, but I believe it saved many lives. We knew they could always catch up later, and better yet, be alive to do so.

Several students and their parents took sick, but we praised the Lord none of our students or their immediate families died.

Without Dr. Bohan's timely warning and instructions in the wake of my father's death, the story could have been much different.

Through the entire time of my convalescence Ma was amazing. Her health stayed strong, and she kept her cheery good nature even when I knew grief was almost overwhelming her.

The snow came, by the foot it seemed, and Ma shoveled it...until Mr. Long, a church member and father of first grader Millie, came by one day and caught Ma shoveling. He stopped her, finished the job, and thanks to several other men of the church she never touched the shovel again...nor have I.

As I gradually gained strength I began to think about what I should do with myself after I was pronounced fully recovered, and could go out again. Only three career choices were easily available for women in those days- wife/mother, nurse, and teacher.

I had experienced some of the first, but that wasn't going to happen again any time soon. Of the other two, nursing required more training than I had, and we really couldn't afford for me to go to nursing school. Ma's military widow's pension, when it finally started to arrive, helped greatly, but that combined with her teaching pay and my widow's pension could do nothing more than keep us even financially.

Teaching was a real possibility, and I knew only a high school diploma and a good academic record were required to start teaching, especially in the country schools. When children graduated from our school they went to High School in Oneida. I had managed to graduate as Valedictorian of the class of 1917--all twenty three of us!

I also had helped Ma in the classroom over the years, and I was well-acquainted with her large books of lesson plans for every subject in every grade. She wanted to make sure her teaching was uniform from year to year without forgetting anything the students needed as they progressed. Many teachers didn't go to all that trouble, and paid the price when their students couldn't complete grade requirements on time. I knew I could do that job, but had to get my full strength back before I started to hunt for a teaching job

These were the things I thought about as day followed day, month followed month, and I slowly, ever so slowly, regained my strength.

*****

Luther: October 1st, 1918, the quarterdeck of USS New Jersey (BB-16), Le Havre.

"I believe the phrase is, it seemed like a good idea at the time!"

The four of us were lying on stretchers on the polished wooden quarterdeck of the United States Navy Battleship *New Jersey*. We had been carried from the ambulances along the dock, and up the slanted gangway to the quarterdeck. There we were gently deposited, to wait for the ship's corpsmen to retrieve us and take us to our berthing area.

Lying flat on my back I had a grand view of the after end of the battleship as it was silhouetted by the waxing moon and strung light bulbs. Jack and I had served in the Marine detachment aboard the armored cruiser *Washington* for almost three years after Parris Island, and even though it was obsolescent by then I admired that ship's symmetry and air of robust competence. This ship was about the same size, but…*oh, my!*

The after turret with its two 12 inch guns rose from the deck on which we lay. The bottom of it looked like every other turret I'd ever seen. However, stuck on top of that turret was another turret, with a pair of 8 inch guns, like a two-thirds version of its lower sister. To top it off (literally), the top and bottom turret were welded together, so the upper one could not even revolve independently of the lower!

I had heard of this class of ship, but never seen one. *Stupid* only began to describe it. Without thinking, my thought turned into speech. "Whatever were those designers thinking?"

Then I heard the reply.

I turned my head and found myself looking up at a Lieutenant Commander. He was of medium height, and looked to be headed toward portly. His dark hair was cut short, and he wore wire-rimmed glasses. He smiled down on us.

"I'm sorry, Commander! I just blurted that out."

"You and everyone else on this estimable bucket of rivets. Don't worry about it."

"Thank you, Sir."

The officer smiled, and looked around at the rest of us as he spoke.

"Not to worry, gentlemen, you're in good hands now, and going home. I am A.P. Kittridge, and please don't ask what A.P. stands for! I am the Paymaster, or more properly Supply Officer, on this luxury barge, and I'll be responsible for seeing you four get home in the maximum of comfort and ease. I have an assistant for this task, but he's off trying to make sure we can take care of your needs in the accommodations we've assigned you. And you gentlemen are…"

I guessed I was still senior. "Sir, I'm Sergeant Luther Barlow, and this is Sergeant Andrew Jackson Sewell, Pharmacist's Mate Third Class Gary Folkerts, and Corporal Matthew Steffen. Were you told we were coming?"

"We were over at Rosyth two days ago visiting the Grand Fleet—comic relief, I think—and we got the message to get right over here to Le Havre, pick up five *Very Important People*, and make knots for the States. As usual, they didn't explain themselves. We got in last evening, and spent last night and today coaling and provisioning. Just finished cleaning the coal dust away as your airship arrived." Kittridge looked down at us, raised an eyebrow, and smiled. "No matter, gentlemen. We'll take good care of you. We may even move you off this quarterdeck eventually…"

He turned to the Officer of the Deck and gave him *The Look*. The Ensign paled in the glare of the bulbs, and literally ran over to the bank of voice pipes against the deckhouse wall. In two minutes a dozen sailors, led by a Chief Corpsman, piled through the watertight door onto the quarterdeck and collected our stretchers. We were carried into the ship, followed by Commander Kittridge.

Our party snaked through around corridors, down a couple of ladders, and eventually arrived at *sick bay*, the ship's hospital. The compartment was relatively large, well-lit, and smelled of disinfectant. We were eased into bunks in a curtained-off area of the compartment.

The corpsmen started to tend to the needs of the other men, and Lieutenant Commander Kittridge pulled up a chair next to my bed.

"I want to check something with you before the other gentlemen come back. I see you have your Bible with you; are you a Believer?"

I was surprised by the question, but answered directly. "Yes, Sir, I am. I ran from the Lord all my life, until I got shot up in Belleau Wood last June. I was lying there and I knew I was dying, and then I heard the Still Small Voice."

"Amen."

"Indeed. He had my attention. He gave me one last chance to trust Him to save me. I really needed saving, and I knew I could do nothing to save myself. So I surrendered, and trusted Jesus. He not only saved me, but here I am!"

"Praise the Lord, Son. I should tell you, I'm just a reserve officer in the Canoe Club. When there's not a war on, I'm Pastor of Appleton Baptist Church in Appleton, Illinois."

"Well, Praise the Lord back! Jack--Sergeant Sewell--and I are from Metamora. We attended, or rather he attended and I ran from, First Baptist Church there."

"So Sergeant Sewell is a Believer too?"

"Yes, sir, and my oldest friend. From things he's said, I think Petty Officer Folkerts is also. I'm pretty sure Corporal Steffen is not; something's bothering him, but I don't know what it is. We just met Folkerts and Steffen yesterday morning."

"Well, you gentlemen will have about ten days to get acquainted. We're under orders to make best speed to Hampton Roads, and our engineering plant is one of the few good things about this ship, but it will still take that long."

"We're really in no hurry, sir; we're just glad to be going home."

"You and me both, Sergeant. I think this bucket will be based stateside until we're decommissioned." The Commander looked over his shoulder. "Ah, my Assistant has finally caught up with us!"

A tall, thin, very young man, with shocks of white-blond hair pointing this way and that, panted his way through the curtains.

"Sergeant, let me introduce my assistant and general dogsbody for this trip. Sergeant Luther Barlow, this is Ensign Homer Wallin. Up until last week he was the Second Engineer on this tub. I consider him responsible for the fine state of the engines and auxiliaries on this ship, and I'm not kidding. He's been detached from the ship, but I'm going to make him work for his passage home. He's going to College on the Government's dime...at M.I.T.!"

Ensign Wallin grinned and blushed as I shook his hand.

Chapter Nine

Luther: October, 1918, at sea aboard USS New Jersey.

An ocean voyage can be a wonderful time of rest and recuperation. Fresh air, sunny weather, and the feeling of leaving the cares of land behind can be regenerative and invigorating. The gentle rolling of the ship as it plows through a calm sea at night can rock anyone, infant to adult, into a sound, restful slumber.

Right.

This voyage was something less than idyllic. We did not see the sun again until the second week of our stay at Walter Reed. Leaden skies, heavy rain, and storm-tossed seas were the rule for our entire crossing. The weather kept us confined to sick bay for the entire voyage. Even the nicest sick bay wears on you after a while.

Plus, because of *New Jersey's* stacked gun turrets, the ship was more top-heavy than the other armored cruisers or pre-Dreadnought battleships in the fleet. That meant she rolled slower, but farther, than most other warships. We took 20 degree rolls routinely, and occasionally we'd go over to 35 degrees. If we hadn't been full of coal, we could have capsized; as it was, we were merely miserable down in sick bay. A rolling ship doesn't bother me too much, but when we started meeting the waves head-on, and began to pitch up and down too, I was in trouble. We were very thankful for the buckets hanging by hooks on our beds.

In spite of the weather, Lieutenant Commander Kittridge and Ensign Wallin were as good as their word that they would make us as comfortable as possible. The food was excellent for shipboard fare, and our Hospital Apprentices and Pharmacist's Mates were uniformly gracious. The sick bay started to fill up with seasick sailors, and others who broke limbs or cracked heads as the ship rolled.

I asked Commander Kittridge if the ship had had any cases of influenza yet; he asked me to keep it quiet, but there had been one suspected case when the ship arrived in Le Havre, but he had been whisked off to the hospital quickly, and so far that was all.

Jack and I had several good Bible studies and seasons of prayer with Petty Officer Gary Folkerts. It turned out he was from Mansfield, Ohio, and was saved in the Apostolic Christian Church. Gary was surprised we knew about the *ACs*, as the group was known for short. A number of German and Hungarian immigrants had settled around Metamora, and had brought their church with them. Their core doctrines and beliefs were the same as ours, but their manner of worship and church polity were different. That didn't bother us, or him.

Gary told us while many young men of the church had volunteered for service, their convictions led them to serve in noncombatant roles only. That's why he became a Pharmacist's Mate…but also volunteered to serve with the Marines. He said he didn't mind being wounded; he was happy to be able to serve his Country, and serve his Lord at the same time. He was *good troop*, Jack and I decided.

Corporal Steffen didn't socialize with us, and spent his time staring at the bulkhead. Gary was from the same platoon, and they were both from Mansfield. He told us about Steffen's reputation as a jokester and a bully. He was also the battalion boxing champion, and was scheduled to compete in the divisional boxing championship before a meeting with a trench mortar shell put paid to that. There was no joking now. The three of us included him in our prayers.

Ensign Wallin spent a lot of time down in sick bay talking with us, tending to our needs, and just skylarking, I think. After two hard years in the engine rooms and standing watches, he said, he was going to enjoy this trip no matter how bad the weather got! He said he was traveling directly up to Massachusetts to start school as soon as we landed, and wouldn't have time to get back home to North Dakota for leave.

"It's worth postponing leave for, though," Ensign Wallin said as we sipped our coffee in the common area of sick bay one afternoon.

"Very few officers get to study at any college and get paid for it, unless it's the War College at Newport. For some reason they must think I need the extra education!"

We both laughed at that.

"You're going to be studying engineering, aren't you, sir?"

Ensign Wallin winked at me. "Let's get this business about titles into perspective, okay? I'm an Ensign; in my trade a Seaman Second usually rates more respect. You are a Marine, and a Sergeant. You've also *seen the elephant* in the most serious way possible. I'm going to be a student; unless I miss my guess you're going to be one too. So around here, I'm Homer; 'Sir' is my father."

"I think you have the right of it, s-…Homer. And I'm Luther. And you're right about the student part. I know what this" I pointed

44

to my leg, "means, and I've accepted it. But I'm still praying about what to do after I'm retired."

Homer took a sip of his coffee. "I understand your indecision. And I'm a believer too. An evangelist by the name of Bob Jones came all the way out to North Dakota to preach, and I realized how lost I was. Went down to the altar and gave my heart to Jesus. Never regretted it, that's for sure! Like the lights came on, and my vision cleared...amazing."

"The same happened to me, believe it or not. I ran from Him until I was lying in Belleau Wood dying. He spoke in the *Still Small Voice*, and gave me one last chance to trust Him. I surrendered, and when I finally woke up in the hospital it seemed like my life had re-started, with everything clearer and brighter than it ever was before. So now, I get to find out what He has for me."

Homer nodded, and took another sip of his coffee. We held on to the table as the ship rolled again. At least we weren't pitching at the moment!

"I talked to our other passenger in the Wardroom, Lieutenant Commander Towers. He told me you had a first-rate mind for engineering and the sciences."

"I don't know if I'd call my mind 'first rate', but I do enjoy working with things, and understanding how and why they work. The Commander was impressed, for some reason."

"I've heard about him," Homer replied, "He's one of the top minds among the Naval Aviators. If he was impressed, there's a reason."

"I'm flattered, but I still need to do what the Lord wants me to."

"Yes, you do, Luther. I'm glad you realize that—although the manner of your conversion would tend to give you that little bit of insight. Where did you say you were from?"

"Metamora, Illinois. A ways east and north of Peoria."

Homer nodded, then set his coffee cup on the table, then picked it up again as it started to slide to port. He continued speaking as he juggled his cup.

"This may mean nothing, or it may mean something important. There's a school in Peoria called Bradley Polytechnic Institute. They aren't more than twenty years old, but they have developed a reputation for first class academics and training in engineering. I actually had them on my short list before MIT came calling."

"I've heard of them too. My Pa said they started as a watch repair school, and branched out. Close enough to Metamora that I could get back on weekends."

We both held on to the table as the ship rolled again.

"Another question," Homer asked, "How did you perform when the studies got intense and the homework piled up?"

"To be honest, I never really had a problem with studying and academics. In fact, my High School teachers begged me to go to college, said I was wasting my life by joining the Marines."

"And you didn't listen to them. Why?"

I took another sip as the ship took another roll.

"Short answer: I was running away. From home, from the church, from the rules, from the Lord. I could run pretty fast in those days."

"And the Lord ran faster."

"Yep. He knew what it would take to make me surrender, and He provided it."

"And now?"

"I'm His. And I like that just fine."

Homer scratched his head, then grabbed the table as his chair almost tipped over. "Won't miss this old bucket in a seaway, that's for sure!" he announced, then caught his breath and continued.

"Now perhaps you can see the options clearer than when you were running. Your teachers, they all had opinions, all had your life laid out in their minds, didn't they?"

"They certainly did."

Homer's face darkened. "My Pa wanted me to be a farmer in North Dakota. In myself, I wouldn't have minded that; however, the Lord worked some other things out, gave me the nudge to join the Navy. I hope Pa gets over it someday."

"My Pa has written exactly one letter since I got well enough to write again, but it was a good one. He told me now he knew the Lord would aim me toward whatever He wanted me to do, and he was perfectly fine with whatever that was."

"That means a lot."

"Sure does," I replied after I drank the last of my coffee, "He had to raise me alone after my Ma died. I know it tore him up to see me run like I did. I'm glad I'm coming home to him."

"I hope I can come home to my Pa one of these days. He hasn't forgiven me yet."

"I'll pray to that end, Homer. In fact, let's pray now."

"Thanks, Luther."

Chapter Ten

Sylvia: April 26th, 1919, the Trimble home, Fremont Road.

Dr. Bohan turned away from me and carefully removed his rubber gloves. Without touching the outside of either glove, he deftly rolled them into each other and dropped them into the glass jar Ma held out for him.

"Ah, thank you, Annette," he said as he tapped the lid onto the jar. "Now if I may wash up while Sylvia is dressing, we can gather in the living room and talk."

In a few moments we gathered in our modest living room.

Dr. Bohan looked at the two of us sitting on the edge of our chairs, and grinned.

"Ladies, I am pleased to announce that as of today, Saturday, April 26th, I am releasing Sylvia from captivity! *Activities as tolerated* is how I'll write it in my notes. Please don't try running any footraces for a while!"

"You can rest assured I won't be trying that!" I said as I laughed.

"Good. Now the other thing. I think we are finally finished with the influenza. We've had three waves of it, and it looks like this last one was the end. It may come back, but I think we're OK for now. I would suggest you only visit folks you know for a month or two, and not get in a large crowd of people.

I winked. "Is the circus coming to town?"

We all laughed again, the stress starting to leave us.

"Going to church is fine," Doctor Bohan continued, "I'm sure you've been missed. Just don't push yourself, Sylvia. If you start to feel tired, stop what you're doing and rest. It's OK to drive now, and even crank the car, but if it won't start right up, just figure on being there a while so you and the car can rest."

"Thank you so much for your care for us, and for the advice to the rest of our Church family, during this time," Ma said. "I'd like to think Bill's passing had some positive affect on our ability to weather that storm."

Dr. Bohan lifted his eyes for a moment, and his grin disappeared.

"Annette, we may never know how much the warning Bill's death gave us contributed to the saving of lives here in Knox County. I was concerned about the influenza, but I never put it all together until that afternoon when you got the letter. And I emphasize: It Was Not Me." He then made the sign of the Cross.

My turn to respond. "I certainly agree with you, Doctor, in all of what you said. God has preserved us for His purpose, that's for sure."

Dr Bohan pulled out his handkerchief and wiped his eyes. "Sylvia, it's moments like these that make me glad I got to be a doctor."

"And now, one last thing," he continued. "I stopped by the Johnson's before I came here, to see how Violet and little Laney were doing. I mentioned where I was heading, and Fred and Violet asked me to invite you two over for a celebration supper at their house tonight, about six. I told them if you couldn't make it I'd swing back to tell them."

Ma looked over at me. "I think we could manage a little bit of an outing, don't you, Syl?"

*****

Luther: October, 1918, shortly after 2 AM, sick bay, USS New Jersey.

BOOM!!!

I jerked awake with the reflexive motion of the trenches. My first instinct was to roll off the bed onto the floor, and roll under it if I had to. Fortunately, the railings on either side of the bed held me in it long enough for my brain to catch up with my reflexes. *What was that?*

As I came to full consciousness I remembered I was in sick bay on a misbegotten battleship, heading home from France to the United States. I then remembered why I was in sick bay, and was thankful again for the railings that kept me from remembering my injuries. All that was well and good, but there had definitely been a gunshot close by, and it sounded like a .45 automatic pistol. The sound still rang through the compartment, but it was fading.

Lights flipped on in the compartment. Shouts and running feet, more shouts and the sound of someone retching. I heard a voice from the next bed. "Luther, you there?"

"Yeah, Jack, what was that?"

"Not sure, but I think someone in here just shot themselves. Look at the overhead."

48

I looked out and up. In an area on the other side of the compartment a stain had appeared on the light green paint of the overhead. A gray stain, with flecks of red.

"Head shot."

"Yep," Jack replied.

I looked again. "I wonder if it was…"

"Looking at angle and pattern of that stain, I think so."

"Oh, no!"

More sailors arrived, and Marines from the ship's detachment. Lieutenant Commander Kittridge came into sick bay at a run, paused by the group of sailors on the other side of the compartment, then turned toward us, panting. He was dressed in uniform pants, a T-shirt, his officer's cap, and tasseled bedroom slippers. We didn't laugh.

"Who was it, sir?" Jack asked.

"Corporal Steffen, I'm afraid. Somehow got hold of a .45," he said, then noticed the overhead. "Did a thorough job with it."

"Is there anything we can do to help, sir?" I asked.

"Not at the moment, gentlemen. We've got to start the investigation, then figure out how to do the burial at sea in this weather. I'll come back when I know more and we'll talk."

"Aye aye, sir," we both said.

With the shock of the suicide, and the commotion of the investigation, we couldn't sleep. A couple of the corpsmen got us up into chairs, and Ensign Wallin (who arrived shortly after Commander Kittridge) contrived to liberate some mid-rats from the nearby wardroom. Gary joined us, and we four sat around a table eating sandwiches and drinking coffee.

"Gentlemen, this is definitely a night none of us will ever forget, and all of us will want to."

"Amen, sir," Jack said, "He must have been one tortured soul. He never did warm up to any of us."

"I just wish I'd talked to him about his soul when I first thought about it," I said. "I was going to do it tomorrow—today, now."

Jack looked directly at me. "Don't worry about it, Luther. I talked to him yesterday morning. He said he was not interested in any of my preaching, and he would thank me kindly if I left him alone."

"Those words?"

"A bit more colorful. I think if I hadn't been a superior non-commissioned officer, he would have been a lot more emphatic."

"Oh, I guarantee he would have," Gary added. He was interrupted by another person joining our group. Lieutenant

Commander Kittridge, now back in uniform, pulled over a chair and sat down at our table.

Ensign Wallin started to jump up, but the Commander put a hand on his shoulder.

"Siddown, Homer, don't expend the energy none of us has got."

A corpsman brought the newcomer a cup of coffee. "Thanks, Corpsman. I really need it right now."

Kittridge sipped the coffee, cradling the cup in his hands, head down. Then, he turned back to us.

"Let me tell you what we know so far. Remember the group of banged-up sailors that came in right after we took those heavy rolls yesterday around Noon? One of them was a ship's Master at Arms. Two of them were escorting a sailor to the brig after a command performance at Captain's Mast, and one took a tumble down a ladder. Fractured his skull, and a compound fracture of his left arm and wrist. Real mess. The Doc had to operate immediately, then put him in the auxiliary sick bay. They stripped off his gear before taking him to the operating theatre. Unfortunately, he had his .45, since the rule of the Chief Master at Arms is to be armed when on duty. Plus, the rule of the same CMAA is the weapon has to be loaded when worn."

"I think I see where you're going, sir," Homer said.

"Yep. Everybody forgot about the weapon, and the Chief Master at Arms—or rather, the *former occupant* of that position—never thought to find and secure the weapon."

"His goose is cooked," Jack muttered under his breath.

The two officers said nothing, but both nodded. Lieutenant Commander Kittridge continued the tale.

"Anyway, Corporal Steffen sees this, takes the weapon (since he could walk better than he let on), hides it, and then when all was dark, he used it."

"How could he have cocked the piece to fire it?" Gary asked. "Several of us tried that on an unloaded—VERY unloaded—point four five. If you wedge it against something that holds it firmly enough, you can cock it with one hand. The rest is easy."

We all pondered the news for a moment.

Commander Kittridge shrugged, and continued. "Anyway, the burial at sea is in about an hour. The Skipper is going to turn the ship to minimize the wave action, and we'll do it from the fantail. We'll all have lifelines around us just in case. The Chaplain's an old friend of mine; he asked if I would do the burial, since I knew the deceased. More like he's so seasick he's afraid he'll pass out and fall overboard!"

In spite of the situation we all chuckled. Commander Kittridge snorted, and continued. "Good man, weak stomach. So I'm doing it. Do any of you know much about the Corporal? Bad as well as good, it would really help if I knew it."

Gary spoke up.

"Sir, I guess I knew him the best of anyone here. He was in my platoon, and his parents are in the Apostolic Christian Church in Mansfield, Ohio, like mine are. He was a couple years older than me, but I knew him well enough."

We all nodded.

"Ever since I can remember he's been a 'bad boy'. Picked fights at school, ran with the wrong crowd, all the usual rebellion things. The more his folks tried to get him to do right, the more he ran from them. That's why he joined the Marines. He told me once he'd just die if he had to live under his parents' rules any more."

"There's a double meaning in that." Jack said softly.

"I agree, but Matthew would never see it. He did OK in the Marines, was a good soldier, but he still ran. He got to where he'd threaten to whip any of us who even mentioned Christ outside of a swear word."

"That's so sad," Ensign Wallin murmured.

Folkerts continued. "He was so wrapped up in that boxing competition that's all he wanted to do off duty. He was good at it, but I think a lot of that was all the *cussedness,* for want of a better word, he had inside."

"Then he took that mortar shell, and everything he lived for was gone. He couldn't box, he couldn't fight the Huns, he couldn't bully anyone. He was through, in his eyes. Way I see it, the Lord gave him a choice, and he chose wrong."

Commander Kittridge spoke softly, "That was the same choice we were all given. Each of us is free to accept or reject His offer. You men took him up on His offer."

I finished the thought, "Corporal Steffen did not.

The four of us sipped our coffee and pondered the Grace of God for a few minutes.

Finally, Lieutenant Commander Kittridge spoke.

"The one principle of Hell is—'I am my own'."

"Sir?" we all three said together.

"One of the saddest quotations I know. It's from *Unspoken Sermons* by George MacDonald, the finest Christian author I've ever read. Not well-known these days, but worth hunting for."

I nodded. "That sure applied here."

"Indeed. Thank you, Petty Officer Folkerts, for your insight, sad as it is. That information will help when I write the letter to his parents. You men are administratively attached to my department for the voyage, so it falls to me."

The Commander sighed, and started to rise from the table.

"Not the first letter like that I've written; not the last either I reckon. Nights like this make me long for the end of this business, so I can get back to what the Lord called me to do…but I guess this is part of His calling, too. And I am blessed to meet gentlemen like you, truly."

"Thank you, Sir," we chorused.

He turned to the Ensign. "Homer, you still going to try to photograph the ceremony with that Graflex of yours?"

"I'd really like to, if you don't mind, sir."

"Then give it a go. Since for some reason we have a photographic darkroom on this barge, maybe I can get a print to send to his family with the letter. The rest of you, I suggest some more sack time. We're supposed to arrive tomorrow about noon, if we don't capsize first! Let's go, Homer."

Chapter Eleven

Sylvia: April 26, 1919, The Johnson farm, just east of the Wagher School.

At precisely six that evening we pulled into the Johnson farmyard. As we got out of the Baby, the Johnson's elderly farm dog Zeke ambled over to check us out. As we scratched him he concentrated on giving me a welcoming sniff!

Fred and Violet came out on the porch to greet us. Fred shook our hands, and Violet hugged us both.

"We are so glad to see you out again, Sylvia!" Violet said, "we've missed you so much around here, seems like it's been a year!"

"Nine months, Violet. I can't tell you how many times I prayed for this day to come! You all were so faithful to come visit me in the *front porch parlor*, but it just wasn't the same."

"I'm kind of glad to have her out from under foot."

"Ma!!"

"Couldn't resist, Syl," Ma grinned.

"Let's go inside, folks. I'm getting hungry."

"Fred!" Violet scolded, smiling.

We stepped inside the house. The Johnson's eldest son, Fredrick Pace Junior, Pacey for short, met us in the front room. A magnificently multi-colored bruise covered his left arm. He looked miserable.

"What in the world happened to you?" Ma asked.

"Betsy, ma'am," Pacey ground out.

"Betsy?"

"Our new buggy horse," Fred explained. "I stopped by Marsh Sale Barn last time I was in Galesburg. Our old horse, Daisy, was getting a bit past it, and we needed a replacement. Betsy looked good, seemed underpriced, I thought, so I bought her. Glad I did, because we found Daisy dead in her stall three days later. But I think we've found out why Betsy was so cheap, or rather Pacey did.

"Is the arm going to be OK?" I asked.

"Dr. Bohan said so. When he was here today to check up on Violet and Laney he looked at Pacey too. Very kind of him."

"Are you going to have to sell the horse?"

"I don't think so, Annette. I applied a bit of the horse training skills I picked up when I worked for old Leroy Marsh back when, and she's settled down for now. Pacey's actually very good with the animals, and I think he's learned a few things from this episode. Right, Pacey?"

"Yes, Pa, I think I have."

I looked at the serious six year old in front of me. "Are you ready to go back and work with Betsy again?"

"Oh, yes, ma'am! I just need to stay away from her back legs!"

I looked over at the doorway as a small child crawled resolutely around the corner of the dining room toward us. He was larger than an infant, but not quite walking yet. He sported a good growth of white-blond hair, and complained loudly about being left out of the festivities.

"Laney, you've gotten yourself out of the pen again!" Violet started to get up, but Fred put his hand on her shoulder, and got up instead. He walked over to the crawling youngster and picked him up.

"Sylvia, I don't think you've met the newest member of our family. This is

Lane Fredrick; we call him Laney. He's our personification of Hope and Change!"

I must have looked puzzled, so Fred continued.

"We *hope* he survives his childhood, as inquisitive and ingenious getting in and out of places as he is…"

Fred took an exaggerated sniff in Laney's direction.

"…and boy, does he need a *change*!"

We all laughed- all except Laney, who continued to cry.

Fred wrinkled his nose. "You really do need a change, young man. No, Violet-I've got it. You're cleaned up to serve dinner." He carried the baby out of the room and into the side room off the dining room.

Ma winked. "You've trained Fred well, Violet."

"Believe it or not, he's always been like that!"

"Just like Bill—," Ma's face darkened.

I stepped in. "Violet, can I help you bring out the food? It's been a long time since I've gotten to do that."

"Sure, Sylvia. Annette, come on out to the kitchen with us, we can all catch up on the latest."

We started for the kitchen.

"WHEEEEE-EWWWWWW!!!" came from the side room.

We started to giggle, then we passed the open door and caught a whiff.

After dinner we sat in the parlor and talked. Since we were talking to the Vice-President of the Wagher School board and his wife, the school came up.

"How far back did the influenza closure put you, Annette?" Fred asked.

"I figure five months. a bit longer if you factor in what the children forgot from the first part of the year. We surely needed to close it, but there's a price to pay."

"Sure is," Fred replied. "How do you propose to make up the time?"

"To a certain extent we can never make up the time we lost. But I've been rearranging lessons among the grade levels, and I think I can get us about where we should be by the beginning of the 1920 calendar year."

"And," Ma added, looking at me, "Now I have a helper!"

"So you're going to work in the school, too, Sylvia?" Violet asked.

"Yes, if you'll have me. I've been looking at my options while I've been down sick. I've also been praying about it. The Lord seems to be heading me toward teaching, and this summer I'll start applying for a position somewhere. Meanwhile, Ma needs the help and I need the experience."

Fred looked at both of us. "You realize we don't have any money to pay a second teacher?"

"Of course," Ma replied, "and we're not asking for payment. We've talked about it, Syl and I, and she wants to do this as a volunteer."

"We'll be fine. Besides, Ma and I both have our—"

I started to say *widow's pensions*, but my voice caught, and I couldn't talk. My eyes started to well up.

Violet came over and patted my shoulder.

"There, there, that's OK Sylvia. We know what you mean. We'll be glad to have you help Annette in any capacity."

Ma reached over to pat me too.

"Thank you Ma, Violet. I'll be all right here in a minute." I was embarrassed to be crying in front of others. I preferred to do my crying in front of the Lord, alone.

At that moment an annoyed sound came from upstairs.

Fred got up slowly from his chair. "I do hope that's not more change!"

We all laughed again, I through my tears.

*****

Luther: November, 1918, The Atlantic, near the entrance channel for the port of Baltimore.

"First time I've ever known the *Canoe Club* to send out a water taxi for someone!" Lieutenant Commander Kittridge remarked, using a slang term for the Navy.

He and Ensign Wallin were standing on *New Jersey's* quarterdeck. Jack, Gary, and I lay strapped into special stretchers on the deck. We were rigged and trussed up for transfer at sea from one ship to another by line.

We had stopped by the sea buoy (the outermost guiding buoy) for the port of Baltimore, Maryland. Coming toward us slowly was a four-stacker destroyer, which would carry us up the Potomac River to Washington.

Lieutenant Commander Towers had also joined us on deck. He was strapped into a contrivance with the encouraging name of *breeches buoy*. He was also going to be transferred over by line, but in a more upright position—if all went well.

I looked over at Commander Kittridge. "Sir, has anyone told you why they're going to all this trouble for us?"

"They have, and it isn't pretty. Baltimore is chock full of influenza. The troopships coming and going in the port are full of it, and people are dying by the hundreds, literally. The Army, in its wisdom, has decreed the ships come and go as if nothing is happening." The Paymaster snorted. "The Navy, and especially the Marine Corps, beg to differ. And they decided to do something about it, at least for you. For some reason they like you!"

Lieutenant Commander Towers spoke up. "That's a first, AP!"

"Now, Jack, not everyone thinks aviators are strange. You ought to try being a *Chop* for a while!" *Chop* is a slang expression for a Paymaster or Supply Corps officer.

"Couldn't do it- too boring. Except on this voyage. What a mess!"

"You said it, Jack. Which reminds me…"

Commander Kittridge took an object wrapped in oilcloth from under his arm, and stuck it in the canvas bag strapped into the stretcher with me. "Sergeant, I had a spare one of these, and thought you might enjoy it. It's that book by George Mac Donald I told you about."

"Thank you very much, Sir," I replied. "I'm sure I'll get a lot out of it."

"You're welcome, son. Oh, if any of you get down towards Appleton anytime, look me up. I expect to be back there sometime this Spring."

"Definitely, sir, though I don't know where we'll finally land," Jack Sewell said.

The destroyer was moving up our port side slowly. Sailors were getting ready to heave lines over.

Commander Towers spoke up. "Hey, AP, are you going to have to go into Baltimore and risk the influenza?"

"No, Jack, the Skipper got orders by wireless this morning. We're going to head up to Narragansett Bay, hole up at Newport for a while, till we see how the epidemic is going to play out."

"Pretty cold up there, if I remember right."

"Yep, but I'd rather be cold than dead."

"That makes two of us, AP."

Commander Kittridge and Ensign Wallin shook hands all around.

"Let me know where you end up at school, Luther," Ensign Wallin said quietly as he shook my hand.

"Will do, Homer. Take care of yourself. I'll pray for your Pa."

"Thanks, Luther."

One by one we were hooked onto the lines, and pulled the forty feet over the ocean between the two ships. Lieutenant Commander Towers came over last.

We waved at the other ship as we both broke away and set our separate courses. Sailors stood by to take us to wherever in the ship they were going to keep us for the short trip upriver.

Lieutenant Commander Towers unhooked the last strap from the breeches buoy, and stepped away from it. He stuck his uniform cap on his head, and grinned.

"These guys mean business. They didn't even dunk me on the way over!"

Chapter Twelve

Sylvia: April, 1919, the Wagher School, Fremont Road, Copley Township, Knox County, Illinois.

(Whew!!)

I was first introduced to Ma's class at the Wagher School that Monday. I stood there next to Ma and looked at the students, and they looked back at me. Ma just said I was her daughter, my name was Mrs. Trimble, and they were to treat me with the same respect they treated her. With these children, that was enough.

Nobody ever asked me any personal questions, especially *Where is Mr. Trimble?* I was sure each student was aware from their parents that certain questions and topics were *not to be heard* from them. I don't know if any of them knew our story, but I never overheard anything.

Ma asked me to take over the first grade reading group. I found I enjoyed sitting in the circle with the 6 first graders, helping and encouraging them as they read. The books were old, but they did the job, and the children liked the stories.

Ma also asked me to give special help to the older students who were struggling with a lesson. Usually I was able to help them over the rough spots; sometimes, I couldn't. In those cases I called Ma over, and watched how she handled the questions.

The month and a half I helped in that classroom was my happiest time since before Hal left for the Marines. I really enjoyed teaching and guiding the children, and Ma said I was good at it. That praise meant even more to me.

The time flew by—at least for me. I was sure the children were chafing at being in the classroom while such a beautiful Spring unfolded around us. The speed with which they left the building at lunchtime and the end of the day was truly remarkable!

In early June the interrupted school year came to an end. We held a graduation ceremony for the eighth graders in the schoolyard, and bade farewell to the rest until September.

Our school year wasn't finished, however. Ma and I went through the school building and deep-cleaned everything. We painted, arranged, replenished supplies. Some of the board members, led by Philip Wagher and Fred Johnson, tidied up the school grounds and painted the outside of the building.

By the end of the second week in June we were finished with the first part of our preparations for the next school year. We would do more in the two weeks before the beginning of school—Ma certainly, and me if I had not found a position by then.

Philip Wagher came to see us as we finished our work on Friday afternoon, June 13th. Philip had founded the school for Copley Township many years before, and was still President of the school board. He looked older every time I saw him, and now used a cane.

He may have been showing his age, but his mind was sharp as always. We sat around the teacher's desk in the classroom, and fielded his questions. He asked about everything that went on in this chaotic year. He asked about the progress of specific students, and behaviors of other students. He missed nothing.

Finally he looked up from his yellow writing pad and looked at us.

"Annette, I am amazed how well you've managed to cope with the most chaotic and fragmented school year I've ever seen! I think, from what I see here, you'll be close to where the class should have been without the closure by the end of this year. That's what Fred said you predicted, and as usual you are right!"

He rubbed his nose with his callused index finger and continued.

"And you did this in the face of—I'm sorry, but I have to say this—the most personally tragic year I can possibly imagine. You've trusted in the Lord, both of you, and He honored your trust."

Ma took a handkerchief out of her dress pocket. "Thank you, Phillip, for your kind words"

"I mean every one of 'em!" Phillip replied, then turned to me. "Sylvia, I'm just as proud of you as I can be! Your work since you've been able to get out has been vital to keep your Ma on schedule to recover from the closure—and to keep her sanity, I'm sure!"

We chuckled at that—he was absolutely right!

"I wish we could hire you too, Sylvia, but we just don't have the money. Wherever you apply, make sure you list me and Fred as references. We'll tell 'em the exact truth—and if that doesn't get you the job, they don't deserve to have you! I know that's a strong opinion, but it's true. And I'm old enough to get away saying it!"

We laughed again. Phillip pointed his finger at the two of us. "Ladies, it is time to rest. I don't want to see you anywhere near this building until at least August first! I suggest you go someplace, see something different, or just laze around! You've earned it!"

"Thank you kindly, Philip, for your confidence in both of us," Ma said, and I nodded in agreement, "And I do believe we'll take you up on your suggestion! We won't be taking any long trips, but we will definitely do some relaxing!"

Philip stood up, slower than usual, leaning on his cane. "Good, good. Now, let's lock up and get outta here!"

We hastened to obey.

*****

Luther: November, 1918, the grounds of Walter Reed Army Hospital, Washington, D.C.

I had to say it. "Strangest hospital I've ever seen!"

We had sailed up the Potomac River to a wharf just east of Washington. Ambulances collected us and took us to Walter Reed Hospital—or at least, that's what they said it was. We found ourselves at a low, brick structure away from the large old buildings of the hospital. We were carried into the building on stretchers, then transferred to wheelchairs of a different design than we'd seen in France.

Jack looked around as we were wheeled into a central living area. "This really doesn't look like a hospital at all. A dormitory of some sort, maybe."

Gary nodded. "Certainly not barracks, either. Looks like we may have our own rooms—that's a change!" he pronounced.

We were wheeled up to a large table with several other patients who were already there. We introduced around; we were from of all branches of the service, including a couple of sailors whose ship had been torpedoed. Most of us were either missing a limb or two, or still sported large casts.

A short doctor in a white coat walked in. "Oh, no, you guys again!" He softened the comment with a big grin.

"We meet again, Doctor Raichart." Jack said in a melodramatic voice.

"So we do, Sergeant—and congratulations on the promotion. I know most of you already from the hospital in France, but for the rest of you lucky fellows I am Doctor Bill Raichart, formerly of Johns Hopkins and Base Hospital number eighteen. My boss, Colonel Finney, sent me back to the States to work on a pilot rehabilitation program for men recovering from serious wounds. You twenty men are the guinea pigs for this endeavor—please hold all *rheeting* sounds until the end!"

Dr. Raichart's sense of humor hadn't changed, or improved. We laughed anyway.

The doctor's grin faded. "And here's the other reason why you're all here, and not over there in the wards," He pointed out the window to the larger buildings. "The influenza epidemic is reaching, well, epidemic proportions. For reasons we won't go into here, the Estimable Brass of the Army have been slow to adopt the recommendations of their medical professionals as to treatment and containment of the influenza. Well, as you gentlemen know, adversity sometimes enhances creativity."

Doctor Raichart walked over to the large table and sat down. He sighed.

"In the vale of logic only decipherable by Senior Military Officers and Department Assistant Secretaries, The High Command would not approve us establishing a special ward of patients needing intensive therapy and rehabilitation, away from the usual wards which are now full of influenza; but they would authorize an experimental unit to test new forms of physical therapy and new kinds of prostheses."

Then, under his breath, "I wonder what would happen if some day one of those Assistant Secretaries found himself in your situation?"

I was surprised Dr. Raichart would say something like that, but then I remembered he was first a Johns Hopkins physician. And a blunt speaker, always.

He continued. "Anyway, gentlemen, you will get the benefit of our little experiment here. You'll have plenty of time to rest, but also plenty of work to do, work that will benefit you for the rest of your lives. Get settled in today, relax, and get oriented; we start tomorrow! reveille will be at seven sharp tomorrow morning, and you'll have an hour and a half to get cleaned up and eat breakfast- that's in this room. 0830 you'll meet your therapists and be introduced to our fine selection of the latest fashions in prostheses! See you then, gents!"

Dr. Raichart waved to us and walked out the door.

Chapter Thirteen

Sylvia: June 15th, 1919, Appleton Baptist Church, Appleton, Illinois.

Ma and I got to church that Sunday to find the place in a happy turmoil. Pastor Kittridge had arrived back in Galesburg from the Navy the day before. He told nobody he was coming, not even his wife! Knowing Deborah, I suspected he was informed of the error of his ways, before she welcomed him home! He bustled around the sanctuary greeting everyone. He came up to Ma and me.

"Annette, Sylvia, I know you've heard it a hundred times, but please accept my deepest condolences for your losses. I just wish I could have been here for you, but—"

"Oh, we understand, Pastor," Ma interrupted, "Don't worry about it! The church folks were so kind to us through everything, and Sylvester Sanford did everything he could to help."

"Deborah's letters kept me informed. I hear Dr. Bohan was a great help too."

"Yes, he was," I said. "He performed the surgery that saved my life, then took charge when we heard Pa passed with the influenza. His actions saved a lot of lives, I'm sure."

"I really like John; I think he's the best doctor in the county. I just wish I could get through to him about knowing Jesus personally."

Ma shook her head. "We just need to keep him and his family in prayer. I know he has one son—a six year old I think."

"Let's do that, Annette. Uh oh, Deborah's reminding me of the time. You know, I've missed her doing that! We want to have you out for dinner soon, ladies; Deborah will set it up."

"Thank you, Pastor. We'd be happy to. Syl, we'd better go find a seat."

"Right, Ma."

It was good to get back in the routine of worship with our church family and Pastor. Sylvester Sanford had done a fine job filling in, but it just wasn't the same.

Pastor Kittridge said he had some preaching saved up from his Navy service, but promised to hold this first service down to only three hours. We all laughed at that, but several folks pulled out their pocket watches.

The sermon topic was "Things I have Learned", and he said it was only a small sliver of what he could talk about. The text was the familiar one from Joshua 24, "Choose you this day whom you will serve", and included illustrations from his experiences. The last illustration was striking.

"In closing, let me tell you a story about four young men I met last fall. Luther, Jack, Gary, and Matthew. These four were all seriously wounded in the great battle of June, 1918, which also claimed our Hal. After a long stay in the hospital in France, We took them aboard the *New Jersey*, and brought them back to the States."

"I got to know these young men on that trip. One, a Sergeant, had been saved for many years. Another, a Navy Pharmacist's Mate Third Class, was also a Christian, from the Apostolic Christian Church in Ohio."

"The other two men were in much the same circumstances, and both had lost limbs- one a leg, the other an arm. They both had the same choice presented, but each chose differently."

"Sergeant Luther told me he had been running from the Lord all his life. He was close friends with the other Sergeant, and they both grew up east of Peoria, as it happens. He said he'd run as hard as he could, but on June 13th, he was very badly wounded. He couldn't run any more; he knew he was dying. And the Lord caught up to him."

Several amens were heard in the sanctuary.

"The Lord, using His Still Small Voice, gave him one more chance to surrender and choose Him. He chose the Lord; he chose life."

More amens.

"He told me that even though his body was still in agony, he was given such a peace and contentment at that moment he is still overwhelmed when he thinks of it. He passed out figuring the next Person he saw would be his Lord. He said he was a little disappointed when he woke up, and saw a doctor in a hospital. He was eager to find out what the Lord wanted to do with him in the future."

"Then there was the Corporal. His family was in the Petty Officer's church in Ohio. Corporal Matthew was running too, to where he threatened to beat up anyone who tried to witness to him. He also was severely wounded in that battle; he lost his arm."

"He had been competing for the divisional boxing championship, and worked for that harder than anything else in his life. Suddenly, that was gone. The most important thing in his life was removed. He too was offered a choice. He chose. While we were battling storms crossing the Atlantic, the Corporal contrived to find himself a pistol. He hid it, and, that night when everyone was asleep, he used it on himself."

I gasped, as did several others in the congregation. *That was so sad...*

"I invited Luther, Jack, and Gary to visit us here any time they were in the area. I hope to see them here some day, and I'd love to introduce them to you. If I don't see them again in this life, though, I know I'll meet them again in Heaven, with Our Lord. It will be a joyous meeting in any event."

"I won't be seeing Corporal Matthew again."

"Choose you this day!"

Two young men and an older woman came forward at the invitation. More than a few in the congregation were crying—as were Ma and me.

*****

Luther: The rehabilitation unit, Walter Reed Hospital.

"Whoever built up that pad on the end of your stump did a pretty good job, Sergeant." Dr. Raichart remarked as he examined my right leg.

"You did that, Doctor," I said.

"So I did. I remember now," the Doctor replied with a grin. "See there, Steve, that is the perfectly prepared receiver for one of your nasty gadgets!"

Steve Mason, a prosthesis specialist from Johns Hopkins and sometime Marine Reserve Captain, squinted one eye at Doctor Raichart.

"Well, Bill, I guess even you can get it right once in a while!"

"Oh, the Blind Pig Effect, eh?"

"Yep." They both snorted, then Captain Mason continued.

"Sergeant, you've been around the good Doctor long enough to know when he's kidding; guess you'll have to figure that out about me. Now I'm not kidding: no matter how you got it, you have just about a perfectly prepared stump, if anything in this sad business can be called 'perfect'. I think we can fit you with something that will not only work, but will be hard to detect by most people."

"Thank you kindly, Sir. I'll be happy with whatever you manage to work up for me."

"I appreciate your confidence, Sergeant, but now I have to earn it. I'm going to take some measurements, and go back and work up a prototype. It won't be perfect the first time, or maybe even the tenth time, but it'll be where we start. Bill, are there any body areas we need to avoid putting straps around?"

64

"No, Steve, I think all the patches will stay on, at least for the time being."

Captain Mason rolled his eyes.

"Sorry, it's just my bedside manner showing through."

"Uh-huh."

Captain Mason got out his measuring tape and a notepad, and measured about every part of my body.

"Captain, why so many measurements?"

The Marine kept measuring as he spoke. "Sergeant, each prosthesis is different and unique to the individual. It all depends on how far up the amputation was made, the quality of the stump, and the overall strength and fitness of the person. Sometimes we have to rig straps over the shoulders to keep a prosthesis on."

"Will I need that? Not that I'm complaining of course."

"I don't think so. Everything looks good for a waistband mounting. What do you think, Doctor?"

I noticed Mason had spoken formally to the doctor.

"Captain, I think that should work fine. There's no other orthopedic damage I can find, and in spite of the extreme severity of his wounds, I think he's made a splendid recovery so far."

"Very well then, Doctor," Mason said as he put the pencil and pad in his pocket. "Sergeant Barlow, let me get my fabricators building a prototype. I suggest you start working on standing on your good leg, and getting around a bit with crutches, in preparation. Can he do that, Doctor?"

"Oh, I think that can be arranged," Dr. Raichart said, with a diabolical laugh.

Chapter Fourteen

Sylvia: Thursday, June 19th, 1919, The Trimble home, Fremont Road.

Our resolution to sleep in every morning lasted exactly three days. Ma and I found ourselves sitting at the breakfast table eating our bacon, eggs, and oatmeal at 6AM the following Thursday. We had both awakened at 5, had our personal time with the Lord, and completed the normal ablutions. Mornings like this we really appreciated indoor plumbing!

"So much for sleeping in," Ma said between bites. "We're just not made for that, I guess."

"Nope. I actually felt worse yesterday morning than I did the night before! OK this morning, though."

"I guess freedom of schedule has a price, Ma remarked, "What are your plans for today?"

"If you don't mind, I thought I'd go to the library in Galesburg and look up some schools to send my application. Do you need anything from town?"

"Hmmm…let me write you a short list for the grocer. I have some things to get for the classroom, but I reckon I'll go sometime next week, and maybe visit Bessie while I'm there. You're welcome to come too, of course."

"Let me see how far I've gotten on the applications, and how I feel."

I knew I was going to be emotional over the next week or so, since it was coming up on one year since Hal was killed. Ma saw my face change.

"What's wrong?"

"Next Monday is one year since…"

"I understand. I've heard the anniversaries of the…event…are the hardest. You just do whatever you feel up to."

"Thanks, Ma. Now, we're invited over to Pastor's house tonight, right?"

"Yes, indeed. Deborah caught me last evening at church. Gave me an invitation card and everything! She gets a little formal sometimes."

I smiled. "That she does. They're an unusual couple to be living out here in the country. I wonder why they chose to move here?"

"I've asked her," Ma replied. "She said two reasons: One, the Lord called AP to be the Pastor of Appleton Baptist Church, which would be reason enough. Two, she said she grew up in Chicago and purely hated it. All the noise, heat, commotion--she loves the atmosphere and people out here in the country. Says it is a great environment to 'foster her writing'."

"I just wish she would use her own name instead of a pseudonym," I said. She had published several Christian historical novels under the pen name *D.F. R. Christman.*

"I've talked to her about that, too. She says some people won't buy a book if they think a woman wrote it. She says that's not in any way Scriptural, and just plain stupid, but there you are. She calls it the *George Effect*"

"Eliot or Sand?"

"I asked her that," Ma chuckled. "I got two answers. First answer: *Yes.*"

I giggled. That sounded like Deborah!

"Second answer: *Cigar.*"

"What?"

"Deborah said the whole business reminded her of that disgusting cigar and its advertising slogan-*I am for men.* She said they could have it and welcome!"

We both laughed. The distributor of George cigars had put up several large painted signs on buildings in Galesburg a few years before. We agreed they were grotesque.

"At least Deborah uses her own initials, and then leaves the readers to imagine what those initials mean."

"Like her husband," Ma said softly.

"Oh, Ma! I laughed so hard I cried when you first told me what they stand for! The poor man…"

"Well, his secret is safe with us- and so is Deborah's. I wonder what she's working on now?"

"Guess we'll find out tonight."

*****

Sylvia: Thursday, June 19th, 1919, The Kittridge home, Appleton, Illinois.

Pastor Kittridge and his wife Deborah lived on the western edge of the village of Appleton, in a log cabin. The outside walls were made of notched logs, anyway. Inside the log walls Pastor and my Pa, along with some skeptical helpers had designed and built a second shell of the house, with a framework of the usual studs stiffened here and there with small steel frames. Over this inner framework went the lath and plaster of the interior walls.

In the center of the one-level house stood a room made of poured concrete, its separate foundation resting on the ground underneath the house. The room served as the bathroom. Pastor called it his *safe room*. He told us he had been in two tornadoes already in his life, and decided the next house he built would have a room they could ride it out in. Some church members who had not experienced a tornado thought this odd, but Pastor told them he had enough money to build a big, showy house they didn't need, or a smaller home that would serve, and keep them as safe as anybody was in this world. Since Pastor built the house with his own money, then deeded the property to the church, nobody ever complained about its eccentricities.

When we arrived at the house we pulled into the driveway behind Pastor's two cars. Not many families in those days had one car, let alone two.

One car was a very ordinary Model T closed sedan. Pastor Kittridge used it for calling on church members. Deborah used it too, but said the Model T was a lot less fun to drive than cars they had owned before.

The other car was a different story. It seems Pastor Kittridge's younger brother, PR (don't ask), was known for making ill-advised purchases on the spur of the moment without consulting his wife. This car had been one of those purchases.

After a short but exciting round of high-speed drives, retrievals when he managed to get it stuck somewhere, and several visits to the Aledo, Illinois Town Constable and Court for traffic violations, the City Fathers of Aledo, and his very angry wife, suggested he divest himself of his acquisition. He had written to his brother AP on the *New Jersey*, and offered him the car for about one-tenth of its original purchase price.

Pastor Kittridge had one weakness, and that was a penchant for *Great Deals*. He wired his brother the money, and early in March his brother delivered the car to the house in Appleton. About that time Pastor remembered he had not informed Deborah, and his frantic telegram informing her of the impending arrival itself arrived about two hours after the automobile. Deborah laughed about it to us, but presented a somewhat different reaction to her husband when he came home from the Navy.

The object of all this entertainment was a 1917 Chevrolet Model D four-passenger roadster. So much had Deborah told Ma when it arrived. I suspected we were about to be enlightened

68

further as Pastor Kittridge almost skipped out of the house and down the walk toward us.

"Annette, Sylvia, so glad you could come visit this evening! I want to show you my new toy."

Deborah stood in the doorway of the house with her hands on her hips, frowning.

Pastor showed us the sleek body, leather upholstery, and the *sporty wire wheels* on the green car. We tried to look politely interested.

"And here is the most unusual feature of this car!" Pastor said as he opened the hood.

Ma asked the obvious. "Pastor, besides an automobile motor, what are we looking at?"

"Annette, this is a very rare Chevrolet V-8 motor!"

"I'll supply the comment for that," Deborah had come down the walk and stood with us. "So what?"

"Dear, this engine is every bit as good as the ones from the high priced cars. It also goes like the wind!"

Deborah rolled her eyes. "He's been reading the sales brochure again. Every time he starts it the thing pops and bangs like it's going to explode."

"I'm working on it, Dear. I know it is something simple—I can fix this!"

"There's something simple, all right. Come on, ladies, let's leave the *ace mechanic* to his meditation!"

"You just wait, Deborah!"

Deborah turned and grinned at us as we followed her up the walk.

After a grand meal of pasta, meat sauce, and stewed tomatoes from Deborah's vast canning stores, topped off with slices of one of her unique breads, we settled back in the comfortable parlor to digest and chat.

"Sylvia, how is the employment search going?" Deborah asked.

"Today I went to the Galesburg Public Library, and wrote down addresses and contacts for the schools in Knox County. I want to contact them all, and see what turns up."

"Do you have a typewriter?"

"Oh, yes. Ma and I would much rather type than write. We both seem to ruin any pen we ever dip in a well!"

"That's the truth," Ma added. "For some reason, I can teach penmanship just fine, but when I try to do it myself I make a mess every time."

"No comments about teaching and doing from the peanut gallery, AP!" Deborah snapped at her husband, who just sat grinning. "I would have been happy to loan you my portable, but if you have a regular one it's much easier to get a quality result."

"Thanks for the offer, but the old Underwood Number Five will do nicely."

"And what are you working on at the moment, Deborah?" Ma asked.

Deborah raised her finger to her lips. "Something completely different for me. Grosset and Dunlap are fine with the work I'm doing now, but I have an idea I want to play with and see if I can master it. By the way, this is secret information!"

"We won't tell!" Ma said.

"I thought I'd try something called *speculative fiction*. What I want to do is imagine this area, this village, this church, about fifty years in the future, and write a novel about the people living here then."

"I can see how you might do that, but I can think of a lot of ways to fail."

"So can I, Syl. That's why I'm approaching this one as an experiment, nothing I have to finish. I think I've been writing more explanations of the book and its times than the book itself. AP and I have had hours of discussions about what life will be like then."

"Assuming the Lord delays His coming," Pastor Kittridge added.

"And AP here has a couple of ideas I really don't want to deal with."

"Like what?" Ma asked.

"Another war, or rather, the continuation of this one."

"How awful!"

Pastor Kittridge nodded. "Yes, Sylvia, it is awful. Horrible. But in my opinion it's as certain as I'm sitting here, barring the return of the Lord. An armistice is just a chance to recover and rearm. They'll be back at it by and by."

"How long do you think we have, Pastor?" Ma asked.

"I honestly don't see it in the next year, or five years, or ten. Give it about twenty years and some different leaders in a few countries, and it will all restart. And this time it will be worse than this last one, by far."

Deborah looked over at me, and waved her hand at Pastor. She saw the tears in my eyes, I guess.

"I'm so sorry, Sylvia! I just wasn't thinking; please forgive me."

"Of course, Pastor. It's been a rough year and a half for everyone."

"I know, and I need to remember that. You, Annette, Hal's best friend Ken Potter's family, and young Jeff Potter! So many are hurting. Like those boys I talked about Sunday."

"At least that story had a happy ending, for three of them anyway. That tale was just fascinating!"

"Those young men were fascinating too, Annette. Wise beyond their years. I am sure the Lord has something wonderful for each of them."

"Were those young men injured to where they'd have to retire?" Deborah asked.

"Two of them for sure. The Sergeant who lost his lower leg and the Pharmacist's Mate—he looked good, but was missing at least a lung. The other Sergeant might return to duty, if his leg finally knits."

"What do you suppose they'll do?" Ma asked.

"Let's see…Luther said the Lord seemed to be leading him toward college and engineering of some sort. Gary the Pharmacist's Mate has a fine knowledge of Scripture, and a tender heart. He's a farmer by trade, but I wouldn't be surprised if he were ordained as a Minister in the Apostolic Christian Church. They are governed by a Board of Elders in each church, but the congregation elects and ordains certain men of the congregation they feel are called to preach and minister."

"That's odd," I remarked.

"It is, but it works well for them. We need to remember the Lord uses people in different ways, but always identifiable according to His purpose. That's a little deep for the conversation tonight, though."

"As opposed to the finer points of operation of the Chevrolet V-8?"

"Don't get started, Deborah…"

We laughed as Deborah gave Pastor *The Look*, then started to laugh herself.

Chapter Fifteen

Luther: Special rehabilitation unit, Walter Reed Hospital.

We spent the winter and most of the following spring in that clinic building on the edge of the Walter Reed Hospital grounds. The weather wasn't nearly as cold or snowy as we were used to in Illinois and Indiana, but it was a damp, penetrating kind of cold. Fortunately, the clinic had a central coal-fired furnace which worked well most of the time.

The food was pretty good, the nurses and orderlies pleasant, and the routine not too challenging…except when we met with Captain Mason and his merry band of *therapists*. The name of the program was Physical Therapy, or *P.T.* for short; this quickly changed to *Pain and Torture*. Six days per week we followed our individual paths to strength, movement, and wellness…to the extreme annoyance of every part of our bodies. Not even Boot Camp brought out the aches and pains like this program did!

However—slowly, so slowly, my ability to move without pain improved.

Gradually some of our old stamina returned. A few aches and pains subsided, to be replaced by new ones. In Gary Folkerts' case, his strength returned fairly quickly, but he had to learn how to get the most out of his one lung, without overdoing it. He wouldn't be running any foot races; then again, neither would the rest of us.

Two weeks after my initial meeting with Captain Mason, he returned, along with one of his technicians, a big man who reminded me of a football player. He introduced himself as Keith Setterdahl, and he brought my new leg!

Sort of…

In spite of Captain Mason's exhaustive measurements, the leg turned out about three inches too long. The socket felt good against my stump, but the resulting list was unacceptable. Keith apologized profusely; Jack thought it hilarious.

Back and forth, rework, retry, rework, repeat. That was the story of my next two months. I got fairly skilled using crutches, and balancing on my other leg, but I really wanted that prosthesis! One day Steve and Keith brought over a prosthesis that fit well and was the right length; however on the end of it was a finely-carved duck foot! I couldn't help but laugh.

Keith promised me the finished prosthesis the next day. True to his word, he returned with the prosthesis, this time with a carved human foot on the end. The prosthesis fit perfectly, so they let me keep it and try it.

Now my work really began—daily instruction and practice strapping on the leg, getting the fit between the stump and the socket right, then learning to stand and walk with the prosthesis. I used a metal frame I could move along with me to keep my balance at first. Eventually I *graduated* to two canes, then one cane. By the end of my stay I could walk on flat surfaces without my cane, although I still needed it to help me balance over gravel and grassy surfaces.

Jack's leg gradually healed, and by the end of April he said he felt like he was ready to go back to active service. Dr. Raichart added *almost but not quite* to that thought. Jack began short, tentative runs around the grounds to try to build up his endurance. A therapist ran with him, watching closely. Jack said he was happy for the company.

In mid-December we were visited by more specialists—the *Occupational Therapy Crew*, as they called themselves. Their job was to help us get our upper body strength back, and teach us skills we could use when we retired. I knew by then I was going to college somewhere, but I was happy to learn new skills while gaining strength.

The therapists learned I played pipe organs; they didn't have one of those available, but asked if I'd be interested playing one of its smaller cousins, a reed organ. I told them I'd be happy to try, but my pedal work (or foot pumping, in the case of this kind of organ) would be a bit limited. They replied that this particular organ would be more of a challenge, because it didn't seem to work, and nobody knew why. I told them to bring it on in…and they did!

The poor box of scuffed wood and cracked leather made no noise except a *whoosh* of leaking air when I first met it. I knew what was wrong—everything—so I set to work. The therapists provided tools and materials whenever I asked for them.

I took the thing apart, found all the leaking bellows and other leather and rubber parts, cut new leather and rubberized cloth, and very slowly put it back together. I learned more about hot glue and accumulated dirt than I ever wanted to know!

Finally, after several mistakes and corrections, I had it all together. By this time I had my leg, so I was able to slowly pump the bellows to start it up. The last time I had touched a keyboard was the previous April, when Marcel Dupré allowed me to play the great organ at St. Sulpice in Paris for a few minutes. This little organ didn't have five manuals and a hundred or so drawknobs, but that first chord from the instrument was more thrilling than the sounds I made that day in Paris.

I suspected I had just acquired a hobby.

A couple of adjustments, and I sat back down to see if I could still play. One piece came to mind—the *Le Grasse* Scherzo in E by Charles-Marie Widor. I had played it at my senior organ recital, and it was a favorite of my organ teacher, Carl Christian Christensen of Peoria. He made me play it from memory, so I still had a good part of it in my mind, I hoped. I hadn't done too badly when I played it on the organ at St. Sulpice; I'd really have to adjust it to make it fit on the one keyboard and no pedals!

I figured it was as good a time as any to find out. I pumped up the bellows, pulled a couple of drawknobs, and began.

As I played, I noticed Jack walk into the therapy room and stand in the corner. He'd heard me play many times before. Then, one by one, most of the rest of the men in the unit came in. They all stood, or sat in their wheelchairs, and listened without a sound.

I fumbled my way through the Scherzo, altering the fingering on the fly to get at least a little bit of the pedal line in. Fortunately, the work is short.

I finished, and found the room was filled with patients and staff, including Captain Mason and Doctor Raichart! They all clapped heartily, and asked me what other music I knew. I told them the only thing I knew right then was that my leg was aching and I needed to get off it for a while. Before the others left they made me promise to play more when I could.

Raichart and Mason walked over to me when the room had emptied.

"Steve, would you say Sergeant Barlow has just discovered a new exercise for his leg?"

"I surely would, Bill, and one that brings with it extra rewards!" Captain Mason grinned at me. "My wife plays the organ. I'll see what kind of music I can borrow from her. I'd guess you only have so many of those memorized!"

"Thank you Sir, I'd appreciate that. And you're right—I have exactly one memorized, and you just heard it!"

*****

Luther, Spring 1919

From the beginning Jack, Gary, and I met on Sundays and Wednesday evenings for Bible study and prayer. Gradually a Sunday routine developed, where one of us would prepare a short message and preach it to the other two while we sat at the table in the dining room. We did this quietly, so as not to disturb the other men; however, soon first one, then another, and another of the men asked to join our group. Before we knew it we had ten of the twenty men in the unit in a service on most Sundays.

At Dr. Raichart's suggestion the refurbished reed organ was moved into the dining room, and I was asked to play for the services too. A couple of stray hymnals appeared in the unit, and we used them for the old familiar hymns. Gary wrote his ma, and she sent him a copy of *Zion's Harp*, the hymnal of the Apostolic Christian church. They normally sang without instruments in their services, so the hymns were tailored for multi-part singing. We sang, and I played, and enjoyed the old hymns of the Faith.

Although we focused on edification and education of the Christians in the group, four of the men trusted Christ as a result of these meetings. What a pleasant addition to the rigorous and often painful work we were doing!

Jack and I found we were competent teachers, but our speaking style did not lend itself to what we thought of as preaching. Gary, however, seemed to have the knack for keeping people's attention, and telling a story to make a point. Jack and I both were pretty sure the congregation in his church back in Mansfield would elect him to minister when they found out about this.

And so the months passed, the holidays came and went, the Armistice was signed, and influenza ravaged the country.

Chapter Sixteen

Luther: May 19th, 1919, the rehabilitation unit, Walter Reed Hospital.

Doctor Raichart called Gary, Jack, and me into his small office that warm Thursday. Captain Mason was also there.

"You're probably wondering why I called you all here,"

"He said in a melodramatic voice," Captain Mason added.

"Steve, this is serious!"

"For these gentlemen, maybe, but not for me."

"That's what you think; I haven't told you all of it either!"

For the first time I saw Captain Mason look abashed.

"Better. Now, Gentlemen, here's all the story I know. Next Monday, May 23rd, we're going to have visitors drop in. Major General George Barnett…"

Uh-oh. My tongue ran away with me. "The Commandant of the Marine Corps?"

"The Very. I see you have the proper appreciation of this August Personage. Steve, you could learn from the apprehension, nay fear, in these fellows' eyes!"

"I will so note, and take it under advisement, O Doctor Bill!"

"One of these days I ought to remind you they gave me a rank too, but it's too much fun this way."

Doctor Raichart turned back to us.

"The Commandant is paying us a visit, along with the Assistant Secretary of the Navy, a fellow by the name of Franklin Delano Roosevelt. And be sure to use all three names. This pair, plus whomever else they bring with them, are coming over to see our operation, and try to decide if they want to expand it, or close it down. They're also coming to leave a few presents, type unknown. You know the sort of stuff they deal in."

I knew—medals. *Uh-oh again.*

"They will tour the entire building, so you know what needs to be done. They will then have a formation out in the courtyard there," he pointed to the unkempt, overgrown area outside his window.

"You aren't responsible for that. I've just let the C.O. of the hospital know who's coming and what they intend to do. I expect some activity out there shortly."

We all laughed, especially since we weren't going to be doing the yard work!

Doctor Raichart was just getting warmed up.

"Also, since you are just about where you're going to stay in height, weight, and number of body parts, the tailors are coming over here in about an hour to measure you for a complete uniform set, in addition to what you've already accumulated. You'll be wearing Full Dress Blues for this visit. Since it's no secret your time here is about done, we need to get the uniforms to you before you either retire or go back to the fleet. Yes, Jack, it's the Fleet Marine Force for you!"

Jack broke out into a huge grin. "Thank you, Doctor, that's wonderful news!"

"Don't thank me yet, Sergeant, I haven't heard which ship you get. I can tell you it won't be the New Jersey; she was decommissioned last week. I heard about your trip back on her; I'm sorry about what happened."

"That was a hard time for all of us, Doctor," Gary replied.

Doctor Raichart looked uncharacteristically serious. "That sort of thing always is. Sometimes you see it coming, and want to stop it, but you can't, Lord knows."

"Yes, He does," Gary said.

Doctor Raichart gave Gary a raised eyebrow, then continued.

"All right, gentlemen, you know as much as I know. You are in charge of the Field Day Exercise with the other gentlemen. Perhaps they'll get their own Christmas presents later. Have at it!"

Dr. Raichart waved us out of his office.

*****

Sylvia: June 22nd, 1919, The Trimble home.

"I'm surprised your Ma let you take the Model T out this far," I remarked.

Helen Smiley had driven all the way out to Appleton to see me that Sunday afternoon. We sat on the front porch, sipping lemonade and talking.

"I've been driving for about a year and a half now. One of the good things about being a little...OK, *stocky*, is I have the strength to manage the wheel and the pedals, and have had for a couple years. Someday I'm sure they'll get around to making a law that says you can't drive below a certain age, but until then I'm going to make the most of it!"

"Pa started teaching me when we got The Baby, but I really didn't have it mastered until a couple years ago. Now I feel I'm about back to where I was before I got sick. You must have been fifteen when you started."

"Fourteen, but close to fifteen. I've done OK so far."

"I'd say you have. How does it feel to have graduated High School at sixteen?"

"I'm surprised they let me do it. But I had all my courses in, took an overload the last two years, and I'm done!"

"I always thought you enjoyed school."

"I do. Did. Just not that school. Too large, too many cliques. I just never felt comfortable at GHS."

"So what do you want to be when you grow up?"

My old friend snorted. "You say that with a sideways grin, Syl!"

"Caught me again, Helen! I know you've wanted to be a teacher since you were about five. Do you still?"

"Oh, yes. I just know better now what grades I want to teach. Someday I'd really like to get a position like your Ma has, in a country school with several grades. That wouldn't bore me."

"I can tell you from experience, it isn't boring! I knew a lot about the school already since I went to it, but it's hard to believe all the things you have to do—and know—to teach in one. I want to get some letters out to some of the school boards this week, and see if I can get an interview."

"I'm a ways from that, yet. I'd like to find a spot as a teacher's assistant, like you did, and learn it that way. May take a couple years more, but I'll know what I'm doing a lot better."

"You know you might not get paid for that—I didn't"

Helen sighed. "I know, but for the right experience I'd do it for a year for free. My folks say I can live at home as long as I like, and that really means a lot. Plus I get along with them, and even with Lester since he's grown up a bit!"

"I always thought Lester was mature for his age."

"Had you spoofed! He just loves to pull little pranks, he calls 'em practical jokes. Doesn't do it so much since he crossed the spark plug wires on the Model T and blew out the coil! That one cost him two months of his paper route money."

"Got his attention, huh?"

"Oh yes...that and the whipping he got helped too. Pa hadn't had to do that for five years."

"I cannot remember the last time I got spanked," I replied. "How about you?"

Helen closed her eyes. "The fourth of July 1912. I lit what I thought was a small firecracker in the back yard, and put a tin can over it. I learned the meaning of *shrapnel* that day…and Pa let me have it. Deserved it too."

"Oh, my! Was anyone hurt?"

"I caught a piece in my arm, that was all," She showed me the scar on her right forearm. "But there were a half dozen other kids in the backyard at the time! Nobody was touched, though. I was amazed."

"So the Lord got your attention?"

"Yeah," Helen replied softly, "What was worse was that up until then I thought I could be good all by myself, and didn't need this *saving* the Preacher talked about. I knew I'd really wanted to raise a ruckus when I lit that firecracker, and that brought me face to face with my sin nature. That is not a pretty place."

"No kidding! I used to be jealous of the school kids getting Ma's attention and I wasn't. It's easy for an only child to get really selfish. I did…until the first Sunday Pastor Kittridge came to the church here. He preached about *secret sins*, and it was just like he'd been watching me! The Lord finally got my attention, and I surrendered…"

I trailed off. I sat for a moment just staring off across the grassy front yard to the corn field across the road.

"What's wrong, Syl?"

"I was just thinking…a dangerous thing. How does what happened to Ma and me square with His purpose for our lives? All this sadness, all this pain—" I stifled a sob.

Helen reached over and put her hand on my arm.

"We see the story as far as He's written it. We don't see the end yet. We're given strength for today, the daily bread. He is working His plan out, whether we see it or not."

I pulled out my handkerchief. "Oh, I know. It's just hard to see where He is going with all this."

Helen sat back in her chair. "Sometimes I wonder if it isn't better if we can't see where He is taking us. We might just see the mountain ahead and miss the blessing over it."

"Or see what is coming and lose heart."

"Before we see the end of it." I decided Helen had the right of it.

Helen stayed for a light supper, and our evening church service. She had brought an invitation to Ma from Bessie to have lunch at their house on Tuesday when she was in town shopping for the school. I was invited, but I said I wanted to stay home and work on my letters to the schools.

Rain began as I was preparing for bed, and continued all night.

Monday, June 23rd, 1919, started out rainy and ended rainy. We had no real wind or heavy rain, but a constant, soaking, drenching rain. The farmers would be very pleased; the rest of us could have done without it. I stayed in all day, and typed letters to school boards.

We burned the kerosene lamps the entire day. The day was dark, dreary, and matched my mood. I didn't cry, but I didn't smile either. The air felt heavy, and slightly numbing. Ma had said the anniversaries would be difficult; she was right. I prayed several times for the Lord to get me through the day and the memories; He did, but I still felt dull and numb. I was thankful I had the energy and health to feel the grief, and slog through it.

Ma spent the day cleaning the house, sewing, and in general catching up with the odd jobs we never seemed to have time to get to during the school year. She said the day was wearing on her too, and took a rare afternoon nap. I kept typing away. I figured I would get a good number of them done, and descend upon the Appleton Post Office on Tuesday or Wednesday.

Late that afternoon Fred and Pacey Johnson stopped by with some early sweet corn. The rain never seemed to bother them, and we sat on the porch for a while watching the ditches fill up. They left in their buggy, and we went back inside.

Chapter Seventeen

Luther: May 23rd, 1919, the rehabilitation unit, Walter Reed.

We got up at dawn to finish the last preparations for the Grand Inspection. I've always been amazed at the amount of work that goes into preparing for one of these events, both the building and our persons. We were all skilled professionals at this sort of evolution, so we were dressed and ready for the show a good half hour before their arrival. At least we didn't have to stand in ranks waiting for them; Doctor Raichart absolutely forbade that draw on our still limited strength.

We stood in the common room and looked each other over for little details we had missed—specks of dirt, Irish Pennants (stray threads from seams or other sewing), and the like.

"Haven't had this kind of fun in a while," Gary remarked.

"Now that we're organized, what do we do?" offered Jack.

"I don't suppose you gentlemen are nervous about this event, are you?" I said out the side of my mouth as I snipped an IP from Gary's jumper collar.

"Terrified," Gary said.

"Petrified," added Jack.

"I'll see you one petrified, and raise you one roiling stomach," I said, and meant it.

"Worse than the New Jersey?"

"You betcha, Jack! These guys are more dangerous than half the German army!"

"Luther, aren't you exaggerating just a little bit?"

"You haven't been the guest of honor at a Marine medal formation, Gary. Just wait!"

At that moment we were interrupted by two men in dress uniforms entering the room. Captain Mason wore a uniform much like ours, except with officer insigne. The other uniform gave us all a start. We quickly came to attention and snapped off a salute.

Doctor Raichart returned our salutes, and turned to Captain Mason.

"See why I didn't want them to know what rank I was? We'd have to be doing that sort of thing all the time and neither they nor I have time to play *watch the birdie!*"

"I see your point, Colonel. People relate to you more as a doctor than an officer."

"That's the whole idea, Captain…at least, relate in the way that will get them well!"

Doctor—*Colonel*—Raichart turned back to us, and declaimed.

"Gentlemen, if I have my way, today will be the first, last, and only day we have to engage in this military show, at least where I'm concerned. I didn't ask for this rank; they stuck me with it! I never told you, but I was head of Orthopedic Medicine at Johns Hopkins before the war. I hope to go back to that job very soon."

He cleared his throat, and continued.

"But for today, I get to play Military. I hope, though, I never forget that you gentlemen—Marines and Navy—along with the others here, that you are the real heroes in this piece. I'm deeply honored to have worked with you, and helped you mend. You're the memories I want to carry away from this time, and I thank you kindly for them!" He turned away, blinking.

Captain Mason started to clap. "Bravo, Bill! I couldn't have said it better myself!"

Colonel Raichart spun around and faced the Captain. "Steve, one of these days I'm gonna bust you down to bedpan washer!" He softened the words with a lopsided grin.

"Right…"

Colonel Raichart turned serious.

"OK, gentlemen, they'll be here in ten minutes, guaranteed. I want you three, along with Captain Mason, to stand with me when I greet them. They'll want a tour, and we get to provide it. The rest of the men will form up out in the courtyard, and try to stay cool until we get out there. The tour's scheduled to last ten minutes, but I've heard the Assistant Secretary likes to talk to people so we may run over. Proper form of address for Mr. Roosevelt is 'Sir', or 'Mister Secretary'. You know how to address the Commandant."

Oh boy, did we!

"And if one of you starts to feel faint, or feel like you'll buckle, step away from the group and go sit somewhere! You'll have to be standing long enough at the ceremony to tire you out; I will *not* have you keeling over on the tour. Got all that, gentlemen?"

"Yes, Sir!" we chorused.

"All right then, pack that last bit of grease into your Military Bearing, and let's go stand by the door."

At exactly ten o'clock four olive green Cadillac touring cars pulled into the drive in front of our building. The first car flew from its front bumper a red flag with fouled anchor and four white stars—the Assistant Secretary of the Navy. The second car flew a red flag with the Marine Corps emblem and four white stars arranged differently from the first—the Commandant. The other two cars stopped behind the first two, and each car disgorged a half dozen men in uniform carrying either Graflex cameras or the smaller Graphic press cameras. *Not a good omen for this ceremony*, I thought.

Drivers ran around to the rear doors of the first two cars, and opened them. From the first stepped a youngish man of medium height in a dark suit. He wore wire-rimmed glasses and a serious expression on his face. He walked over to the second car as two men got out.

The first man to exit was older, with graying light brown hair combed over to the right, a well-trimmed gray moustache, and another serious expression on his face. That would be Commandant Barnett.

Behind him stepped a somewhat shorter, wiry man of about the same age. He wore horn-rimmed glasses, and had a body carriage more military and ramrod-straight than any I had ever seen before, even my Drill Instructors. His uniform sleeve almost didn't seem big enough to carry the chevrons he wore. The Marine Corps didn't have a billet for Sergeant Major of the Marine Corps, but from what I'd heard this man performed those duties for the Commandant. I almost feared him more than the Commandant!

The little party formed up and walked up the widened sidewalk toward where we stood. Taking our cue from the Colonel, we came to attention together, and snapped our salutes together. The Commandant and the Sergeant Major returned the salutes; Mr. Roosevelt nodded.

"Welcome to our unit, gentlemen!" Colonel Raichart said.

"Thank you, Colonel," the Commandant said. "Knowing your love of Military Protocol, I figured you'd have the place wired and sandbagged."

Colonel Raichart blushed deeply; it seemed he was *known in high places*!

Mr. Roosevelt snorted, and then spoke.

"General Barnett warned me about you Johns Hopkins fellows, but I see he was mistaken. I'd really like a tour of the place, if you don't mind!"

Now it was the Commandant's turn to blush. The three of us, and for once Captain Mason, kept poker faces, somehow. If nothing else, this was High Class Entertainment.

"Certainly, Mr. Secretary. If you gentlemen will step this way," and Colonel Raichart led the group into the building.

Tours, like inspections, can be unpredictable—no, make that *always are*.

No matter how hard and how long you clean, paint, press, or polish, something always happens. Early on we learned to do the very best we could, and then just let it go. Unlike the unsaved, we knew the Lord would take care of the situation as He saw fit, so after a certain point we just had to give it to Him.

This tour proceeded without surprise until we came into the commons room. Mr. Roosevelt had been looking closely at each room, and especially at the equipment the therapists used with us. Now he entered the commons room, looked around, and visibly startled. He walked quickly away from the group, over to where the organ sat along the wall.

"So this is where you ended up!" he said as he put his hand on the recently-varnished case. The Assistant Secretary turned to us, wearing a wide grin.

"This little organ sat in the chapel over at the Navy Department when I got there a few years ago. It wouldn't play, and nobody seemed to know how to fix it. I noticed it was gone a few months ago, and I figured, sadly, it had been discarded. I am so happy to see it here! I had heard someone here restored an organ, but I didn't know it was this one. Who did it?"

So much for no surprises. I stepped forward. "I rebuilt it, Sir."

"And you are..."

"Sergeant Luther Barlow, Sir."

"So you're Sergeant Barlow! I'm very happy to meet you!" Mr. Roosevelt walked over to me and shook my hand. "I've heard about you, Sergeant."

Oh, no. "I'm happy to meet you too, Sir."

"I understand you play the organ, too, Sergeant."

"Yes, Sir, a bit."

"More than a bit, Sergeant! I'd really like to hear what that organ sounds like, if I could impose on you to play something right now."

Me and my big mouth. "Of course, Sir. If I may?"

"Go right ahead, Sergeant. We have a few minutes before the ceremony, don't we, General?"

"Of course, Mr. Secretary. Colonel, I wonder if you have a head around here that hasn't been declared off limits?"

"Of course, General, right this way," Colonel Raichart said, and pointed.

"Thanks, Colonel. Sergeant Major, what about you?"

"No thank you, Sir, I'm fine. I'd really like to hear the Sergeant play."

"Suit yourself," General Barnett said as he moved with alacrity through the door, followed by Colonel Raichart.

This exchange gave me time to walk over to the organ, pull out the bench, and sit down. *Now what?*

I suddenly remembered two things, and they were critical. First, I quickly prayed that the Lord would give me the strength and skill to play in this situation, and let me remember whatever it was I was going to play.

Then, I realized the only piece I really had prepared was that little scherzo by Charles-Marie Widor. Captain Mason's wife had given me a small pile of very nice music, but I had not had time to memorize any of it.

All this went through my head in the ten seconds it took to walk to the organ and sit down. The others in the party walked over and stood a few feet away—except for Mr. Roosevelt, who came and stood at the side of the instrument, where he could see my hands. *No pressure here, Barlow!*

Nothing for it now. I started pumping, and pulled three drawknobs. I placed my hands on the keyboard, Fervently thanked the Lord in my mind for giving me something to play, and…played.

Since I first played the Scherzo on this organ I'd had time to recast the music to get the most out of one keyboard and very limited voicing. My audience listened intently as I played, flipped drawknobs in and out, and generally resembled the one-armed paper hanger of lore.

I finished. I bowed my head for a second as the onlookers started clapping, and thanked my Savior for getting me through it.

Mr. Roosevelt reached in and shook my hand. "Thank you so much for that performance, Sergeant! I am so happy to see this organ finally restored to its full function!"

"Thank you, Mr. Secretary."

Mr. Roosevelt turned to the group. "Sergeant Major Simmons, do you still have that little wheelbook you always carry?"

"Sir, yes Sir!" Simmons replied, as he fished the small spiral notebook out of his pocket.

"I need to borrow it for just a moment, if I may." The Secretary took the notebook from the sergeant major and tore out a page. He pulled a pencil from his coat pocket and began to write, speaking as he wrote.

"Please see this organ returns to the Navy Department Chapel when it is no longer required at this place. Franklin D. Roosevelt, Assistant Secretary."

He looked up. "That ought to do it. Sergeant Major, would you see this is fastened to the back of this organ please?"

"Of course, Mr. Secretary."

"Thanks, *Sar-Maj*,"

I had gotten up and returned to the group by this time.

Roosevelt turned to me again. "Sergeant, I understand you lost a leg below the knee—is that correct?"

"Yes sir, my right leg."

"I watched you walk during the tour, Sergeant. I couldn't tell which leg was the prosthesis. I also couldn't tell as you pumped this organ. By the way, will you be able to play the pedals of a pipe organ with that prosthesis?"

"Mr. Secretary, I really don't know, and won't until I have some time to practice. However, given my experience with pumping this one, I'm optimistic, Sir."

"I think you have reason to be optimistic, Sergeant. When you are retired, if you ever get up around Hyde Park, I'd love to have you come up and play the organ at my church up there."

"Thank you, Sir. I'll keep that in mind."

The Assistant Secretary sounded sincere, but I wondered how much of that speech was the politician speaking. In any event, I doubted if I would ever get up to Hyde Park.

Mr. Roosevelt wasn't quite finished. "Captain Mason, I understand you are responsible for the construction and fitting of prostheses here, and developing the therapy the men receive to use them. Correct?"

"Yes Mr. Secretary."

Captain Mason was all business, and all Marine; up till then I'd wondered if he could be both at the same time. He had turned an interesting shade of white, though.

"I have gotten many letters from our young men who have been fitted with prostheses you designed and your team built. I have yet to receive one with anything but fulsome praise for your work. If, God forbid, I ever have need of the services you provide, I want you providing them!"

"Thank you, Mr. Secretary."

I want to give you my personal 'Well Done', and that of Secretary Daniels,

Admiral Benson, and General Barnett."

"Thank you very much, Mr. Secretary."

"What did I just approve of, Mr. Secretary?" General Barnett asked as he came back into the room.

"I just gave our collective 'Well Done' to Captain Mason for his physical therapy advances, and work on prostheses."

"Oh, most certainly, sir," the Commandant nodded, then turned to Steve. "Captain Mason, you now know one of the things we're going to talk about in the formation out there in the courtyard. Are we about ready to start that evolution?"

Colonel Raichart responded. "Mr. Secretary, General, if you'll give us about five minutes to get these men out there, and everybody lined up, I believe we could start."

"Make it ten minutes or so, Colonel. I need to go where the General did."

"If I may come with you, Mr. Secretary,"

"Of course, Sergeant Major. Thank you all for a fine and informative tour, and thank you, Sergeant Barlow, for reacquainting me with an old friend, who has found her voice." Roosevelt then walked quickly through the doorway, followed by Sergeant Major Simmons.

Definitely the politician speaking there, I thought.

As the formation began my leg was starting to feel the effects of the walking and pumping. The Assistant Secretary complimented us for our strides toward recovery and rehabilitation, and praised Colonel Raichart and Captain Mason for their pioneering work. He made no commitment to keeping the unit open, but I really didn't expect him to. At least we knew he wasn't promising us something he couldn't deliver.

Then to the clicking of camera shutters four of us were called to the front—Captain Mason, Gary, Jack and me.

General Barnett moved slowly from one end of our little line to the other, accompanied by Sergeant Major Simmons, who held a box with the awards. Secretary Roosevelt read out the citation, General Barnett took a smaller box the Sergeant Major handed him, and pinned the appropriate medal on our tunics.

Captain Mason got it first. He received a Navy Cross for assisting at an aid station very close to the front for several hours under enemy artillery fire during the Battle of Belleau Wood. He told us later he was just visiting the station to observe when a major German counterattack began, and simply lent a hand while the casualties came in. He didn't mention the shrapnel wounds he received when a shell landed in the middle of the aid station, which he ignored until he finally fainted from loss of blood; the citation added that little detail.

Pharmacist's Mate Third Class Folkerts also received the Navy Cross, for repeatedly going in front of a German machine gun emplacement to treat and retrieve fallen Marines, until he himself was critically wounded. Gary stood ramrod-straight as the Commandant pinned the medal on his tunic, but tears streamed down his face. The Commandant ignored the tears; I suspect they weren't the first he'd seen under those circumstances.

Next Jack received the Navy Cross, for charging the German machine gun

position on June 12th, where he'd been wounded. I remembered that occasion very well, since I had been the one who caught him as he fell, and ended up carrying him back to the aid station. Someone must have been watching us, and put him in for the medal; he surely deserved it.

The Commandant and the Sergeant Major came to me.

We saluted. I stood as still and straight as I could , as the camera shutters snapped. At least we were outside so the photographers didn't have to use flash powder. I noticed my leg was starting to ache more.

The Commandant nodded toward Mr. Roosevelt, who began to read.

"The Secretary of the Navy is pleased to award the Navy Cross to Sergeant Luther Howard Barlow, U.S. Marine Corps, for exemplary heroism while serving with Company H, 2nd Battalion, 6th Regiment (Marines), 2d Division, A.E.F. in action in the *Bois de Belleau*, France, June 12th, 1918. Sergeant Barlow disregarded his own safety by going out under a heavy shell and machine-gun fire three times, to carry wounded comrades to the battalion Aid Station, each time returning to continue the fight. Sergeant Barlow's actions were directly responsible for saving the lives of his three fellow Marines."

As General Barnett pinned the medal on my tunic, I had the stray thought that Mr. Roosevelt had a unique accent and inflection to his voice.

I shook hands with the General, and we saluted, all according to the usual protocol. I must have shown some unconscious relief that the ordeal was over, for at that moment General Barnett whispered four words I will never forget.

"I'm not finished, son."

Though my face and posture remained frozen, my heart sank to my toes. I knew what was coming next- knew it, and had prayed it would never come. This one the Lord chose to answer in a way other than how I wished.

88

The Commandant nodded to the Assistant Secretary again.

"The President of the United States of America takes pleasure in presenting the Medal of Honor to Sergeant Luther Howard Barlow, U.S. Marine Corps, for extraordinary heroism while serving with Company H, 2nd Battalion, 6th Regiment (Marines), 2d Division, A.E.F. in action in the *Bois de Belleau*, France, June 13th, 1918. After his platoon had taken a position along a railroad embankment, Sergeant Barlow, accompanying his platoon leader and two other Marines to reconnoiter the ground beyond, was suddenly fired upon by an enemy machine gun from 50 yards. The first burst of fire from the enemy machine gun killed or wounded the platoon leader and the other two Marines. From a standing position on the railroad track, fully exposed to view, Sergeant Barlow opened fire at once, but failing to silence the gun, rushed forward with his bayonet fixed, through underbrush toward the gun emplacement, throwing several well-aimed hand grenades while firing first his rifle, then his pistol, at the emplacement. Sergeant Barlow succeeded in eliminating the enemy machine gun emplacement with the final grenade he threw, falling directly in front of the gun with his right leg nearly severed below the knee and with several bullet holes in his body. His unselfish and sacrificial action enabled the rest of the platoon to rush forward, and continue the advance."

General Barnett turned to Sergeant Major Simmons, and took the medal case from him. He turned, opened the case, and placed the wide blue ribbon of the medal around my neck. I remained frozen in place.

The General reached out, and shook my hand, as the shutters clicked. Sergeant Major Simmons also shook my hand; he did not do that with the other recipients. Both men then braced, and initiated a salute—to me. Another tradition of this medal. I returned the salute.

The formation was dismissed, the Secretary, the General, and their party departed. We all filed back into the building that had been our home for so long, and we would soon be leaving. My body went with them, but my mind was far away, back in France.

Chapter Eighteen

Sylvia: June 24th, 1919, the Trimble home, Knox County, Illinois.

Tuesday the 24th began with a beautiful, brilliant sunrise over the rolling farmland. The sun streamed in my window as I got dressed and made my bed. I stepped into the hallway and saw Ma preparing breakfast in the kitchen. We sat down to eat to the sound of cattle and horses in the farmyard a field away from our house.

"What a beautiful morning!" Ma exclaimed.

"After yesterday, it certainly is!" I replied with equal fervor.

"For the first time since we finished at the school I feel really rested. It's a good day to go shopping and visiting. Are you sure you don't want to come with me?"

"I'm tempted, Ma, but no thanks. I really have to get these letters out as soon as I can, to get my name in front of the school boards before they start hiring."

"How many have you done already?"

"I have fifteen finished and in their envelopes. I have another fifteen addresses of boards to go, then I will put on the stamps and take them to the Post Office. I'd like to get them done and out before the Post Office closes this afternoon, so I'll try to be ready to go by the time you get home."

"That sounds fine. I should be home by mid-afternoon so you can take the Baby to Appleton."

Ma finished her oatmeal and started to pick up the dishes to put them in the sink.

"Ma, just leave those in the sink. I'll take care of them later. They'll be a nice break from typing."

"Thank you, Dear. Is there anything you need from town?"

"Nothing I can think of. I think we're set here for a few days."

"All right, then. Let me check my lists....yes, I think that's everything. Can you think of anything else we need to talk about?"

"No, Ma, I think we've covered it all."

"Well, I'll be off then. See you later. Love ya, Syl!"

"Love you too Ma. See you."

Ma cranked the Baby, and left. I decided to take care of the dishes first, and cleaned a bit in the kitchen while I was at it. Then, since there was nothing hurrying me, I tidied up some in the rest of the house, until I realized I was just putting off sitting down at the typewriter.

Got to get at it. I pulled out my list of addresses and names, and sat down at the typewriter. The next time I looked up I had six letters done, and an hour and a half had passed. *Time for a break.*

I made sure I was presentable and walked out to the mailbox. The mail had arrived. A note from Helen, thanking us for having her out on Sunday. A letter from the Navy Finance Center in Cleveland, verifying that we were still living at our current address (There was a joke in there someplace, but I decided not to think too much about it!). The *Galesburg Evening Mail* from yesterday, of course. And that was it.

I walked back to the house, taking time to enjoy the warm breeze, and the pleasure of unhurried life. Back inside, I decided to fix lunch a bit early. I wanted to fix something I could only make when Ma was not home- I made a peanut butter sandwich, and fried an egg to put between the two slices of bread with peanut butter. Ma hated even the thought of that combination, but I had liked it since I was a child. *No accounting for taste,* I guessed.

While I ate I read the paper, or rather what little of the paper was worth reading. The Evening Mail had a reputation for purveying an inordinate amount of gossip and fluff along with its news. They also had a penchant for front page editorial cartoons: today's portrayed the League of Nations as a giant prize-fighter, with President Wilson announcing the 'champion'. That one was wrong on several levels, in my humble, unasked-for opinion. Ma shared my opinion; one of her errands this day was to stop the Evening Mail and start receiving their competition, the Republican Register. *Time for a change,* I thought.

I did read where there was a very bad automobile wreck just south of Appleton Sunday afternoon, and a woman passenger had been killed. Helen and I had seen people rushing that way shortly after three, and wondered what had happened. I started to read the story, but stopped short before I got to the worst of the details. There were many ways to kill oneself in a car, and these folks seemed to have found one of the nastiest.

I leafed through the rest of the paper, and noted for about the thousandth time the annoying practice of writing advertisements, usually for patent medicines or other hokum, and inserting them in amongst the regular articles to make them seem like real news.

So much for the paper. I folded it back up, and put it on the table next to Ma's Morris chair for her to read when she got home.

After the requisite clean up and ablutions, I sat back down at the typewriter. The afternoon on the Fremont Road passed very quietly, only the occasional passing of a horse and buggy or a car to compete with the wind blowing through the growing corn, and the sounds from the nearby farmyard. I remember thinking this was quite the idyllic afternoon, and thanked the Lord for letting me experience it.

I was still typing away at about a quarter past three when I heard a Model T pull up out front. I got up to look out the window, and saw Pastor Kittridge's sedan pulled up just past our driveway. Pastor and Deborah were in it, but made no move to get out.

That's odd...

A moment later a Model T touring car with the top up stopped directly in front of the house. In it were Bessie and Helen, but Helen was driving. I began to get an unsettled feeling in the pit of my stomach, but I couldn't figure out what was causing it. What was really strange was nobody moved to get out of their cars.

Another moment, and the Baby puttered up the road, turned into the driveway, and stopped by the garage. I waited for Ma to get out, but instead a man in a dark suit opened the door, and stepped out. He moved to the other side of the car and opened the passenger's door. A small boy got out. I noticed he had a head of curly blond hair, and a very serious expression on his face. The man and boy started for the front porch.

It was then I recognized Dr. Bohan. I had not seen him so formally dressed before. The first wisps of terror wafted across my vision like the beginnings of a conflagration.

The others got out of their cars, and all converged on the front porch. Numbly, I determined I should go out and meet them. I opened the door.

"Sylvia, may we come in?"

"Of course, Doctor. Hello, everyone. Please come in."

Helen told me later my voice was a monotone, devoid of any hint of emotion.

The group entered the living room. Everyone stood. Nobody spoke.

Doctor Bohan finally began. "Sylvia, please sit down. Please."

I sat.

"Sylvia, this is the hardest thing I think I've ever had to tell anyone. Please forgive me if I lose control while I do this. Your mother—"

I shuddered and drew a long breath, but did nothing else.

"passed away about twelve thirty this afternoon. She was eating lunch with Bessie, and she suddenly collapsed."

I felt like I was floating, even though I sat in the Morris chair. I didn't cry, then. I looked around at the group gathered around me, and noticed everyone, including Doctor Bohan, had reddened eyes, and wisps of tears on their faces.

The rational part of my mind decided it needed more information. I must ask for it.

"Could I hear the details, please. I believe I can weather the shock as well now as later."

Doctor Bohan looked at Bessie, who looked back. He nodded, and she spoke.

"Annette had visited the two newspapers, and a couple of stores, then came over to the house for lunch. We were about halfway through when she suddenly looked at me. Her eyes went wide, she said, 'Oh-I', and then her eyes shut and she fell off the chair! I screamed, and Helen and Lester came running. We got her onto the long sofa, and I called Doctor Bohan."

At that point Bessie choked up and began to sob. Helen took up the story.

"While my Ma was calling the doctor, Lester and I tried to do what we could. I felt for a pulse and found none. She also was not breathing. There was nothing else we could do, so we prayed and waited for Doctor Bohan."

The doctor sighed, and continued.

"My son and I were having a game of checkers and waiting for my wife to return from the store when I got the call. Young John here is set on becoming a doctor himself, and always asks to come with me on calls. Today he got his wish, sad to say."

"We got to the house in about seven minutes. When I got there, your mother was as Helen described. No pulse, no breath, no blood pressure. Do you want to hear the clinical details, Sylvia?"

"Yes, Doctor, tell me everything, please."

Doctor Bohan took a breath, sighed, and continued.

"I found a marked swelling in the abdomen, and evidence of frank blood in her throat and mouth, also in the nasal area. From the examination, and what the Smileys have told me, I think Annette had a sudden, catastrophic rupture of the aorta, the main supply artery of the heart. I would suspect an aneurysm has been growing for some time, and today it ruptured. In that case, death would occur in a few seconds. There was nothing anyone could have done, not with the skills we have now."

"Wouldn't she have noticed something was going wrong?" I felt detached from what I was saying, and was surprised to hear such a calm, lucid question coming from my mouth.

"Not necessarily. Aneurysms can have symptoms, or never give a hint of their existence until they do what this one did."

"Ma took a nap yesterday. She never takes naps."

"Yes, that might have been a symptom, but then again it might not. There was no way we could have predicted this. She was 50, is that right?"

"Fifty-one last March 8th."

"So young, but the Lord can call us anytime He pleases." Pastor Kittridge spoke for the first time.

"Yes, He can. He did." I guessed the logical part of my brain was still in business. Time to start dealing with the practical matters.

"What happens now?"

"I took the liberty of having her taken to Horton and Foley on South Cherry Street." Doctor Bohan replied, "I have found they are competent, and will work with the church on the funeral. Is that acceptable Sylvia? Pastor Kittridge?"

We both nodded our assent. Helen picked up the thread.

"I will be staying with you till after the funeral, and as long as you need me after that. I can help with the details, if you want. We're all here to help you get through this, Syl, now and hereafter. We mean it!"

I saw all their heads nod in agreement. Time to reply.

"Thank you for all you are doing for me, and for Ma. I know the Lord keeps us in His hand, and I'll just have to cling to Him, and let you dear friends help me." I trailed off.

At that point young John, Doctor Bohan's son, came over to where I was sitting. He looked so earnest, so sad, in his white shirt and short pants. His curly blond hair went every which way, but seemed to fit the rest of him perfectly.

He put out his hand. "Mrs. Trimble, I am so sorry about the passing of your mother. I hope some day to be able to prevent deaths like this one, but for now all I can do is offer my sincere condolences."

Such a profound speech from someone so young! I swept him into my arms for a hug, which surprised him. As I hugged this young boy the tears I had tried to defer came streaming forth. I could not control them.

"I'm so sorry, John! There's nothing I can do about all these tears."

"That's all right," the little man said as I released him. "If I am to become a doctor, these are the situations I must deal with. Someday I'll be able to."

As Deborah, Bessie, and Helen crowded around and hugged me, I saw John Bohan, Senior, crouch down to eye level with his son.

"John, I told you when we left the Smiley house that this would be the most difficult call I've ever had to make. Now you see why; can you handle this, young man?"

Young John looked his father straight in the eye.

"Yes sir, I can," he whispered.

Chapter Nineteen

Luther: May 23rd, 1919, the rehabilitation unit, Walter Reed.

About midnight I sat at the large table in the common area of our unit. My bare legs—or rather, my bare leg and prosthesis—peeked out from under my robe. I sat sipping coffee and looking at… nothing.

"Up a little late, aren't we, Luther?"

Jack padded out of the living area. His slippers made a scuffing sound as he walked over to the sideboard, selected a coffee mug, and poured a cup. He sat down at the table.

We sat there a few moments in unaccustomed silence.

"Spill it, Luther. It's The Medal, isn't it."

"I don't deserve it, Jack."

"Why do you say that?"

"Do I have to tell you? You know what it was like out there…"

"You need to hear it from yourself. Then, we can talk about it."

"That sounds complicated."

"You'll find it gets a lot simpler once you say it." As usual, Jack made sense.

"Okay. I'll not say anything about the NC, since all the rest of you got it too, but for more worthy things than me."

"That is debatable, Luther, but not right now. I'll grant you that one."

I sipped my coffee, and continued. "When I was on that railroad embankment I was mad—mad at all the killing, and mad that the Captain and my two men got hit. I remember thinking I had to get rid of that machine gun. Then something snapped, Jack. I don't remember doing the things that citation says I did. The next thing I knew I hit the mud, and the pain started. How can I get The Medal for something I don't even remember doing?"

Jack cradled his coffee cup in both hands as he spoke.

"Two reasons as I see it, Luther. One, whether or not you remember deciding to charge that machine gun, you did it. Somebody saw it, and wrote it up. Your actions speak louder than your memory."

I thought about that for a moment. "I guess you're right, Jack, but whatever I did, I sure never did it just to get a medal out of it!"

"No sane man would. It may be just as well you don't remember what you did, maybe save you from a few nightmares."

I nodded. My oldest friend continued.

"And my second point. What happened when you fell in the mud dying that day?"

I closed my eyes. "The Lord got my attention."

"And?"

"I surrendered."

"And?"

"He saved me."

"Spiritually and literally?"

"Yeah, Jack. He did both."

"So whether you remember how it happened or not, God's plan was for you to end up in the position where He could get your attention. As a side-benefit, you did something that made you a hero, albeit an unconscious one."

"That's an unusual word you used, Jack."

"Unconscious?"

"Albeit."

Jack laughed. "It just came to mind, and I used it. Fits though, doesn't it?"

"It does....and you're right, of course."

"Of course, I am."

"Don't push it, Jack!"

We both laughed, quietly so as not to wake up the others. I took another sip of coffee, and looked out the window at the scattering of lights illuminating the Walter Reed grounds.

"I still don't want to call attention to myself with that medal around my neck."

"Sorry, Luther, but you're pretty much stuck with it. When you're retired, you won't be wearing anything other than dress uniforms, and that means either the ribbons or the medals. And now I get to say something you've said to me on many occasions: *Suck it up, Marine!*"

"Touché."

Jack grinned at me. I knew he'd been waiting to say that for a long time.

"Cheer up, Luther. You'll be the hit of the festive occasion, the perfectly dressed retired Marine at the wedding. You do have a sword, don't you?"

"If my footlocker ever turns up, I do. I still don't think I'll advertise my availability for Arch of Swords duty, though."

Jack picked up our empty coffee mugs and walked over to the sink.

"Suit yourself. One of these days, though, you may find yourself the groom! You won't be able to duck it then- although I have to note the number of eligible ladies who would put up with your tinkering and organ playing has got to be vanishingly small!"

"You might be surprised yourself some day."

"I agree. Tell you what, let's defer that discussion until it happens."

"I'll remember you said that. And Jack, thanks for helping me get this sorted out in my mind."

"My pleasure. Just remember, no matter what, you are representing the Lord, and the Corps."

"Yeah. In that order…"

"Yep

*****

Sylvia: The Trimble house, now Sylvia's home, Fremont Road.

I never realized the amount of work dying made for those left behind. The next week of my life, until the funeral on June 28th, was at once both hectic and interminable.

Ma told me once that with Pa in the Marines, she never knew when something would happen to him; she had also seen death come in an instant in her classroom. I remembered that terrible day, and its aftermath. So both my parents had made arrangements. Helen took me to Mr. Mogler's law office in the Carr Building in Galesburg first thing the next morning to start processing the wills.

All that week Helen got me where I needed to be, and made sure I did what I had to do. She drove us into Galesburg several times to take care of business, and talk to the undertakers.

I remained numb, in a mental fog, able to act but really not to *feel*. After the initial cry with young John Bohan, I didn't cry. I figured I would after the funeral at some point, but I didn't know when.

Pastor and Deborah visited us daily, and talked over the arrangements with me. Ma was to be buried in the Hagenfield Cemetery, close by the school and the Johnson farm. The funeral would be at the church.

The morning of the funeral was warm and humid, with a low hanging overcast. The dank air seemed to weigh on me like a heavy blanket, with no breeze to bring relief.

Horton and Foley did a good job on Ma. In the casket, she looked as good as I could ever remember seeing her. Unlike some of our more morbid friends, we did not have a photograph made of her lying in the casket. I wanted to remember her, as I remembered Pa, from the photographs we made when they were living.

I found my thoughts wandering from one subject to another as we waited for the funeral to begin. I felt I was a detached observer, noticing and evaluating each detail around me without emotion. In my mind I knew this was an avoidance, and a defense, against overwhelming grief; I accepted that evaluation, and also knew at some point the grief would be expressed.

I think just about every family in the church, and all the families of the school children, attended the funeral. Several others I did not know introduced themselves. One older man, balding, slightly stooped, shook our hands and received a hug from Helen. She said he and his wife were good friends from the church in Galesburg. After it was all over I could not remember any of the strangers' names.

Lee Wright also attended. I wasn't surprised, since Hal had worked for him at the cycle shop, and his mechanics maintained the Baby. I saw him talking with Pastor Kittridge, and idly wondered if Pastor was picking Lee's brain about that little project in his driveway.

Pastor's message to the assembled mourners was short and to the point. We live and die at the Lord's Word. We're going to live someplace forever, so we'd better not delay our choice to trust Christ, and be ready to depart at any time. Annette was ready for the Call, and she is with Jesus.

Pastor had talked to me about that last day of Ma's life, and he used that conversation at the end of the message.

"For many of you what I've said here are truths you've heard from childhood. But consider—have you ever thought of it from the point of view of the one who is now deceased? I've talked to Sylvia, and I can tell you Annette got up Tuesday morning feeling better than she had felt in a long time. School was out, the first preparations were done for next year, and she had gotten some well-deserved rest. She was praising the Lord for the opportunity to be alive on that beautiful day, and for the opportunity to go shopping and visiting."

"She talked things over with Sylvia, and they determined there was nothing more they needed to talk about. Annette's last words to Sylvia were, 'Well, I'll be off then. See you later. Love ya, Syl!'"

"To which Sylvia replied, 'Love you too Ma. See you.'"

"Neither of them knew the next time they would see each other alive would be in Glory, or at the Rapture of the Church. But what

99

they said to each other was utterly and completely true, true in every particular, true for Eternity."

"And here is the question I ask you: 'If you died today, where would you go?'"

"You can know."

We followed the horse-drawn hearse to the cemetery. We were second in line; Helen had to make most of the trip in low gear to avoid overrunning the hearse, and the moto-meter showed the engine flirting with overheating.

I stood there, in the front row of mourners, as we sang a few of Ma's favorite Gospel songs, and Pastor read the committal service. Then the casket was lowered into the ground, and several of the men began to cover it over with dirt. I noticed Philip Wagher and Fred Johnson talking softly to each other off to the side from the main group of mourners.

*****

Saturday, June 28th, 1919, before the funeral.

"The Service Manual you ordered is in, AP. Clare wanted me to tell you since I was coming out here today."

"Thanks, Lee, although I am afraid it's just going to be an accessory to sell with the car."

"Giving up this soon?"

"I'm at my wit's end. Every time I try to start it, the thing bangs and pops and backfires something ferocious. Nothing I've done makes any difference. I can't even take it out of the driveway, much less into Galesburg for your men to look at it. And Deborah's threatening to make me sleep in the thing!"

Lee Wright snorted at the last comment. Usually he would laugh out loud at something like that, but he really didn't feel like laughing today. Nobody did.

"Wouldn't do you much good anyway. We never sold any of them, and I doubt if any of my mechanics have ever even seen one. I wasn't selling Chevrolets when they were new, so I don't have the service manual or special tools for it either. That's just one strange bird."

"It sure is! I don't know what made my brother buy it...or me buy it from him!"

Lee Wright raised his index finger. "AP, I've known you long enough to know you just can't help yourself if a rat-killing deal comes your way! And if that thing would run, you got that kind of a deal."

"Maybe I can sell it to someone who can make it run—I can't. Deborah's never going to let me forget it, either."

"Tell me about it! Clarice is the same way with me. Here's an idea—I'm going to a dealer's meeting in Peoria next week. I'll mention your car to some of the dealers if you'd like. It's unusual enough someone may want one just for it's curiosity value!"

"Thanks a bunch for doing that, Lee! I don't want to cheat anyone though-I intend to tell them the whole sad story!"

"I understand, AP. And talk about sad stories," he gestured toward the coffin.

"I just feel so bad for young Sylvia," AP replied, "The Lord's got something great in His plan for her, but it's got to be tough to take that on faith right now."

"She's had some hard knocks; she's a tough girl. I think she'll make it."

"Lee, just being tough won't do it. Some day I'll tell you a story from my time in the New Jersey to illustrate. And thanks for coming out here today to support Sylvia. I have to go start the funeral now. See ya."

"Same to ya, AP."

*****

Later, at the cemetery.

"We're in trouble, Fred," Philip Wagher whispered to Fred Johnson.

The two men were standing just off to the side of the knot of mourners, watching as several men began filling in the grave at the Hagenfield Cemetery. Philip was the founder of the school and President of the school board; Fred was Vice President and heir apparent to the aging founder.

"We sure are," Fred whispered back. "I told the board members we'd meet at my house when this broke up. Is that still OK with you?"

"Just fine. We need to decide today if at all possible."

"The Lord's handed us a good one this time, Philip."

"That He has. But I also think He's provided the solution."

Fred nodded. "Do you think she'll be able to pull it together after all the tragedy that's hit her in the last year?"

"Fred, I really think so. That young lady has spunk, and resilience. She proved it this spring. I think she'll rise to the challenge."

"I pray so. Not like we have any alternatives I can see."

"Nope."

Chapter Twenty

2 PM, after the funeral dinner, the Johnson farm house.

Eight men and one woman sat on chairs pulled into Fred and Violet Johnson's parlor. Pacey and Laney were upstairs with Campbell Miller's wife Doris.

The one woman in the group was Violet Johnson. When he was elected Vice President of the school board, Fred had insisted Violet be included as his assistant. She was not an official board member, and could not vote; she could advise and suggest to the board, both directly and through Fred. This was an unusual arrangement, but had worked well for years when Philip Wagher's wife Mabel was alive.

"Fred, please tell the board what you and I are recommending."

"OK, Philip. Folks, here's the situation. At the moment we have no teacher for the school. Philip and I have prayed about the situation—pretty intensely prayed about the problem, and we both feel the logical person to succeed Annette is her daughter, Sylvia. We all know her, she knows us and the children, she is the one most familiar with Annette's lesson plan books, and she helped get the school back together after the influenza, starting in April."

"Is there anyone else we know who could do it?" Bud Long asked. "How about Mrs. Kittridge?"

Violet Johnson spoke up. "I'll answer that. Deborah has said to me on numerous occasions that she is sure she knows why the Lord hasn't given them children—she just doesn't have the patience to work with them day after day. She said she tried teaching Bible School one time at the church they came from, and only lasted one day! She would never agree to teach at the school."

"I've had similar conversations with Mrs. Kittridge," Philip said, "So she's out. Anybody else?"

The silence in the room gave the reply.

Philip Wagher continued. "All right folks, I move we hire Sylvia Mates Trimble as the teacher for the Wagher School, same pay and provisions as Annette had. All those in favor....."

"Wagher's Rules of Order," came a stage whisper from the side of the room.

Philip grinned. "I believe Pastor calls it the Navyman's Golden Rule. Whoever wears the gold—he tapped his shirt cuff—makes the rules!"

Laughter filled the room.

"That was needed, folks," Philip said when all was quiet again. "Now, all in favor of hiring Sylvia, say 'aye'."

All were in favor.

Philip spoke again. "Thank you folks, for your support. Now we have to figure out how to go ask her."

"I took the liberty of informing Miss Smiley that there would likely be visitors later this afternoon. I think she figured out what we were thinking, but said she wouldn't say anything to Sylvia, and would make sure they were home."

"Thanks, Fred. Ahead of the game as usual! Now, whose buggy gets the call for this trip?"

Campbell Miller spoke up. "Let me drive you over there. I just got the Model T last week, and I haven't gotten tired of driving the thing yet!"

"Much obliged, Campbell. Fred, could you and Violet come with us, please?"

"Of course. Oh—meeting adjourned. We'll tell you how it went tomorrow after church."

*****

Sylvia: 2:20 PM, Sylvia's home.

Helen and I sat at the kitchen table in the house on the Fremont Road. I guessed it was my house now; the paperwork said it was, my mind just hadn't caught up with the fact.

We both sat with a cup of coffee in front of us, and just stared off. We had been given a small funeral dinner by some of the ladies of the church, but neither of us ate much. We weren't hungry now either.

We stared out the window to the west, where dark clouds brooded low on the horizon. *That must be the storm that's been threatening all day*, I thought.

The activity of the preparations for the funeral, and the legal work to get everything closed out or transferred, had kept the part of my mind that was functioning occupied during the past week. Now it was all done, and I felt…empty. I did not know what I should do next, and had no desire to find out. I just sat.

Helen said this was just a stage of the grieving process, and I would feel better eventually. I knew she was right, but there was a certain comfortable feeling in the lethargy at the moment. Besides, she was acting the same way.

A Model T came along the road in front of the house, and turned in to the driveway. The sound died.

"I wonder who that might be?"

"I don't know, Helen." I thought I'd had enough visitors to last me a while.

"Come on, Syl, lets go see."

"Whatever." I got up with a groan, and walked to the door. On the porch stood Philip Wagher, and Fred and Violet Johnson.

I spoke. "Hello, folks. What brings you over this afternoon?"

"Campbell Miller's Model T, but that's not important right now."

"Philip!" Violet Johnson said, and poked him in the arm.

I wasn't surprised Philip would come out with a line like that in response to a harmless question. I really believe he'd have made a good vaudeville comedian. And Violet did exactly what I'd seen Mabel do dozens of times!

"I'm sorry folks, I just can't resist a good straight line. We are here on business, though; may we come in?"

"Of course! Come right in."

Helen and I led the party into the living room, and we all sat down. I began to suspect why they were here. A tingle of *something* began to stir in my mind.

"Who's watching the boys, Violet?"

"Doris Miller is. Campbell volunteered to drive us over here, and she said she'd keep them occupied for a bit."

"May I get you folks some coffee?" Helen asked.

"In a couple of minutes, if that's OK, Helen. We need to get something settled here first. Fred, you're on!"

Fred Johnson took a breath, and began.

"Sylvia, you know the bind we're in. Violet and I, and Philip here, have been praying hard since last Tuesday. There's only one possibility we have peace about. After the funeral, the School Board met. The decision we came to was unanimous. Sylvia, will you accept the position of teacher at the Wagher School for the next school year? Salary and terms the same as your mother received."

I sat back in the Morris chair. In the fifteen seconds between the end of the question, and my answer, I considered several questions, and came to answers for each of them. The visitors could see I was thinking, and they let me think.

Can I do this job? Yes.

Do I want to do this job? Oh, yes!

Do I need a job to do? Certainly.

Is the salary acceptable? Yes, especially with my pension.

May I take this job, Lord? Is it Your will? 'Called according to My purpose...'

May I make one condition? Yes.

"Mr. Wagher, Mr. and Mrs. Johnson, your confidence in me means more than I can tell. Yes, I would be honored to teach at the Wagher School next year. I have one condition, though..."

Philip spoke. "Name it, Sylvia. If it's within our power, we'll do it."

"I want to employ Helen here as my unpaid teacher's aide and assistant."

Helen's mouth dropped open, and it was her turn to collapse back in her chair. I didn't get a chance to surprise her like that very often!

"Helen, is that something you want to do?"

"It sure is, Mister Johnson! I've wanted to be a teacher since I was five. I graduated from high school a year early, so I could get a position as a teacher's assistant for a year or two to learn the trade. And I don't need any payment, as long as I can find someplace to stay."

"You can stay here, Helen. I have room, I have food, you can go home on the weekends if you want, it would work out great!"

"Well, Philip?"

"I think that is a grand idea, Fred! I wish we could pay you, like I wished we could pay Sylvia, but we can't. If you're willing to accept that, then welcome to the family!"

"Thank you Mr. Wagher!"

"It's Philip...to both of you."

"And we're Fred and Violet, like we've always been!"

Helen and I shook the men's hands, and Violet hugged each of us.

Philip looked around. "Now, Helen, I could use that cup of coffee, if you don't mind. I think these two could stand one too—Fred, perhaps we should bring poor Campbell in before he thinks we forgot him!"

We all laughed, even me a little, and Fred walked out on the porch to wave Campbell in.

Chapter Twenty One

*Saturday, June 28**, 1919, 1:40 PM, suite 500, Bank of Galesburg building, Galesburg, Illinois.*

Donald Wain, Vice Admiral (retired), Navy Supply Corps, owner of Wain Engineering Corporation, stared out the window of his office on the top floor of the tallest office building in town.

Don had just returned to the office after attending a funeral at Appleton in eastern Knox County. He did not know the deceased personally, but she and her daughter were close friends of his Navy colleague and friend AP Kittridge, Pastor of the Appleton church, and his remarkable wife Deborah.

Don's wife Pamela was unable to accompany him on the trip. Her medical conditions made travel by car and walking over uneven ground difficult, so she usually managed her affairs by phone, and by visits of friends to their house.

This day, however, Pam was also waiting at their home for the arrival of two more close friends, and one new vested partner in the corporation. The company executive officer, Dick Meriden, and corporate counsel Margaret Rawalt Bailey—the inimitable *Maggie B.*—were escorting the new company accountant and her daughter to Galesburg from *elsewhere.*

Don looked out the windows in the spacious corner office. Across Main Street to the north stood a ragtag collection of small stores, a livery stable, the town's best laundry, and the Lutheran church facing Ferris Street. Across Kellogg Street to the west squatted the grimy bricks and dirty windows of the elderly Illinois Hotel. *Henry Hill's buying it to replace it with a modern arcade,* Don thought, *and good riddance to that* bedbug boudoir! He stopped, and looked down at the polished office floor. *I'm sorry, Lord, I really shouldn't be that uncharitable. People You love live in that place.*

Don looked up and out again. The view from this building really was panoramic, at least to the north and west. Very different from the view out these windows when he helped an old friend clean the building as a teen-ager in the seventies.

The telephone on his desk rang. He pulled it over to him and lifted the earpiece. "Don Wain...oh, hi, Love! Have they arrived yet?" He listened. "OK, I'll wait for them here."

He nodded absently, staring out the window again. "Right. Glad I went, but sad, Love, just sad. Schoolteacher out by Appleton, dropped dead of an aneurysm. Lost her husband to the influenza, and her daughter lost her husband at Belleau Wood, and nearly died of sickness herself."

Don listened some more. "Yes, Love, we'll keep an eye on the daughter and see if we can help. She's best friends with Helen Smiley from church." Another moment, "OK, Love, we'll bring Jackie back to the house and find some dinner tonight. How's Evelyn managing?"

Don listened, and smiled.

"Great, you two have fun and we'll see you in a couple hours. Love you! Bye."

Don hung up the phone. *We'll have a better communication system when we have our own building, eventually*, he thought to himself.

He pushed the concealed button under the middle of his desk, and a door in the top pivoted up like a sewing machine cabinet. A glowing colored screen came to life, and a keyboard rose and lit up. Don pulled a small oval object from its holder and moved it around on the desk. *Might as well get some work done while I wait*, he thought to himself, then spent the next ten minutes playing Solitaire on the optimistically-named *ThinkPad*.

Don heard the beep indicating the elevator had stopped at the floor, then the tiny red light hidden at the corner of his desk indicated entry into the outer office. He folded the *ThinkPad* back into his desk and squared his shoulders. A few seconds later the inner door opened, and three persons entered the office.

Two of the newcomers Don knew well. The elderly man who opened the door stood a couple inches over six feet. The wrinkles of experience framed clear blue eyes and a modest nose, and the tanned bald head with just a trace of gray fuzz around the ears left the impression of quiet brilliance. Richard Meriden, executive officer of the corporation, lived up to the billing.

The two women with Dick also exuded competence, but differently from their escort, and from each other.

Margaret Rawalt Bailey—*Maggie B.*, attorney at law, stood five foot three inches tall. Stocky, with coarse features, she wore her graying auburn hair short, and spoke with a lawyer's fluency. She practiced law in Chicago, and as Wain Engineering corporate counsel regularly visited Galesburg, and the other facilities of the corporation. She had met the third woman and conducted her through the journey to here and now.

The third woman stood slightly taller than Maggie, and while also stocky moved with a *fluidity* neither of her escorts could match. Her face seemed unusually round, her gray eyes steady, framed by wrinkles brought by years of alert observation in bright sunlight. She also wore her hair short, and carried herself as if she was used to being a *presence* wherever she went. *The most competent trio I know*, Don thought as he stood and walked around his desk.

"Welcome, *Captain*," Don said as he shook the new arrival's hand.

"Thank you, *Admiral*," Jacqueline Brighthonor, Captain, United States Navy (retired), replied.

"How was the trip?" Don asked as the newcomer sat in the proffered chair.

"Not difficult, but certainly jarring," Jackie replied, "Walk into a room, shut the door, a light comes on, open the opposite door—to *here*! Like the cat shot you know is coming, but the thing fires about one second before expected."

The two old Navy hands lapsed into the jargon of the Navy of their *first* careers, referring to the catapult launch of an aircraft as a *cat shot*.

Don nodded. "I always sat in the back of the CODs, so every launch was a surprise."

"*Chops* in the back, *drivers* in the front," Jackie grinned at the dig she'd just made at Supply Corps officers, riding in the *carrier onboard delivery* (COD) aircraft.

"Right, *Air Boss*," Don replied, referring to her position on the aircraft carrier she'd just retired from. "Have you made arrangements to keep proficient while you're working out here?"

As Don and Jackie spoke, Dick and Maggie retreated to their desks in the outer office.

"Yes, I have," Jackie replied, "I have a standing weekend reservation for that sweet little T-34 Charlie you keep at the municipal airport *back there*. I figure one weekend a month should do it."

"Great! That's why we bought one when they were retired out of *Naval Air Training Command*. You know, eventually we'll have our own aircraft out here."

"Why not right now, Don?" Jackie asked, "We can import about anything we want, can't we?"

Don's smile faded. "No, Jackie, two reasons. First, we don't want to draw attention out here, at least not yet. Right now, if we can't keep the technology firmly hidden, we can't import it. Later, as we get more established and see how this universe is going, we can introduce the advanced technology, gradually. We don't need to be thought of as some Buck Rogers saviors of mankind—that's not our mission, at all."

Captain Brighthonor nodded. "That brings up a question, Don, but what's the other reason for going slow on aviation?"

Don glanced out the window to the west. *That wasn't there a while ago*, he thought, then turned to the retired Naval Aviator.

"Second reason, Jackie—the current aircraft are not something I'd personally want to ride in, let alone ask one of the *vested partners* to fly! The airframes aren't so bad, but the aero engines of this time are just horrible! We won't get anything good enough for our safety until the Wasp and Whirlwind radials arrive in the middle twenties."

"Are we going to help that along?" Jackie asked.

"We're going to push that development as hard as we can, as *consultants*, and eventually start inserting better engines into the stream, but not yet. Tell you what—my friend Lee Wright is sponsoring a little air meet just east of town this Wednesday. I'll take you out there and you can see the *state of the art* for yourself. Up for that?"

Jackie grinned. "I think I could be persuaded, Boss. You don't mind if I call you that, do you?"

Don grinned back. "That's fine, Jackie. Or Don, or whatever. We're not formal out here—all working for the same true Boss, and that's not me!"

"Good. Now I have a question for you, Don."

"Shoot."

The recently retired Naval Aviator took a breath, then fixed her gaze on Don.

"Why are you doing all this back here, in this universe? I've been briefed on how *certain persons* were contacted by those parties whom the Lord had allowed time travel, and asked to come to this universe, in this time, and serve. I know why I decided to come out here," a tear formed in Jackie's right eye, she ignored it, "but that doesn't answer the big question—why are we, why are *you*, spending all this time and treasure for these people, in a different time and different universe? What is the goal of this operation? You do have a goal, don't you?"

Don sat motionless, staring at his new accountant, for a long moment. Then he blinked, and flexed his hands.

"Would it change your decision to come work for this company if I told you we have no goal for its existence?"

Jackie squinted one eye at her new commanding officer. "No, first because I have my own reasons for wanting to do this, independent of yours. Second, because I don't believe you, *Admiral*."

Don's expression remained neutral as he stared back at Jackie. Then, he broke into a wide grin.

"Good shot, Jackie! The accountant for this company needs to be able to tell when I'm not being straight with her, and call me on it. She also needs to be able to tell me when I'm being unrealistic or...*stupid*, and lay it on the line with me."

"How do I fare?"

"Excellent on both counts! Pam's relayed the stories you told her about your time on *Kitty Hawk*, and as skipper of *VRC-30*. If I ever need to be put in my place, I'll trust you to do just that, smartly!"

Jackie grinned. *I wonder if Pam told him the other story, about when Eddie was killed?* she thought behind the grin, then put that out of her mind.

"Very well, Don, I'll be sure to do that when it's needed. Now, the *question*?"

Don swiveled slightly in his chair, and glanced out the west window again. *Uh, oh,* he thought, then faced the waiting Jackie.

"We're going to have an interruption in a couple minutes, but let me answer you first."

"I've been watching it too. Go on."

"Our official purpose is to do everything we can with our knowledge of what is coming to this universe to ease the effects of the events, and deflect the worst of the effects if we can. I and the others were inserted into this universe to experience truncated careers in our specialties, and become thoroughly at home in the time, and now we're building our infrastructure to begin to affect the country and its natives in a positive way. Does this make sense, *Captain*?"

Jackie snorted. "Just barely, *Admiral*! You need someone to take your *pronunciamientos* and turn them into English for the rest of us. I guess I just got handed another collateral duty, right?"

Don stared at his new accountant, then laughed. "Pam told me you'd be perfect for this job, especially when I got too windy! Yes, that's another duty of yours, and I will be most grateful for your help!"

Jackie smiled again. "Good, Boss. Now another question—with the company building major bases in Tennessee and—gag—*North Dakota*, why did you put the headquarters here?"

Don raised his eyebrows. Now, Jackie, Hoople is a very nice little place—on the railroad, yet far away from nosy neighbors. It's a great place to spend a vacation, especially next year when we get *The Spa* up and running!"

"Like a winter vacation in Antarctica, but I understand why we want the secret facilities there. But the *question*, Admiral?"

"All right, Jackie, here it is. Besides being on two railroads, and having room for an airfield, Galesburg's my home town. I grew up here, lived here most of my life *before*. I always enjoyed researching the history of the place, especially of the time we're in now. That gives me a little head start toward assimilation. I've never been a joiner, but I joined the Galesburg Club here, and made sure I included the current and coming major players in my circle of friends. As we buy property here, and start doing things in and for the community, I'll have the credibility I'll need to start influencing first the city, then the country, toward what will get them through the coming years."

"But you do realize as soon as you start playing in this little sandbox, events are gonna start to shift away from *the script*—what happened in the other universe."

Don glanced to his left out the window again. "The *butterfly effect*? Of course. However, the raw material—the personalities involved, and the larger events we can't change—will still be the same. And remember, the Lord put us here to do this job, and He'll send people and opportunities our way, things we can't even imagine at this early stage. Loads of fun—and remember, we'll still have support from *elsewhere* up the line."

"OK, Don, I get it, and I'm ready to pitch in and help. But right now, I think we ought to deal with whatever that is coming up out of the west."

They both looked out the window. The black line reaching to the horizon from north to south was noticeably higher in the sky.

"Ever seen that before, Jackie?"

"Nothing like that, not even when a typhoon was coming in the western Pacific. Too big for a tornado."

Don stood up. "Hey, guys, come in here please," he called toward the outer office.

Dick and Maggie came in. "What, Boss?" Dick asked.

"Look out the window. Ever see anything like that?"

Dick shook his head; Maggie paled.

"*Derecho*, Don. Straight line winds of a storm front, makes that bowl-like cloud horizon to horizon. Bad as a small tornado, but much larger. Went through one in Kansas once. We gotta get to safety pronto!"

Don thought for a few seconds, then started for the door. "Come on, folks, hide out at my house. Safe room in the basement, or slip through the *transfer room*."

"Will we make it before it hits?" Dick asked.

"I think so," Jackie replied. "I've been watching it. Speed of advance is about forty knots. I'd say we have maybe a half hour tops."

As the group strode toward the elevator, Don had a thought. "Dick, since we haven't got the top on your new car yet, you put it in the garage when we get there. I'll leave mine outside."

"But that Baby Grand's your favorite," Dick replied.

"And that Model D Chevy of yours has a *283 and Powerglide* in it! I'd rather not explain that to anybody in town just yet, and if it's wrecked somebody will see."

The elevator door closed and the car started down.

"And if the Derecho blows the garage down?"

Don shrugged. "Then we have a lot more to worry about than the car."

*****

Sylvia: 3:20 PM, Sylvia's house, Fremont Road.

The visitors left shortly after finishing their coffee. They wanted to get home before the storm hit. Helen and I sat on the porch and watched the storm as it rose from the western horizon and marched briskly toward us. We were talking about our new careers and plans for the school, but we quieted as the storm approached.

The clouds looked like the side of a giant upside-down bowl, stretching from horizon to horizon. The leading edge was curved, smooth, and very sharply defined. Behind the leading edge of the clouds, blackness stretched from cloud to ground. Lightning flashed in the clouds. The whole mass seemed to be coming on quickly.

"Looks like the end of the world, doesn't it, Syl?"

"You said it, Helen. Except the real end is fire next time."

"Right." A moment and Helen spoke again.

"You don't happen to have a storm cellar, do you?"

"Actually, we do. We use it as a root cellar."

"I wonder if it might not be a good idea to relocate there, seeing that thing will be visiting in a few minutes?"

"I believe that is a wise suggestion. Let me get a lamp and we'll take these chairs with us. The cellar's out behind the garage."

We kept up the pretense of speaking matter-of-factly, but we were both really scared. I'd never seen a storm like this before, and time was short.

I stepped in the house, picked up a small kerosene lamp, then joined Helen as we carried our porch chairs back to the door of the storm cellar. I opened the door, lit the lamp, and we stepped down into it. As I set the chair and lamp down, and turned to close the door, I felt the first gust of cold wind sweep past the opening. I closed the door and barred it, then joined Helen in the dimly lit cellar, to wait—for what, we did not know.

Ma and I had kept the cellar clean, and disposed of bugs as we stored and moved canning jars and boxes there. The room was small, but cozy, and felt relatively safe.

"Now I can think of a dozen things I should have brought down here with us," I remarked. "Too late now."

"I think this is just a precaution, Syl. I didn't see any tornadoes headed our way."

"But with it so black under that cloud, I wonder if we'd have seen them?"

"Point taken. Just have to trust the Lord to take care of us."

The wind began to howl outside. The door of the storm cellar rattled.

I started to laugh.

"What's so funny?"

"I was just sitting here thinking, *A little storm, so what? No problem!* Maybe that's a change in perspective after all the things that have happened in the last year."

Helen nodded, then we looked toward the door as the wind rattled it. I decided to ask Helen something.

"Did you know those people were coming to visit us this afternoon?"

Helen smiled. "You got me! Fred warned me they might come calling later this afternoon. He didn't say what about, but I figured it out. He told me not to tell you, and I didn't."

"But you didn't see my *condition* coming, did you?"

"Nope, I had no clue. Glad you thought of it, though."

"So am I. We'll have a great time if we don't blow away!"

We heard several crashes close by, and a grinding screech from farther away. The lamp flame flickered as the wind blew through the cracks around the door. Suddenly the wind eased, and we could hear gushes of rain striking the door, and dripping through the cracks.

"That's all for the wind, I guess," Helen remarked.

114

"Praise the Lord!"

"For sure," Helen echoed.

After a half hour the storm passed, and we came out of the storm cellar. To the east the sky was still black; the sun shown to the west. The only damage we could find was one of the doors on the garage hanging by one hinge; I could fix that easily enough. Looking up and down the road I could see tree branches, bits of tin, and occasional unidentifiable lumps strewn around. Pa had not wanted trees in our yard for just this reason. Except for a couple of trees down in the schoolyard, the school looked intact. The Johnson's farm house beyond the school looked OK too.

Helen came up beside me. "I bet all the electric power is out in Appleton," she said with a lopsided grin.

"Right. If they had electric power there, I suppose it would be out. Oh—maybe all but one. Pastor Kittridge has a Delco Light plant, if he can get it running!"

"He has problems with mechanical things?"

"Only when he buys something he thinks is a great deal. He bought a car sight unseen from his brother while he was still in the Navy. Now it sits in his driveway, and pops and bangs when he tries to start it. I heard him telling Lee Wright this morning that he's in way over his head."

"Can't Lee or his men figure it out?"

"Not this time. It's a Chevrolet V-8, and none of them have ever seen one."

"Chevrolet made a V-8?" Helen asked.

"Yes, but nobody bought them in the middle of a war, and they dropped it. Pastor gets all moody when something mechanical defeats him, and this one truly has."

Helen picked up a stray tree branch. "What does his wife say?"

"You haven't gotten acquainted with Deborah Kittridge yet. She's very smart, and speaks her mind. I heard Pastor tell Lee she was threatening to make him sleep in the car!"

"Would she do that?"

"To make her point, yes!"

We both giggled at that one.

Chapter Twenty Two

Luther: Tuesday, June 3rd, 1919, The rehabilitation unit, Walter Reed.

"Well, everything looks fine, Luther. You're good to go!"

Steve Mason leaned back in his chair as I rolled my right pant leg down.

"Thanks again for everything, Captain—"

"Steve, Luther. You'll notice neither one of us is wearing a uniform at the moment."

"So we're not…Steve."

We were both in civilian clothing- suits and ties, with a white lab coat in Steve's case.

I had almost completed my processing for retirement from the Marines, and this was the last meeting before I caught a ride and headed for Union Station in downtown Washington, and home. I was also the last appointment for Steve, as he was headed downtown that afternoon to catch a train for Baltimore—a much shorter trip than mine!

All my uniforms and other gear had been packed and shipped several days before. I would only carry one large suitcase with me. It would be a bit heavier because I had been issued a second prosthesis, and I wasn't able to risk losing that!

The unit had become quiet and lonely the last couple of days. Gary left first, on his way to Mansfield, Ohio, and his farm. I suspected he would meet with his church's Board of Elders, and then the congregation, in the near future; he could no more quit preaching than quit breathing, as he told me. He added that he had very nearly done the latter, and had no desire to repeat the experience any time soon!

Jack was next. He left to catch a train to Key West, Florida. His ship turned out to be the newly commissioned battleship *Idaho*, and she was down off the Keys *working up;* he would join her there. He told me he'd write, but not to expect anything for a few months as he was going to be very busy sorting out the Marines aboard. On a battleship, Marines manned one of the fourteen inch gun turrets, and as a gunnery specialist he had a hunch he'd be spending a lot of time in 'their' turret.

So it was just Steve and me, for the moment.

"Now, don't forget, I want to see you once a year to check the prosthesis, and to inspect that stump. From what you've said getting to Baltimore shouldn't be a problem. Of course, all our services are free. We service what we sell!"

"Sales pitch time again, Steve?"

Doctor Raichart stepped into the examination room. He was also dressed in a suit and tie, with a white coat.

"Bill, we've sold this person the goods already! I'm just making sure we give good service."

"Well, the proof of the pudding is in the walking...or something like that. How are you, Luther?"

"Just fine, Doctor. I can't believe this day is finally here."

"Neither can I, Luther. Let's see, you woke up on June 25th....and it's now June 4th. You've been around for....oh, just call it a year! The last dog and all that..."

"I guess I am, aren't I?"

"Yep. Tomorrow a different bunch takes over this building. They haven't told me who, and I haven't asked. Oh, and the movers came this morning to pick up the organ. Mr. Roosevelt's note made sure of that! Maybe you'll get to visit it again some day."

"Maybe, Doctor, but not anytime soon."

"Indeed. Now, do you have any final questions for us? Don't hold back; you won't see us again for a year unless something goes badly wrong."

"Yes, Doctor, Steve, I do have one question. Would it be possible to wear my prosthesis in a tank of water, and can I do that without damaging it?"

Steve spoke up. "Planning on taking up swimming? You can do that just fine without a prosthesis."

"No, not that. It's just when I get home, I need to get baptized at church, and I could really use two legs when I go into that tank."

"Baptized? Weren't you baptized when you were a child— sprinkled or something?"

"No, Steve. First, the church I was brought up in didn't sprinkle. Second, baptism is for someone who has trusted Christ as their Savior. When I was back there, before I joined the Marines, I wasn't one of those people at all! Since I am now a believer, I need to do this."

Steve's eyebrow raised, and he nodded. "Ok, now I understand. I'm Catholic—our process is different. What you can do is use your second prosthesis to go into the water. It is sturdier than your primary one, and built to stand more strenuous, extreme activity. As soon as you're out of the water, take that prosthesis off, dry it with a towel, be sure your stump is dry, and put on your normal one. That should do it."

"Great! Thanks again for everything, Steve. Especially thank your wife for the music! And you too, Doctor Raichart."

Doctor Raichart put himself in the third chair with a small grunt, then looked straight at me.

"Don't mention it, son. I suppose I should tell you something, and I guess now is the time. When you woke up, I said something about being honored to work with you. Well…when you were brought in, you didn't know it, but your story came in with you. I had a hunch you were headed for *The Medal*, and I determined to do the best I could do to help you be able to get it standing up and breathing, instead of having it presented to your Pa. I guess I succeeded…" He turned away and pulled out his handkerchief.

Steve continued. "You've noticed Bill gets a little choked up from time to time. Anyway, let me tell you what a pleasure it's been to get you set up with your leg, and help get you strong enough to use it. I want to see you at Johns Hopkins every summer from now on, to make sure you stay happy, healthy, and mobile!"

"OK, I'm back now," Doctor Raichart said. "I echo what Steve so eloquently stated. If something goes wrong, get hold of us. Come see us once a year. And have a great life!"

I shook hands with Doctor Raichart and Steve Mason, and they clapped me on the back. "With the Lord guiding me, I hope to do just that!"

*****

Luther: Illinois, and home.

After a reasonably comfortable two days in transit courtesy of the Baltimore and Ohio, New York Central, and Rock Island Railroads, I arrived at the riverfront station in Peoria, Illinois the morning of Friday June 6th. Pa was there to meet me.

Amid the usual hugs and greetings, we reunited. I hadn't seen him since I stopped in on my way to New York to catch the ship for France, about two lifetimes ago. We had been friendly enough then, but I knew he was very concerned for my soul, and my safety, then. Now those concerns were moot.

We walked out of the station to his Oldsmobile touring car demonstrator. I hefted my suitcase into the back, and climbed in. Pa started the car, and we headed toward the Franklin Street Bridge to cross the Illinois River toward home.

"I see the Franklin Street Bridge hasn't collapsed while I was away," I said with a grin as we started across it.

"Hush your mouth, Son!" Pa replied.

We went through this routine every time we had to cross the bridge. This bridge replaced one that was supposed to replace an ancient wooden bridge next to it.

That first replacement bridge lasted exactly twenty days before it collapsed early one morning in 1909. They had to hurriedly refurbish the old bridge, nicknamed *old toothpicks*, and continue to use it until the *replacement* replacement bridge was finished three years later.

I vividly remembered being brought down to see the wreckage, and having to travel over that terrible old bridge. I think that is what started my nervousness around bridges. I could stand on the heaving deck of a ship in the middle of the ocean without fear, but put me on a narrow bridge over water and I was Not Happy! Of course Pa thought it hilarious...and our *shtick* began. Our passengers never thought it that funny, for some reason

We crossed the bridge and continued our climb out of East Peoria toward home.

"Looks a lot busier than when I left," I remarked.

"Everything's grown tremendously in this area since the war. All sorts of industries, businesses, and people—lots of people. Even seen some growth out our way."

"I hope the town hasn't changed its personality."

"It really hasn't. We're far enough away from the city to avoid most of its bad influences...but close enough to commute in a good car!"

"And that's where Barlow Motor Company comes in."

"You bet, Son! We're getting plenty of Model T trade-ins these days. People want something a little more comfortable than a *flivver*. Old Henry won't see it, though—not till his sales crash."

"So you still see the opportunity, then?"

"More than ever! And we can do it the old fashioned way, by giving the customer an honest reliable vehicle at a reasonable price, and by not playing games to cheat them. Some of the city dealers got greedy during the war; they're going to regret their shady dealings, I think."

"Pa, I've been looking at the papers, and those trade magazines you sent me, and I think I know what kind of a car I want to buy."

"I'm almost afraid to ask, Son, but what?"

"I'd like one of those Chevrolet V-8s!"

Pa drove in silence for a moment.

"You know, Son, that's a pretty good idea. Those cars were a lot better than their sales numbers showed. They were just too expensive for the folks who buy Chevrolets. If it had been an Oldsmobile, I think it would've sold even better than this model 45 V-8 here," He patted the steering wheel of the big touring car. "There aren't many of those model Ds around, and people are scared of them, so they're cheaper."

"That's what I figured too."

"Let me keep my ear to the ground, and see what some of the other dealers turn up. If we run across one at the right price, you can move on it. Until then, just drive one of the used cars on my lot."

"Thanks a lot, Pa. I really appreciate your confidence in my decision."

"That's not the only decision I have confidence in, Son."

"I know, Pa."

"How are you going to handle that this Sunday?"

"First off, tomorrow I intend to go see Pastor Reem. I need to make a public profession of faith, and get baptized. Then, we'll see if the congregation wants me to join the church."

"That's a wise course. They all heard about your salvation, of course; this just brings it home to them."

"I agree. Although I'll be going to college, maybe at Bradley, I'll still be home on weekends I hope. It would be good to be a member, especially after running for so long."

"You know there was a big piece in the paper about you, and a picture of you getting the Medal of Honor."

"I wish they hadn't done that, but I couldn't stop them."

"You still think you don't deserve that medal?"

I sat a moment, watching a freight train pass us on the track next to the road, forming my answer.

"Yes—and no. I know the Lord made it happen to me to draw me to Him, and He made me do the things I got the medal for. I still don't remember doing them, though. Jack helped me work through things, and he really helped me accept it."

"I'm so glad Jack was there for you. He's become like a second son to me since his folks passed a few years ago."

"I think he feels the same about you, Pa. He's on the new battleship *Idaho* now, but said we wouldn't hear from him for a while as they were working up to join the fleet."

Pa chuckled. "I still can't get over naming a battleship for a landlocked state! Not like they could sail over there from Bremerton or anything!"

We both laughed at that, as we covered the miles toward home.
*****

Luther: Sunday, June 8th, 1919, First Baptist Church, Metamora, Illinois.

"Thank you, Luther. Upon your profession of faith, so movingly just given, I baptize you in the name of the Father, the Son, and the Holy Ghost."

Pastor Reem clamped the handkerchief over my nose and sent me backward into the water. Two seconds later he brought me back up, sputtering like everybody I'd ever seen get baptized did. To a chorus of amens I stepped slowly out of the tank, and up the steps to the little room behind the choir loft where we changed.

I took off the robe and dried off before sitting down on a chair and unstrapping my prosthesis. I was drying it with a soft towel when Pastor Reem came into the room to change. He squished as he walked.

"Hip boot leaked again," he muttered, "Don't know why I even bother."

He pulled off the boot and poured about a quart of water out into a pan.

"At least I got smart and left a pan up here. Wear old shoes too."

Pastor saw I was about done drying the prosthesis. "Luther, may I take a look at that, please? I've never seen one like that."

"Sure, Pastor," I handed it to him. "It's my secondary one. The therapist at Walter Reed said to use it for the baptism, then switch back to my normal one."

Pastor looked at the prosthesis as he held it in his hands. "Never seen one so well-finished. And so light, too! And this is your *secondary* one?"

"Yep. Here's my *good* one." I handed it to Pastor and began putting the special cushioning sock over my stump.

"If any of these things could be called *beautiful* this one could" he said as he examined it.

"Well, as a reminder of what the Lord had to do to get my attention, I'd say it is beautiful, too."

Pastor handed me the prosthesis, then continued to dry himself while I strapped it on.

"So, what are you going to do now, Luther?"

"First, get accustomed to living in the civilian world again. That won't be so hard, since regulations in the hospital were pretty relaxed. Then, go to college. The Lord seems to be aiming me toward some sort of engineering."

"Not the ministry, then?"

"No, not full-time, anyway. While we were at Walter Reed, Jack and I, and another young man from the Apostolic Christian Church in Ohio, took turns preaching to each other on Sundays. Ended up with half the patients in the unit worshiping with us, and four saved."

"The Lord gave you an effective ministry, then?"

"Yes, but we didn't start out to do that—it just happened. Jack and I learned we were really more suited to teaching than preaching. Gary—the *AC* fellow—was the preacher in our little band."

"Well, we need engineers and teachers, of course. Perhaps later you could teach a Sunday School class around here, if you want. Do you still play the organ?"

"Oh, yes," I grinned, "I restored an old reed organ while I was at Walter Reed. They called it *occupational therapy*, but I called it *tedious fun*. I played it for our services after I got it working."

"Speaking of organs, once you're a member…which should have happened out there by now; the Deacon Board chairman was going to keep the people over and vote on it! Er…what was I talking about, Luther?"

"The organ."

"Oh, yes! Once you're a member you can have at ours any time! It hasn't been played regularly since Mrs. Arbuckle passed away. I'm sure the congregation would love to hear it again!"

"I'll be happy to see what I can do with it, Pastor." And I would, too—although if it was as decrepit as I remembered it, I had a long road of woe to travel until it was playing again.

I finished tying my tie, and Pastor Reem dropped his waders in a wooden box. "Ought to just bury those things, but I guess I'll try patching them again."

We walked down the stairs and out into the sanctuary, where most of the congregation had stayed to shake my hand. I was glad to be home, and glad not to be wearing the uniform, and *The Medal*. I knew someday I would have to wear it, but not today.

Chapter Twenty Three

Don Wain and others: Saturday, June 28th, 1919, 5:15 PM, North Broad Street, Galesburg.

"Will you look at that," Dick Meriden whispered in awe, shaking his head at the wreckage in the front yard.

Donald Wain leaned on the railing and stared, mouth open. His wife, Pamela, looked out at the scene for a moment, then felt for the porch chair next to her and sat down heavily, wiping her hands on her apron.

Maggie B. craned her neck as she observed as much detail of the scene as she could from the safety of the porch. *Never know if someone'll sue over this*, she thought.

Retired Navy Captain Jackie Brighthonor held her daughter Evelyn's hand. The thin nine year old leaned over the rail. "Mom, may I go look closer?" she asked.

"Ev, I know you want to look closer, but none of us are going off this porch until the power company people say it is OK. You could get electrocuted."

"Oh, Mom! May I go back to my book then?" the dark-haired nine year old asked—in Mandarin Chinese.

"Yes you may, Ev, but please use English here—the others do not know Chinese."

"Sorry, Mom—I forgot," Evelyn said in English, then skittered back into the house.

The *display* in the front yard did not move.

One of the glories of Galesburg was the multitude of huge elm trees lining the older streets, and populating the parks. The largest of the elms had graced the Lombard College campus since 1868, and its siblings stood on terraces everywhere. Except in front of the Wain house, now.

The massive elm had not resisted the straight line winds of the derecho, and toppled over across Broad street. Its upper branches almost reached the house on the other side; the roots plucked out of the ground stood as tall as the porch roof. Its fall had dropped power and telephone lines, splintered a telephone pole...and flattened the Wain's Chevrolet Baby Grand. Only the hood and front wheels appeared at one side of the massive trunk of the fallen tree. The rest was under the trunk.

"Now I see why you wanted my car in the garage," Dick remarked.

"Glad we did that," Don said, then sighed and gripped the porch railing tighter.

"Why didn't you put it in the driveway?" Pamela Wain asked.

Don turned to face his wife. "We only had a couple minutes before it hit, and Dick was behind me. I figured I'd do a U-turn and park it in the street."

"A good idea, dear, except when it's not," Pam replied, then turned to Jackie. "Things usually aren't this exciting."

"I hope not," the newly-arrived accountant replied. "Sorry about Ev's lapse there."

"No problem. How is her language study going?" Pam asked.

"Pretty well, actually. I hope we'll both have some opportunity to practice it here."

"I'll introduce you to Yu Chen, and her daughter Li Chen. We ate at their restaurant when you visited."

"Thanks, Pam, we'd love that," Jackie replied.

Maggie B. turned from her survey. "Hey Don, how are you fixed for insurance?"

"OK, I think," Don replied, "I'll go see my insurance man tomorrow morning, if I can catch a ride."

"He'll be busy, I think," Maggie said, and leaned on the porch railing. "Straight to the junkyard?"

Don scratched his head. "Maybe not, Maggie. The front end still looks OK—If I can find a good body I might be able to have the motor and transmission put in it. I'll have Lee Wright drag it down to the dealership, and see what happens."

"Right. Like someone's gonna have a Baby Grand blow its engine and fall into your lap? Dream on, my *foggy froggy!*"

The others chuckled at Pam's comment.

"Now, Love, let's just see what turns up," Don turned to his wife, "Stranger things than that have happened."

"Like us here?"

"Exactly, Love!"

A large touring car edged up to the scene from the right. It stopped just short of the tree and wires. A big man in a bowler hat and raincoat leaned out of the driver's side. "Hey Don, is that your car under there?"

"Yes it is, Omer! Quite a sight, isn't it?"

"I've been driving around, and that's the worst I've seen yet! I'll go find my photographer, and have him come take a photo of the mess before the light fails. It'll go on the front page of the *Register*, if you don't mind."

"Sure, go ahead. Just tell him to watch out for the power lines."

"I will. You're all OK, right?"

"As OK as we ever are, Omer."

The big man laughed. "Good for you, Don! You can still joke with your car turned into a pancake."

"Might as well—it's only stuff."

"For sure. Thanks, Don. Dale will be here directly." The car backed slowly away from the scene.

"Do you really mean it?" Pam asked.

"Mean what, Love?"

"About it only being stuff?"

Don turned to his wife. His hands clenched and unclenched twice, before staying open. "Yes, Love, I do. Sometimes it's harder than others."

"I know, Dear, and it'll all work out," Pam said, then slowly got up. "Back to the kitchen—glad we've got a generator since the power's out."

Maggie B. turned. "Let me help you, Pam."

"Thanks, Maggie," Pam replied, then accepted Maggie's arm as they walked slowly toward the door.

As they went back inside Jackie spoke. "Who was that man, Don?"

"Omer Custer. Owns a bunch of things in town, including the *Republican Register* newspaper. He's gonna have his photographer take a picture of the *pancake* and put it in the paper."

"One of those *people* you've made friends with?"

"Exactly, *Captain*. He's an honorable man, even though he used to be a brawler in the old days."

"Wouldn't want to get on his bad side, even now," Dick remarked.

"Even though you were trained by the *Special Operations Executive*?

Dick nodded. "Right. We were trained in assassination and sabotage, not brawling. If we ever got into a knock-down drag-out we'd already failed."

"I hear ya," Don said, then turned to Jackie. "Sometime get Dick to spin a few yarns with you. I suspect you have some stories to tell too."

"I'm sure I do." *And one I won't tell anyone else besides Pam,* Jackie thought.

*****

Sylvia: the house on the Fremont Road.

125

I was amazed at the change in my mood between Saturday afternoon and Sunday morning. I had a job, and a friend to help me. I guess it was true what I read so often in Scripture: In my bereavement the Lord still provided! I knew the euphoria would wear off eventually, but Helen and I both enjoyed it while it lasted.

Helen's folks came out Sunday afternoon to see how we were faring, and Helen told them the news. Bessie was thrilled, and said she and L.M. had been praying something like this would happen. The logistics of coming home to Galesburg on the weekends had to be worked out, but Bessie said they had a couple ideas in that regard. As usual L.M. didn't say much; Helen told me his work schedule as an engineer was so chaotic his normally quiet disposition was made even quieter by exhaustion.

We arranged to drive into town Wednesday to do some shopping, and pick up some of Helen's things at her house. We figured a few trips over the next month and she would be all set.

Tuesday brought the first *Republican Register*, and news of the Saturday storm. This paper actually used a word I had to look up in the dictionary: *derecho*. A very large storm with high straight-line winds, with the front of it looking like an inverted bowl—yep, what we saw that afternoon. Dominating the front page was the photo of a touring car that looked just like *the baby*, with a huge tree trunk lying over the passenger compartment, everything behind the steering wheel squashed like a bug! So much for that car.

So we had things to do, and a mission in our lives again. I knew at some point more grieving would come, but I determined to carry on until then.

*****

Deborah Kittridge and others: Tuesday, July 1ˢᵗ, 1919, 10:25 AM, Appleton Baptist Church parsonage.

The knock on the door on a Tuesday morning surprised Deborah Kittridge. She stopped treading the sewing machine, marked her place on the pattern, and went to the door.

"Lee, what a surprise to see you this morning!" Deborah's mouth twisted into a smirk, "Are you here to drag *AP's Folly* off our property?"

Lee Wright laughed, happy to be able to laugh again after last Saturday, and also bring good news.

"No, Deborah, not today. But, I think I might have a lead on a way to get that car off your hands. Is AP home?"

"Sure is. He's in the study…studying, or sleeping, or something."

She turned around "AP!" she bellowed. Lee couldn't help but let out a snort.

"I can't resist using my *husband call* when he's holed up back there!"

"I can understand that." Another giggle.

AP appeared behind Deborah. He was dressed in overalls and a T-shirt.

"Hi Lee! Sorry I'm not very presentable; I was going to go out and cut some weeds in a little bit. Come on in!"

"That's OK, AP. I can't stay—gotta get back to the shop. I've been at a dealer's meeting in Peoria since yesterday. I was talking to the dealer from Metamora, and would you believe his son has just been retired for wounds from the Marines, and is looking for a Chevrolet model D!"

AP grinned. "What's the dealer's name?"

"Howard Barlow, Barlow Motors."

"His son is Luther Barlow, and I know him! He was one of a special party of six, or rather five—long story, we brought back from France on the *New Jersey*. Luther was heading to Walter Reed, and he's missing his lower right leg. He wants a Model D?"

"He does. He's done his research, his Pa says, and he's very serious."

"I believe it. He's one sharp young man. I think he's going to go to Bradley and study engineering. If anybody could make that sorry vehicle run again, it'd be him. And his Pa is a dealer?"

"Has the whole General Motors line. Very successful too. But he said Model Ds are thin on the ground in the Midwest."

"Can you contact them and tell them about the car?"

"Already done. Howard knows where you live, and what the car looks like. I said the car was pretty low miles, but popped and banged when you tried to start it. I said nothing about price of course."

"All I want to do is get my investment back…"

"And ensure your future sleeping arrangements!"

"Deborah!" AP exclaimed, before he and Lee started to laugh.

"Men! I know how to contact Clarice, you know."

The men sobered up quickly.

"Lee, did you tell him to come over and look at it?"

"I did. Howard told me to tell you he and his son will be over tomorrow morning sometime to look at it. He said they have a way to get it back to Metamora if they need to. He also said he had the manual for the car, and his son was reading it."

"If I know Luther, he'll have the thing memorized by the time they get here! If you could call Howard over in Metamora and tell him tomorrow morning, or whenever they could get over here will be just fine. If I'm not here, Deborah will know where I am and can run me down."

"Literally?"

"Deborah!"

"All right," Lee chuckled as he spoke. "I'll be happy to do that. And I really do need to git."

"Run while you can…"

AP rolled his eyes. "Seriously, thanks a bunch, Lee. I owe you for this one!"

Deborah grinned as Lee turned to leave. "He certainly does!"

*****

Noon, Wright-Allensworth Motor Company, 247 East Simmons Street, Galesburg.

Lee Wright's business partner Rolland "Rol" Allensworth was waiting for him when he walked in the door to the dealership.

"Two things, Lee. First, we dragged in *Don's Pancake* this morning. It's in the side lot."

Lee looked out the west window of the showroom. There sat the poor flattened 1914 Chevrolet Baby Grand. It looked even worse than it did on the front page of the Evening Mail. "Anything salvageable?"

"Tom says the engine and transmission look fine. The hood and radiator are OK, maybe the front suspension. The rest of it is done."

"OK, I'll call Don in a while and confirm what he wants us to do with it. Next item?"

"Carl Swanson's coming in at one. He wants to talk about a car trade. He just bought a brand new Model T coupe yesterday afternoon."

Lee sat down at his desk and beheld the pile of papers in his in-box. "Why would he want to trade this quickly? Even a Ford is a new car for longer than that!"

"He found out this morning there's going to be three Swansons in a few months."

"Oh. Makes sense. Interesting how such happy news can ruin a person's whole day."

"You said it, Lee!"

Lee sat back in his chair and scratched his thinning hair. "Hmmm. We just took in that '17 Dodge touring. Really nice car—maybe we can trade him for that."

"We're into that Dodge for about three hundred," Rol said, looking at a paper on his desk. "The Ford would have cost right at five hundred since it's a closed coupe. He paid cash. I think we can deal."

Lee nodded. "Sounds like an interesting day. Before I tend to those two, let me call Howard Barlow in Metamora before I forget. His son wants a Model D, and AP Kittridge has that one he can't get to run."

"AP could stand to catch a break," Rol commented.

"Yeah, before Deborah makes him sleep in the thing!" Lee snorted, then picked up the earpiece.

Chapter Twenty Four

Luther: June, 1919, Metamora, Illinois and elsewhere.

The Monday after I arrived home, after making sure I could drive with the prosthesis, I took one of Pa's used cars into Peoria and toured the Bradley campus. I was suitably impressed. I liked the small class size and the way all classes for the applied sciences department were located near each other. The labs seemed well-equipped, and the instructors I met were friendly. The Lord gave me peace about the place, so I collected a set of application paperwork and headed home.

I had requested a transcript of my High School Grades, and my retirement papers from the Marines arrived while I was working on the application. Of course, my awards were listed on the retirement papers, especially *the medal*, but If I couldn't hide their existence I wasn't going to point them out either.

It was bad enough my retired identification card had the notation 'MH' on it, which told anyone in on the system that I held *the medal*, and therefore was given certain privileges.

I also had a significant boost to my retired pay from that little circumstance, not that I was going to worry about the money one way or the other. We were not wealthy, but we had enough not to worry about it. Paying for college was not a concern, and I could buy anything I *needed*.

Another day I drove into Peoria to visit my old organ instructor, Doctor Carl Christian Christensen. I found him, as usual, at the large Moller pipe organ in the sanctuary of First Congregational Church on the Hamilton Street hill. Carl was a lanky man in his middle sixties, with a fringe of white hair around a bald head. He hadn't aged that I could tell.

"Ah, Luther, I heard you were back," he spoke with his trademark Danish accent as he put out his hand. "I am glad you survive that terrible war, and I congratulate you on the Medal of Honor!"

"Thank you, Sir, it is very good to be back," I said, side-stepping the part about The Medal.

"Call me Carl, please. Your father tells me you wounded were. You lost a leg?" Every once in a while he'd scramble word order when he spoke.

"Yes, ...Carl, my right leg below the knee. That's one reason why I wanted to come see you; I'd like you to check my pedal work and tell me how I can improve it."

"I can do that, Luther. Sit up there on the bench and give me a few chromatic scales, starting at the bottom, as quick as you can, say three octaves."

As I climbed onto the bench Carl added, "Pull one of the 8 foot stops; they're easier for me to hear these days."

He had me repeat the chromatic scales ten times. By the end of the exercise I was amazed how much faster and more accurately I was able to sound the pedals, even with my prosthesis.

"You've lost some speed and accuracy with the prosthesis, but not enough worried to be," Carl pronounced. "I think you will be able to manage all the music within your overall skill level. Now let me hear you play something. How about that Scherzo?"

"That one I can give you!"

I pulled the old familiar stops on the Moller, and began to play. Carl stepped away from the console and listened closely to the sound from the organ case while I played.

When I was done Carl actually clapped!

"Bravo, Luther! I do not think you have lost any of your skill on the manuals. How did you manage to retain it?"

"When I was convalescing at Walter Reed in Washington I rebuilt an old pump organ, and then played it in the unit often. Actually, the Scherzo was the only piece I had fully worked up for most of my time there."

"You kept your skill, and that is what matters. The pedal work will improve, or you will make allowances." Carl sat down on the front pew, and motioned me to follow. "Now, what are you doing with the rest of your life?"

"I'll be going to Bradley Polytechnic in the fall, studying engineering."

Carl nodded. "And I understand something else was settled on the day you were wounded?"

"He got my attention, Carl."

Now the elderly organist grinned. "He has ways of doing that. You were given a choice, were you not?"

"I knew I was dying, but He gave me one last chance to trust Him. I surrendered, and He saved me."

Carl looked beyond me, where the large stained glass window split beams of colored sunlight on the pews. He sighed.

"I was not brought to the point of physical death, but He brought me face to face with my sin," Carl said softly. "I was engaged to play the organ for a series of meetings in New York City, conducted by a man named Dwight Moody. You may have heard of him…"

I nodded.

"I tried to put what he was saying out of my mind and concentrate on my playing, my *professional persona*. The second Friday of the meetings I could stand it no longer. At the altar call I abandoned the organ and fell on the altar. Mr. Moody dealt with me, and I surrendered. To this day I am amazed that Jesus would save someone as foul as me. But He did."

"Amen, Carl. He did it for me, too. I thought when I faded out afterwards I was on my way to Glory. I still am, but I woke up in a hospital."

"Was that a disappointment?"

"Yes, it was. But He's blessed me so much already since then I know He'll do with me what He wants, and it'll be very, very good."

Carl grinned. "I praise the Lord He has you in His hand now. And…I have an idea."

Carl pulled a key ring from his pocket and removed a key.

"This is the key to the side door over there. Take it, and whenever you have a few moments, or feel the need to get away, come here and play. All I ask is you write in the log here when you come and when you leave, and if you detect a problem with the organ, leave me a detailed note about it so I can get it fixed. Later on, if you want to try fixing the problems, do so, but only when someone else is here. I will not have you getting stuck in the organ case!"

I took the key. "I will surely do what you've asked, Carl, and I thank you more than you know for the opportunity to play here again!"

"You are entirely welcome, Luther. One more thing—please make sure you shut off the organ before you leave. I do not want to burn this building down by something left on!"

"Of course, Carl." I knew the congregation loved their ornate old church building, but since the first time I came for a lesson I thought it was a fire trap just waiting for a chance to burn down. I also resolved never to visit after dark. Truth be told, the place always scared me just a bit.

*****

Luther: Tuesday, July 1st, 1919, the Barlow home.

132

I was sitting at the kitchen table working on the application to Bradley Polytechnic when the telephone rang. I answered it.

"Luther, I have great news! I was talking to Lee Wright from Galesburg at the dealer's meeting last evening, and he told me about a Model D Chevrolet he knows is for sale. In fact, it could be quite a deal. Do you know someone in Appleton named A. P. Kittridge?"

"I sure do! He was the Paymaster on the *New Jersey* when we came back from France on her. He said he was Pastor of Appleton Baptist Church in civilian life. He has a D?"

"He does. I gather he bought it sight unseen from his brother while he was still aboard ship. It is in his driveway. Lee says it starts, but then pops and bangs and cannot be driven."

"That sounds like maybe a spark plug misfire or something. When can we go see it?

"How about tomorrow? We'll take the service car and drive over there. Take a set of dealer's plates, and the towbar if we need it."

"That would be great, Pa! I have the service manual here; I'll do a little boning up on the ignition system just in case. Besides, I'd really like to see Commander Kittridge again."

"Great, Son. I have a bit more work to do here, and I'll be home in about an hour. I think I'll take the service car home with me."

"Is it still the Model 51?"

"Sure is. No sense getting rid of something that works, right?"

"Right, Pa. See you in a while!"

Next morning, after a quick breakfast, we loaded a few tools and a can of gasoline into the back of the service car, and left for Appleton.

The service car had an interesting history. It had started life as a 1915 Cadillac Model 51 touring car, the first year of the Cadillac V-8. The previous owner put less than 500 miles on it before he made a slight misjudgment in speed…of an oncoming interurban motor of the Illinois Traction System. Said oncoming motor and several grain cars mangled the back end of the car's body and flipped the car off the right of way like a piece of paper. Fortunately the driver was only slightly injured, but the car appeared to be a total loss.

Enter my father. He bought the wreck, dragged it to the shop, and over several months he and his mechanics took the remains apart, straightened the frame, and reconstructed the body as a two-seater enclosed coupe, with a small carrying bed behind the driver's compartment. They gradually added a towbar mounting, extra lights and light truck tires. The dealership used the car as its mobile repair shop and towing machine. When I was home on leave from the Marines I found the car fun to drive in spite of its size.

Today I was content to let Pa do the driving, at least on the outbound leg of the trip. We started towards the Illinois River behind the agreeable rumble of the big V-8.

"I always did enjoy driving this car, Pa. You and the men did a good job on it."

"We just went through and refurbished it. New clutch, new brakes, bigger generator and so on. If you'd like this instead of the Chevrolet I think it could be arranged. I have a 1918 model in the back of the shop we've been working on. It's ready to be put back together into another one of these anytime."

"Thanks for the offer, Pa, but I'd really like the Chevrolet if I can manage it. Did old man Hagrelius misjudge the interurban again?"

"No. This one came from Pekin, and an Illinois Midland steamer caught it."

"I'm surprised there's anything left of it."

"Trains on that line run so slowly it only pushed it out of the way…after it turned the back end into a ball of metal. Nobody hurt, happily."

"And we get another one to experiment with."

"Right. But these exercises do have a purpose. We need experienced body repairmen to fix our customer's cars, and between the newness of the trade and the war, we've had a hard time getting and keeping them. So I arrange these *exercises* and let the young men learn the trade with them. Better to ruin one of those than a customer's car!"

"Good idea, Pa."

We reached the lowlands just north of Peoria Lake, and began driving on a narrow road toward the river. I realized where we were heading.

"Pa, do we have to go this way?"

"We do if we want to get there this morning. The traffic in downtown Peoria has gotten much worse since the war, so bad the locals call it *rush hour*. I'm not getting in that if I can avoid it by going this way."

"But this bridge—"

Pa turned to me and grinned. Sometimes he could be downright cruel!

At the end of the narrow road—causeway, actually—sat a small house next to the end of a very long, very narrow truss bridge. This was the Upper Free Bridge. It had been built in the 1880s, and showed its age.

The bridge tender looked down the span, checked for traffic at the other end, and also river traffic, then waved us on. We started over the one lane bridge.

Pa laughed. "Son, you got through the Great War, sailed stormy seas on your Armored Cruiser, and survived being shot up, but you close your eyes and grip the side of the car door like you're going to pass out when we go over a little bridge!"

"Right, Pa," I said through clenched teeth.

"Suit yourself," he replied, and began describing the scenery as we drove over the gently swaying spans.

One of these days, I thought.

Chapter Twenty Five

Luther and others: Wednesday, July 2nd, the parsonage, Appleton.

After my little adventure with the bridge, we climbed out of the Illinois River valley and set course west on the graded gravel road to Galesburg. Pa said he had heard of plans to pave the road with concrete in a few years; that would certainly make it easier to get from Peoria to Galesburg. Today, though, the ride was agreeable and relatively smooth.

We passed the old stagecoach stop of Kickapoo, then across Kickapoo creek on another rickety bridge and through Brimfield. We turned off the main road into a succession of country lanes which brought us to another bridge, over the Spoon River. I managed to keep my eyes open on this one, to the further cackles of my Pa. We stopped at the crossroads outside of Appleton to let an older Chevrolet pass in front of us, heading north.

"That's unusual," Pa said as he noticed the two young women in the car as it passed.

"They seem to know where they're going."

"So they do. And that's one good-looking Baby Grand."

Leave it to an automobile dealer to notice the *car*.

We passed through the village, and came to a single story home made of…logs? We turned in the driveway, and there was our quarry!

"There it is, Pa, as advertised."

"Not bad, Son. Wire wheels too. This could be interesting…"

We walked up to the door and knocked. A tall woman with dark hair in a bun answered the door. She reached out to shake our hands.

"You must be the Barlows! I'm Deborah Kittridge, AP's wife. Come on in, and I'll get him. He's back in his study, pacing the floor like an expectant father! Please sit down—I'll be right back!"

We sat down in the Kittridge parlor.

"Unusual." Pa remarked.

"Sure is," I replied. "Homey and relaxing though."

"The greeting, or this room?"

"Yes."

Deborah Kittridge came back in the room with AP in tow. I stood up, followed by Pa.

"Luther! How grand to see you again!" He pumped my arm vigorously and clapped me on the shoulder.

"I'm really glad to see you again, Commander!"

"Forget that *Commander* stuff. It's AP, or Pastor, if you prefer."

"AP sounds fine to me. Let me introduce my father, Howard."

"Very pleased to meet you, Sir," AP said as they shook hands. "Your son and I had a very unusual trip home on the *New Jersey* last year. It was a pleasure and an honor to know him."

"I'm kind of proud of him too, even if he does chicken out when we go over a little bridge!"

"Pa, the Upper Free Bridge is not a *little* bridge! And I admit, it scares me to death."

"It does that to us, too, Luther. Deborah and I won't go near it."

"Speak for yourself AP; I think it's quaint. And quit rolling your eyes!"

AP grinned—she'd caught him in mid-roll as he stood behind her back.

Pa brought us back on course. "AP, could we have a look at the Model D?"

"Of course, Howard. Let's go see the poor beast..."

"At last, he sees it as it truly is..."

"I was only kidding, Dear!"

"Right."

I decided this couple were made for each other, and fun to watch.

We trooped out to the car. AP opened the hood on either side, and latched them together so they wouldn't fall back down.

"If I may just look the car over for a few minutes please," I asked.

"Of course. Take all the time you need."

Everyone stepped back and let me inspect the car. Inside of fifteen seconds I saw what might be the trouble. Two spark plug wires next to each other on the left side didn't look the same as the others—they looked like they were on each other's plug. That would certainly cause the misfire. I carefully inspected the rest of the car. It looked very clean, and very good.

As I was going round the car I noticed Deborah giving precisely the same inspection to our service car, even quietly opening the hood on one side. Pa was too busy watching me to notice her. I wondered if she were doing the same sort of calculating I was. Since I knew what a horse trader my Pa was, and also that it was getting towards time to let the service car go, I had a hunch what was going to happen. First, though, I had to sort out the Model D.

I turned to AP. "Could you try to start it, please?"

"Surely."

He got in, pumped the foot feed a few times, pulled out the choke, adjusted the spark, switched on the key, and hit the starter button. The engine groaned as it turned over, then caught. It immediately started popping and banging, and the whole car bounced as it shook. I quickly made the 'cut' motion with my hand, and AP shut it off.

"Confirm ignition off?"

"Ignition off."

Now for the test. I unscrewed the tops of the two misplaced spark plug wires—they were loose, another clue—and switched the wires. I tightened the plug tops down, tighter this time, and stepped back. I turned to AP, who still sat in the driver's seat.

"Try it again, AP."

AP repeated the starting procedure, and after two revolutions the engine leapt into life—without banging! It missed slightly for a moment as the two misfiring plugs cleared, then purred at a steady slow idle.

We all had huge grins on our faces—all except AP Kittridge. He just stared at the engine, mouth open.

"How…did you know that?" He finally gasped.

"I had a hunch that might be what it was, from the description you gave Lee Wright. So I memorized the firing order and cylinder orientation before we came this morning. The two wires I switched just didn't look right like they were, and the tops were a bit loose. Now that I look closer, the firing order would have been off the other way."

"How could that have happened?" AP still looked shaken.

Pa answered. "My guess is someone switched them on your brother as a prank. Or maybe his wife got fed up and decided to take *direct action*."

"Now there's an idea!" Deborah interjected.

I decided I liked that woman.

Pa continued. "However it happened, it happened. And since nobody around here is familiar with one of these motors, nobody caught it. Don't beat yourself up over it; this sort of thing happens even in the shop back in Metamora. We just learn and move on."

I had to be honest. "AP, now that it's running right, do you really want to sell it?"

AP Kittridge looked over at the idling auto, and sighed. He turned back to me.

"Yes, Luther I do—and relax Deborah, I really mean it! I bought this thing outside of the Lord's will, because I thought it was a Great Deal. While it may be that for you, or somebody else, it wasn't for me. So it needs to go, and only for how much I have in it."

Crunch time. "How much is that, AP?"

"One hundred fifty dollars."

I saw Pa startle. I kept a straight face, but I was shocked. The car only had 500 miles on it. Even as an orphan, the normal value was several times what AP wanted.

Pa spoke first. "AP, I can count on one hand the number of times I've said this in sixteen years in the car business, but you're not asking enough for this car!"

"I know, Howard, but I also know the Lord is teaching me a lesson with the thing, and I really want to learn it this time. Besides, I really did only pay a hundred fifty for this car. My brother took the big loss."

"Just out of curiosity, did your brother also learn from his experience?" I asked.

"Nope. His wife just wrote Deborah that he's gone and bought the biggest Harley Davidson motorcycle he could find!"

We all laughed till we nearly cried.

"You know," Deborah said as we started to recover, "I may have a solution to this predicament. I suggest, Luther, you and AP take the Chevrolet for a short drive to check it out and make sure it is what you want. Meanwhile, I will take a short test drive in that Cadillac behind it. Would that be acceptable, Howard, assuming you come with me?"

Now it was our turn to stare open-mouthed at a grinning Deborah Kittridge.

"AP, you know I always enjoyed that Locomobile and those other big cars we've owned. I've never told you this, but I've always admired the V-8 Cadillacs. I thought if I sold enough books, I might get one someday. It's not been a priority, of course, but it has always been in the back of my mind. Here's a unique example of one, that seems to be in good condition, but isn't ostentatious like Cadillacs usually are. Howard, were you planning to take that vehicle out of service in the near future?"

For once Pa was rattled. "Er, yes, Deborah, I actually have its replacement

being finished in my shop right now."

"Might it be for sale, then?"

"It might."

"Then let's take our test drives, and meet back here in a few minutes to talk."

We all nodded. I retrieved the dealer's plates from the service car and put them on the Chevrolet, Deborah climbed in the driver's seat of the Cadillac, and we were off in opposite directions.

I took the V-8 through the village and out the north road. For having sat for several months, it felt remarkably solid and steady.

"I have to ask—what got into Deborah back there?"

AP turned toward me and spoke up so I could hear him over the wind.

"You have to understand how Deborah operates. She is very smart, very poised—*self assured* I think is the term. She comes to her own conclusions and isn't shy about sharing them. I think that's what first attracted me to her. She's just...*unique*. She drives me crazy sometimes, but I love her very much."

"I can see that, AP...although your conversations back and forth can get interesting."

"We've always been like that. It's all in fun—most of the time."

"Would she really have made you sleep in the car?"

"Lee told you that, did he? Well...to prove her point, yes, she would have!"

"Wow!"

"Oh yes...then about three AM she'd have dragged me back in the house, and we would have made up. Making up with Deborah is *always fun*..."

"I caught that, AP. And I'd say you two are made for each other!"

"We've always thought the Lord exercised His sense of humor when He put us together. And we wouldn't have it any other way!"

After about twenty minutes we drove back to the house, and pulled up in the street, since the service car was already in the driveway next to their Model T.

"Well, what do you think?" AP asked.

"AP, this car is just what I want. I'll take it, assuming we can come to some deal when we get in the house."

"I have a feeling Deborah has already made the deal, and will merely inform us of it."

I nodded and chuckled. "I think you're right. Let's go see what she has decided for us!"

Deborah Kittridge had, of course, already sealed the deal with Pa. She informed us we were making an even trade of the Chevrolet for the 1915 Cadillac service car. I could take the Chevrolet now, and Pa said we could deliver the service car to Appleton as soon as the new one was finished—about a week, he figured. Pa would remove the towing equipment and the lettering

140

on the side. Deborah asked that the extra lights remain. If something happened to the service car between now and then, we would renegotiate or pay the asking price for the Chevrolet. Pa and Deborah had already shaken on the deal, so AP and I really had nothing to do!

They invited us to stay for lunch. I accepted, but Pa said he needed to get to Galesburg and see Lee Wright about something, and maybe he'd take Lee to lunch. Pa left in the service car, after emptying the can of gasoline into the Chevrolet.

Lunch with the Kittridges was delightful. Deborah was an outstanding cook, and the conversation was very pleasant. I wished I lived closer to this intriguing couple. I suspected his church was a good one too.

Before I left to go back to Metamora, I used their facilities. I was surprised at the thick walls surrounding the bathroom, and the feel of the floor as my prosthesis walked on it. It seemed to be made of concrete!

"I must ask, why the unusual bathroom? Is that concrete?"

"It sure is!" AP replied. "When we built this house, I had that room put in special. It is made of reinforced concrete, and the base of it sits on its own foundation under the house. That's our *safe room*. I've been in two tornadoes in my life, and we decided we didn't want to be blown away with the house next time a tornado hits. And I thought we were going to have one last Saturday night, too! We used that room—and were glad to have it!"

"That was quite a storm Saturday night. Straight line winds, though."

"I'm glad it held off as long as it did. We had a big funeral that morning—the teacher at the school where most of my members' children go suddenly passed. She was only 51, and the Lord saw fit to take her."

"That's rough, AP! What are they going to do?"

Deborah answered. "The school board asked her daughter to take over the school. She helped her Ma get the school going again after it was closed for the winter due to the influenza. She's smart, and very competent. Poor girl—she lost her husband at Belleau Wood, then her father to the influenza, now this. And she was down for months with a sickness that nearly killed her."

"I know some of that pain myself; I was wounded in that battle. But the Lord also got hold of me that day I was shot, and He saved me! And here I am."

"I told your story, and that of your friends, the first Sunday I was back."

"I suspect you also mentioned Matthew."

"I did. Well, we can praise the Lord He saw you three fellows through, and here you are, off to college."

"Right. And now I'd better be off or I'll catch the downtown Peoria traffic during 'rush hour'!"

"You ought to live out here," Deborah said as she shook my hand. "This is *rush hour*—one horse and buggy!"

We all chuckled.

"You never know, Deborah," I replied.

The trip home was uneventful. AP had changed the oil and made sure the radiator was full, so the car purred contentedly. Of course, I took the Franklin Street Bridge home. I could handle the see-through grating of the bridge deck much better than the swaying vibration and creaking of a certain *other* bridge!

Chapter Twenty Six

Sylvia: Wednesday, July 2nd, 1919, midmorning, the Fremont Road, Knox County.

Another beautiful day! Helen and I planned to drive into Galesburg to shop for groceries and school supplies. We were invited to lunch with Bessie and Lester, and figured we'd bring back more of Helen's things.

We got going a bit earlier than we planned. Doris Miller had driven by in their Model T, and told us Pastor and Deborah had some early sweet corn for us and the Smileys. We headed over to Appleton first to pick up the corn.

Deborah and AP were unusually excited when we stopped by. A man and his son from Metamora were coming to look at the Chevrolet. AP said the son was Luther from the story of the young men they brought back on the *New Jersey*. I wished I could meet him, but we were on a tight schedule and had to get to Galesburg.

As we came to the main crossroads just outside town I saw a strange looking vehicle stopped at the intersection. It looked like a closed coupe with a low open box behind the front doors. Large and dark green, with writing on the side.

"Helen, can you see what it says on the side of that thing?"

Helen craned her neck around as we crossed slowly in front of the vehicle. "It says *Barlow Motor Company, Metamora, Illinois, Service Car.*"

"They must be the ones coming to relieve Pastor of *AP's Folly.*"

Helen giggled. "I wouldn't be surprised. Who's calling it that?"

"Deborah, who else?"

"I sure wouldn't want to get on her bad side!"

"I've never heard her say an unkind word about anyone…except her husband. That's a special relationship!"

"I don't know them well enough yet," Helen said, "Are they really fighting?"

"Oh no, not at all! It's just that they both seem to enjoy a good bicker, and aren't afraid to speak their minds—or be the punch line in a joke. If they can have fun with each other, they do; when things get serious, they are all business and a perfectly matched team."

Helen thought a moment as I turned onto the Fremont Road and headed toward Galesburg. The wind blew from the south through the open car, and she had to speak up to be heard.

"I saw that a week ago yesterday. When we first stopped at their house, Deborah came to the door all cheery and joking. As soon as she saw our faces, she instantly changed. She took charge, and quietly suggested we all come over to see you."

Helen paused a moment, then continued.

"After what had happened, we were all distraught, and unsure how to approach you. Doctor Bohan was even a bit frantic. The only two members of our little party who didn't lose control at some point were Deborah….and young John Bohan!"

We gained speed down the North Creek hill as I pondered what Helen had said.

"I understand Deborah maintaining control—I've seen her like that before. But young John? I'm amazed. And he was so serious when you came to tell me—" I gulped.

"I know," Helen replied, "I've never seen someone so young be so focused on what he wants to do when he grows up. I don't think Doctor Bohan is encouraging him to be like that: he just *is*. If he's still like that when he grows up, I want him to be my doctor!"

"Me too. Hopefully that'll be quite a few years off yet. And his father is the best doctor I know."

"I agree."

As we started through the multiple curves of the Fremont Road toward Galesburg I noticed the *MotoMeter* on the radiator was reading a little high. I wasn't surprised, since we had just climbed the hill from Appleton. As we picked up speed the temperature dropped back into the normal range.

We crossed the East Galesburg road and began the two mile run to the edge of the bricks of Fremont Street at the city limits.

"Look at that!" Helen yelled as she pointed just to our right.

A yellow aeroplane with writing on its side skimmed over the road above our heads, and came to earth just beyond the fence to our left.

"Wow! I read they're using that field as a landing ground now," Helen said, looking over her shoulder at the aeroplane, now on the ground

"If I'd seen it coming it would have scared me to death!" I exclaimed.

"Assuming it didn't hit us."

"Let's not think about that!"

As we came to a stop at the intersection of Fremont and Lincoln Streets, the vibrating rumble of the bricks was replaced by a different sound—a constant ticking sound from the Baby's motor. I saw a little smoke coming from under the front end of the car.

144

"Uh-oh," I muttered.

"Is that what I think it is?"

I gently touched the throttle, and the ticking increased in speed and sharpness.

"Yep. That's a connecting rod—I've heard that sound before."

"What do we do now, Syl?"

I remembered what my Pa taught me. "We drive, slowly and carefully. We pretend the motor is balanced on eggs. We keep the revolutions as low as we can, but not lug it. That way, if we do throw the rod, it won't shoot out too far, maybe not even through the block. And…we pray."

Helen nodded. "I've been praying. Where do we take it?"

"Wright-Allensworth on Simmons Street. Pray that Lee can do something about this without it bankrupting us."

*****

Don and Jackie: Wednesday, July 2nd, 1919, 10:35 AM, the streets of Galesburg.

"So what are you going to do for a car, Don?" Jackie asked as they walked out of the Bank of Galesburg building.

"Not sure yet, Jackie. I could walk over there," he pointed to the Wright-Allensworth building, "and buy anything on the lot, but I don't have peace about that. I also want to buy something that Art, our *export director*, can peddle for a good profit up the line. He's given me a list of cars to look out for, and I've sent him a couple already."

"I saw those in the balance sheets," the newly arrived accountant remarked, "Nice return on the investment. But you can't keep borrowing Dick's Chevrolet forever."

"I know, and Pam keeps reminding me. I have to get something by the end of the week. I might just buy something new from Lee and store the remains of the Baby Grand. But for now, Dick's car will do."

"I called Lee Wright this morning. He has several used cars I might be interested in—or maybe you. A Model T coupe with *five miles* on it, traded in yesterday—growing family surprise. Plus a couple unusual Oldsmobile V8s."

Don grinned. "That's an interesting collection. Maybe we can stop by this afternoon after the air meet."

145

The two walked up to the blue *chummy roadster* parked in front of the Hotel Custer. Don opened the door for Jackie, then moved around to the driver's door.

"Aren't you afraid someone will steal this car and find out what's in it?" Jackie asked softly as Don slid in.

"Nope, first because it looks like every other car of the day. The disc wheels hide the front brakes from view. Then the locks on the hood keep anyone from looking inside. We think it'll do."

Don slipped the key into the ignition switch and turned it. The motor started instantly with a quiet putter. "Dual exhaust like the original. Tuned so it sounds almost but not quite like the original." He flipped the turn signal switch and moved the shift lever on the dash. He looked behind the car, and pulled out.

"So this is basically a *stealthy street rod* from our time, right?" Jackie asked.

Don grinned. "Right. Not enough of these on the road for anyone to know what they're supposed to sound like, so we can get away with it. Built as tough as our people in Hoople could build it, to stand the awful road between here and Peoria. Dick and Estelle love the car."

Don stopped, then drove slowly across Main Street as the arm on the traffic signal changed. "So, have you and Ev found a place yet?"

"I think so," Jackie replied, "decent house over on West South street. Close to Knox, not ostentatious, Ev can go to Ayers Primary. Nice neighbors."

"Looks like you'll only have one dog with you."

Jackie snorted. "Yeah. Pam just loves little Teddy, so looks like you're a new doggie daddy! Can you handle him?"

Now Don chuckled as they stopped for a passing train on the Santa Fe. "I think so. He *is* a cute little guy. How'd he lose the eye?"

"Infection, I think. The vet said it was pretty bad when he removed it. I told you the breeder was getting ready to kill him when we came to see his sister. We fixed that! They get along with each other, but both seem to like their private time. He'll do fine with you guys."

"Probably the only shih tzus in this part of the country," Don said as the caboose passed. He moved the shift lever into drive and crossed the tracks. The car accelerated up the low hill.

"So what are we going out to see this fine morning?" Jackie asked.

"Lee Wright's sponsoring a little air meet just east of town. A couple of Curtiss *Jennies*—JN-4s—are flying down from Chicago, do a little barnstorming, advertise what's coming for the town.

"I see. And Lee's going to be a *dealer*?"

"Yep. I don't think the sales will amount to much, but he'll be able to promote aviation around here. If all goes according to script, Ruth Law's flying circus will base here next summer. That'll be a real treat for the aviators around here."

"Do we have any pilots in Galesburg?"

"Three that I know of. Phil Bertschi and Cully Olson instructed for the Air Service in the war. Julian Mack did that for the Navy. They fly out of the Monmouth airport until we can set up a field here. Lee and I have arranged for their services when Curtiss finally sends Lee a couple planes."

"I need to thank you again for *arranging* my Aero Club license."

"No prob, Jackie. You'll need that *provenance* when we start flying our own ships. You have way more than enough qualifications; we just *inserted* you into the pilot queue a bit early. 1915 should do the job."

"Will anyone ever question my license?"

"Nobody will *quite* remember giving you the test, but you're on every record they keep of their pilots. Like my complete Navy history is *written on stone tablets* in their records. Plus, the Lord is the One who makes folks remember...or not remember."

Jackie chuckled. "That's a blessing, Boss. But back to the aircraft Lee's going to sell—are we ever gonna buy one?"

Don turned right onto Losey Street and passed the side of the Cottage Hospital.

"Not right away, Jackie, but we will before he gives up the franchise. I won't have one with an OX-5 motor—they're just an engine failure waiting to happen! Once we establish a reputation for advanced research, we can put a Continental or Lycoming flat four in one, call it experimental, and get away with it."

"And long term?"

"I have clearance to try and develop a relationship with Hugo Junkers over in Germany. His F-13 and later are the best airframes we'll see for the next ten years. And from what I've read, he might be persuaded to come over here and build 'em. Those airframes would be perfect to fly some *experimental* PT6A turboprops!"

Jackie grinned. "I've daydreamed over the years about putting turboprops in those early all-metal birds. I think we could have

147

some winners there! But can we *inject* those engines into this time?"

"Too early to say," Don replied as they drove under the first CB&Q viaduct on Losey. "The guiding rule is to introduce things slowly enough that people see them as breakthrough engineering, not stuff out of time. Also, we have to be able to build the new equipment—engines in this case—with the technology and metallurgy of this time. Again, I'm not Buck Rogers."

"Or *Duck Dodgers*," Jackie said with a giggle.

"Right, *Captain*."

Don turned left just past the second viaduct, and headed northeast on the angled Lincoln Street. Jackie wished she hadn't worn a hat, as the wind kept trying to flip it off her head.

Don looked toward the oncoming intersection with the Fremont Road. "Hey, here comes the other pristine Baby Grand in the county. The girl whose mom just died owns it."

As the two cars passed Don and Jackie waved, then startled.

"You hear that?" Jackie asked, "A rod's about to let loose in the motor! Smells hot too."

Don sniffed, then nodded. "For sure! They weren't smiling either—bet they're trying to limp it in to Lee's. We'd better follow them!"

Don came to the intersection and whipped the Chevrolet into a U-turn in the middle of it. The back tires chirped as he accelerated out of the intersection heading back southwest.

"Nothing like a *hot rod*," Don said as they came up behind the other car.

*****

Sylvia: Lincoln Street, Galesburg.

"Clear both ways, Syl." Helen said.

I pulled out carefully onto Lincoln Street, figuring to take the least traveled streets, and only one railroad track. As we drove the ticking became louder, and turned into tapping. I could see more smoke behind us.

A car passed us going the other way. The occupants waved, then stopped. In my rear view mirror I could see the woman passenger looking back toward us.

"That was Don Wain from church," Helen said, "The woman with him isn't his wife." Helen stretched to look behind us. "He's making a U-turn at Fremont, coming back toward us. Moving fast."

"Do you suppose they realize we're in trouble?"

"I think so, Syl. Tell you why later."

The blue roadster pulled up to within a car length of us, and matched our speed. "Looks like he's going to follow us."

Helen nodded. "Good. Need all the help we can get!"

I eased the Baby right onto Losey Street, and drove west under the two viaducts, and on past the Cottage Hospital. The blue car stayed right behind us. I turned left on Kellogg Street, and headed downtown. Fortunately I was able to cross the Santa Fe tracks without either of us having to stop.

The tapping was getting louder by the minute. I began to smell hot engine oil, and the MotoMeter started to climb. This was going to be close. *Lord, please let us get this car to the garage!*

I had to stop for the traffic signal at Main Street. It seemed like an hour before the signal arm moved. When the way was clear, I eased the car forward as the tapping became a banging. I turned right on Simmons Street and saw parking places ahead of me in front of the Wright-Allensworth building. I gave the Baby a bit of gas, then pushed in the clutch and turned off the ignition. We coasted into the farther parking place and stopped. The blue car pulled in behind us.

"Thank you Lord!" Helen and I said together.

Chapter Twenty Seven

Sylvia: Wright-Allensworth Motor Company, Simmons Street, Galesburg

We slowly got out of the car and looked at the smoke wafting from under the front end. The occupants of the blue car walked up to us. I recognized the slightly stooped, balding man from the funeral.

"That was close," the short, stocky woman with the man observed, "When we went by we saw the smoke and heard the noise, figured we ought to follow and make sure you got here OK."

"Thanks," Helen replied, "But who are you, ma'am?"

Don started to speak, but the woman cut him off. "I'm Jackie Brighthonor, Wain Engineering's new accountant. Don was taking me out to watch the flight ops, er, planes at the landing field."

"I'm Helen Smiley, and this is my best friend Sylvia Trimble. I guess Don told you about us?"

Jackie shook our hands as Don looked around and scratched his head. "Yes, he did. I'm very sorry to hear about your mother, Sylvia."

"Thank you, ma'am. The Lord is working it out, although I'm not sure how this," I pointed at the still-smoking car, "fits into His plan."

Jackie looked straight at me. She reminded me of my high school principal, only kinder. "I'm sure it's in His will, so let's see what happens when Don gets his wits back together." She grinned at her escort.

A stocky young man in suspenders and wearing an eyeshade stepped out the showroom door. "I sent Claire to the back to find Lee, he'll be up in a minute. Hi, Sylvia! I wasn't expecting you in here today!"

"Hi, Rol. I wasn't expecting to stop here either, but we sort of had no choice."

"So I see—and heard," Rolland *Rol* Allensworth said, pointing at the Baby. "What happened?"

"The motor started making noise as we were driving into town," I replied.

"And we saw them and followed them in. Glad we did!"

"I guess so, Don," Rol replied, "And you must be his new accountant."

"Right. Jackie Brighthonor," she said, and put out her hand. "I called this morning."

"Yes, indeed," Rol turned back to me. "Sylvia, who's your friend?"

"This is my best friend Helen Smiley. Helen, this is Rol Allensworth, Lee Wright's business partner."

"Glad to meet you, Sir," Helen said as they shook hands.

"Smiley...Oh, yes! Oh—never mind. Sometimes I tend to talk to myself." Rol reddened.

Lee Wright came out the showroom door. He looked a little disheveled; I'd rarely seen him like that. Behind him walked two of the shop's mechanics, one carrying a fire extinguisher.

"A regular party out here, I see," Lee greeted us. We took turns introducing the newcomers. "Now, what's up, ladies?"

"I think the Baby is about to throw a rod. It started ticking at Lincoln Street and the Fremont Road. I used every trick I knew to nurse it in, and we barely made it."

"We met them on Lincoln Street and decided to follow them in," Don added.

Lee looked at Don with a slight grin. "That figures. Sylvia, would you mind if we try to start it and get it onto the lot? Easier than pushing it."

"Go right ahead, Lee—I think the damage has already been done."

Lee pointed to the bricks under the motor. "Looks like you have an oil leak."

"We didn't have that before."

"Didn't think so. Now, here's what we'll do. I'll get in and work the controls. Warren, you crank please. Bandy, get ready with the fire extinguisher. The rest of you might want to stand back. Got it?"

We all nodded. "OK, let's do this," Lee announced.

Lee and his men took stations around the Baby. The rest of us stood by the corner of the building—except for Don, who stood on the sidewalk near the open hood of the car.

Lee moved the controls. "Go ahead, Warren."

The burly mechanic grasped the crank and pulled up. As usual, the Baby started on the first try. However, Lee must have set the throttle too high, for the motor instantly tried to race at full speed. I heard a terrific bang, smoke boiled from the front of the car, and the plate glass showroom window shattered. Everyone instinctively jumped away from the window, then realized Don had landed face down on the sidewalk.

The shorter mechanic sprayed the smoking motor, and as the last of the glass tinkled on the showroom floor I saw Jackie and

Helen rush over to Don. He stirred, rolled over and got up slowly. Aside from a couple of scrapes on his hands, and a tear in one pant leg, he seemed okay.

Lee got out from behind the wheel and surveyed the damage without a word.

He turned to Don. "You OK?"

Don nodded, and looked down. "I guess my pants will never be the same."

"You did look pretty scared," Jackie added softly, then snorted.

"Well, that answers all outstanding questions. Sylvia," Lee announced, and turned to his mechanics. "Get the others and push it into the lot when it cools down please. Rol, have Claire call the glass company, then join us in my office. The rest of us need to do some thinking."

We all trooped into Lee's office, bringing folding chairs with us. After a moment Rol stood in the open doorway.

Lee Wright sat in his chair with his eyes closed, tapping a pencil on his desk top. As he tapped, Jackie looked around at the rest of us, then spoke.

"I have an idea. Sylvia, can you drive a Model T?"

"I think so. I've driven Helen's parents' Model T a few times. They're different, but I think I could get the knack of it."

"You could teach her, couldn't you Helen?"

"Oh, yes, Jackie. No problem at all," Helen said decisively.

"I think I know how to do this," Jackie said, "Lee and Don, listen up."

This woman is used to telling people what to do, I thought, then Jackie continued.

"OK. Lee, you told me this morning you took in a Model T coupe with only five miles on it yesterday, right?"

Lee nodded.

"Very well. I propose we trade Sylvia that Model T for her car. Even up, no cost to her. Don pays the difference, and pays Lee to have his running gear transferred to her old vehicle. Deal?"

I sat there, stunned. "That would be wonderful, Jackie! But...can you speak for Don like that?"

Jackie grinned. "Of course, I'm his accountant! Right, Boss?" she turned to Don and raised her eyebrows.

Don said nothing, but nodded and kept fiddling with his pant leg.

"Deal, Lee?" Jackie asked.

"Deal!" Lee dropped his pencil on the desk. "We'll get the paperwork started immediately so the ladies can be on their way."

152

"Meaning *I* get the paperwork started," Rol grumped, a smile pulling the sting.

"Great!" Jackie stood up. "Now, while Rol is doing that, I want to see those two Oldsmobile V-8s you said you have."

"Er, of course, Jackie," Lee seemed startled, but recovered quickly. "Let me get the keys and we'll go out to the lot."

Jackie headed for the side door. "Come on, Don, one of these is for you. Pam said so!"

Don got up and followed Lee and Jackie out without a word.

*****

Sylvia: Forty five minutes later, the side lot, Wright-Allensworth Motor Company.

Helen and I stood looking at my new car.

"Everything's ready to go," Lee announced, "All your things are transferred from the other car, the license plates are switched, and you have a full tank of gas."

"Thank you so much, Lee! You too, Don—and please tell Jackie thanks too."

"I will, Sylvia, as soon as she gets back from the test drive." Don held up a finger. "One more thing—Lee, I want to offer the ladies a ride in one of those Curtiss aeroplanes you're going to sell! We talked about offering that to people who buy your cars, and I think these two might be interested. What do you say, Lee?"

"I'm fine with that, Don, as soon as I actually receive one of the planes," Lee said, "Ladies, would you be interested?"

I shook my head. "Not me, thanks anyway gentlemen. I've got plenty at the school to keep me busy. Maybe some other time."

Helen spoke up. "Lee, Don, if I might, I'd really like to take you up on the offer. "I've always wondered how it would be to fly, and I'd like to see if I could be a pilot some day. I'd love to try it!"

"Then you shall, Helen, just as soon as Lee gets a plane!" Don grinned. "Now maybe you ladies will want to continue your shopping trip."

We shook the two men's hands, and climbed into the Model T. Helen talked me through setting the controls, Lee cranked, and with waves we headed out of the lot. We'd decided to skip the rest of the shopping and go over to Helen's house for lunch as planned.

"You think Don meant what he said about the aeroplane flight?" I asked Helen as we passed the library.

"Sure do, Syl," she replied, "That's what I was going to explain when he followed us in. Don and Pam are just...*unusual*. They always go out of their way to help people, in the church and town. Whenever they say they'll do something, they just *do* it. If they say I get to fly, it'll happen."

"Jackie really took charge after the motor blew up. She's used to telling people what to do, that's for sure."

Helen nodded. "No kidding! I'd heard from Pam she and her daughter were coming, but hadn't met them yet. Wonder what she did before she came here."

"No idea, but I'm sure glad we met them!"

We pulled around the block to park in front of the house. We parked behind a seedy-looking Model T touring car.

We got out of the coupe and were halfway up the walk before Bessie realized we were there. She came out on the porch, and exclaimed, "Land sakes, girls, what happened to the Baby?"

I couldn't resist the opening. "We washed it, and it shrunk."

Over lunch, we told the whole story. Bessie was amazed, but grateful the Lord not only kept us safe, but dropped a new car in our laps.

In the middle of lunch L.M. came home. He took a quick shower to wash off the locomotive grime, and joined us for a sandwich at the end of the meal. We got to repeat our story to him. He grinned at Bessie as we told about the new car, then they winked at each other. *Here we go again*, I thought. Helen was looking at her plate and didn't see the exchange.

As we got ready to leave, Helen spoke. "Ma, the new car is too small to carry much stuff, so we'll have to make a few more trips into town to get it all moved."

Bessie raised one eyebrow. "Oh?"

L.M. stood up. "Girls, let's go outside."

We went down the front steps and trooped to the terrace. L.M. pulled something from his pocket and flipped it to his daughter.

Helen looked at what she had caught. "A key, Pa?"

L.M. grinned, "Fits that." He pointed at the ragged touring car in front of my coupe.

Helen gasped, and wobbled. For a teen-ager in those days, *any* automobile was infinitely better than *no* automobile!

Bessie explained. "This was owned by one of L.M.'s engineer friends. He traded it in to Wright-Allensworth, so L.M. went and bought it yesterday. Mechanically, it's perfect—the previous owner said so, and we also had it checked. It will serve you for a long time. It only *looks* like it's been stored in a barn for twenty years!"

L.M. stood grinning at his daughter. "It also has a self-starter," was his only comment.

Helen finally found her voice. "Thank you, Thank you, Thank you!" She

hugged each of her parents in turn.

Then her practical side took over.

"Pa, how much did you pay for this car? I need to know."

L.M. kept grinning. "Fifteen dollars. A *rat-killing deal*."

Helen looked at her parents, and I saw a glint in her eye.

"So does that mean I'm going to find dead rats under the cushions?"

L.M. and Bessie were still laughing when we pulled away from the curb in our new (to us) cars.

Chapter Twenty Eight

The people at church that Wednesday night rejoiced when Helen and I told the story of our motoring adventure that day. Adding to the festive atmosphere was the news that AP had finally disposed of the *Wheeled Planter* (Deborah's description) in their front yard. The story of the young man who fixed the car in about thirty seconds added to the laughter—at Pastor's expense, of course. He took the ribbing with good-natured grace, and mentioned in his message how the Lord used the experience to teach him a lesson…again.

In some of the things she said Deborah implied that the last chapter of this tale had yet to be written; we didn't quite understand what she was referring to. She said we'd find out by and by.

By and by turned out to be the next Wednesday evening service. Helen and I had spent the day poring over Ma's lesson plan books, and we were pretty tired. Not tired enough to miss church, though.

We arrived early, and found Pastor and Deborah getting out of the odd-looking vehicle we'd seen in Appleton the day of our adventure!

Helen beat me to the mark. "What *is* that thing?"

Deborah Kittridge turned around, smiling. "The *rest of the story*!"

"Now what did Pastor buy?" I asked.

Deborah laughed. "For once, it wasn't AP. I bought this!"

She laughed again when she saw our reaction.

"I said last week we got rid of the *wheeled planter*, but didn't finish the story. While the young man was looking over the *planter*, I was looking over the vehicle they came over in—this one. The young man's Pa is a car dealer over in Metamora, and this is—was—their service car. They rebuilt it from a wrecked 1915 Cadillac. I've always wanted one of those, but wasn't about to spend the money for one. So I made a deal: we traded even up. And they delivered it today."

I thought about that a moment. "So who got the better deal, Deborah?"

"We both did. Luther got the car he wanted, and unlike someone we all know and love," she looked over at Pastor and shook her head, "he'll actually be able to keep it running. The mechanic who brought this over says he checked the *planter* over and it's in fine shape. Good for him! And I got something that is fun to drive and actually useful. We both won!"

"It's unique, that's for sure," Helen said.

"I think it is kind of sporty, to go buzzing around the countryside in, but also has a solid utility to it. I call it my *sport-utility vehicle*."

"That's a catchy phrase," I remarked. "I don't suppose the companies would actually build something like that."

Deborah laughed. "Not hardly, Syl! They're too busy either building Model Ts or trying to build things to replace Model Ts. Give 'em a few years to dethrone Old Henry and maybe they'll start building cars like this."

"Is that a thought from your book research?"

Deborah grinned, shifted her eyes from side to side, and put her finger to her lips. "*Shhh.*"

"Right!" I giggled.

As we were going in the church Helen asked, "What was that 'book research' about?"

I leaned over and whispered in her ear. "She is a published author. Right now she's researching something called 'speculative fiction', and trying to predict how life will be around here in forty or fifty years. It's very *hush-hush*"

Helen nodded, but still looked puzzled.

*****

Luther: August, 1919, Metamora and elsewhere.

The first of August brought my acceptance letter to Bradley Polytechnic, in their General Engineering program. I decided not to specialize in one area, even though that seemed to be the trend. I wanted a broader knowledge of the subject; I'd seen enough dead-end career paths in the military, horse cavalry being the most obvious.

One key to success at college, I knew from my military experience, was a quiet, relaxing place to hole up and study. I absorbed information best in an environment without distractions…but with distractions available if I needed a break. One thing I knew for sure—a college dormitory room did *not* meet that requirement! I'd have to rent a room off campus, and it had to be the *right* room. A bad choice here would be as distracting as living in a dormitory!

157

I realized I needed to give this matter to the Lord. The same morning I asked Him for guidance in this, Pa brought the subject up at breakfast.

"How is your room search coming?"

"Not good, Pa. Everything I've seen in the paper touts how close they are to the social life of campus. Nobody talks about quiet places for study."

"They're looking for the young students who've never been away from home before. Ply them with promises of good times and a carefree life."

"You got it, Pa. Any school can be a *party school* if that's what you look for."

"And that's not what you're looking for."

"Right again. I want to get as much out of this opportunity as I can, and where I live is going to be a help or a hindrance. I want it to help."

Pa raised an eyebrow. "Are you open to suggestions?"

He knew I did not like to listen to his advice when I was growing up. My next comment proved things had changed.

"Yes, please, suggest away!"

Pa smiled. "I was down at Strickfaden's garage in East Peoria yesterday. Newt's been refurbishing used cars for us lately, especially Fords. I got to talking with his chief mechanic, Charlie Templeman. An odd duck, but a fine mechanic. I mentioned your going to Bradley this fall, and he said his wife takes boarders in their house on Bourland, close by the school. He said she is really careful about who she accepts, and aims to make it a place for studying, not partying. I told him I'd tell you."

I put down my fork and grinned. "Pa, you've just given me the best lead I've had yet! Do you have the address?"

"One Twenty One South Bourland. They have a phone—the number's three one four zero four."

"I'll give her a call, then. Did Charlie say what his wife's name is?"

"If I remember right it's Agnes."

I stopped wiping my mouth. "You said Charlie is an *odd duck.* What way?"

Pa pushed his chair back as he thought.

"First, from what he's implied in conversations, I don't think he's a Believer. Then, he doesn't seem to take much care with anything but his work at the garage. Never heard a word about his home life until yesterday."

"Well, he must trust his wife if he lets her handle the house arrangements like that."

"I guess so, but something else…" Pa thought for a moment. Then he snapped his fingers.

"I've got it! Except for direct questions about the cars he's working on for us, all he ever talks about is himself. What he's done, how he thinks. Acts like everybody else is *wallpaper!*"

"I've met people like that in the Marines. If they were setting type, they'd run out of *I*."

Pa snorted. "Didn't see that one coming!"

I grinned.

A call to the number Pa gave me resulted in an 11AM appointment at the house on Bourland. The Chevrolet V-8 purred right along as I covered the miles towards Peoria. Pa's mechanics had checked the car thoroughly after I brought it home, and pronounced it in excellent order. I praised the Lord for providing me a reliable vehicle—and one I enjoyed! I knew a car made a truly lousy idol, and suspected it had served that purpose for one person already, maybe two. AP Kittridge was definitely happy to be rid of it…and I was happy to have it.

I motored up the Main Street hill and headed out toward the school. I turned left off Main street and drove slowly south on Bourland Avenue. At the first side street I parked in front of the corner house. The yard was small, but well kept. The neighborhood seemed remarkably quiet, considering its nearness to the school.

I walked up the front porch steps at exactly eleven o'clock. The door opened before I could knock, and a woman of indeterminate age stepped onto the porch. She was a bit shorter than me, somewhat stout, with brown hair streaked with gray up in a bun. Her gray eyes seemed to bore straight through me.

"I'm Agnes Templeman," she said and put out her hand.

"I'm Luther Barlow, the one who called about the room. My father talked to your husband, and he suggested I contact you."

"So he told me. He doesn't usually advertise for me; he must have been impressed in some way. Come in, and we'll talk."

"Of course."

We walked through the entry hall and into a fairly large room containing a large dining room table, several chairs, and an upright piano against the inside wall. Mrs. Templeman offered me a chair at the table, and we sat down. She began speaking without preamble.

"In order to save time and disappointment, let me tell you my rules first off. No smoking, drinking, or lewd behavior. We keep the house quiet for the other roomers. If you're going to be eating a meal here, please tell me at the start of the day so I only prepare as much food as we need. Rent is due one month in advance; if you choose to leave, I require one month's notice. Please be respectful of the other roomers, and my family, at all times. Those are my rules; do you have any questions?"

That was quite a speech, and just what I was hoping for. "No, ma'am, those rules are acceptable in all particulars."

Mrs. Templeman's eyebrow raised slightly. "Very well, Mr. Barlow, may I see your acceptance letter to Bradley, and some other form of identification and character reference?"

I pulled out my letter of acceptance, and my retirement form from the Marines. I also included a letter of reference Pastor Reem had written for me.

Mrs. Templeman looked over my acceptance letter in detail, and set it aside. She read Pastor's reference letter, and nodded.

She then picked up my retirement form. She started to read, then gasped. Her eyes went wide, and she re-read a section. She put the paper down slowly.

"Sergeant Barlow. I remember reading about your award in the paper. Two of my brothers were in that battle. David and John have told me about it, probably more than I needed to know. I am honored you are considering living here."

"Ma'am, please don't talk about this to the other roomers. I know it will probably come out eventually, but I really would rather it didn't right away."

Agnes nodded. "I understand, Mr. Barlow. Some things are best left unsaid for a while, until we are able to talk about them with less emotion. I will say nothing except to my husband and son. I know Forrest won't say anything; I'm not so sure about Charlie, but he is not here enough to say much to the boarders."

"Thank you, ma'am."

"Call me Agnes, Mr. Barlow. 'Ma'am is *Charlie's mother*.'"

I couldn't help snorting; I didn't expect that twist.

The slightest hint of a smile passed across Agnes' face. "Mr. Barlow, as you travel through this world you will encounter some persons who live for others. You can tell the *others* by their hunted expressions. Hopefully you will not meet that *example*."

I nodded. I wasn't sure if she had just made a joke, so I stuck to formalities. "And I am Luther. It would be my pleasure to stay in this house."

Agnes looked surprised. "You haven't even asked the rent!"

"I strongly suspect it will be an appropriate amount. I should also tell you now, if you don't mind I'd like to keep the room rented throughout the year, even if I am not physically here. After the last few years, I really don't want to change scenery, especially when I've found the ideal studying spot."

Mrs. Templeman...*Agnes*...stood up. "that would certainly be fine with me, Luther. Let me show you the rest of the house, and you can choose your room. I have three available at the moment."

A small boy in short pants and a white shirt opened a sliding door and came up to us. He carried a book about half his size.

"Luther, this is my son Forrest. Forrest, this is Mr. Barlow. He will be renting a room from us while he attends Bradley."

The young boy—he looked about seven—shook my hand. "Happy to meet you, sir."

"The same, Forrest," I replied.

"I think you'll find Forrest is a very quiet little boy. When he's not reading, he's tinkering on things."

"Agnes, I was just like him when I was young! Growing up around an automobile dealership, I just naturally started tinkering early on. I don't have time to do it like I used to, but I get by when I have to."

"In that case, I warn you: Forrest may ply you with questions about anything and everything!"

The young boy blushed and lowered his head.

"That's fine. I think I can make a little time now and then to do that. After I graduated from High School my Pa said he about went through school all over again answering my questions!"

Agnes and I laughed, and Forrest smiled.

The three of us walked through the kitchen and looked at the room opening to the side of the kitchen. We looked out the back door at the small but manicured back yard, with two garages facing the side street.

We returned through the kitchen, and started up the narrow stairs to the second floor. My stump started aching with the climb, and I had to lean on the railing more than I wanted.

Agnes noticed. "Oh, my! I forgot you were missing a leg—I remember reading that. You really should take the room off the kitchen; it would be so much easier on you."

I got to the top of the stairs, and turned the hallway corner before I replied.

"Hmmm. Is there a bathroom on the first floor?"

"No, just the one off this hallway—oh, I see." Agnes frowned.

161

Time to reassure. "I want to live here even with the stairs. I think it will be a matter of practice, and gaining a little strength. I haven't had to manage stairs since physical therapy at Walter Reed this spring. I need to get back to exercising, especially since I'll also have to deal with stairs at the school. Let's see the other vacant rooms, if I may."

"Of course."

As we were walking back along the hallway a door opened, and a very short, elderly woman stepped out. My first thought was she looked like a young girl who had aged without growing up. She was dressed neatly, but in an older style.

"Oh, Marie, let me introduce our new boarder. This is Luther Barlow. He will be attending Bradley this fall. Luther, this is Marie Heath. She's lived with us since we moved to Peoria ten years ago."

Marie stretched out her hand. "I am very glad to meet you in person, *Sergeant* Barlow! I remember you from the newspaper article when you were awarded the Medal of Honor. I am so pleased you've chosen to live here!"

"Thank you, ma'am," was all I could think of in reply.

"It's Marie, always Marie! May I call you Luther?"

"Of course, er, Marie."

"I'm sure we'll get better acquainted as time goes by."

So evaporated my desire to live quietly in anonymity.

I decided to take the room off the kitchen. It was a bit larger, and while the noise from the kitchen could be heard through the door, it also had an outside entrance, which made it easier to come and go quietly, and get out in case, God forbid, the house caught fire. The edict of no smoking in the house reduced, but did not eliminate, that threat.

Agnes quoted me the monthly room and board. It was in line with what I expected, and well worth it; I paid the advance rent and deposit on the spot. I arranged to move a few personal items in over the next couple of weeks, which would be easy with an outside door.

She also invited me to stay for lunch, and I enjoyed a very nice meal with Agnes, Forrest, and Marie Heath. The other boarders worked during the day, and only ate breakfast and supper at the house. I wasn't sure how my schedule would fit, but Agnes assured me she would be able to keep me fed if I kept her informed.

After lunch at the Templeman home, I stopped by the Admissions office at Bradley to make sure I had done everything they needed. I then visited Carl Christensen at the Congregational church. On the way home I managed to get to the Franklin Street bridge at *rush hour,* and was pleased to find my Chevrolet handled stop and go traffic as competently as it did everything else. My leg, though, had definitely had enough for one day by the time I got home!

Chapter Twenty Nine

Sylvia: The Wagher School, Copley Township, Knox County.

July simmered into August, and we began the march toward the first day of school. Helen and I worked at the school nearly every day, checking off items on the Start Of School Checklist. Ma had every preparation written down and scheduled, and although I knew she varied the routine when she had to, she tried hard to keep to the schedule. So did we.

On Monday August 18th we had a special meeting with Philip Wagher, and the Johnsons. I had never attended one of these meetings, but Ma told me this meeting was very important. She never said more; I now found out why.

We met around the work table in the school building. Philip started the meeting with prayer around the table; unusually, this included even the women in the group.

"I know it is unusual to have men and women praying in the same meeting, but this is an unusual meeting. I feel we are all on the same team here, both teachers and board members. We all need to beseech the Lord every day to give us wisdom and strength to accomplish our mission—the preparation of our precious young people. Besides, I invoke Pastor's *Navyman's Golden Rule...*"

We laughed, and Philip continued.

"Now, Sylvia, I know you know about this meeting, but you have never heard what it is about. That's because this is a *confidential briefing*. Nothing we say here goes beyond this room, and is never mentioned to anyone else other than the persons in this room. This is to maintain the privacy of our students and our families. You need to know what is going on with each of your students, and their families, in order to effectively teach them, and to counsel and support not only them, but their families. Am I clear so far?"

"Yes, Philip," Helen and I said.

"Good, good," Philip grinned. "Fred and Violet will now give you the information you need to know before school starts. Please do not write anything down, but commit all this information to memory, or remember the information exists, and ask Fred or Violet if a question comes up. Okay, Fred, show time!"

Fred and Violet spoke about each child and family we would have in the school for the coming year, and told us every bit of information they knew about each family. Helen did not know most of the families; I did, and I was amazed at the trials and struggles they faced. We also heard detailed information, as far as the Johnsons could determine, about the abilities and struggles of each child we would have. I was amazed at the depth of information the Johnsons (and Philip, though he did not speak) had amassed. I also noticed the Johnsons gave the same information about their son Pacey, who would be coming to the school for the first time this year—and themselves. No wonder all this was confidential!

Finally, Fred and Violet finished. They both emitted a big sigh and crossed their eyes, then started giggling!

"That part of the briefing is optional," Philip remarked dryly, with a grin.

"Do you have any questions, ladies?"

"Not right now Fred. I think we have enough of it to know when we get confused, and ask."

Helen nodded in agreement.

Philip leaned back in his chair, and a look I hadn't seen before moved across his face.

"And now I have something to say that I haven't even told Fred and Violet about. You know I haven't been getting around so well lately. I figured it was just the aging of a fellow in his seventies. Well, it's not. I visited Doctor Bohan a couple weeks ago, and he did some checking."

Philip looked directly at each of us in turn, then continued.

"I have cancer, folks, and probably about six months left in this life."

All of us showed shock on our faces; Helen and Violet started to weep quietly. Fred and I just set our jaws, and looked steadily at Philip.

"Hmmm. For the record, that's about the reaction I expected from each of you. Everybody reacts differently to sudden bad news, as we've learned all too often the last couple of years. My advice is to trust the Lord, and let Him handle the grief—not just here, but in all the other areas you have dealt with, and whatever is to come. Cry when you need to; feel sad when you need to; carry on with life. And realize your mood may change at no notice, and that's OK too. Talk to each other, comfort each other, keep close to the Lord; that's the Scriptural way to handle it."

We nodded.

"Now the second part of this little speech," Philip pulled a piece of paper out of his pocket and handed it to Fred. "Fred, this letter is my resignation from the presidency of the School Board, and the Board itself. In it, I recommend the board elect you as President."

Fred took the paper and put it in his pocket, as Philip continued.

"I've arranged to go live with my grandson Victor and his family; they've been begging me to do that for years, and now it's time. I will be closing out the homestead, and making sure my will is up to date. And I'll be looking forward to seeing my Lord and Savior in the very near future!"

We all just sat there, either weeping or staring. Finally Fred shook himself and spoke.

"Philip, we've been worried about you for several months—"

"And now your worries are gone!"

"Philip!" Through her tears Violet reached over to poke Philip.

Philip smiled. "Thank you, Violet. Mabel would have done the same thing for a line like that!"

Helen and I made our way back to the house in silence. We went in, I stirred the fire in the stove, and put the pot of coffee on to boil I'd prepared earlier. In a few minutes we sat at the kitchen table, each cradling a mug of coffee, and our thoughts.

I finally broke the silence.

"What a way to start the year."

"I guess we not only give them a change of teachers, but a change of the board too."

"I don't think the students will be affected that much. They know me, and I've already adopted most of my Ma's teaching style. They'll learn about you soon enough…"

Helen twirled her imaginary mustache like a melodrama villain, and we both giggled.

"Exactly!"

"I couldn't resist, Syl."

"I like the way you think. Don't know if the kids will…"

"They'll learn."

"I guess they will. This will be fun to watch."

We giggled again. I guess we needed the release. When we finally quieted down, I continued.

"The children really don't have contact with the board, so they shouldn't notice the change. The parents, though, they'll be stunned. Philip's run the school since before most of them were born. They're likely to feel like their anchor's come off, and they're drifting. I guess that's why Philip has been preparing Fred and Violet for the job."

"I wonder if that Confidential Briefing was the last test for them before Philip cut 'em loose?"

"I think you're exactly right, Helen, now that you mention it!"

"Well, for better or worse, we know where we stand."

"Yep."

A moment later Helen smiled. "I got a note from Lee Wright in the mail today."

"Oh?"

"We have an appointment at one o'clock tomorrow afternoon in Galesburg."

"Oh, we do, do we?"

"Actually, it's for me, but I figured you'd want to ride along."

"What are you talking about?"

Helen's grin widened. "Lee's first plane has finally arrived. I get to fly tomorrow!"

Lee Wright and Donald Wain had offered both of us an aeroplane flight when I got the Model T. I had declined, but Helen had accepted with enthusiasm. I'd forgotten about it until now.

"That's great news…I think. Are they flying from the field over by Lincoln street?"

"No. They're using a field at the end of North Seminary Street. Longer and flatter, I guess."

"So we just show up?"

"I guess so. I'll wear my culottes, of course, but otherwise the note said just come on out."

I thought of something. "Helen, have you told your parents yet?"

Helen took a sip of her coffee. "I was tempted not to say anything, but the Lord reminded me I needed to be honest all the time. I told them when I was at home last weekend."

"How'd they take it?"

"Ma is concerned, but says she won't stop me. Pa just sat there for a moment, then he got a big grin on his face, and said he wished he could trade places with me for the trip! I guess he's always had the same dream to learn to fly. Running a fast locomotive is fun, he said, but just isn't the same."

"Maybe some day he can."

"I sure hope so! This time, though, I get the fun."

"So you do. I'll be happy to watch, and not participate!"

"Suit yourself."

Helen looked into her coffee mug for a moment, then continued.

"Syl, I was going to wait until the day before school to give you something, but I think now's the time. Hold on a moment."

She left the room, and came back with a cardboard box, wrapped in brown paper.

167

"I was going to gift wrap this, but I think it will be OK as it is."

I took the package from Helen, and started to unwrap it. I opened the end, and gasped.

"Helen!"

"That's my name, last time I checked," she said with a grin.

I slowly pulled the object out of the box. A wooden plaque to hang on the wall, in two pieces, the smaller to hang below the larger. The top object was a carved Marine Corps insignia, about a foot in diameter, made of a dark polished wood.

The smaller object was a star, painted gold. The symbol of a Marine loved one, killed in the war. It was designed to hang from a hook below the insignia.

My eyes started to fill. "This is beautiful. Where did you find it?"

"My Pa asked his friends who'd been in the war. They gave him the name of a carver in Chicago, and when he was laying over there a while back he contacted him. This is the result."

"Thank you, Helen—and thank your Pa for me too! This is beautiful…and will help me to remember."

"You're welcome, Syl. I just had to get this for you, for the classroom."

"I'm glad you did. I'll put it right behind my desk. If any of the children ask, I'll tell them to ask their parents."

"Good idea. You don't need to be blubbering in front of the students."

"Like I'm doing now?"

"Like you're doing now. And that's just fine."

Chapter Thirty

Don and Jackie: Late August, 1919, the streets of Galesburg.

"Do you think we'll make it out to the airfield *this* time?" Jackie asked as the two stepped out the side door of the Bank of Galesburg building.

"Hope so," Don replied, "This should be more interesting than the one we missed."

Jackie glanced at the slightly stooped balding man at her side. He didn't see her flash a sideways grin. "Yes, I suspect so. How many people are flying this afternoon?"

"Only Helen. We wanted plenty of time for the *extra maneuvers,*" Don looked up at the marquee of the Orpheum theatre, "Ah, Marx Brothers again. Got to remember that. Would you and Ev like to see 'em too? Since Pam is ill there'll be space in the box."

"Let me see how things shake out the next couple of days. I've wondered how funny they were in person."

"It's vaudeville. Spotty performances, even by the greats. Small house, or a rowdy one, and their timing goes. Not so bad at the Orpheum; the Auditorium on Broad street has too much echo, not to mention a nasty smell. The Gala can be a snake pit some days."

Don and Jackie walked up to the Oldsmobile coupe parked in the usual spot in front of the Hotel Custer. "Thanks for letting me go first with the mods, Don. The Hoople folks did a great job."

"No problem. You and Ev need to be safe in the car, and that plate glass had to go."

"I'm glad, don't much fancy getting shredded in an accident." Jackie walked around to the driver's door and unlocked it. She opened the door and pushed a button. "Did I really need power door locks?"

"Naah," Don replied, opening the passenger door, "the guys just wanted to see if they could do it. Easy."

Jackie started the Oldsmobile V-8 and pulled away from the curb. "You say we have more vested partners coming?"

"Right. Three guys are retiring from the Navy this month and coming aboard. Captain Matt Plotczyc is retiring from this time, and Master Chief Sammy Allen's coming from our time."

"Sammy? Great! I worked with him on *Kitty Hawk*," Jackie said, "Leading chief in the aviation department. Smartest electronics geek I ever met, degree from M.I.T. to boot, but whenever I talked to him I felt like I was in a Warner Brothers cartoon!"

Don chuckled. "Yeah. I kept expecting him to pull out a carrot and chomp on it. He got a lot of teasing over the years—won't have that here. Mary Beth and the kids are coming out too—she told Pam how much she wants to experience life out here after living in Yokosuka for so long."

"Smells are about the same," Jackie remarked as she drove across Main Street. "Who's the third one?"

"A GS-15 civil service fellow who worked with me *uptime*. Elwood Foutch. Finest logistician I ever met, and a master woodworker to boot. Amazing cook, gardener, I think he talks to animals. Very quiet around humans though--I think he was teased a lot growing up because of his appearance. Reminds me of a hobbit."

Jackie started to giggle, then stopped. "That's awful! Kids can be so cruel."

"Yeah," Don replied, "He told me his childhood was pure torment, only the Lord kept him from going crazy."

"Master Chief Allen told me the same thing," Jackie said, then snorted. "So we're going to have three *characters* working for us?"

"Yep. The guys wanted someplace where they could do what they love without having to deal with the *notoriety*. And they are masters of their professions."

"This job is getting to be more fun every day." Jackie smiled.

Jackie threaded the dark green coupe through the Galesburg streets, and came out on a dirt road heading north out of town. In the distance they could see a biplane and several cars on the left

"Hard to get used to this road not going all the way north," Don remarked.

"Is this where the permanent airfield is going?" Jackie asked.

"Not on the west side—too close to town. Maybe on the east there, between here and the railroad track. Several fields around town are suitable, but the city doesn't have the money to buy good farm land for a field."

"We do."

"Right, Jackie. We'll probably buy our own field once we start collecting aircraft. The script says the city will buy a field on the west side of Henderson street about 1930, then one farther out of town twenty five years later. We'll see what happens here."

Jackie drove along the dirt track at the northern edge of the farm field and pulled up by the cars and the plane.

"JN-4, one each," she remarked as she shut off the car and opened the door, "Wind's from the right direction."

Don looked at his watch. "We're here an hour early, Jackie. Why did we have to get here this early?"

"Glad you asked, Boss." Jackie replied, and opened the trunk. She pulled out a bundle with straps…and a flying helmet. To Don's surprise, she then pulled her dress off over her head, revealing the green *flight suit* without insignia underneath. She pulled the rubber bands off the leg cuffs and let the suit legs drop to their normal position.

Don's face paled, then turned red. "Jackie, what did I say about flying behind an OX-5?"

Jackie's grin turned vulpine. "You gonna try and stop me, *Admiral*?" She shut the trunk lid and walked toward the aircraft.

Don shook his head and followed her.

*****

Sylvia, about 45 minutes later, the streets of Galesburg.

Helen drove us to the landing field in Galesburg in her Model T. The poor thing shook and rattled like it was on its death ride, but the motor purred happily, and Helen said it drove like a new car. I figured as long as the body (with us in it) didn't part company with the frame, we were OK.

We came in the Fremont Road, then up to Seminary. We turned right, and followed the street to where it became a dirt road veering to the left. We saw a collection of cars at the end, and drove toward them.

I happened to look out to my right. About ten feet higher than we were, and coming right for us, was an aeroplane! I had no chance to yell out a warning to Helen before the plane passed directly over our heads. I could smell hot oil in the wind it stirred up as it passed over.

I looked over at Helen. She was driving along, looking straight ahead, as if nothing had happened! Helen glanced over at me with an evil grin.

"You knew that thing was coming, didn't you?"

"Guilty as charged. I saw it coming and figured it was about to land. I also figured I could get to the other side of the field before it got here. Didn't quite make it."

"You certainly didn't! Weren't you afraid we'd get hit?"

"Nope. This road's off the landing field."

171

"Too close for me!"

Helen grinned again.

"If that didn't scare you, you have the nerves to be a pilot!"

"I think so, Syl. I just need to see if I have the reflexes."

I thought a moment, as we pulled up beside the other cars. "You're serious about this, aren't you?"

"As a heart attack. You don't have the bug; you might not fully understand. No offense."

"None taken. And here comes the contraption."

The Curtiss JN-4 *Jenny* rolled up to the small group of onlookers, and turned to face the field. With a couple of pops the engine shut down. A man in a flying helmet stood up in the back cockpit and climbed over the side. From the front cockpit clambered a shorter, stocky figure in odd green coveralls. I was surprised to see Jackie Brighthonor, Don Wain's accountant, when she pulled off her flying helmet.

We joined the onlookers as the two pilots walked up.

"That was fun," Jackie announced, then turned to us. "Hi, ladies! Ready to fly, Helen?"

"I think so, Jackie. Which one of you will be the pilot?"

Lee started to speak, but Jackie interrupted him.

"Change of plans, Lee. Cully Olson here is a fine pilot, but I think I'd like to take Helen up myself, if you don't mind."

Don and Lee looked at each other, then at their pilot. "Cully, is she qualified to do that?" Lee asked.

Cully Olson smiled and nodded, revealing an uneven set of teeth. "She certainly is. She handles the ship like she's half bird! I'd like to take lessons from her myself."

"Well, Don, what do you say?"

Don scratched his head. "Lee, she's going to do this no matter what *we* say. Her Aero Club license says she's been qualified for a while. They'll be just fine—go for it, ladies!"

"Will do—soon as the engine cools enough to top off the gas," Jackie said.

Another person got out of her car and stood with us.

"Ma!" Helen hugged her mother. "What are you doing here?"

"I had to come out and see my daughter fly! I brought the camera so we can show LM. He got called out or he would have been here too."

Cully handed Helen an aviator's helmet. She put it on. "This fits fine."

Helen turned to Don. "Are you really going to let me do this?"

"You can still back out, Helen."

"Not on your life, Don! If you're ready, Jackie, let's go!"

The two ladies walked over to the plane and talked quietly while one of Lee's mechanics filled up the plane's gas tank from a couple of large cans. I couldn't hear what they said from where I was standing, but Helen was nodding and grinning. Bessie walked over to them and took a couple of photographs.

Jackie helped Helen into the back cockpit. She watched as Helen put a gadget of some sort around her neck, and then climbed in the front cockpit. Jackie put a similar gadget around her neck, then looked out toward the mechanic at the front of the plane.

When Jackie nodded the man heaved on the propeller. After two tries the engine roared into life. Helen waved as the aeroplane started to move to the north end of the field.

The aeroplane turned, the engine noise got louder, and the craft bounced its way down the field. Halfway down the field it rose into the air and climbed steadily. I found my grin was mirrored by everyone else on the field. I could imagine how Helen felt!

For the next hour Helen and Jackie flew around the area—sometimes out to the west, other times right above us. Several times the aeroplane touched down as if to land, then the engine got louder and it climbed away again. Twice it did land, then taxi to the other end of the field and take off again. Don, Lee, and Cully Olson watched closely and muttered comments to each other; I couldn't hear what they said.

Eventually the aeroplane climbed, and looped twice! I wondered how Helen's stomach took that. The craft then gave an impromptu air show above our heads, each maneuver performed twice. Sure more than a ten minute flight around the city!

Finally the aeroplane lined up with the field, and again came down to a smooth touchdown. This time, they finally taxied back to where we were standing.

When the propeller stopped Helen jumped out of her cockpit even before Jackie had started to get out. I wondered if she had to get sick and was desperate to get away from the plane. Instead, she whooped and hollered like I'd never heard her yell before. She finished with, of all things, a gymnastic back flip! I was stunned, but the other onlookers started clapping.

Helen literally bounced as she strode over to us. She couldn't stop grinning.

"How was it?" Lee asked.

"Just like I'd imagined it! Better, actually—I could do the maneuvers!"

"You did WHAT?"

173

"Flying, Syl! After that first touch and go out there, I was flying the plane! The approach, the landing, the takeoff—everything! I actually can do this!!"

Jackie came up to us. She was grinning too.

"How'd she do, Jackie?" Don asked.

"Outstanding! She did all the maneuvers I asked of her, and much more smoothly than I would have expected someone who hadn't been up before. We went further, and after a demonstration touch and go, I gave her the controls. As you saw, the first touch down she bounced a little bit—but I bounce all the time, so what?"

"Just gotta make sure you come down as many times as you go up," Lee said with a wink.

The rest of us giggled or snorted, but Jackie shot Lee *the look*.

"Right," Jackie continued, "Anyway, you saw how she did the rest of the flight. I took her through some elementary aerobatic maneuvers. I'd do one, then she'd do it. I have *never* seen someone be able to do those maneuvers on their first flight! She also handled the final landing, calm and cool as a cucumber, never mind how she was when she got out!"

Don and Lee looked at each other, and nodded. Lee turned to Jackie and spoke clearly.

"Jackie, what would you say of Miss Smiley's prospects as a pilot?"

Jackie drew herself up to attention.

"Sir, I estimate Helen is about three hours of flying time away from soloing. Once she has soloed, I would expect about another forty hours of lessons, plus the same amount of practice time until she is ready to be examined for an Aero Club license. From there, the sky is literally the limit!"

Helen turned and hugged Jackie. She then turned back and hugged Lee. She then hugged her Ma.

"Thank you so much for giving me this opportunity! I'll finish the course when I can afford it, now that I know I can do this."

Don got a funny look on his face. "Not exactly, Helen."

Helen's mouth fell open; her eyes flashed. "What? Why?"

Don smiled and took off his hat. "What I mean to say is, your course of instruction, up to and including getting your license, has already been paid for!"

Again, Helen looked stunned. "What? Why? How?"

Lee turned to me. "Does she always get this way when she hears good news?" he whispered.

Cully whispered before I could, "You'd better be glad your wife isn't here right now. She'd slap that grin right off your face!"

174

We turned to Don as he continued.

"Helen, Wain Engineering Corporation is paying for your instruction. The Company is always looking for talent, and you've certainly got it! Your instructors will be Cully and Jackie here, and maybe a couple others. All we ask is when you get your license you fly for us—for pay—on weekends and during the summer when you have time.

Helen looked over at Don, obviously bewildered. *Too much emotion at one time*, I thought.

Jackie spoke up. "When your schedule permits, and we have an airplane and pilot available, we're ready to make you a pilot!"

Helen started to sob.

After the flying Jackie insisted on taking Don back to his house. Sitting in the living room with Pam and Evelyn, she sipped her tea and asked a question.

"All right you two, how did you know Helen would have the aptitude and desire to be a pilot? I could believe you just wanted to be hospitable and offered the airplane rides when we bought the cars, but then you set this up today *assuming* she'd be a natural pilot and have the desire to become one—that's hard for me to swallow! Especially since you were *right!* So what gives?"

Pam set down her teacup. "God told us."

"He *what*?"

"He told us," Pam repeated. He speaks to us through His Holy Spirit, *still small voice,* you know. When He does this Don and I compare notes; if He told us both the same thing, we run with it."

Jackie took off her glasses and massaged the bridge of her nose. "When does He do this?"

"Dreams, usually," Don said, "Occasionally when we're awake and busy doing something else. Always quiet, never anything that contradicts His Word or His overall plan. Been happening since before we were approached to come out here."

Jackie just stared at the other couple.

"I'm really glad to hear that!" a young voice piped up, "I thought I was the only one that happened to."

Now the others turned to the young girl sitting on the love seat between two shih tzus.

"You never told me this, Ev! How long has this been going on?"

"Ever since I got saved, Mom. At first I thought that was how the Holy Spirit talked to everyone; then I wondered when you never said it happened to you."

Jackie looked at her daughter, and sighed. "Now I'm beginning to wonder about *me*. Should I have been hearing that Voice too?"

"Not necessarily," Pam replied, "The Lord gives different abilities depending on the purpose He's called us to. We do what we do; you manage numbers and people, fly and fix complex aircraft. I don't know what Ev will do, but He does."

Jackie nodded. "All right, Pam, I'll take your word for it. I know He made it abundantly clear Ev and I should come out here when I retired. So far we've really enjoyed it," She looked over at her daughter, who smiled and nodded, "So I think we're still in the Lord's will. It's just so *different*—pleasantly different, though."

"We're glad you're here too, Jackie," Pam reached over and patted her hand.

Don sat quietly, frowning. "Love," he said finally, "Did you say something about Jackie *fixing* aircraft?"

"You want to explain, Jackie? I need to visit the *little room*," Pam replied, then got up slowly and shuffled off down the hall.

"You remember I broke my back in a landing accident on *Forrestal*, right?"

"Pam's mentioned that, but I don't remember the details," Don said.

"While I was recuperating the Navy sent me out to Newport for a slot at the Naval War College. That's where I met and married Eddie, and where you," she nodded to Evelyn, "were *commissioned*! For all that, I was still bored, so I went and got my A&P—*aircraft and powerplant* mechanic license. Great occupational therapy, and I've kept it up."

Don shook his head. "Jackie, you continue to amaze me!"

"Good," the company accountant said, "and by the way the next JN4 Lee gets in is mine. Signed the papers, put down the deposit. Mine will be an *H* model with the Hispano-Suiza engine in it though—until I swap it for something modern. See what I can make of it."

"Are you sure, Jackie? That's a lot of money for you personally. Will you have enough time to take care of it here?"

Jackie frowned and shot Don *the look*. "You make it sound like I brought home a *pony!* We can easily afford the airplane and a new engine. I'll keep it in Monmouth until we get a field here. And I will *not* have to shovel out its hangar every day!"

Don and Jackie laughed, but Evelyn looked serious. She spoke clearly, softly.

"Mother, could we perhaps get a small horse for me to ride? They're not very expensive. I promise to take care of it every day, and even shovel out the barn!"

Jackie looked at her daughter, mouth open. Evelyn stared back at her, then started to laugh. "Fished you in!" she announced.

Chapter Thirty One

Luther: Saturday, August 30th, 1919, First Baptist Church, Metamora.

My life was about to change dramatically. Next Monday I would begin my studies at Bradley Polytechnic. I had moved my things into the side room of the Templeman rooming house, and would begin staying there during the week. I felt at loose ends that weekend; I was not accustomed to being between projects.

Well, not *totally* between projects. Over the past two months I had been working on the organ at First Baptist in Metamora. This was the infamous 'Old Squeak', and I had made it my mission to bring it back to life. So far, I had been partially successful. I had tinkered, nursed, and soldered dozens of small tubes from the organ console to the wind chests. This organ sported a tubular pneumatic action, where pressing a key opened a valve, directly sending pressurized air to one or more pipes. In *theory*, that is.

In practice, the mechanism was notoriously unreliable, hard to service, and forced the organist to constantly change the timing of pressing the keys to compensate for delays in opening the pipe valves. Nobody built organs like this any more, but unfortunately the Estey Organ Company had built this one, and we were stuck with it. The sound of the organ when everything was working had always been one of my favorites—rich, melodious, perfectly balanced. The problem was getting everything to work at the same time.

The sum total of my efforts to date sounded less than impressive. I had gotten the main and swell keyboards more or less reliable for about half the available stops. I also had about half the pedals working most of the time; that was enough, at least for the music I intended to play on the thing.

When I told Pastor Reem of my progress on Old Squeak, he asked if I could be ready to play a morning service offertory by the end of August. I agreed.

Silly me.

I was amazed that Saturday the 30th to find the organ actually working properly, as I practiced the piece I had selected for the offertory. Among the scores Captain Mason's wife had given me was a very pretty prelude on the hymn tune *Be Thou My Vision*, by Healey Willan. I decided to use it because it was a very pretty piece, showcased a tune I had always liked, and…it required no

178

more of the organ than I had working. It was also a quiet, reflective piece; if the congregation expected me to start off with a piece of bombast, they would be surprised.

That Saturday afternoon I checked every tube, connection, and pipe I would be using. I then played the piece four times, and all was perfect! I wish I could have recorded it.

I shut off the organ, locked up the church, and went home, confident I had done all I could to make the next morning's offertory a success.

*****

Luther: the next morning.

Bright sunlight streamed through the windows of the church that Sunday morning. Yesterday's unseasonably cool weather had given way to a very warm and humid day. Fans waved in the congregation's hands as we proceeded with the morning service. Dennis Lepper, the church's music director, accompanied the singing on the piano. I could have joined in, but I still didn't trust the organ, even after yesterday's perfect response.

Finally, it was time for the offertory. While Pastor Reem prayed, I made my way to the console, and clambered onto the bench. I faced toward the organ, away from the congregation, because of the short maximum length of the tubes when the organ was built. I could see the pulpit through a small mirror.

Finally the prayer was over. I made sure the right drawknobs were pulled, found my place on the keyboards and pedals, and began.

This piece starts whisper quiet, and very restrained. All was well so far...

The first hint of trouble started as I began the next section, after changing two drawknobs. I started to play, and noticed a high-pitched overtone, a *cipher*. One by itself wasn't surprising. As long as that was all I got we were still OK.

Suddenly, other ciphers started to sound. Most were in the upper registers, but some were not. Harmonies became tangled dissonances. I was not pressing the keys, but pipes were sounding anyway.

I later discovered a series of tube connections had failed, admitting pressurized air to places it should not have been visiting. This in turn caused other failures.

179

That was later. Right now my playing had dissolved in an uncommanded series of howling pipes and whistling tubes. I couldn't play any more, and just stopped in the middle of the piece. I shut off all the stops, hoping that would calm the tempest; it did not.

Suddenly all the pipes stopped sounding, and the cacophony was replaced by a very loud, flaccid, buzz. It sounded just like a social indiscretion from the digestive system of the largest giant twisted fairy tales could conjure up! I sat frozen for five seconds, unwilling to believe my ears. Finally, my hand darted out and I pulled the power switch for the blower.

Even then, the overwhelming *raspberry* did not end. The whine of the blower turbine slowly spun down and stopped, but the buzz did not stop until the air pressure in the organ bled off completely.

Finally, dead silence in the sanctuary. I rested my head against the music rack on the console. A robin chirped in the tree outside an open window. Pastor got up slowly from his chair and moved to the pulpit. He took off his glasses, rubbed his eye and pinched the bridge of his nose.

"Thank you, Luther. That was *special*...."

The sanctuary erupted in gales, peals, storms of laughter. I turned around, got off the organ bench and held on to the side of the console as I bent over laughing. There was simply nothing else I could do.

Old Squeak had done in another organist.

Amazingly, Pastor Reem was able to preach his prepared message after that episode. It was a good one, too.

After the service he invited me back to his study for a few minutes, both to unwind and to dissect the *event*.

"So 'Old Squeak' does in another organist," Pastor said as he poured a cup of tea for me.

"I just feel terrible about that performance, Pastor. It just rolled me over!"

Pastor poured himself a cup of tea, and sat down in the chair beside me, before he replied.

"First, Luther, don't feel bad about what happened today. That happened to Mrs. Arbuckle at least four times I can remember, the last about six weeks before she passed."

"How did she handle it?"

"The first time she jumped off the bench, ran out to the foyer, and cried her eyes out. It took *The Deb* talking to her to finally calm her down."

"You still call your wife that?"

"Not to her face—I value my life!"

I nodded. "You know, you're now the second Pastor I know who has a *formidable wife* named Deborah."

"Oh? Who's the other one?"

"AP Kittridge, from Appleton."

"I know him. *The Deb* and I had dinner with them at a conference in early June. He'd just gotten back from the Navy."

"I met him on the ship that brought us home from France. Then, he was the one who owned the Chevrolet I'm driving. I met that Deborah when Pa and I went to pick it up."

"He mentioned that car. His loss, your gain."

"I think so, although he was very glad to be rid of it. He said he bought it sight unseen, while on the ship, and outside of the Lord's will. The Lord brought that to his attention."

"He has a way of doing that."

"That He does."

I took another sip of tea. "You always have the best tea, Pastor."

"*English breakfast.* Good stuff from the pot."

"Pastor, I should tell you the Lord used that little *situation* this morning to remind me I need to give everything to Him, especially performances."

"Didn't do it this time?"

"Nope. I had to get it right in the silence, while you were going up to the pulpit."

"Good. Sometimes, we serve best as an object lesson to others…or *high class Vaudeville!*"

I almost sent a swallow of tea out my nose at that!

"Where were we?" I asked when we had both composed ourselves.

"We were talking about Mrs. Arbuckle and the *Amazing Squeak,*" Pastor replied.

"I'd better watch how I sip this! Seriously though, what about the other three times?"

"She did what you did—sat there and then started laughing."

"Might as well laugh; doesn't help to cry."

"Got that right! Any idea what happened this time?" Pastor asked.

"I've been thinking about that since it happened. It worked perfectly for four run-throughs yesterday. Today—maybe because it is much warmer and more humid, that threw something out of balance, and one thing broke, which started the chain. I could hear things going bad in the chests as it progressed-I think that first failure brought on the others, like a line of dominoes going down. A main wind line to the sixteen foot wind chest did the rest—I opened the trap door to the chests and saw it right away."

"That's quite a litany of disaster, Luther. Recommended treatment?"

"The organ pipes are excellent, the sound of the instrument is superb, when and if it works. I recommend keeping the pipes, and getting new actuating mechanisms, maybe the whole console too, this time electro-pneumatic. Or—a company down by Saint Louis is working on an all-electric mechanism. The only wind is what sounds the pipes. I like what I've read about it; if I get some time I could go down there and see what they're up to."

Pastor took a sip of his tea. "And how would we pay for the rebuilding?"

"At the moment, Pastor, I have no idea."

"I guess the thing will sit there until the Lord arranges what to do about it. I don't think you'll have the time to do any more to it during the school year."

"You are so right about that!"

"If I can be of any help, Luther, don't hesitate to ask."

"Thanks, Pastor. We'll see how it goes."

"Good," Pastor said as he levered himself to his feet. "We might as well go home. I have to face *The Deb* for that remark after your offertory."

"I figured you'd say that, and you did! I thought it was about all you could say after a performance like that."

"I saw the look on *The Deb's* face; she was Not Amused. I'm in for it!"

"You have my sympathy, Pastor."

Pastor Reem grinned. "One of these days, you'll have this problem!"

"Are you prophesying?"

"We'll see, won't we!"

Chapter Thirty Two

(If you just want to read the exciting parts, please skip to the next chapter!)

Sylvia: August 25th, 1919, The Wagher School.

There we stood, and here they came.

Helen and I developed a routine to start each school day, and we tried it out this first day. I based the routine mostly on how Ma had done it, but added a couple of my own twists. Our resulting presence in the classroom was measured, effective, and more than a little bit theatre!

From the first day I always held a yardstick in my right hand. I have come to think of the yardstick as the *Teacher's Secret* Not *Weapon*. It is long for pointing, it makes a nice tapping sound, and makes a very satisfying *THWACK!* when slapped against something hard. I recommend one of medium strength, so it looks like it would hurt if applied, but is weak enough to snap immediately if it accidentally hits something or someone. The trick is to *imply* the yardstick could be applied to a miscreant, but never actually *use* it. When you find one you like, get enough to last you a while; I went through about five per school year.

To go with the yardstick, we perfected *The Look*. This was a facial expression designed to convey to the new student *this teacher means business*. Equal parts set jaw, deadpan expression tending toward a frown, and a piercing stare when needed. Helen had a much better *Look* than I did, so I practiced mine in front of a mirror to bring it up to her standard. We would stand next to each other, glowering into the mirror, and see how long it would take for one of us to start giggling and break the glare. If the children had seen us thus engaged, the game would have been over; of course, they never did!

This first year was about like all the others. Some children filed in, sat down, and looked like frightened rabbits. Others came in with an obvious *attitude*, sitting at their desks, looking around like they were daring someone to challenge them. Thanks to our *confidential briefing*, we had at least a vague idea what might be causing them to display this *attitude*, and we worked with them accordingly.

Still others came in, did everything just perfectly, and looked around to see that everyone saw how perfectly they behaved. Those children defined *smug* nicely, and tended to seek our attention more than the others. They may have considered themselves *teacher's pets*, but we didn't. Their realization of this fact was jarring to them, and entertaining to us!

We saw all the strengths, weaknesses, emotions, foibles—the sum total of human behavior—on a small scale in our classroom. Add to this the immediate spiritual state of each child—saved or lost, seeking or running—and we had a school full of challenges that first year, and every year thereafter.

What a privilege...and what a responsibility!

Helen and I spent much time in prayer every day for our students and their families, in addition to preparing for each day's class for each of eight grades, and each child's particular needs.

People who haven't taught in a multiple grade classroom look upon those of us who have in awe. 'How do you ever find enough hours in the day?'

We found that if we spent the time we needed to spend in prayer, and concentrated on the immediate needs of our students, all the rest of it just fell into place. We didn't have much free time, but we got everything done that was important. Having Ma's lesson plan books to teach from was a Godsend, of course!

Discipline wasn't much of a problem, at least for us! Children always misbehave sooner or later; they're humans, after all. Once we stopped the behavior, or broke up the fight, or whatever, usually all we had to do was keep the miscreant separated from the rest of the class (but still visible) for a period of time. Some teachers still used dunce caps; Ma never did, and neither did I. And a child never went to the corner for problems with their schoolwork. I wanted the children to *want* to learn, not *fear to fail*. I had a stool available for each corner of the classroom; I never needed more than three of the four at any given time. On the rarest of occasions I still used the paddle, but usually that intervention was reserved for the parents.

The second part of the discipline system was the *note home*. I kept a stock of half sheets of paper, and sealable envelopes, in my desk. When someone misbehaved to the point I needed to let their parents know, I would write *the note*, and seal it in an envelope. The looks the children gave me when I handed them *the note* were highly entertaining; Helen and I had to keep a poker face on those occasions. The notes were always delivered, and since we had informed each parent of our communication system before school started, the child always brought a note from home acknowledging receipt of *the note*, and occasionally offering comments.

When I describe the fun we had while teaching in those years, I don't want the reader to think we had fun at our students' expense. We loved our children dearly, and wanted nothing more than their success in life, whether they stayed on the farm or moved to the city. More important, we also prayed for them to be Born Again. But there is a certain humorous element in teaching, as in any important endeavor. My Pa explained that part to me when he became a Marine Drill instructor during the war, and I always enjoyed hearing Ma tell of some of her stranger experiences in class. Both professions were as serious as they could be, but could be cat-crazed funny too!

We had to maintain our serious outer demeanor to maintain class decorum and discipline…but sometimes, after the last child left for the day, we'd talk about what happened and dissolve in laughter! Sometimes we just had to rear back and let it fly. This was why, when I became a building principal, I always pulled the fire alarm for the drills myself; I also turned towards the wall so they couldn't see my evil grin!

Almost all of our children and their families attended Appleton Baptist Church, so our day included prayer and Bible reading in the routine. Occasionally a student would come to us with a spiritual question or problem, or we might notice changes in behavior indicating all was not well with a child's heart. In those cases we would try to discover what was going on, and either counsel the child ourselves, talk to their parents, or consult with Pastor and Deborah. Occasionally we would involve Fred and Violet Johnson, especially if it looked like something was going on in the family to upset the child. We were prepared to do whatever it took to help our students trust Christ and live for Him, as well as learn what they needed to get along in this world.

Our school year included a two week 'vacation' sometime from late September to late October, to let the children help with the corn harvest. We were ready to do this whenever the farmers and Fred Johnson agreed the crops were ready. As long as we knew the time was coming, we could arrange our lessons to smoothly resume whenever the children returned. Happily, we never had another interruption like we had with the influenza.

The Lord blessed us greatly in another way—we did not lose a child to illness or accident while I was the teacher. In those years this was almost unheard of. We were all very grateful to the Lord for His mercy in allowing us not to have to deal with the death of a student. I understood this from a very personal perspective, and also knew it would not continue indefinitely.

185

The routine of school, home, church, and the occasional visit to town or other unusual event, continued year after year, season after season. The work was sometimes hard, the hours always long, but provided the fabric of our lives for the next six years.

After two years Helen felt she was ready to launch into a classroom on her own, and found a position in the Galesburg schools. Ironically, the position was at Ayers Primary School, located on the grounds of the High School she so disliked! In spite of the location, she was thrilled to have a classroom of her own, and after a time of adjusting her methods to fit the larger class and fewer grades of the city school, she excelled. She also remarked how much fun it was to be working with her personal role model, the teacher who mentored her through her rough high school years. Although I did not know her personally, I felt like I knew Miss F. Lillian Taylor through Helen's stories about her.

After Helen left I had to adapt to not having an assistant in the classroom, and another person living in my house. I felt lonely at times, but with the commotion of the classroom, the nearness of neighbors and friends, and of course my prayer life, most of the time I was able to get along fine. The grieving of the events of 1918-1919 gradually faded, only coming back to visit me occasionally. Knowing that would happen, I was able to pray, and cope.

Philip Wagher passed at the end of November, 1919. Again we traveled slowly to the Hagenfield Cemetery, and again the men spaded dirt over a casket. We all grieved for the man who made the school possible; we then carried on, as he would have wanted us to.

So passed the years, quiet and unvarying, except for a few interesting episodes from time to time.

*****

Luther: Bradley Polytechnic Institute, and elsewhere.

I often hear people my age talk about the stresses and trials of their college years. To hear them talk, the time was a never-ending ordeal of staying awake in droning lectures, filling binder upon binder with illegible notes, and nodding off while trying to study a textbook at 3A.M. That always sounded like torture to me. If, as I often found, the former students had spent most of their time on anything and everything else but their studies, it was truly *self-torture*.

I have always been blessed with a quick, retentive, memory. I could read something once, and retain it forever. I kept expecting to run out of space in my brain for the things I read, but I never did. That was an incredible blessing to me, as I dove into my complicated studies.

As a Marine I learned the value of time allocation, scheduling, and getting proper rest whenever possible. The military life demands focus of attention and mind on whatever problem is at hand; keeping focus while on a ship, or in a combat situation, both add extra skills and require different levels of focus. College, I found, required a little bit of all these skills. Somehow I managed to adapt, and I can honestly say I never found myself exhausted, or at the end of my emotional rope, during my extended college career. Really!

I was pleased to find I was able to produce the innumerable papers a college education required with speed and precision. For this ability, in addition to the Lord, I was grateful to my far-seeing parents. Back in 1904, when my Pa first branched out beyond bicycles and started selling automobiles, he saw a need for increased efficiency of his office staff. Since the ladies in the office were also friends of Pa and Ma, they also wanted to make the work as easy as possible for them.

Pa heard about an instrument called the *Blickensderfer electric typewriter*. At Ma's urging, he decided to risk $125.00, a large amount at the time, and purchased one of the machines. He also bought a parts list, service manual, and some key wearing parts of the machine. He told me he had the idea of distributing the machines, if the one he bought proved out. The machine worked far beyond his expectations, and allowed a typing speed unheard of in those days; however, the office ladies were terrified of working around electricity, and refused to use it!

Pa took it back home, and we used it there; I typed my high school papers on it. The company stopped making them, probably because people were afraid of them, but Pa managed to purchase some more parts, and several unsold machines, at a very attractive discount. They normally used ink rollers instead of ribbons; however, Pa purchased several experimental kits to convert them to use a standard typewriter spool ribbon. Over time Pa and I developed the skill to service them, and they have continued to serve us well ever since.

I brought one of our Blickensderfers, or *Blick Electric* for short, to my room at the Templeman house. Agnes was fine with it, since she was used to Charlie working on odd electrical devices around the house. Forrest was enthralled with the machine, and would sit by the hour watching me type a paper. And I typed quickly, probably aided by the dexterity I had developed playing the organ. Paper production became almost a pleasure…almost, but not quite!

The one part of my college career that suffered was my social life—I didn't have one. I went to school, came back to my room and studied, and went home most weekends. I knew the other people in the house, but I couldn't say we socialized. They had their lives and I had mine, and that was it.

In retrospect, I think it boiled down to priorities: I had a set of priorities for my life, based on the Lord's will as He revealed it to me, and He gave me peace about them. Within those priorities, I worked hard; outside of those priorities, I guess I was pretty much oblivious. My Marine training tended to increase this tendency toward, to use a longish word, *parochialism*. I didn't dislike my classmates; I just didn't have time to get involved with them. Perhaps I should have made time; however, so far I think things have turned out OK.

When the time came to declare a major, I found myself led to declare two—General Engineering, with no specialty noted, and Geology. Why Geology? Well, I'd always been interested in how the surface of the Earth could tell us what lay beneath it, if we knew what to look for. The Lord created this planet with a set of rules and laws, and the planet carried them through from crust to core. At least, that's how it seemed to me. So I wanted to learn more about the subject.

A double major increased my work load, and ultimately kept me at Bradley for five years instead of four, although the last year I only attended classes two days a week. Fortunately, money was not an issue; and after my experiences on and after June 13th, 1918, I figured I had as much time as the Lord decided I needed.

It helped to have a comfortable place to live for those years. I also note here that besides being a gracious and solicitous host, Agnes Templeman was an outstanding cook…although she had two unusual kitchen practices.

First, she never measured anything. I stood in awe as I watched her making things in her kitchen—a pinch of this, a dash of that, half an old coffee cup of something else, and the result was always marvelous! When I try to cook I have to measure everything— twice!

Second, she never washed her pots and pans! She'd wash the rags and towels she used to wipe them out, but then she'd put the utensils away without ever getting near the sink. She always did this, and had done it for years. This screamed loudly in the face of my knowledge of microbiology and disease transmission (granted they weren't my specialties). However, as far as I know none of us ever got sick from food poisoning while we lived in that house! Don't ask me why, except, once again, the Grace of God.

So passed the next five years, productive but quiet, except for a few interesting episodes from time to time.

Chapter Thirty Three

Pam Wain and Jackie Brighthonor: Monday, July 19th, 1920. The Wain house, North Broad Street.

"Are you sure you won't come with us to watch Helen fly?" Jackie Brighthonor asked.

"Not today, thank you," Pam Wain replied, "I'm fighting a lovely gout flare, and you know what *colchicine* does to me!"

"I do indeed," Jackie said, then changed the subject. "You don't mind Ev hanging around while we're gone, do you?"

"Never!" Pam replied, "She always has a good time when she's here. We talk a lot, and she loves digging through our records and video collection. She also loves to walk Teddy."

Jackie shifted in her chair. "She does that for Missy, too. Good thing—my back starts to ache when I walk too much." Jackie decided to mention something that had been bothering her. "You know she calls you *Auntie Pam*?"

Pam's brow furrowed. "I've heard her, and I'm honored. Does it bother you? I can tell her to stop—"

"No, no, don't do that," Jackie replied, then sighed. "Ev tells me about what you two discuss. You've filled in a lot of the *gaps* in my parenting skills. I was at sea so much of the time, I guess I missed some of those milestones. My mother raised her when Eddie and I were deployed, then Chaplain Martindale's wife, Ro, watched her after Eddie was killed and Mom had her stroke. I don't know if she even thinks of me as her mother, really."

Pam smiled, and put her hand on Jackie's. "Oh, she does, you don't have to worry about that! She's very proud of all you've accomplished, both in the Navy and here. She tells me she really feels at home in this time, and in her circle of friends. She talks about learning Mandarin with Li Chen, Yu Chen and Lee's daughter—I think she's her best female friend. And as far as boys..." Pam shrugged, "She tells me she is very good friends with Jeff Potter from church."

Jackie nodded. "She's told me all of that. Do you suppose she thinks of Jeff as a *boyfriend?* She's never had those crushes we had when we were her age."

"I don't know," Pam replied, "She says she communicates with him, knows what he's thinking. She believes there's a genius hiding in that young man, if we could only figure out how to help him communicate."

"I wish Everett and Flora would let him go to school," Jackie said, "but then I think about how schools in this time deal with kids who are different, and I wonder if he isn't better off where he is, at home. The only school I think I'd trust him in would be Ayers Primary, with Lillian Taylor, and he's almost too old for there now."

Pam nodded. "Wherever he went, it'd have to be someplace where he can be as different as he needs to be. What do you think we have here—Asperger's Syndrome?"

Jackie took another sip of tea. "Seems logical, Pam, but he's got that lack of speech. Ev says he can only speak three or four words at a time, and then only when the subject is very important or very emotional. That's not classic Asperger's—although we probably shouldn't be calling it after someone who's barely out of high school right now!"

Pam and Jackie chuckled. "I guess not," Pam said, then thought of something she needed to ask. "Changing the subject, you know Ev's going to start asking questions about *relationships* here soon. If she asks me, do you mind if I answer her straight? I don't want to be teaching her stuff you would normally teach—"

Now Jackie patted Pam's hand. "Don't worry about that, Pam! You just tell her anything she wants to know, as long as it's not something you'd be embarrassed by. And she already knows where babies come from—she told me she read it in *Encyclopedia Britannica*!"

"Not the 1911 version," Pam winced, "That thing's too stodgy—and chock full of errors."

"Nope, the *Ultimate Reference Suite*. I wanted it for the historical stuff, so I brought it back on one of the laptops. It's still wrong-headed, but the information's accurate."

"In that area anyway," Pam chuckled. "And by the way, I told Ev I would keep whatever she told me secret, unless it puts her in danger; then I'll tell you."

"Ev's told me that too. I'm so glad you're here to mentor her!"

Jackie's comment was interrupted by a flushing sound from down the hall.

"Ah, the king is off his throne," Pam said with a giggle.

Don sauntered into the living room. "Did I miss anything?"

Pam winked at Jackie. "We were just talking about Jackie taking you up for some aerobatics when Ruth and Helen get back from the test."

Don turned red and tried to loosen his collar with a finger. "Not on your life, Love! Especially not in a *Jenny*!"

191

"Now, Boss," Jackie interjected, "My *Jenny's* perfectly safe! That Rotax engine hasn't given a bit of trouble. Let me take you up some time."

"No, no, and no, ladies! Today we're going to cheer Helen on, and let her and Ruth Law share the joy. Oh—love, I figured we'd invite Jackie and Ev, Helen and Syl, plus Ruth Law and our new aviation manager Gil Foster over for dinner this evening. We can get it *catered*. OK?"

Pam stood up and faced her husband. "Thank you for informing me exactly *six hours* before you expect me to serve dinner! That's assuming I can stay out of the *loo* long enough. Good thing all I have to do is make a call, go downstairs to the *transfer room*, and wheel the cart with the food up here. Plus, Ev's here this afternoon and she loves to help. No thanks to you, mister!"

Don started to say something, but Jackie spoke over him. "Who's supplying the food this time, Pam?"

Pam snorted. "I'll call *upstream* and have 'em send over something from *The Colonel*. Our guests will have no clue!"

"Gonna leave it in the bucket? Eeep!"

"Of course not, Skeezix!" Pam snarled as she pulled her hand away from Don's ribs. "Now, you two get a move on—they're supposed to be at the fairgrounds in a half hour! Let me get busy on the dinner—Ev will be back from Teddy's walk in a few."

"All right Love," Don sounded subdued, "and I'm sorry I didn't warn you about the dinner—I just thought of it while I was dressing."

"More like daydreaming," Pam said, and the couple kissed, "Now you two go and enjoy the air show."

****

Sylvia: 1:50 PM, Monday, July 19th, 1920. District Fairgrounds, Grand Avenue, Galesburg.

"Helen, tell me again why we're going out to the Fairgrounds."

"I haven't told you the first time, Syl! It's a surprise—you'll see!"

"That's what I'm afraid of. I've seen a few of your surprises."

"You still haven't forgotten that time on Seminary Street, have you?"

"I was scared half to death! I'm just glad I wasn't driving when that plane went over us."

"Well, don't worry about that today. The roads don't go that close to the field—oops!"

"So we *are* talking about flying again, aren't we? I knew it!" I used my Stern Teacher voice, but grinned to pull the sting.

"OK, you got me. It's flying. The day I've been working and waiting for is finally here, after almost a year!"

"License test?"

"You bet! Lee and Don arranged it. I'll be flying off the backstretch of the track."

"Seems like a funny place to fly from."

"It's a half mile long, dead level, and cindered. None of the other fields around here are any more than that—fields, usually muddy."

"You told me nobody who's taught you can give this test—somebody's rules?"

"Yep, the Aero Club of America...quite a title, but nobody else issues a license people will believe. Have to have it to participate in air meets."

I turned to look at my passenger, "You're not going to be some daredevil, are you?"

"Me? Perish the thought, Syl! I just want the license so I have some credibility if I do a little flying for pay in my spare time."

"We have spare time?"

Helen half-turned toward me, pouting, "Some day, maybe. Possibly? A little?" she asked in a whining little girl voice.

"You do *plaintive* really well, Helen!" I said, then we both laughed. We'd been busier the past year than we ever dreamed of when the school board hired us after Ma passed. We'd done OK, but spare time was a precious thing during the school year.

"So who is giving you the test?"

"Lee won't say. He just said I'd be *pleasantly surprised*."

"Is that why we took my car instead of yours?"

"Well...yes. The usual crowd knows the rattletrap I drive, but if this is someone really new they'd take one look at us in that thing and laugh me off the field!" Helen got a funny look on her face. "I can't afford to have that happen."

"A bit nervous?"

"A *lot* nervous. Those flying machines are about the lousiest idol that's been invented yet, but I really want to succeed in something very few people my age, and fewer women, can do."

"Have you gone to the Lord about this?"

"Yes, Syl. He's kept the door open this whole year, when I had to squeeze in lessons an hour or two on the weekends. He's got a purpose in it, I'm sure...and He's allowing me to have fun doing it. So on I go!"

"Is your ma coming out to watch?"

"She wrote and said she couldn't—her sciatica is acting up and she's spending a few days in bed."

"I'm sorry to hear that. We'll go see her when you're done."

"That'd be great, Syl, thanks."

We drove through the gate and toward a line of cars and a few aeroplanes just off the second turn of the track. I recognized Don and Jackie, Lee Wright, Cully Olson, and a few others; that was all. Then we pulled in and parked at the nearer end of the line of cars and shut down.

Jackie saw us get out. "Hi Helen, Sylvia! Come on over and meet our guests."

We walked over to the little group. Jackie and a shorter man in flying helmet and leather jacket met us.

Jackie began, "Ladies, I'd like you to meet Gil Foster, former Air Service pilot and flight instructor. He's going to manage our aviation section up in Chicago. This is Sylvia Trimble, teacher, and our victim, er, *examinee* for the day, Helen Smiley."

As we shook Gil's hand I noticed Don roll his eyes behind Jackie's back.

"Quit rolling your eyes," Jackie shot back at Don, who reddened.

"Are you giving me the test today?" Helen asked Gil.

"Not me," he said with a grin, "Here comes your examiner."

A tall, thin woman in a flying helmet walked over toward us.

"Hello, ladies! I'm Ruth Law. Which one of you is Helen?"

I looked over at Helen. She was looking paler than she had been a moment before. She stood stock still, her hands trembling; her lips moved, but nothing came out.

"Since Helen seems to have lost her voice," I said, "I'm Sylvia Trimble, and this frozen statue next to me is Helen Smiley, your pilot for today."

Ruth Law grinned as she shook our hands. "I'm used to that sort of reaction by now. Helen, I've heard good things about your flying. Are you ready to demonstrate for me?"

Helen found her voice. "Y-Yes, Ma'am," she squeaked.

Ruth smiled again. "Relax, Helen, I'm not an ogre! And it's 'Ruth', not 'ma'am."

Helen nodded, still looking a bit flustered.

"Better. Did Lee give you the list of maneuvers we'll be performing today?"

"Yes m—Ruth. I have it right here"

"Are you prepared for them?"

"Yes, Ruth, I am."

There was the old Helen back! I thought.

"Then let's be about it!"

The two turned and walked toward the nearest aeroplane, another Curtiss JN-4. As they climbed into the plane, Ruth in front and Helen in back, I turned to Jackie. "Who is that woman? She sure rattled Helen!"

"That's Ruth Law," Jackie replied, "the most famous woman pilot in the country! She holds several world records for women pilots, and at least one for both men and women. She's one of the Aero Club's Master Examiners, and if she says you get a license, you get a license!"

"And the other way 'round?"

"Oh, yes. She has a reputation as a tough examiner. Helen will have to work hard today."

"Why is someone so famous here in Galesburg?"

Jackie took off her sunglasses to look at me. "She owns her own flying circus—daredevil stunts, racing, and so forth. She's decided to base here at the fairgrounds this summer while they go around the Midwest and give shows. They just got here last week."

"Oh," I said, and turned back to watch.

Once Ruth and Helen were seated in the aeroplane, they fastened the speaking tube, called a *gosport* for some reason, between them, and prepared to start the engine. I noticed Helen gave all the directions to the man who spun the propeller.

The engine fired right up, and with a thin wisp of exhaust smoke the plane taxied away toward the end of the backstretch of the track, now the runway.

Jackie turned to the rest of the group. "Ruth will have Helen perform every part of the flight today, and will grade her on her performance. I have the script here, and I'll watch them with the binoculars, and comment."

"Yes, Jackie, please do," Don said, and traded his binoculars for the clipboard with the script.

The plane turned at the end of the runway, the engine roared, and it came back toward us. It lifted off smoothly and began to climb, turning south and east away from town. Jackie followed the flight, and made comments to the rest of us while Don checked items off on the clipboard.

A few minutes and a page of check marks later Jackie suddenly said, "Uh, oh."

I looked up at the plane, high in the sky just southwest of town. I saw a puff of smoke, and one or two things other than smoke, come off the plane. In a few seconds the sound of the engine coming back to us changed from a droning buzz to a *clank-BANG!*, then silence.

"What happened, Jackie?" Don asked.

"I think they just had the engine come apart on them," Jackie said quietly. propeller too."

Cully shook his head. "I've seen that happen a couple times with OX-5s. Something seizes, the crankshaft snaps and the prop goes sailing away, taking the front of the engine with it."

I saw Jackie bite her lip, then, "Lord love a duck, I called her a *victim!* I was just joking like we always do. And now—"

I started to pray hard.

"She's still straight and level," Lee said.

"Roger, copy," Jackie spoke the odd phrase, "It's still under control. They've turned back toward the field and are losing altitude. It'll be tail heavy because of the stuff they lost. Thoughts, Gil? Cully?"

Out of the corner of my eye I saw Cully take out his handkerchief and wipe his forehead before answering. "They can make it back. They have enough altitude, and they haven't spun in, so whichever one is flying has a pretty good idea of their speed. Gil?"

"Agree, Cully. I'd come in high, and side-slip the excess altitude once I was sure I was going to make it. Worked for me back when."

"Me too—several times," Cully said.

"And me," Jackie added, "If the ship gets too far out of balance she won't be able to control it."

"Looks like they're trailing something," Don said, squinting.

"Fuel—not surprised," Jackie said, "Praise the Lord it's not on fire!"

I could see the crippled plane lining up with the end of the runway/backstretch.

Jackie spoke. "Time to side-slip…..now!"

At that instant the plane's left wings dipped, and it lost most of its height in a couple of seconds. The plane straightened up, swept over the track fence, and touched down smoothly. The plane rolled up to us and passed, slowly losing speed.

As it came up to us I heard several people in the small crowd swear, and a man with a 'Press' ribbon on his coat snapped the shutter on his Graflex.

Lee Wright took out his handkerchief and wiped his brow as the plane rolled past.

"Will you look at that!"

I stared open-mouthed at the apparition rolling past us. The propeller, radiator, and part of the engine were just gone! I saw tears in the fabric of the wings and tail surfaces, where parts of the motor must have struck them.

In the front cockpit Ruth Law was moving her head slowly. Blood covered her head, her flying helmet partly torn off. In the rear cockpit I could see Helen looking from side to side as she watched where the plane was rolling. It stopped a hundred yards down the track. We headed that way.

By the time we got to the plane, several men were lifting Ruth out of the front cockpit. She was moving, a good sign. Others brought a first aid kit and stretcher, and two of the men started bandaging her head.

Helen was climbing out of the rear cockpit on her own. She took out a handkerchief and calmly wiped a few spots of blood from her blouse and face. She pulled off her helmet and started to wipe it off.

"I see you decided to end the examination early, Helen. Is there a problem?" Jackie asked, a deadpan look on her face.

I could see the twinkle in Helen's eyes as she replied.

"We were flying around up there, and an argument developed just ahead of us. After a short discussion, the propeller decided to pack up and leave, taking a few friends with it. We then though it best to return to the field for consultations."

Helen told me later this sort of macabre understatement was the usual way pilots discussed their more hair-raising experiences. I guess it beat fainting, or crying hysterically.

What I didn't realize was the man with the Graflex had taken several more photographs of the scene, and heard their conversation. I must say he reported it accurately when his article appeared in the *Register* the next day, along with the photos!

Meanwhile, the men finished bandaging Ruth's head. Two picked up the stretcher, and headed toward a nearby car. Ruth whispered something, and pointed; the men brought the stretcher over to us. She looked at Helen, and whispered.

"Thank you...Helen...saved my life. You...pass. License...in the...mail."

Helen nodded. "Thank you, Ruth," she said softly. The men placed Ruth in the car, and she was gone.

Jackie sidled up to me. She looked over at Helen, and spoke softly. "I've seen the look on her face before—had it myself more than once. In an hour or two, maybe a day or two, she's going to have a very emotional reaction to what happened here. When she does, someone needs to be with her, to help her cope. She'll get over it, but it'll be rough for a bit. Can you stay with her? Maybe stay at her house overnight?"

"Sure, Jackie. I'll get her over there."

"Good," Jackie said, "When she's back together tell her I'd like to take her flying in my aeroplane on Saturday. Have her come by my house around eight. OK?"

"Sure," I replied, "happy to."

"Thanks, Syl. Now you might want to get Helen out of here before she starts to come apart. I'll help if you want."

"OK, thanks, Jackie."

We moved to Helen's side, and started her toward the car.

Chapter Thirty Four

Luther: Thursday, July 22nd, 1920, First Baptist Church, Metamora.

"Well, that was *special*," John Wick remarked as he pulled the blower switch on Old Squeak.

Pastor Reem, my Pa, and I all added a chorus of laughs to the slowly dying flatulence of a ruptured air line—again—in the organ of the First Baptist Church of Metamora.

"Gotta laugh because you can't cry?"

"No…John," I managed to get out between snorts. "You just said exactly what Pastor Reem said from the pulpit when Old Squeak did that to me on a Sunday Morning not quite a year ago!"

Now John joined in the chortles. We finally calmed down a minute after Old Squeak had finally stopped buzzing.

John shook his head. "You weren't kidding about that thing, Luther! I don't think I've ever heard a tubular pneumatic fail so quickly, and so completely. And you say you fixed it again since the last time?"

I answered as I was wiping my eyes.

"Even though I wasn't going to try playing it again, I went through and re-soldered all the ruptured connections, and wrapped the wind supply tube with rubber and hose clamps. I wanted you to hear as much of the pipe sounds as you could before it died."

"Much obliged," the president of Wicks Organ Company in Highland, Illinois, replied. "That work let me hear enough to tell me you have a wonderful set of pipes in this organ. The balance is perfect, even when the chords coming out are interesting…"

We all chuckled again. John Wick continued.

"I also see your estimation of the sound potential of this organ is spot on. I wish Estey hadn't tried to go cheap on the wind chests and pneumatics—every one of their organs from that time has the same batch of problems, though yours is the worst I've seen. Fortunately there is a solution, and it's the one you suggested—save the pipes and junk the rest!"

"Come on in here," Pastor Reem said. He beckoned us all into his study, offered us seats, and shut the door.

"I have to say those of us here completely agree with your assessment, Mr. Wick. And we'd like nothing better than to solve the problem the way you and Luther have suggested. The problem is the one you'd expect—money. About how much would a job like this cost?"

John Wick opened up a folder. "Pastor, I figured you would ask me that. When Luther came up to see us earlier this month, he gave me a detailed list of the ranks, divisions, and sections of the organ as it is now. He also gave us a rough drawing and measurements of the installation. Looking at it now, I can tell you he was as accurate as one of our own designer/estimators. Luther, I'm glad you're going to college, but if you weren't I would hire you right now!"

"Thank you, Sir. May I keep that in mind?"

"I hope you do! Although, after you see my estimate, the others in this room may be less willing to remember me!"

Pastor Reem laughed. "Don't worry, Mr. Wick, we'll remember you in any event."

"Thank you, Pastor—I think. And it's *John*, by the way, to all of you!"

"In that case, John," Pastor Reem said, "give us the bad news please."

John took a sheet of paper out of a folder he was holding and handed it to Pastor.

Pastor Reem studied the document, with Pa looking over his shoulder. He then handed it to me. I scanned it quickly—*about what I figured. But where would the money come from?* I wondered.

Pastor Reem scratched his bald head, took a deep breath, and spoke.

"John, your estimate looks good from a practical standpoint. No sense changing the pipes if they're good, and we disassemble the monster for you, that's fine. Four Thousand Seven Hundred Fifty sounds reasonable, and jibes with what Luther has told us. Unfortunately, we just can't afford to do this right now."

My father finally spoke. "Oh?"

I knew my Pa, and so did Pastor Reem. We both started to smile. That word, plus a slightly raised eyebrow, meant a surprise was coming—and we both knew what it was.

"Gentlemen, I've been thinking about doing something for the church in memory of my late wife and Luther's mother, Rita. She always loved to hear that organ, even when it was about as sick as she was. She was thrilled when she learned Luther was starting to take organ lessons, towards the end. For a memorial to her, I think I could find a little money to put toward the rebuilding of the organ....oh, maybe about five thousand dollars."

He said it so quietly it took a few seconds for the full import of his words to sink in. Pastor Reem and John Wick stood to shake his hand and clap him on the back. I hugged him, and couldn't resist a comment.

"So I'm not getting that in the inheritance?"

Pa glared at me in mock anger.

"Certainly not, Son! You'll earn your own money, somehow or other! In fact, for that crack I hereby appoint you Chief Organ Dismantler!"

"Thanks a bunch, Pa…although I think I might find a way to enjoy that job!"

"Figured you would, Son. Gentlemen, let's get this deal finalized so my son can start his new job!"

And that's how I spent the rest of the summer of 1920—tired, hot, filthy dirty—and loving every minute of it! I and my willing band of volunteers carefully removed and tagged every pipe in the organ, removed the wind chests, and created a trailer full of twisted lead tubes and sheet metal ducts. The local junk dealer was thrilled to get those, probably the only time since their manufacture they had made someone happy.

Twice during the process we sent a freight car full of pipes and miscellaneous parts down to the Wicks factory in Highland, near St. Louis, to be reworked. We kept the electric blower, and gave the organ console to a church in Streator whose Estey console had been damaged in a fire. Thus all of Old Squeak got put to some good use—and the rebuilt organ would be installed, if John kept to his schedule, the following June. That gave me a year to work up an inaugural program, and with my school work I found I needed every bit of that time!

*****

Sylvia: Thursday, July 22, 1920, a little before 4PM, Main Street, Galesburg.

Helen had indeed come apart after the forced landing during her license test. By the time I got her to her folks' house and she had told the story to her mother, Helen started to shake and cry. I put her to bed and fixed supper for both of them, then stayed overnight.

After three days of rest she was back to normal. I retrieved her from her folks' house that afternoon, and drove downtown. Star Grocery on the square was selling out and moving since the building had been sold, so we figured we could pick up a few bargains. People, cars, and horses crowded the downtown, and we were just cruising the streets in a slow line of vehicles, looking for a place to park.

"The street's crowded this afternoon. Wonder why?" Helen asked.

"I don't know, but I'd guess it's a nice day, it's between harvests, and the farmers all decided to come to town at the same time. I can't recall the traffic ever being this heavy, though."

"No holiday, and the district fair isn't for another month. Oh, that reminds me—Jackie stopped by the house yesterday morning and confirmed we're going flying Saturday morning—I'll meet her at her house around eight. Then Ruth Law came over in the afternoon, and we had a long talk."

"Is she OK?"

"She thinks so. She said Doctor Bohan told her not to fly for a couple weeks until her scalp healed and he could take out the stitches, but that was all. She was quite impressed with our favorite doctor!"

"I'm glad. What else did you two talk about?"

Helen pointed up ahead. "There's one just leaving! I'll tell you later."

I eased the Model T coupe into a parking place on the east edge of the Public Square park. We would have to scoot across traffic to get to the grocery, but I was just happy to get the spot close by.

We got out, and started to walk towards the grocery on the north side of the square. We took about three steps when I heard a commotion back on Main street. Helen and I looked over, then quickly moved back to the car.

"Oh, no!" Helen exclaimed, with good reason.

An aeroplane was flying west on Main Street…at about the height of a two-story building! Right up Main Street it came, wings barely missing the tops of the buildings. Sometimes the wings were below the level of the top of a building as it flew by. Fortunately the street was wide, and the plane stayed just above the top of the telephone poles and their tangled wires.

Below the plane, chaos. Streetcars stopped with a lurch; some people got out and ran to the curb, others just craned their necks out the windows. People on the sidewalks looked up and ducked as it flew past. We could hear screams, shouts, and curses wafting through the air, getting louder as it approached. All over the street draymen and buggy drivers tried desperately to hold their horses and keep them from bolting.

Helen motioned me over closer to the car. "Here, get ready to get on the hood if a horse bolts this way. I'll get on the car next to us. Too far to the trees, and I can't climb anyway!"

We stood and watched the unfolding scene, ready to move if we had to.

The plane finished its traverse of Main Street and flashed over our heads, clearing the tops of the trees in the park and the Union Hotel roof by a few feet. It continued toward the gas works down by the Santa Fe tracks.

"Its one of Ruth's planes. I recognize the markings."

"Why would she do something so stupid, right after getting all that free publicity with your flight?"

"My guess is she doesn't know about it- or maybe knows about it now. She has some pretty odd birds flying for her, and when the cat's away, et cetera…"

"Well, someone is going to have to face the music, if he doesn't crash first!"

As we were talking, the plane reached the gas works, and made several tight turns around the tall masonry smokestack of the works. It then headed back toward us.

We saw where it was heading as it brushed the treetops over our heads again. "The courthouse!"

The plane flew past the tower of the Congregational Church, right up the streetcar line on South Broad street, and just over the trees of Standish Park. It then banked to the left and threaded its way around all four sides of the county courthouse, lower than the top of the courthouse bell tower.

"Someone's in trouble now. Talk about annoying the Judge!"

"Got that right, Helen! Do you see him? I've lost him."

"No, I think he's gone. Didn't hear a crash, so maybe he got away clean."

Main Street was slowly starting to return to normal. Fortunately, no runaway horses made it as far as the square, so we were safe.

Helen nodded her head off to our right. "Look over there," she whispered.

The same reporter who had been at the fairgrounds was packing his Graflex camera into its case.

"I wonder if he got a tip that there'd be something to see here about this time?"

"Wouldn't be at all surprised, Syl. And since Ruth is officially out with her injury, she can say she didn't have anything to do with it."

"Would she do that?"

"She'd have to, whether she did or not. I'll explain on the way home."

"Yes, let's get the groceries and get on the road. The Big Store can wait."

An hour later we were back on the Fremont Road heading home.

"So how did the talk with Ruth go?"

"Fine, Syl. She really meant it when she said I'd saved her life. She wants me to fly with them before school starts—get some experience, she said."

"Are you going to do it?"

"I think I will—a little bit anyway. Saturdays, and maybe one day at the District Fair. I don't want to let up on our preparations for class."

"Sounds good—no flying like we saw this afternoon, though!"

"You said it! I like straight and level, and just a little higher up than a second floor window!"

We laughed as I accelerated down the North Creek hill, crossed the creek, and started up the other side. Helen was unusually quiet as we climbed the hill.

"All Right, Helen, spill it! What else did you two talk about?"

"Ruth said something very interesting in our conversation. She said that was the first time she'd ever had an emergency while she was flying that she could do absolutely nothing about. She was too hurt to put on a big front like all pilots do after we got down, but it really bothered her later. Was still bothering her."

"Sounds like an opening to me."

"Yep. I told her I have Someone who holds me in His hand all the time, and through that whole crisis I knew He was guiding me. And if He did decide to take me home then, I still won for eternity! Ma came in and heard that, and told Ruth how she and Pa felt the same."

"How'd she take that?"

"She didn't laugh it off, that's for sure! She said her own mother hadn't spoken to her since she took up flying...and marveled that my Ma could feel that way about it. Ruth said she had never heard anything like my relationship with Jesus before, and she'd grown up in a church—Universalist, as it happened."

"Sure wouldn't have heard it there! You tell her the rest of it?"

"I sure did," Helen replied, "She listened carefully—she's very sharp. She said she wasn't ready to *do that* just yet, but she said she'd think carefully about it."

"You think she will?"

"I'm going to pray that way—just have to. Oh, I gave her a Bible too. Had a spare, and she didn't have one."

We came to the Appleton Road intersection.

"That's all we can do, Helen."

"All you can do, Syl. I can throw a little flying in too!"

We were laughing as we turned in the driveway.

Chapter Thirty Five

Jackie and Helen: Saturday, July 24th, 1920, 8AM, Jackie Brighthonor's house, West South Street, Galesburg.

"Welcome, Helen, glad you could make it," Jackie Brighthonor said as she answered the front door. "Come on in, I'll be ready soon as I use the *loo!*"

As Jackie disappeared down the hallway Evelyn came from the back of the house, Melissa S. Tzu trailing in her wake. "Hi, Miss Smiley, how are you?"

"Fine, Ev, thanks. How are you and your helper?" She bent down to scratch Missy, who flipped over on her back.

"We're fine," the thin eleven year old replied, "Enjoying the summer while we've got it!"
"So what are your plans for today?"

"I'm going to hang out here for a while, finish my homework, then your mom's invited me for lunch."

"I had breakfast over there this morning, and she told me. I'm glad you two get along."

Evelyn nodded. "We always have a good time—and Lester's good company."

"Lester?" Helen frowned, "Are we talking about the same *Lester,* my brother?"

"Right," Ev replied, "He's always decent with me."

"That's it—you're not his older sister!"

"I know, and I also know your mom reminds him of that when she doesn't think I can hear!"

Helen and Evelyn laughed, then Evelyn smirked. "I think you'll enjoy the flight today—Mom's got some surprises for you!"

"Surprises?"

"Don't give the game away, Ev!" Jackie said as she came back into the room.

"I'm not, Mom—I didn't say what *kind* of surprises!"

"They're all good," Jackie added, then picked up a leather briefcase. "Let's go, Helen. Hold down the fort while we're gone, Ev!"

We will, Mom," Ev replied, then looked around. "I guess *I* will—Missy's gone back to bed!"

The two pilots laughed as they walked out the door.

The road to Monmouth seemed to stretch farther than usual that July morning.

"I'll be glad when we can get a permanent field near Galesburg," Jackie remarked, "I don't like to spend time driving when I could be flying." She held the steering wheel of the Oldsmobile coupe lightly with one hand.

"Could we use the District Fairgrounds?" Helen asked.

"Unfortunately, no," Jackie replied, "Ruth needs all that space for her flying circus this summer. Then, in a year or two the fairgrounds will be closed and the area sold for a housing development."

"I haven't heard anything about that," Helen said, "How do you know about it?"

"That's one of the things we'll talk about today as we fly. Let's wait till we get to the field."

Helen nodded. *What is she getting ready to spill?* She asked herself.

"Well, here's my hangar," Jackie said as they stopped beside a white frame building without windows.

"Looks more like a house, except for no windows," Helen said.

"I wanted it to blend in with the rest of the buildings around here. I also wanted to minimize threat of break in or vandalism. No windows helps. Since it's also my workshop, it has a few extra amenities."

Jackie unlocked the side door and the two stepped in. Jackie flipped a switch, and the inside filled with cool light. Helen saw a JN-4 with an odd looking nose in the middle of the concrete-floored hangar, with other things stored around the walls. In the back a doorway led to a short hallway with three doors off it. Several locked cabinets also lined the wooden walls.

Jackie led the way over to a table holding two canvas packs. She took a booklet from beside one of the packs and handed it to Helen.

Helen, these are Irving Model A parachutes," Jackie pronounced. "The one on the left is mine; the one on the right is now yours. Here are the use and care instructions." She handed the booklet to a surprised Helen.

"W-Why?" Helen stammered.

"Because as an employee of Wain Engineering, you deserve to be kept as safe as we can make you. With these aircraft, the odds you'll need to get out of one of 'em quickly sometime are about a hundred percent. This will save your life—it's saved mine."

Helen flipped through the booklet, then looked at Jackie. "Thank you. This is a real surprise!"

"More to come," the older pilot said, heading for the hallway. "I have to change—back in a couple minutes."

Helen turned over the parachute and started to figure out the straps attached to it.

"Back," Jackie announced. Helen turned to look, and her mouth dropped open.

Jackie stood before her in the green coveralls she had worn when she first took Helen up. However, the coveralls now sported...*what?*

Jackie grinned. "Looks a little different, eh? Let me explain the *adornments*."

Helen just stared as Jackie pointed to various things.

"This garment is called a *flight suit*, she began, "although certain members of the surface ship Navy refer to those of us who wear it as *green bags*." Jackie snickered, and after a moment Helen smiled.

"Those patches on your suit are very pretty," Helen said, "You didn't wear them when you took me up that day."

"No, I didn't," Jackie replied, "because they're not just decoration—they represent what I did before I came out here. I want to explain them to you, to get the discussion started."

"What discussion?"

"You've asked about my training, and these patches tell the story." Jackie continued, pointing to her right shoulder, "This is the patch for *Fleet Logistics Support Squadron Three Zero*, usually called *VRC-30*. We flew people and critical supplies on and off aircraft carriers at sea. I flew a tour as a pilot with the squadron, returned as Executive Officer, and became Commanding Officer when the previous C.O. died suddenly of a heart attack. I served a tour and a half as squadron C.O. Helen, you might want to sit down—you're getting wobbly."

Helen sat down in a nearby folding chair with a thump. Jackie, smiling, continued.

"Next, on my right front is a patch given to me by the Grumman Aircraft Corporation when I logged my four thousandth flight hour in their aircraft, the C-2A *Greyhound*. That's what it looks like from the front. Beautiful bird, even though it has a fuselage the size of a small barn!"

Helen just stared at Jackie.

"Now, on my left shoulder above the American flag is the patch of the aircraft carrier *USS Kitty Hawk*, named after the place where the Wright Brothers first flew. I served as Assistant Air Officer on her, until the Air Officer became ill, then I became Air Officer, or

Air Boss, in charge of all the aviation work done on the carrier, until I retired last year and came out here."

Helen finally spoke. "I've seen pictures of the Royal Navy aircraft carriers, but we don't have any yet. How could you do all this when we don't have carriers?"

Jackie nodded. "Where—and *when*—I came from, we had them. Let me finish up here, then I'll explain. On my epaulettes here," she pointed to her shoulders, "are my rank insignia—I could always tell 'em to *watch the birdie!* And on my left front here is my name tag." She pulled it off her flight suit and handed it to Helen.

Helen stared at the tag. Underneath an embroidered set of Naval Aviator's wings she read:

Jacqueline Brighthonor
CAPT USN   *Big Bird*

"*Big Bird* was my Navy call sign, or nickname," Jackie added, "My maiden name was Byrd"

Helen handed the name tag back to Jackie, looked her square in the eyes, and spoke.

"What universe are you from, anyway?"

"Let's get the airplane preflighted, and I'll tell you."

*****

Jackie and Helen: On the way to Chicago.

The modified Curtiss JN-4H plodded toward Chicago behind the muffled buzz of the *vastly different* motor.

"That Rotax is way more reliable than the Hisso this ship came with, but it doesn't help the speed any," Jackie remarked through the intercom between the ladies' helmets. "Now that I've explained what's going on, do you have any questions?"

"Oh, do I!" Helen replied, the microphone in front of her lips picking up her voice clearly. "First question: If you come from a universe with the same people in it, don't you know what's going to happen here way before it does?"

Jackie thought a moment before replying.

"Yes...and no. The big things that happened back there are likely to happen the same way here. We have a list of those events we call *the script*, and we try to predict what's going to happen here, at least for the big events. For instance, World War One happened on schedule, and close to the way it did back where we came from."

209

"That makes as much sense as anything else you've told me so far, Jackie. What about the *no*?"

"We've found some events and people don't turn out like they did where we came from. For example, the Democratic Party Convention earlier this month nominated Cox and Roosevelt for their ticket, and not Wilson—that happened in our universe. However, in our history Wilson had suffered a severe stroke in 1919, and though he tried to influence the convention they ignored him. Here he's still in good health, pounding around the convention trying to get nominated for a third term, and they *still* ignored him! So it's the same thing, only different—sorry, I just had to say that!"

Helen snorted. "This whole business is like that!" She was silent for a moment. "What about *me* in that other universe? I *am* there, aren't I?"

"Yes, you are," Jackie replied, "but as far as I know, you didn't fly. Don says you taught him history and geography in the middle 1960s, but he doesn't remember much about you, except you lived in your folks' house on West South street, never married, and had a mean right hook to whack students when they misbehaved!"

Now Helen laughed—the sound distorted as the intercom tried to transmit it. "I don't hit students here—never will, by God's Grace!" Then Jackie could hear a catch in her voice. "But does that mean I'll never get married here?"

"I don't know if you will or not," Jackie replied, "but the one thing I do know is you're doing things right now you never did there—most girls your age would never dream of doing, let alone have a chance to make a second career if you want. Your life is completely different from the Helen Smiley in that other universe. I don't know if you'll ever get married, but you sure *could*!"

Jackie began to descend toward Checkerboard Field, visible through some haze in the distance.

Helen finally spoke. "Thanks for telling me straight, Jackie. I'll be a while sorting it out, but I think I see my place in all this. And I won't talk about it to anyone, not even Syl."

"We'd really appreciate that, Helen," Jackie spoke softly, the intercom amplifying her voice so Helen could hear. "I think some day Syl might become involved with our organization, but not just yet. I think you understand why all this can't become common knowledge."

"I do," Helen replied, "and you might be surprised how well I can keep a secret."

"I'm glad," Jackie said with a chuckle, "now let me show you the quirks to landing this beast, and we'll go have lunch with Gil. He's one of our partners, and knows everything I've told you today."

*****

Jackie, Helen, and Gil: Saturday, July 24th, 1920, 1PM, a diner near Checkerboard field, Maywood.

"This food's not bad," Jackie remarked as she dug in to her baked perch.

"Only place in town I know of that does fish right," Gil Foster added. "How's your pork chop, Helen?"

Helen raised a finger before she swallowed. "Great, Gil! Cooked just like I like them."

Gil Foster met Jackie and Helen when they landed, and drove them to a nearby restaurant. Jackie took off her patches and stowed them in the airplane before they left the field.

"So you're from this time?" Helen asked.

"Right," Gil replied, "After I was released from the prisoner of war camp I was brought back to the States and discharged. I met Dick Meriden while I was over in France, and he got me an interview with Don. They decided they liked me, and hired me. I've been briefed on the company and its mission, and now it's time to go to work!"

"What are you going to do up here?" Helen asked.

"Little bit of everything. I'm going to be what we call a *fixed-base operator*. We'll provide supplies and services to plane owners, probably buy and sell used aircraft, and sell new airplanes if we can find a company we can work with that isn't building junk."

"How's that going to help Wain Engineering in the long run?" Helen asked.

"We get our foot in the door of the aviation world," Gil replied, "People will think of us as the place to go for airplanes and supplies. Then, when we're established, we can start introducing new bits and pieces for existing aircraft."

"And if we can cut some sort of deal with Hugo Junkers, we can partner with him to bring out truly advanced ships, with motors that don't self-destruct!" Jackie added.

"I'd really like that! Where's my place in all this?"

211

Jackie put down her fork. "On weekends, and during the summers, we'd like you to ferry airplanes around the Midwest, whatever Gil has going at the moment. You can use my ship to fly up here as needed. That'll get you time in many different aircraft, and increase your piloting skill relatively quickly. Just keep wearing that parachute!"

"Oh I will, no doubt about that!" Helen smiled. "I think I'm gonna enjoy this."

"Maybe, maybe not," Jackie said, "When you're not flying for Gil, I want to give you as much advanced training as I can. Flight planning, weather knowledge, a little of the physics of flight. Help you fly with your *brain*, besides the seat of your pants!"

"That'll give me something to think about besides teaching."

"Right," Gill said, "I've heard teaching is hard work; you might need something to take your mind off it once in a while."

"Plus," Jackie added, "eventually you'll be able to teach others how to fly, and give the Aero Club exam. It may not pay much, but I think you'd enjoy the challenge!"

Helen swallowed the last bit of pork chop. "How can I ever thank you for giving me this opportunity?"

"Keep doing what you're doing," Jackie put her hand on Helen's shoulder, "and keep helping Sylvia in that classroom. I think you'll have your own classroom somewhere soon enough."

"And you get to fly us home," Jackie added.

*****

Sylvia, supper that evening.

"So, how did the flying with Jackie go?" I asked as we sat at the supper table.

"Better than I could ever have imagined, Syl!" my old friend replied, "I have a job flying for Wain Engineering and Gil Foster weekends and summers. I'll be learning advanced skills from Jackie when I'm not ferrying planes all around."

"Not much time for yourself."

"No, but my two jobs are so different I'll be able to rest from the one while doing the other."

"So which is first priority?" I asked.

"Teaching, no question," Helen nodded her head once. "That's how the Lord set it up, and I'm not going to change it on Him."

I picked up the dishes and walked to the sink. "I'm sure glad you're staying here another year. I've really appreciated your help—and company."

"Me too, Syl. Maybe next year I can find a position. But for now, I'm just so blessed, in ways I can't even describe!"

Helen joined me as we washed the dishes.

Chapter Thirty Six

Sylvia: Saturday, August 16th, 1920, just before 3 PM, District Fairgrounds, Galesburg.

I was sitting in the stands at the District Fair on a hot August afternoon, wondering how I managed to get talked into being there. Helen had asked me to come with her for the afternoon, and even though we only had two weeks till the start of school, I agreed. I wanted to support Helen in whatever she was doing today…but she wouldn't tell me what that was!

I figured she was flying with Ruth Law's circus in some capacity this afternoon, but so far all I had experienced was a succession of livestock exhibits, home economics projects, new automobiles, crowds of people, heat, and flies—lots and lots of flies! I was sitting down, but my hat wasn't large enough to keep the sun off my face and neck, and I sunburn easily. I also did not enjoy trying to keep flies out of my Coca-Cola.

While I was engaged in my little pity party (I knew it was wrong, but I couldn't help it!), another woman climbed the bleacher steps and sat down next to me.

"Hi, Jackie," I said, "Surprised to see you here this afternoon."

"Had to come out and watch the flying," Jackie replied, pulling a small fan from her dress pocket. I noticed her skin seemed well-tanned, and the skin around her eyes wrinkled as she smiled. "Where's Helen?" she asked.

"She told me she'd see me later about a half hour ago," I replied, "I don't know where she went."

"I'm sure she'll turn up. Ev's with Don and Pam Wain around here someplace. Oh—looks like the next event." Jackie pointed to the field.

Three people in flying gear walked over to two JN-4s parked in the infield. I thought the first person might be Ruth Law, judging from the person's height; the others I couldn't tell from where I sat. Two people got into one plane, one into the other. The ground crew swung the propellers, and the two planes taxied out on the track. They took off together, and began to circle the fairgrounds, gaining altitude.

They passed over the infield of the track, one just below the other, several times. Then, a rope ladder dropped from the back cockpit of the higher plane, followed by the occupant of that cockpit! He climbed down the ladder until he was hanging just below the body of the plane.

I didn't think Helen was the person over the side, but I wasn't entirely sure!

As the planes circled the fairgrounds, the person over the side of the first plane gradually worked lower on the rope ladder. Then, as they swept over the infield again, the second plane moved directly underneath the first. The person let go of the ladder and dropped into the rear cockpit of the second plane!

"Neat trick," Jackie observed.

"Helen tells me that's a pretty routine stunt for the flying circus. I sure wouldn't want to do it!"

"Me neither," Jackie said with a snort, "I'd rather stay in my airplane."

The two planes circled the field once more, then the top plane climbed and turned away, circling off to the north. The second plane picked up speed, and climbed.

That pilot then began a full set of aerobatic maneuvers—loops, dives, climbs, and other gyrations I had no clue what they were called. Every so often the pilot would just roll the ship upside down, flying along like that for a few seconds until the engine started to sputter, then roll upright again, eight times by my count.

"That plane's got a Hispano-Suiza engine in it—I can tell by the sound," Jackie said, "More power for the aerobatics, and a lot more reliable."

The pilot then climbed for two or three minutes, then sent the plane into a spin over the open field just south of the grandstand. The crowd wasn't expecting that, and I heard gasps and a couple of screams around me.

"Atta girl," Jackie said softly.

I turned to Jackie. "Is that Helen flying?"

"Yes. She told me not to tell you unless you asked."

The plane recovered and pulled out about as high as the plane that flew up Main Street the previous month. As the plane flew past the grandstand at that same height, the pilot—Helen—lifted an arm and waved to the crowd. The occupant of the rear cockpit just sat and stared straight ahead. I noticed some sort of substance on the side of the aeroplane right under the rear cockpit I hadn't seen before.

"Is that stuff under the back cockpit what I think it is?" I asked Jackie.

"Yep," Jackie replied, then smirked. "Mission accomplished. Explain later," she added.

215

The other Curtiss came up behind the aerobat, and flew just behind the first plane. The two planes circled once, and landed almost together on the backstretch of the track. They turned, and taxied up in front of the grandstand. The engines cut off at the same time.

Loud applause started as the three aviators got out of the aeroplanes. The first one took off her flying helmet, and waved. It was Ruth Law, as I figured.

The second one, who had transferred between planes, took off his helmet, and waved. This was a young man I did not know. He looked just a little pale, for some reason. It appeared even daredevils could get airsick!

The third person, the pilot of the lower plane, stepped out, took off her helmet, and waved to the crowd. Of course, it was Helen!

The crowd cheered loudly for Helen and her performance. She bowed a couple of times, then the trio headed off to a tent in the infield as another JN-4 was being started.

Jackie stood up and motioned to me. "Come on, Syl. Helen asked me to bring you to the infield tent when she was done."

"OK Jackie, just let me finish this Coke."

"Finish it on the way. Let's go!" Jackie spoke in her *command voice*.

So off we trudged, down the bleachers, through a gate in the fence, across the track, and over to the tent. Jackie pulled open the flap, and I went in.

Helen jumped up and ran over to hug me. "I did it, Syl! Ruth said my flying in the transfer, and the exhibition were flawless!"

"That's right," Ruth said from another chair. "Helen, you had that routine nailed!"

The third aviator just sat in his chair and groaned. He wiped his brow with a handkerchief.

Ruth looked over at him and snorted. "You had it coming, Al! Gorge yourself on fried oysters and chocolates at the buffet tent, then expect to go flying! No wonder you turned that ship into a *Vomit Comet*!"

I giggled; I'd never heard that phrase before, but it sure fit!

"It wasn't supposed to be an aerobatic display, Ruth."

"Al, I've told you time and time again to be ready for *anything* in my shows! You were about as ready for that routine as I was last month when you flew up the main street of this town, which has so graciously let us base here and use their fairgrounds, you flew up their street at *naught feet*!"

Ruth folded her arms in front of her and gave Al *The Look*.

"As I said, Al, you're a great pilot, but you had this one coming!"

Al hung his head. "I'll be gone by dark, Ruth."

"Don't you dare! I want you to improve, as a pilot and as a *man*. If I didn't care, I'd just kick your can out of here. If you didn't care, you'd just slink off like a whipped cur! I care; do you?"

Al looked up at Ruth. I think I saw his eyes filling.

"I'm sorry, Ruth. I wasn't thinking. And I'll stay, if you'll let me."

"Yes, Al, I'll let you stay. Now get out of here and go get cleaned up. You fly in an hour!"

Al scrambled to leave the tent.

Ruth Law looked at the assembled group.

"I believe that settles the matter. Helen, I'm glad you and Sylvia were downtown when *The Al Wilson One Man Terror Squad* came through. I hope what I said, plus your really grand aerobatic routine, not to mention the fun of cleaning up that aeroplane, will have the right effect. If it doesn't he will go away, and that will be that!"

Helen beamed again. "Thanks for all your kindness, Ruth."

"Thank *you*, Helen, for *your* kindness…and that little matter about a month ago!"

*****

Sylvia and Helen, later that afternoon.

We were on the Fremont Road, driving home. The drive would have been boring, but Helen and I were talking.

"Once again, you've impressed me. I had no idea you were so good at that kind of flying. Is that what you've been learning the past year?"

"Some. I wanted to learn the aerobatics mostly for fun. What I really concentrated on was flying across country, learning the aeroplane, and learning to watch the weather for danger. And learning what to do in an emergency."

"I guess you learned that pretty well!"

"I guess I did, what they taught me. Now Jackie is going to give me the *advanced course* over the next few years. She wants me to be ready for anything when I fly for them."

"Most pilots don't plan for emergencies?"

217

"Nope. Most of 'em only think about the fancy maneuvers, and getting up in the *freedom of the sky*! That's fine, until something breaks. And with those OX-5s, something *always* breaks."

"If they're so unreliable, why are people still using them?"

"Jackie isn't—she's got an experimental engine in her Jenny that's very reliable. And I was flying Ruth's best airplane, with the Hisso engine."

"And everybody else?"

Helen snorted. "Because the government built umpteen thousand of them for the war, and the war ended. Ruth said it only cost twenty five dollars to buy a brand new engine to replace the one we blew that day! Put it in, test-run it once, and fly—that's what they do."

"Not very safe, is it?"

"Not at all! Could be worse; Hall-Scott made an engine for these things that was so bad the government just collected them all and scrapped them!"

"What a waste!"

"War wastes—but let's not talk about that right now, Syl"

I was perfectly happy to change the subject.

"There's another reason I won't fly with Ruth full time," my friend continued, "She's great herself, but some of her people I wouldn't trust with my hat, much less with my life."

Helen moved the pedal to low as we approached one of the sharp corners on the Fremont Road. As we accelerated out of the turn she spoke again.

"Besides, Al Wilson tried to put the make on me."

"What?"

"Yep. Asked me for a date. Several times. Seemed loath to take 'no' for an answer. I finally had to get direct."

"You can do that pretty well; I've watched you in the classroom."

"That's the voice I had to use, with the face to match. That settled it."

I thought of something, and turned to Helen with a grin. "So there was *extra motivation* for your performance today?"

Helen giggled. "Oh yeah! Ruth and I talked about that stunt he pulled last month. She really didn't know about it until after he did it, and she had to do a lot of apologizing to the City Fathers to stay at the fairgrounds. She wanted to teach him a lesson, and knew she had to get his attention. That's where I came in. The aerobatics were pre-planned; I threw in the inverted flight when I heard what he ate for lunch."

218

"Was that what I thought it was on the side of the plane?"

"Oh, yes! He kept yelling for me to stop—I could even hear him over the engine—but I ignored him. I made sure the slipstream would carry...*it*...down and behind me. Caught a whiff every now and then."

"But couldn't he have taken over the controls?"

"Oh, no! When they do that stunt they take out the control stick in the back cockpit. Otherwise, when the visitor drops in there he could jam the stick over accidentally....or miss the seat."

We both giggled as we thought of that result.

"Anyway, Helen, I hope he's learned his lesson!"

"Which one—don't fly low over Main Street, or don't mess with Helen Smiley?"

"Yes."

Helen laughed. "I'm sure he got the second one!" She sobered. "As for the first...Ruth said she's seen his type before. He also hits the bottle too much. She figures she'll have to fire him soon, hopefully before he kills himself flying in her company."

"Or kills a passenger."

"That too. Ruth is sure one of these days the Government is going to step in and require standardized licenses for pilots. She maintains high standards for the people she tests for the Aero Club, but anyone with a little money can buy a plane and go flying. Or go kill themselves. That's why I wanted the Aero Club license."

We passed the road to the Hagenfield Cemetery. I always glanced down that road—I'm not sure what I expected to see.

"You sure you want to keep doing this?" I asked Helen.

"Yes, I do. It's not my first priority of course—my teaching is. But the Lord's let me keep this on as a second job, I guess you could say. I enjoy it, and I try to be careful at it. Careful pilots tend to last longer, and the Lord has me in His service anyway, so I'll keep it up on the side."

"What about marriage?"

"What about it?"

"Someone might come along some day."

"So he might. Might happen to you, too."

"I've already been married."

Helen looked over and saw my face.

"Syl, you never know when someone special will come along. Could happen to me too...and I figure when it happens, we'll know it."

"I guess so. It's not like I have any fanciful notions about married life..."

"I should say not!"

"Guess we just wait on the Lord, and see who He drops into our lives"

"Like Al Wilson dropped into the back seat of the Curtiss?"

We both laughed at that.

Helen stopped at the Appleton Road, then eased across.

"Helen, you realize Fred, Violet, and the School Board pray regularly for us."

"That the Lord will bless our work at the school?"

"That...and that we'll each find the Lord's choice for a mate."

"Figures. Guess we'll see, Syl."

"Guess we will."

Chapter Thirty Seven

Luther: Thursday, August 4th, 1921, right after lunch, Johns Hopkins Hospital, Baltimore.

Steve Mason watched me walk, turn, crouch, and perform several other gyrations with my prosthesis in the examining room.

"OK, Luther, that's all. Go ahead and put your pants back on while we talk."

I retrieved my trousers while Steve wrote on his clipboard.

"I meant to tell you, Bill sends his regards. He's teaching in the Medical School all day today and couldn't get away. He said to let him know if the prosthesis goes on backward now!"

"Believe it or not, I've actually done that a few times! Middle of the night, not really awake, you know."

"You're not the first one. Did you walk in circles then?"

We laughed at that one. Then, I got serious.

"How does it look, Steve?"

"Really great, Luther! The changes we made to the socket last year are holding fine, and haven't deteriorated. Next year we'll do another pair of prostheses, since they wear down over time. You'll keep your old ones, of course, and use them if you need to. Can't have too many spares!"

"I'm surprised they aren't worn out by now."

"They're pretty sturdy, and to be honest, we overbuilt yours, not knowing how active you'd be with them. The only wear I see is a little on the edge of the sides of the foot. That's odd; most of the time they wear more on the toe and heel."

"I wonder if it's my organ playing?"

Steve snapped his fingers. "That's got to be it! We don't have any other *customers* who are organists. I'll mention it in my notes here. Are you able to play the pedals OK?"

"Believe it or not, yes," I replied, "I have to make sure the prosthesis is centered on the stump, and the straps are placed right, but then I can go almost as fast as I did before. And if I have to, I can compensate for the pedal parts. I'd better be able to; I'm supposed to play the dedication recital of our church's rebuilt organ Sunday the 14th!"

"Is that the 'old squeak' you told me about last year? I told Francine the story about your offertory disaster and she almost fell off her chair laughing! With you, not at you—she's had it happen several times herself! She purely hates tubular pneumatics."

"So do I. We fixed that, though- the new chests are by Wicks, with their new Direct Electric action."

"I've heard of them. Any good?"

"I think they're the best available, and I went to them first when we decided to do something permanent about Old Squeak. The owner wants me to work for them."

"Will you?" Steve asked.

"I think in another year or so, part time maybe, if my classes keep going like they have."

"And how are your classes going?"

"Much better than I ever expected. I have to work, but it's not drudgery. And I'm understanding what they're teaching."

"Have you come up with a specialty yet?"

"Not really. I've gotten most of my mathematics courses out of the way, and started to take courses in specific areas-everything from hydrodynamics to electronics. Believe it or not, it's all interconnected."

"I've found that to be true in my field too."

"Same Builder."

Steve nodded. "I guess so. Say, can you stick around a while this afternoon? Francine wants us to meet her at our church for some *organ bashing*, and then come to dinner afterwards, if you're available."

"I'd like that, Steve! I don't leave until tomorrow morning. Did I tell you I'm stopping at Mansfield, Ohio, to be in Gary Folkerts' wedding? Jack Sewell's on leave from the *Idaho*, and I'm meeting him there. Then we go back to Metamora and he gets to help in my recital on the 14th!"

"That's all great news! Does Jack know he's helping?"

"No, but he's pushed presets for me before. He reads music; used to play a little trumpet in High School. He needs the practice."

"Are you gentlemen doing the Arch of Swords for Gary?"

"Well...yes. First time I'll be in my uniform in public since I retired. I had to pick up a few items out here for it."

"You sound a bit tentative, Luther. Is The Medal still bothering you?"

"A little. Jack helped me work through it after I got it, and time puts things in perspective to a degree."

"The last thing I wanted was the NC for that little business at the aid station. But...I figured for better or worse, they caught me, so I might as well just go with it! If I may give advice..."

"I understand, and I agree. I don't know which bothers me more, getting back into the uniform for something as *militarily precise* as the Swords, or putting that Medal with the Blue Ribbon on again."

Steve closed the cover on his clipboard. "Look at it this way. Are you in charge?"

"Not this time; Jack's senior now."

"Then make sure you're one of the last two. What's a whack on the bottom among friends?"

We both laughed.

Francine Mason was the regular organist at the Catholic church they attended in a suburb of Baltimore. We spent a delightful hour and a half playing for each other, with Steve lounging on the front bench listening.

She played some of her standard service things, and I played a couple of the pieces I had worked up for the recital. I also improvised a bit, to get a feel for the big Skinner organ. It had a lovely tone, but was a handful to control. I didn't envy Francine trying to play anything but routine services on it.

I also played a few Gospel hymns on the organ, probably the first and last time that ever happened! Francine particularly liked "The Old Rugged Cross", and I sent her a copy when I got home. Unfortunately I couldn't sing the words for her. I have the singing voice of a half-strangled toad, and he was most happy to be relieved of it! That's why I never got into song leading. I could do everything a song leader does except sing the songs myself, which just doesn't work in a service.

Over dinner at a nice restaurant, we talked organs and music. Steve had an interest in the music his wife played, sang in their choir, and contributed to the conversation from a singer's viewpoint. I couldn't find an opening to present the Gospel, unfortunately.

Next morning I was off on another cross-country train trip, courtesy of the Baltimore and Ohio Railroad. I arrived in Mansfield early Saturday morning, and met Gary at the station. Jack arrived a few minutes later from Chicago.

We collected our baggage, and piled into Gary's Dodge Brothers sedan. He showed us the church- a typical Apostolic Christian building with Eastern European touches, and then took us by to meet his bride and her family, with whom we'd be staying. We found his betrothed was named Elizabeth Anna...Steffen. Matthew had been the oldest child in the family. After an awkward, stammering moment, we were put at ease by Mr. and Mrs. Steffen, and the other children. They said they had grieved, and had been given the peace of the Lord about the matter. And that was that.

223

Jack and I enjoyed watching the family interact, especially the prospective son in law interacting with his betrothed. They did not touch; their conversation was unusually formal, but every so often we'd see them giving each other *That Look*…and figured out that conveyed all they needed to say to each other! This was going to be a fun wedding.

Later that evening, after the bride-to-be and the other children had gone to bed, Jack and I sat with the Steffens in their parlor, sipping herbal tea.

Mr. Steffen spoke. "Now, in the privacy of this room, we'd like to hear the story of the time you were with Matthew—all of it, even the death. Gary has declined to speak of those times, except in the most general way. The letter we received from Lieutenant Commander Kittridge was a great blessing in our time of grief, but we understood there were some details he did not feel at liberty to disclose. Now we need to hear them."

I looked at Jack, and he looked at me. Taking turns, we told the tale, from meeting Gary and Matthew in Colonel Finney's office to that meeting around the table on the *New Jersey*, the morning after he did it. We left nothing out. Mrs. Steffen gasped when Jack described the stain on the overhead, but they insisted we continue. They shed no tears; they'd already done that years before.

When we finished Mrs. Steffen looked out the parlor window at the gas-lit street. She then turned to us, and spoke softly, with an accent I could not place.

"Thank you, gentlemen, for telling us this information. It is as we imagined, unfortunately. Thank you, Sergeant Sewell, for making one last effort to talk with Matthew about his soul. Do not feel bad, either of you, that he would not listen. We, and the church, prayed continually for his salvation, and tried to reach out to him, but he would have none of it. The harder we prayed, the faster he ran. Gary was right; after Matthew was wounded, he could run no more. And as Commander Kittridge said, he was presented with a choice. And because our Lord gives us freedom to choose, he chose. And here we are. Luther, Gary tells us you had something similar happen to you; please tell us about it."

I recounted my life of running from the Lord, how He got my attention, and my life since I chose.

The Steffens nodded gravely. When I was done, Mr. Steffen spoke.

"Glory to God! We are so glad you made that choice, and were born again! We wish Matthew had done the same, but we rejoice in your salvation, and your calling according to His purpose."

The Steffens spoke formally, but we could tell they meant what they said from their hearts. Jack and I compared notes later, and agreed we were humbled in the presence of this family, who trusted the Lord through that kind of experience. We could learn from them.

*****

Luther: the next morning.

Even though Jack and I had grown up with a number of AC friends, we had never attended their services before, and never been to one of their weddings—one and the same, for the weddings were held on Sundays after the afternoon service. This, like so many practices of the AC church, was rooted in practicality, in this case getting everything done on one day, so the people who had to travel in by horse and buggy only had to make one trip.

The standard Wedding Day consisted of a church service in the morning, a dinner routinely produced by the ladies of the church (and, like every group of AC women I've ever met, they could really cook!), and an afternoon service directly after dinner. Added today was the wedding ceremony and reception after the afternoon service. It made for a happy day, but a long one.

It was particularly long for the bride and groom, who had to go through the normal Sunday routines knowing what was coming at the end of the day! Gary's day was further disrupted when he found out the minister in the rotation scheduled to preach the morning service had been admitted to the hospital overnight, and Gary as the next up had to take over at short notice to preach the morning service! He was also dressed in his Navy Dress White uniform, which made his presence in the pulpit that morning doubly unusual. Gary was up for the task, though; he preached an excellent message that morning.

During the noon meal, various church members came by and spoke with Jack and me. We discussed various topics, but nobody said anything about the war, or our medals. I suspected Gary had a word with the congregation before our arrival. I felt uncomfortable in the stiff dress uniform again; Jack was much more used to the uniform since a lot of what the Marines did on a battleship involved wearing the dress uniform. At any rate, our uniforms would need to go to the cleaners when the day was done.

After the second service, Gary and Elizabeth Anna walked by themselves to stand before the minister who preached the afternoon

225

message, and repeated their wedding vows. I was impressed by the simple yet solemn service.

After the reception came the Arch of Swords. Jack led the detail; I got one of the two spots closest to him. The other members of the detail were Marine friends of Gary's from the platoon he served. Two of them were men he had rescued in the action where he was wounded, and won the Navy Cross.

To the untrained eye we performed the drill very well, but each of us knew where we messed up, and would practice some more on our own before trying this again. I must report, however, we performed the whack on the backsides without error! Gary hadn't warned the congregation about that!

After the Arch of Swords, everyone went home…except Elizabeth Anna now went to a new home, with Gary. Very quiet, very economical…and very appropriate.

The next morning Gary and Elizabeth Anna drove by in his Dodge to collect Jack and me to take us to the train station! I was amazed by this, but according to Gary farm work had to take priority, and a honeymoon away from the farm just wasn't going to happen for a while. Fortunately, the congregation left them alone after the reception, so they could get started on their new life together with a minimum of disruptions—except us.

Eventually we shook hands all around, got our baggage aboard the outgoing B&O express to Chicago, and took off. We sat in our seats in the day coach for a few minutes in silence, as we left the city of Mansfield behind. Finally Jack's mouth quirked, and he spoke.

"Mighty nice of Gary and Elizabeth Anna to take us to the train station."

"Yeah, especially since they seemed so tired…"

"You noticed that too?"

"Hard not to, as much as both of them yawned."

"Could hardly keep their eyes open, Luther."

"Nope. Their color sure seemed good though, so I guess they weren't sick."

"Now that you mention it, they did seem to be glowing a bit…"

Jack and I looked at each other, and laughed for ten minutes straight.

Chapter Thirty Eight

Sylvia: Thursday, June 16th, 1921, around 10 AM. The Fremont Road.

Life was changing again for me this summer. Helen had applied to teach in the Galesburg schools, and had left early this morning to go to an interview with a building Principal. I was going to have to adjust—not only to running the classroom by myself, but living alone too. I had gotten used to Helen living in the house, and though we would see each other often I would still miss her.

This morning I was headed over to Appleton with some asparagus from my *specialty* garden for Deborah. For some reason that vegetable grew happily in the soil of our yard, where even dandelions were stunted. After years of trying to make other things grow, Ma had given up and become the asparagus supplier to the church. I had continued the arrangement, trading asparagus for some of the wonderful fresh produce the other members grew.

I closed up the house and walked to the garage. Starting the Model T was an unvarying ritual, performed by millions all over the world. Mine always started, but cranking it got old. I would miss that old beat-up touring car of Helen's, and its self-starter. The first rule of my car was always to back it into the garage, so I didn't have to crank in the dark.

I slowly pulled out of the garage and stopped to close the doors, then got back in to go. When I got to the foot of the driveway I looked both ways as usual. To the east, I saw a small figure running up the road toward me. At first I couldn't make out whether it was an animal or a person, so I decided to wait until I knew for sure before I got out on the road.

The figure resolved into little Laney Johnson, all of three years old, running down the road for all he was worth! I knew from Violet that Laney was a very good boy who never did anything impulsive or malicious; this behavior was unheard of. Something must be wrong.

I set the hand brake and got out of the car. Laney saw me and started waving his little arms and yelling. Mercifully, there was no traffic on the Fremont Road that morning.

He ran up to me. I crouched down and caught him in my arms. His white blond hair flew in all directions, and he kept panting, out of breath.

"Laney, what is the matter?"

Between gasps, Laney spoke single words.

"Mama...sick...hurt...come...quick!"

I scooped him up in my arms and deposited him on the passenger seat of the Ford. I ran around to the driver's side and got in. A Ford will get moving quickly when properly persuaded, and that morning I persuaded.

We pulled into the Johnson farmyard at a rush, with a liberal application of the Rocky Mountain brakes. I jumped out of the car and ran around to get Laney out, but he had already opened the door and jumped down. We ran to the house, and entered through the open front door.

I heard a moan coming from the side bedroom, and a child's voice. "Who's there?"

"Sylvia and Laney!" I yelled as we moved toward the room.

I found Violet Johnson stretched out on the bed, holding her expanded stomach. I felt a chill go through me as I realized she could be experiencing what I had suffered three years before.

Her other son Pacey was standing by his mother. It looked like he had been crying, but now he only looked scared.

"Violet, what can you tell me?"

"Just hit me about a half hour ago...terrible pain...I don't think it's labor...constant."

"Where's Fred?"

"South...forty...with...Sigmar...and...Billy."

I turned to Pacey. "Are you able to run that far to tell them what's going on?"

"Yes, Ma'am!"

"Wait a minute before you go. Violet, we need to get you into my car. We'll take Laney and go to the Cottage Hospital in Galesburg. From there, I can call Helen or Bessie to come help us. We need to get you to the hospital right now!"

Violet shuddered as another spasm of pain traveled through her.

"OK, let's try this, Violet. Ready, set, Up!"

With me helping, Violet lurched to her feet. She leaned heavily on me as we slowly walked through the house and out to the car.

Pacey tried to help as I half-lifted Violet into the car. She dropped into the seat with a groan.

"OK...Thanks...Syl...Pacey, go tell...Pa...where we...are going."

"Yes, Ma!"

Pacey ran off down the lane between the cornfields.

I put Laney in the center of the seat, and cranked the car. The cranking actually helped me calm down—about the only good purpose I've ever found for the action!

I got in, and we took off toward Galesburg. As we got close to the Appleton Road, I saw a vehicle turn off the Appleton Road toward us. It was the unmistakable car of Deborah Kittridge! We met and stopped in the road.

"I decided to bring you over some rhubarb and pick up the asparagus since I was going to town. Syl, what's going on?"

"Violet has terrible pain in her abdomen. Laney ran down to get me. I'm taking them to the Cottage Hospital. Pacey ran off to get his Pa."

Deborah, as usual, snapped into her 'all business' mode. "Right. Got it. Where is Fred?"

"Violet said south forty, with Sigmar and Billy."

"I will pick them up and take them to the hospital, after I go by home and tell AP. I expect to be there within the hour. I'll be praying as I go. Now scoot!"

With that, Deborah let out the clutch and took off with her back tires spitting gravel.

"That's our Deborah!" I said as I started again. Violet nodded, and managed a small grin which turned into a grimace as another wave of pain arrived.

Laney held on to his Ma's arm as we bumped along the graveled road. Violet leaned back in the seat, and occasionally groaned or gasped. I am not usually a fast driver, but my Pa had taught me how to safely drive an automobile faster than normal. I made good use of the two speed axle for the straight sections, and pulled on the Rocky Mountain brake lever when we came to the corners. Fortunately, we met no traffic that morning.

In the moments between praying for Violet to be OK, praying that Pacey would find his Pa, and praying we'd get around the next curve, I evaluated what I knew about Violet's condition. I was pretty sure it wasn't labor, even though she was about eight months along, more or less. She kept holding her right middle abdomen; when I had my attack I had screaming pain all over, not localized. This looked more like it was her appendix, or something. Maybe the baby annoyed it with his or her kicking; I remembered that feeling. I felt a twinge of sadness at that, then almost giggled. The old emotions weren't quite under control today!

Again I took Lincoln Street to Losey Street; I didn't want a train to slow us down. When we got to the hospital I ran inside and got the nurses; they brought a wheelchair to the car, and lifted Violet into it. Laney went with them into the building. I parked the car and trotted in.

The Head Nurse, whom I remembered from my stay here, walked up to me. She smiled.

"Are you here to sample our hospitality again, Sylvia?"

"Not this time, Gloria. I brought in Violet Johnson, the mother of one of my students. She is about 8 months pregnant, and began having severe pain this morning. Her other son ran down the road and found me."

Gloria's smile vanished.

"That's starting to sound like you when your Ma brought you in. I hope we don't have a repeat of that! Any idea where the pain might be centered?"

"She keeps holding her upper right side. She hasn't said specifically, though."

"Hmmm... appendix, maybe. You're fortunate, Doctor Bohan is just finishing a surgery upstairs. I told him we had another case for him down here, and he'll be along in a few minutes."

"Thanks a lot, Gloria. Did you see which room they put her in? I need to mind Laney, her youngest. We brought him with us."

"Does her husband know?"

"The older boy, Pacey, ran off to find him. Our Pastor's wife happened by in her car as we were leaving; she said she'd bring them in. I'll stay in any case."

"Good, Sylvia. Glad to see you by the way, and in slightly better circumstances than last time! They're over in room two."

"Thanks, Gloria."

I walked to the room, and went in.

Doctor Bohan came into the room about five minutes later. He shooed all of us out except one nurse, then he asked Gloria to come in and they closed the door.

I held Laney by the hand as I walked to the main desk, and asked to use the phone. I got Helen; she said she'd just gotten home. I told her what had happened, and she said she'd come over right away.

Right after I finished the call, Doctor Bohan came out of the examination room. He motioned us to another room on the other side of the hallway.

At that moment Deborah Kittridge walked swiftly into the lobby area, trailed by Fred and Pacey Johnson. She saw us, and strode over.

"As advertised, we are here! What's the situation?"

"Doctor Bohan has just finished examining Violet, and asked us to come into the room over there."

"OK. AP will be here in a few minutes. Let me take charge of Laney while you and these two go in to see the Doctor."

"Right. Laney, please stay with Mrs. Kittridge."

"Yes, Ma'am."

That *teacher* voice works every time!

Fred and Pacey followed me into the room. Neither one of them had yet to utter a word.

After he closed the door, Doctor Bohan turned back to us.

"If there is any good news in this situation, it's that I think Violet is suffering from acute appendicitis. That's dangerous, but we can fix that. And we have to, right away. If the appendix ruptures, the risks go up like a rocket. So I have to operate immediately."

Fred Johnson finally spoke. "What about the baby, Doctor?"

"The baby's heartbeat is good, and the little one is sure mobile in there! That's an excellent sign. What I'll do, is check the situation carefully once I get inside. I will probably go ahead and take the baby by cesarean section. She's far enough along that I don't think there will be any problems; no guarantee, of course."

"We'll pray to that end, Doctor."

"I know you will, Fred. Now let's go in and tell Violet what's going on."

We went in to Violet, Doctor Bohan told her what was going to happen, and we prayed with her briefly. Then, the nurses whisked her upstairs in the recently installed elevator to the operating theatre.

As we came out to the lobby/waiting area we met Pastor Kittridge coming in, closely followed by Helen. Fred and the boys decided to wait for the surgery to be over, along with Pastor Kittridge. Deborah suggested Helen and I come with her for lunch. Since there wasn't anything else we could do at the moment, we took her up on her offer.

Chapter Thirty Nine

Sylvia: Thursday, June 16th, 1921, American Beauty Restaurant and elsewhere.

We three got into Deborah's *sport utility* Cadillac. Deborah started the car, and we pulled out onto Seminary Street heading downtown.

"There's a new restaurant downtown I want to try; I've heard good things about it. Lunch is on me, by the way!"

"You don't have to do that, Deborah," I said.

"Time to celebrate, Syl! I just got a check from my publisher, and need to put it in the bank anyway. I was headed into town when I ran into you on the road."

"In that case, we surely thank you," Helen said.

We stopped for a train at the Santa Fe tracks heading downtown. I noticed something strapped to the steering column of the car I hadn't noticed before.

"Deborah, what is that gauge?" I pointed.

"Oh, that's a tachometer. It tells me how fast the engine is going. That way, I don't overspeed or lug the engine when I'm driving."

"Is it really useful?"

"It was this morning!"

We stopped at the Bank of Galesburg and Deborah deposited her check. Then we walked next door, where a sign proclaimed 'Newly Opened: American Beauty Restaurant'. We went in.

The dining room was long and a bit narrow. We slid into a booth near the back. Since it was just before the lunch hour, we were glad to have gotten in before the crowd

A gentleman in an apron came to take our order; I found out later he was the co-owner, Paul Poulos. At Deborah's suggestion, we ordered the chicken croquettes, which she said were one of their specialties.

We prayed for the food in advance, and included Violet and the Johnson family. Then, as we waited for the food I asked Deborah a question.

"How did you manage to find the Johnsons, drive to Appleton, then to Cottage, and get here that fast?"

Deborah grinned. "Well, I did cheat a little. Campbell Miller brought his Model T out to the south forty to carry tools to help

Fred and Sigmar fix some fence, and he offered to go to Appleton and tell AP. Made pretty good time, too…for a couple of Fords."

"You still had to be flying to get here as quickly as you did…those funny looks on Fred and Pacey's faces didn't have something to do with it, did they?"

Deborah giggled and took a sip of her water.

"I will only say that the top speed of the Cadillac model 51, which the specifications say is 70 miles per hour, is a bit understated."

"You didn't-!"

"77 on the long straight stretch of the Fremont Road."

Helen looked thoughtful. "The Curtiss I fly will barely make that, on a good day with a tailwind."

"I think the mechanics in Metamora did a little tinkering on their Service Car. It's always been faster than claimed, and handles better too."

I decided to hand Deborah a straight line. "So Fred and Pacey weren't so impressed with the rate of travel?"

"On the contrary! I've never before had the pleasure of a grown man and a boy begging me to slow down before I killed them."

Helen and I giggled.

"AP just shuts his eyes and prays…"

We started to laugh.

"…loudly."

We finally had to stifle ourselves because the other diners were starting to look at us funny.

"Deborah, I've never met anyone who could tell a funny story like you, especially on a day like this." I said softly.

Deborah sobered. "To tell you the truth, I had another reason to drive like that. When they got in the car, those two were as frightened as I've ever seen a human. They were terrified of losing Violet. I knew eventually the Lord would get through to them that she's in His hands, and He's taking care of her; until then, they were just about to melt down in panic. I decided to give them something else to worry about for a few minutes, until their hearts caught up to where the Lord wanted them to be. Worked, too!"

We were silent for a moment, then Helen spoke.

"With all due respect, Deborah, that is just about the looniest explanation of an action I've ever heard." *Pause.* "I love it! Gotta remember to try it myself some day!"

We all laughed then, as our food arrived on the arm of a rather perplexed Mr. Poulos.

"So, I haven't asked for a while, how's the writing coming along?" I asked as we started to eat.

Deborah's grin gave us the answer, but she elaborated.

"Great, Syl! That check I just deposited is the largest one I've ever received for my writing. After the Lord's tithe, it is still more than twice as large as my whole income from writing in every other year!"

"What happened?" I asked.

"I am still with the same publisher, but I am doing work for a writer's group working exclusively for that publisher. I am not allowed to go into specifics, but we produce books in series for the youth market. Ghost write 'em, actually. Several different series."

"You mean like the Har—," I began.

Deborah held up her palm. "Shhh! Whether it is or not, we can't even breathe a name of someone's series in public! Can't start speculation."

"I'm sorry, Deborah!"

"That's OK, Syl—you didn't know. I'm probably saying too much now, but I think I can keep it generalized, if you'll let me run with it that way."

"Sure, no problem. I heard nothing…," Helen said.

"Me neither," I added.

"Good. At any rate, I've been putting out about a book every six weeks."

"Wow!" Helen and I said together.

"Wow is right! Between the actual writing, and correcting the galley

proofs, all my free time is spent. I've put a lot of hours on the DelcoLight plant typing into the night too."

"Is it worth all that work?" Helen asked.

"I think so. Even though I am writing under a pseudonym, and not even my usual one, I'm still gaining lots of experience in writing, and *scripting*, my books. That'll come in handy in the future. Only one problem, though…"

I didn't know if this were real, or a setup for a punch line; Deborah was capable of both. "OK, I'll bite. What's the problem?"

Deborah was silent for a moment.

"You thought I was setting you up for a punch line?"

I blushed. Helen giggled.

"I wish I were, but for once I'm not. All that typing is really bothering my hands and wrists. It's starting to limit how much I can work per day. All the great book plots around won't help if I *can't type*!"

"Is there anything you can do?" Helen asked.

"I could hire a secretary to take down the books from dictation, but that costs more than I make. Or…"

I turned to Helen. "Here's where she tells us what she's already done!"

"Syl, one of these days you're going to turn up in one of my books!"

"With pleasure!" I fired back.

"You're getting entirely too good at this."

"Too much sparring with me," Helen volunteered.

"That must be it" Deborah declared. "Well, however you learn it, that skill will come in handy when you're keeping your husband in line! Works for me!"

"You sound confident husbands are in our future."

"I really am, Syl. I don't pray about it every day, like certain of our student's parents do," She winked. "But I have brought it to the Lord on occasion. He's given me peace that the situation will be handled according to His purpose, and that's good enough. He's given me that peace about other things, and they've come out fine. I rescued AP from bachelorhood, after all!"

We laughed at that, but also gave some thought to what she had said.

"Anyway, back to the matter at *hand*…"

Deborah expected a groan, and we gave it to her. She continued.

"I have found what I think is the solution. An electric typewriter! It does the hard work; all I do is press the keys lightly. Logical, isn't it? But would you believe there is exactly one brand of electric typewriter in existence that actually works? And they just stopped making them!"

"Why would they do that? Aren't there thousands of people who need one?"

"You'd think so, Syl, but three problems. One, price: $125.00. That's steep. Two, voltage. The voltage of electricity in homes is finally getting standardized in the cities, but while they were trying to sell the things nothing was standardized. They could make it to use any voltage and current, but not all of them and make any money. Plus, I need one for 32 volt direct current so it'll run on the DelcoLight. If we get power from Galesburg it'll be 120 volt Alternating Current. Complicates things."

I followed what she was saying, but just barely. That was usually taught in High School.

Deborah took a sip of her tea. "Three, fear—good 'ol unreasoning fear. Typists didn't want to be working so close to electricity. Afraid it'd leap out and strike 'em dead, I guess. So the company never sold enough to make money on the project. So they've stopped making the things."

Helen supplied the next straight line, with a wink. "So you won't be able to get one?"

I giggled again—I knew where this was heading.

"It so happens I contacted the company…the Blickensderfer Typewriter Company. That one's so weird I can't even use it in a book! I contacted them, and they gave me the name of someone in the area who has become the *de facto* distributor of some of their remaining stock of machines. He can fix them too, they said. And I know him!"

I took the bait. "New advanced product, nobody wants it, only one person can supply it, and you already know them. That sounds like a book in the Tom Sw—"

"Shhhh!"

I grinned.

Deborah nodded to me. *"Touche'*. I wouldn't want to be the first child in your class who tried to match wits with you!"

"Haven't had anyone really try yet…but I will."

Helen interrupted. "All right, you two. Let's get back to the story; I want to order dessert!"

We both grinned at her, and Deborah continued.

"The Electric Typewriter King of Illinois is…Howard Barlow! The same Howard Barlow who's a car dealer in Metamora, whose son relieved AP of his little indiscretion a couple years ago! Howard says that car is running fine, by the way."

"How'd he end up with typewriters in a car dealership?

"I asked him that, when I wrote him last week. He said he bought one in '04 for his office ladies, and they were too scared of it to even try it! He and his son have used one for years, and when he learned they were going to stop making them, he wired the company and they made a deal. Actually, I guess it was a rat killing deal."

Helen choked and sent her water out her nose.

"Are you all right, Helen?"

After a moment Helen was able to speak. "Wow! I wasn't expecting that one. You just reminded me of a joke I made when my folks gave me my car. I found out Pa paid next to nothing for it, and asked him if I'd find dead rats under the seats."

Now it was Deborah's turn to laugh and cough. "Did you?" she finally asked

"Eight cents and a petrified chicken leg."

"All right, I give," Deborah said a moment later when she could breathe. "You two have learned how to gang up on me. My work here is done."

A deep breath, then, "Anyway…in a few days I'm driving to Metamora to actually try one of the things, and if I like it I bring one home. 32 volts version for the Delco Light, of course. He says he has one. I'm actually looking forward to the trip."

"Not as fast as you went today, I hope."

"No, Syl, that speed's for emergencies only. And we had one today. I suppose we ought to get back, in case the gentlemen want to get something to eat. Helen, let's see what's on their dessert menu."

We each tried two pieces of filled chocolate candy for dessert— hazelnut cremes with drizzles of white chocolate on top, made in the restaurant. They were exquisite, as was the rest of the meal. We hoped the place would stay around a while.

We returned to the hospital to find the men and boys still sitting quietly in the waiting room. Pastor said they had prayed for quite a while, and then just sat there, not knowing anything else to do. For once, Deborah made no comment to that.

While we were standing there Doctor Bohan came out of the elevator. His shoulders slumped, but he had a smile on his face.

"Well, folks, it was the appendix. I'd say it was about an hour at the most from rupturing. Sylvia, I'm very glad you got her in here so fast! The surgery was routine, once I saw what we had. She is still unconscious, but resting comfortably. She should stay here for about a week, then not lift anything more than about ten pounds until I tell her it's OK."

Everyone looked relieved. Fred spoke for all. "Thank the Lord the news is so good, Doctor! We're sure grateful you performed the surgery."

Doctor Bohan's mouth quirked. "Aren't you forgetting something?"

I knew what he was getting to, but I kept a straight face.

"Fred, you have a daughter."

The men and boys looked like they'd been slapped, then they started talking all
at once, slapping each others' backs, and shaking Doctor Bohan's hand.

All except Laney. He smiled, but he toddled over to the three of us.

Deborah crouched down and took his hands.

"Laney, what do you think of all this?"

237

"Baby sister. Where's Mama? When can we eat?"

We three bent over laughing again. I guess Laney had his priorities straight!

Chapter Forty

Luther: Saturday, August 23rd, 1921, First Baptist Church, Metamora.

The last chord of Healey Willan's *Introduction, Passacaglia and Fugue in E flat minor* died away in the almost empty sanctuary.

I took out a handkerchief and wiped my forehead as my audience of two clapped vigorously.

"Great job, Luther!" Jack Sewell exclaimed as he clapped me on the shoulder. "I think you finally have *Old Squeak* whupped!"

"I surely hope so, Jack. After all that work, I surely hope so."

The third member of our little party spoke.

"Did either of you hear any anomalies during the concert?" John Wick looked concerned, as befit the President of the Wicks Organ Company of Highland, Illinois. This was his baby too, after all.

"Not a thing, John. How'd the presets feel, Jack?"

"Smooth as can be, John. As far as I could tell, every voice cut in and out just like they should."

Jack had resumed his customary role of preset pusher, stop adjuster, and *calming influence.*

"That's just wonderful, gentlemen!" John said. "I think we're good to go, then."

"You are staying for the recital, aren't you?"

"Oh, I wouldn't miss it, Luther! Besides, Carl Christensen wants to talk with me about some modifications he wants to make on your old nemesis over in Peoria."

"That old Moller always treated me right, John. *Old Squeak* was my nemesis!"

John laughed. "That it was, Luther!"

"But I think I've gotten the payback. Look at this."

John bent over to examine the small brass plate affixed to the console underneath his builders' plate:

In memory of
'Old Squeak'
The Previous Organ. 1900-1920.
Rest in Pieces.

John snorted and held his sides laughing.

"I think he approves," Jack observed.

"So he does. I hope Pastor does."

"Your Pa bought the thing, I don't think he'll mind."

"After what Old Squeak did to poor Mrs. Arbuckle and me, it's only fitting!"

John finally found his voice.

"That's the funniest thing I've ever seen on an organ! I love your sense of humor! By the way, if the job on the organ in Peoria pans out, Carl wants you to superintend it."

"I'd love to, John, but when will I find the time?"

"He says it is something he can play around, literally, so you may take your time, at least until next summer."

"I'll have to thank him for his confidence in me, John, no matter what happens."

"You can't fool your organ teacher, Luther. He knows you very well, and he's kept up with your work on this instrument. For all practical purposes, you superintended this job...and did half the work!"

"I thank you again for the opportunity, John. Not to mention those two little *gifts* in there!" I pointed to the organ case.

"And I thank you, Luther, for all the work you put into this installation!"

When John saw how much work I was doing on the organ—hard, dirty, tedious work, to tell the truth—he told me to stop in to see him when I was in Highland the next weekend. I had become very familiar with the Chicago and Alton Railroad timetable as I traveled from Bloomington down to Highland. I visited at least once a month to check on the organ's progress, and make decisions about the voicing and layout of the organ as it was erected and test run in their shops.

One day John led me upstairs to *the attic*—I guess they call it a *loft* when it's that big. Thousands of pipes of all sizes and materials were stacked in the place, each one tagged with detailed information of what voice it was, what note, and where it came from. The sheer *smell* of the place was incredible—like every old organ case in the world crammed into a single location! I'll never forget that glorious odor. I thought it was *glorious*, anyway.

We walked the narrow aisles between stacks of pipes until we came to two groups of pipes next to each other. One set were shaped reeds, an eight foot stop; the other set towered over everything else in the room.

"How would you like these two ranks added to your organ, Luther?"

I gaped. Christmas this early?

"How...Why?"

240

John grinned. "In this trade, we end up with a lot of extra pipes, as you see. These two ranks came from an Estey of the same age as yours. I remember them—first rate voices. Thirty two foot Contra Bombarde, and a really nice Vox Humana. Your organ is excellent, but that Vox Humana you have is really a poor mutation. And everybody can use a good blasting Bombarde! You've done so much work on this job, I think it's the least we can do to fill in a couple of gaps for your trouble."

And so we acquired two very nice new voices for our organ. I had not told Pastor Reem about the additions, and made sure I didn't use them when he was around. I even asked that two blank drawknobs be installed for those voices so nobody knew they were there; I'd install the engraved ones myself after the recital. The recital would be the *surprise introduction*.

I was starting to get hungry. "You ready for supper, Jack? John?"

"Thank you kindly, Luther, but Carl Christensen asked me to dinner this evening. He said his son is back from New York, and is interested in hearing about what we do."

"I know he has children out east, but I've never met them. That should be an interesting evening."

"It should. Leave it to me to talk about these gadgets at meals! My wife purely hates when I do that!"

"It appears she's not here this afternoon," Jack remarked.

"If she were, I'd hear about it!" John laughed. "See you gents tomorrow!"

"Later, John," Jack and I said together.

"So what's for dinner, Luther?"

"Let's go over to The Nook. It's just up the street, and the food's good. We can walk there."

"Fine by me. Lay on, MacDuff!"

Jack knew we both had that sort of sense of humor. We locked the church and walked up the street in the late afternoon quiet.

"Prosthesis bothering you, Luther? I see you're limping."

"A little. All that pedal work takes its toll."

"You gonna be OK for tomorrow?"

"I think so, if I don't do anything stupid. And wipe that look off your face!"

Jack kept grinning.

We went into the small restaurant and sat down. The waiter came, and we ordered. Since the owners were first generation immigrants from Scotland, the food reflected that cuisine. Corned beef and cabbage sounds mundane, but these folks really knew how to prepare it.

As we waited for the food, we talked.

"Luther, I don't know why I'm asking this, but how did you decide to play those particular pieces tomorrow?

"You're asking because you want to partake of my superior knowledge."

"Nobody likes a smart aleck!"

"I guess they don't. Let me think a moment and I'll answer that. Here comes the food anyway."

After the food arrived and Jack prayed, I continued.

"This may sound like a lecture so I apologize in advance. The offertory for the morning service was easy: unfinished business. *Old Squeak* got me when I tried to play that in 1919, and it's time to finish it."

"It is really nice, Luther. Beautiful, I guess. I can't imagine how you felt when *Old Squeak* wrecked it."

"It wasn't anything like being shot up, but I did feel betrayed. And very embarrassed. And thanks again for the idea of that brass plate!"

Jack snorted. "One of my better ones, I think. But go on, please. I'm actually finding this interesting—I wonder what's wrong with me?"

"Probably too much living in a gray metal can on water. Anyway, for the recital, I want to show off as much of the character of the organ as I can in the limited time I have. It's probably been ten years since anyone heard those pipes as they really sound, and I want to reacquaint them. Plus introduce the new members of the family!"

I'll be watching out the corner of my eye when you let loose with that Bombarde! There'll be reaction, that's for sure!"

"About three minutes into *Fiat Lux*, I figure. Just push preset four and stand back!"

We both laughed in anticipation.

"Back to the subject. I wanted to alternate slow and quiet with faster and louder, for contrast. The organ has a lot of beautiful soft ensemble sounds in it now—that Vox Humana really helps them coalesce. People sometimes think organ playing is all scream and bombast. That's for calliopes, not organs. Usually."

"You're going to have some fireworks in the Willan, though."

"I am, but not so much. My first thought for the finale was a sonata by Guilmant with even more blast. But the more I worked on it the less I wanted to use it."

"Why'd you choose the Willan?" Jack asked.

"I've been working on it since Francine Mason gave me the score when I was at Walter Reed. I think it'll help the congregation appreciate that organ as an aid to worship, not just an expensive toy. So I changed the finale."

"I can't follow the Willan like I can the others—too complex for my simple ear."

"I couldn't either, Jack, but it's grown on me."

Jack pulled out his wallet. "Let me buy, Luther. I don't get to do it very often.

"Thanks, buddy. I guess there really is such a thing as a free lunch!"

"Dinner, Luther."

"Whatever," I grinned.

That evening, after Pa and Jack had gone to bed. I couldn't get sleepy. This happened often the night before a recital. It's funny—even the night before that fateful day in June 1918 I dropped off to sleep in the trench almost immediately for the short time we had to sleep, but before one of these I just couldn't do it. I got up, fixed a pot of coffee, and sat down with a cup and my Bible.

I finished my Bible reading, prayed, and still didn't feel sleepy. I looked around the room idly, and saw the book by George MacDonald AP Kittridge had given me when I was leaving the *New Jersey*. I took it off the shelf and started reading.

What a marvelous book! MacDonald really expressed the relationship between God and man in a way I had always thought of it, at least since I'd been saved, but never quite put into words. The whole Gospel situation, from lost to saved, from rebel to Son, became much clearer for me. I wished I could thank AP for giving me this book; I thought one day I'd have to drive over to Appleton and thank him in person.

I stayed up much later than I should have, but I knew it was worth the inevitable exhaustion the next day. I also knew that exhaustion wouldn't hit until after the recital. I'd just have to be extra careful not to nod off during Pastor's evening message!

Chapter Forty One

Don and Jackie: Sunday, August 24th, 1921, 8:40 AM, east causeway of the Upper Free Bridge, Peoria, Illinois.

"I can't believe you actually drove over that awful bridge!"

Jackie Brighthonor, retired Navy Captain, aviator, and accountant for Wain Engineering, took a deep breath and let go of the dashboard grab bar she'd been clutching a *bit* too tightly.

"No problem, Jackie," Don Wain replied, shifting into second for the drive across the long narrow causeway. "The script says that thing isn't coming down until a towboat hits it in the forties. Because of the war they rebuild the bridge, only to have it get hit again by the *same* towboat, and that's the end. We're fine now."

"And what if the script's wrong here?"

"Then you'll keep me afloat as you swim to shore."

"That's what *you* think, Admiral!" Jackie gave him *the look*, "I can't swim either."

Don shook his head. "Why did two people who can't swim join the Navy?"

"*I* wanted to fly—and I always wore a life jacket!"

"How'd you pass the swimming test?"

"Same way you did—learn enough to pass, then never do it again." Jackie shifted her lower back. "Almost did once, but I never did hit the water."

"When was that?"

"Tell you later." *That's one he's not hearing today...along with how Eddie died*, Jackie thought. "You haven't told me how your vacation to Hoople went."

Don pulled out onto the graveled road to Morton and beyond before he answered.

"Pretty good. The Spa's up and running now, and the immersion bath did its thing—I feel another ten years younger. The base is building up, and we've started on the long runway."

"And Pam?"

Don looked over at his accountant as he spoke. "The same, Jackie. Fifteen minutes in she started to get the allergic reaction again. Spent the rest of the time recovering from it. She's decided not to try it any more."

Jackie nodded. "She didn't give me the details, just said she's done. What's wrong, Don?"

Don waited till a freight train passed on the track to the right of the road before replying.

"The Breckinridges say about half of one percent of everyone put into the baths have some sort of allergic reaction. Some can be treated, but some just can't. They don't know why that is."

"So twenty-fifth century medicine still falls short of perfection?"

"Yep. We're humans, and anything but simple creations. Amazing to me the Lord lets that technology work as well as it does."

"But Pam—" Jackie felt a lump in her throat, "What's going to happen to her?"

Don stared straight ahead, jaw set. "At some point she is going to die, Jackie, like we all will. Her normal lifespan will apply, however long the Lord gives her. She believes that will be sooner, rather than later."

"Will any of that medicine help her?"

"The normal crop of medications, both from our time and later," Don replied, "Just the infusing nanite bath won't work for her. That's the prevention part of their medicine—the treatment part still works."

Jackie pondered what Don said for a moment. "So you two just keep going?"

"Right. If the Lord wants any of us here, nothing can kill us. If he wants to take us Home, nothing can keep us here. Not even the baths of *the tank*. She understands that, and accepts it."

Neither spoke for the next ten minutes. Finally, Jackie broke the silence. "So, why are we driving this far just to go to church and an organ recital?"

"Several reasons, and you'll be involved as our accountant."

"Figured that, *Admiral*. So what are the reasons?"

First, I love good organ music. Don't get to hear it very often, so it's a treat to hear a recital like today's. Second, I want to get acquainted with John Wick."

"Who's he?" Jackie asked.

"President of Wicks Organ Company. They make an all-electric pipe valve and stop control system that's the most reliable anyone will *ever* make. When we rebuild our music hall I want one of their organs in it."

Jackie snorted. "We don't own a music hall."

"The Lord's given me peace that we will, three to five years out. Just don't know which one yet, although I have a hunch it'll be the hall next door to our offices."

"The *Auditorium*?," Jackie frowned. "That place is a wreck—you've said so yourself!"

"So I have. Structure's sound though. If we can buy it for next to nothing we'll gut it and put in a new interior, use what we can of the old stuff, and put in all our *imported* electronics, with an organ second to none!"

"How do you know it'll be available?"

Don pulled up to the four way stop in Morton. He replied as the modified Wills Sainte Claire V8 glided through the intersection and headed toward Metamora.

"Sid Nirdlinger owns it. He's got it leased until the spring of 1925. We've talked, and I have first right of refusal when the lease is up, sooner if they default for some reason. That's plenty of time to plan the rebuild."

"Hmmm… When were you going to tell your accountant, *Admiral?*"

Don winked. "Oh, about right now."

Jackie fixed her most baleful gaze on her boss. "I will have a word with Pam. She may introduce you to something new—the word *no.*"

"*Yes?*"

"No!"

"Yes!"

"No! And barring that, here's a little something Eddie and I used to do," Don noticed a shadow passed over Jackie's face before she continued. "When one of us said something really silly, the other would poke them in the ribs. The silly speaker would say *Eep!* to acknowledge their error. I poked Eddie way more than he poked me."

"And Pam knows this?"

"She does. Consider yourself warned."

I wish I hadn't told him that, Jackie thought behind her grin, *Now I have to try to put Eddie out of my mind all over again!*

*****

Luther: Sunday, August 24th, 1921, First Baptist Church, Metamora.

Pastor Reem asked me to sit on the platform for the first part of the service that morning. I couldn't tell if he wanted to make sure I didn't trip on the platform steps, or he just wanted to show me off.

246

The sanctuary filled rapidly. From my vantage point I watched the teenagers filter in from their class downstairs, and sit in the back on the left. As usual, one of the deacons planted himself right in the middle of their pew, to maintain order. Other people arrived in a steady stream, and found their customary spots.

I picked out various unfamiliar faces in the crowd. Jack sat in the front pew, where he could watch me; he wouldn't come up to help until the recital in the afternoon. A slightly stooped, balding man and a shorter, round faced woman also sat in the front pew. They looked familiar, but I couldn't place them. The man took a small wooden box from his pocket and set it on the pew next to him. *That's odd*, I thought.

Carl Christian Christensen sat in the middle about five pews back, where the acoustics made the organ sound clearest. A younger man in a suit sat with him—his son, I guessed.

My father sat in his usual spot about halfway back on my right. However, a petite blonde woman sat with him! I did not recognize her, and he'd never told me he was seeing anyone. I knew he spent frequent evenings away from home, but I figured he was working late at the shop, or making sales calls, or something. I began to suspect I had been spoofed!

Just before the service started, a family came in and sat in the back—Charlie, Agnes, and Forrest Templeman, and Marie Heath! I had mentioned in passing the upcoming recital to Agnes, but I had no idea they would come to it. I beckoned to Jack, and he came up to the platform.

"Jack, see that strange family back there? That's the Templeman family; I rent my room in Peoria from them. The smaller elderly lady is Marie Heath, one of the boarders. Could you slip back there and invite them to dinner with us? I'm buying of course."

"Sure. Right back!"

I saw him approach them and speak; after a moment Charlie nodded. *That's done*, I thought.

At that moment Pastor Reem walked to the pulpit and the service began. Our pianist and Music Director, Dennis Lepper, accompanied the singing. He was thrilled I had finally prevailed over the late, unlamented *Old Squeak*, but preferred I play its replacement.

We proceeded through the usual accouterments of a Sunday morning service. Pastor Reem got up, gave some prayer requests, and then added one more announcement.

"I hope all of you will come back at two this afternoon for the inaugural recital on the Rita M. Barlow Memorial Organ. Luther tells me he has a few numbers picked out to try on it…"

Pastor let the rustle of suppressed giggles subside before he continued.

"But he will be playing the offertory this morning after I pray. Two years ago next week he tried to play this offertory on Old Squeak, and we remember the result…"

More giggles, not quite suppressed.

"Well, he's asked if he could finish the offertory this morning, and I think it's very appropriate, on this interesting day. Now, let's pray."

As Pastor prayed I again climbed the low steps to the choir loft and sat on the organ bench. The new console faced the North side of the sanctuary, and since it was connected to the organ case by a cable, not tubes, it could even be swiveled a bit, depending on what it was being used to accompany.

I pushed the first preset. Jack would be doing that for me in the recital, but this morning the job was all mine. I asked the Lord to bless my playing, and get me through the rest of the day.

Pastor finished. I began.

The familiar quiet melody of *Be Thou My Vision* drifted into the sanctuary. The organ performed perfectly, and I managed to keep up with it. I deliberately arranged the voicing so I didn't use the two new stops; although, as the piece progressed, I did have a mad urge to yank the Bombarde drawknob and let them have it!

The piece came to its gentle, quiet close. *Thank you Lord!…*

I canceled the presets and slid on the organ bench to come down to the front pew. At that moment Pastor Reem said four words that stopped me cold.

"Stay up there, Luther."

I looked over at Pastor, and little wisps of fear started to seep across my vision.

"One of our guests this morning has given me a note. In it, he asks if you would please play an improvisation on the next hymn, the last one before the message. He asks further that when you have completed your improvisation, if you would please play the hymn through once as it is written, then accompany the congregation as I lead all three verses of it."

Oh, my.

I hadn't even looked at the hymn board this morning, since I wasn't accompanying and never sang the hymns—I really do have a voice like a half-strangled toad. I looked at the board, and saw the hymn was number one hundred eighty one. Let the Lower Lights be Burning. The same tune whose alternate words had so impressed me the week before at Gary and Elizabeth Anna's wedding.

Pastor continued. "This is an unusual request for a Sunday morning service, but this is an unusual Sunday morning service. We will do as requested. Luther, are you clear on the instructions?"

I looked at Pastor and nodded slowly.

"Very well. You may start when you are ready."

I turned around and slid back square on the organ bench.

The mechanics of an improvisation are fairly standard. The usual drill is to take the familiar tune, and alter it through a number of variations, changing the melody, rhythm, and tonal quality of the song in successive phases, until eventually one comes out at the far end back pretty much where the tune began. Dennis Lepper told me the musicians who play 'jazz' music go through the same process, only paying more attention to rhythm changes and more dissonant modern chord progressions.

None of that made a bit of difference at the moment. I had ideas, but I found my emotions starting to stir for some reason, and I began to fear I couldn't put together a coherent improvisation.

I was learning...

Lord, let this be Your doing, to give You glory; I can't do this myself!"

Instantly I had peace that, whatever happened in the next few minutes, it would be His doing. I pushed preset number six, took a long breath, and launched into the deep.

An interesting phenomena I have noticed as a performer is the ability to occasionally step out of the performing moment and listen to what I am playing from the point of view of an interested observer, while simultaneously playing the music myself. This usually happens when I know what I am playing so well I can afford to let most of me keep playing while some part of my consciousness steps back and listens.

I found myself in that position this morning, but it wasn't because I knew what I was playing so well; in fact, I'd never heard it before! Something deep in my subconscious, prodded by Someone I knew well, was doing the playing, and to a certain degree I was just along for the ride.

Once I got used to the sensation, I listened with interest to the developing piece, and explored its motivation with yet another part of my mind. The circumstances of my conversion, and subsequent recovery to this point swept past my mind as if in a long scene

249

from a motion picture. My feelings of relief, gratitude, and love for the Lord appeared, affected what I was playing, and moved on. The happiness of Gary and Elizabeth Anna came to mind, and contributed to the piece.

I was surprised to see me pressing preset number four at this point. So much for planning; here comes the Bombarde! I let loose with a phrase on the pedal with the Bombarde; Jack said later there was an audible thud in the sanctuary as the congregation startled and jumped in their pews!

As the music subsided from that surprising climax, I found myself asking the Lord if, perhaps, one day I could experience the joy Gary and Elizabeth Anna felt that day they were wed. *Where did that come from*? That thought had never entered my conscious mind before that I could remember, but it certainly did that day!

Unbidden, Scripture came to my mind. "Likewise the Spirit also helpeth our infirmities: for we know not what we should pray for as we ought: but the Spirit itself maketh intercession for us with groanings which cannot be uttered. And he that searcheth the hearts knoweth what is the mind of the Spirit, because he maketh intercession for the saints according to the will of God."—(Romans 8:26,27.)

I guess that was what was happening at the moment, as the music part of me was playing shifted again. To my astonishment, I then heard another tune beginning to interweave itself with the one I was supposed to be playing. I found myself producing in the reed chorus *Let the Lower Lights Be Burning*, while above that, in obbligato, *It Is Well With My Soul* on the Vox Humana!

That combination is not supposed to work—the first song is in 3/4 time, the second in 4/4...but there they were, combined in about the most beautiful mixture I'd ever heard! I thanked the Lord for the privilege of hearing this outpouring of emotion, produced from the heart through a big machine.

Again, Scripture came to mind—the last verse of the passage before: "And we know that all things work together for good to them that love God, to them who are the called according to His purpose." (Romans 8:28).

After the climax of the combined songs, the music started to fade as I took stops off the combination, one by one. Finally, in the softest of diapason groups I played the combined songs once more, as a valedictory chorus, I guess.

The improvisation ended. I pushed the combination preset for a moderate full organ and began to play the song 'straight', as requested.

I stole a glance to my right. I saw a lot of little white somethings waving among the congregation—handkerchiefs, it appeared. I knew the piece had been massively emotional to me— but to them too? I guess it spoke, as the Lord had wished. Jack told me later he had timed it at exactly eight and one half minutes.

Pastor got up, also with a handkerchief in his hand, and led the singing. That singing seemed a little muted, like people were having trouble finding their voices. If I'd had a singing voice, I would have had trouble with that myself.

What a blessing! What a privilege! Thank you Lord! was all I could think.

Again, Pastor managed to preach his prepared message that morning, and again it spoke to my heart. He ended with a strong call to come to Christ for salvation, and several people came forward.

People crowded around me after the service, and told me how my playing had touched their hearts. I lost track of how many times I said, "The Lord did that, not me.", but they thanked me anyway. I prayed I would never forget Who did it, though.

Pa and the blond lady came up to us as the crowd was starting to thin. He introduced Mrs. Inge Rasmussen from Washington, widow and head of the library in that town. We shook hands, and I noticed the broad grin on her face. *Something's definitely up*!

Pa confirmed Jack and I would eat supper at the house this evening, with him and the visiting Inge.

Strangely, Carl Christensen and his son did not stay to greet me, but rather sent me a note by Pastor thanking me for the playing this morning, and promising to be at the concert in the afternoon.

The Templeman family and Marie were waiting outside the church, and after introducing Jack we walked over to The Nook, where I had reserved a table for Sunday dinner.

As we stepped into The Nook, I noticed the couple from the front row in church sitting at a table near ours. As we came in they stood, and the man stepped over to me.

"Mr. Barlow, I'm Donald Wain, owner of Wain Engineering Corporation in Galesburg, Illinois, and a friend of AP and Deborah Kittridge." Motioning to the woman accompanying him, he continued. "And this is Jacqueline Brighthonor, the company accountant. My wife Pam dearly wanted to come to hear you today, but she is ill."

"I'm filling in for Pam today, and please call me Jackie," the shorter woman said as she shook my hand, "We truly enjoyed your playing this morning, especially that improvisation! I trust the recital will be even more spectacular."

"I hope so, er, Jackie, but that was the Lord doing the improvising, not me."

"I know," Jackie said softly, "If we let the Lord work through us, He amazes us every time. I know He's done that for me."

"May we join your party, Mr. Barlow? We've already ordered and will pay for our own."

I glanced at the table. "Of course, Mr. Wain. May I introduce everyone?"

"Yes, please do—and call me Don, please."

I began by introducing my father and Inge, then Jack. I came to our other guests.

And here are friends of mine from Peoria—Charles and Agnes Templeman, their son Forrest, and Marie Heath—Mister Wain, are you all right?"

Don had dropped to the floor like a sandbag hit him! Jackie was just able to break his fall enough to keep him from hitting his head.

"Bring a chair, please," Jackie spoke just like the Major commanding the Marine detachment on *Washington* so long ago! I grabbed a chair and set it next to the two. Jackie reached under Don's arms and hauled him up far enough to lever into the chair. She then stood close to keep him from sliding out.

She had the strength of the Major too!

After a moment Don opened his eyes part way and turned his head slowly to look around. "What happened?" he croaked.

"You keeled over as Luther was introducing the Templeman family," Jackie said in a quiet voice.

"Oh…OK." Don looked over at the Templemans. "I am so sorry, folks. Every once in a while my blood pressure takes a tumble and so do I. I believe I will be OK here in a minute. And I am very happy to meet you all."

I saw Jackie squint one eye, and stare at Don for a moment; then she grasped his chair. "Since you're in the chair you might as well scoot up to the table and stay there."

"Thank you, *Captain*. I'm feeling better now. Thank you for picking me up."

Don still didn't sound very sure of himself as Jackie helped him scoot to the table. "Don't mind him," Jackie said to the rest of us, "Sometimes he says things that don't make any sense. He's a retired Navy Vice Admiral, but obviously I'm not a *Captain*!"

With that we all sat around the table. Pa prayed for the meal, and eventually the food arrived and we dug in.

252

During the meal and conversation, Don listened, and said very little. Jackie spoke more often, but mostly we listened to *the monologue* from the other end of the table.

Don and Jackie excused themselves, saying they needed to get back to the church to rest a bit before the recital. They seemed friendly, but I really couldn't find out much about them during the meal.

Finally, I went up to the cash register to pay for our group's meals. The short, swarthy owner of the restaurant waved me off.

"Sure 'an that other couple in your group already paid for all 'o ye! You dinna owe a cent!"

I thanked the owner, and shaking my head returned to the table.

Chapter Forty Two

Dedication Recital
of the
Rita M. Barlow Memorial Organ

First Baptist Church
Metamora, IL
Sunday, August 24th, 1921
Luther Barlow, Organist

Programme
Offiering in Morning Service
Prelude on Slane (Be Thou My Vision)
Arrangement by Heathe Williams
Improvisation ot Morning Service
Let the Lower Litghts Be Burning
P.P. Bliss

Organ Recital SP.M.
Fiat Lux
Theodore Dobois
Fantaisie 16-14-Adagio
Cesar Franck
Scherzo In E "La Grasse"
Charles Marie Vidor
Grand Choeur
Cesar Franck
Cannon en ut Mineu
Theodore Salome
Menuet from Suite Gothique
Leon Boellmann
Introduction: Passacaglia and Fugue in
Eflat Minor
Healy Willan
Encore
Priere A Notre Dame
Leon Boellmann

Metamora, IL. First Baptist Church, August 21, 1921

"Luther, when you called me up to the platform you called the Templemans a *strange family*. How right you were!"

"That wasn't how I meant it at all…although now that you mention it, it kind of fits."

"Kind of nothing!" Jack sputtered, "How do you ever stand being around Charlie?"

"He's almost never around, is how. He has a room over Strickfaden's Garage in East Peoria, where he works. He stays there during the week—to *save gas* he says."

"More like save your sanity!"

"Amen to that!"

Jack and I were finishing our after lunch ablutions in the bathroom at church. We were making sure our hair was combed, and no *social indiscretions* peeked out anywhere.

Jack shook his head and rolled his eyes. "Luther, I don't think I've ever met anyone as stuck on themselves as that man, not even in the Marines! Lunch was one nonstop monologue. Every time one of us would ask a question, or try to change the subject, he'd run right over us!"

"Agnes tells me he's always been that way."

Jack raised his eyebrows. "Why in the world did she marry him then?"

"I wondered too, so one day I asked her. Short answer: he was the first one who asked. She also thought she could change him—and we know how that ends up!"

"That's really too bad. She and the boy seem like nice people."

"Oh, they are! Forrest peppers me with technical questions all the time—he's *radio-mad*, got a library table of the stuff in their parlor, even as young as he is. Always trying new circuits and ideas."

"Amazing he hasn't burned the place down yet," Jack remarked.

"Oh, he's zapped himself a few times, but so far he only uses batteries. The first time he gets an AC to DC converter power supply he could really light the place up! He is careful though—just never cares what anything looks like, as long as it works."

"Never make a Marine, I'm afraid!"

"Too true, Jack."

As we dried our hands, Jack changed the subject.

"Did you notice how Marie managed to keep up her end of the conversation in spite of Charlie's efforts to upstage her?"

"She always does! And you used the right word. She's a retired actress, from the days when groups of actors toured constantly, giving performances in every little town you could name. She definitely has *stage presence* even now—and I bet nobody ever upstaged her! We've had some good talks...although she manages to change the subject whenever I start to mention the Gospel."

"Bet she's more polite about it than Charlie."

"Marie's always polite...and always cooking up the next line. She's good at her trade, even now."

"I sure feel sorry for them though, Luther. Charlie acts like he just stepped out of the funny pages—or out of a Vaudeville act!"

"I'd like to say he has a more affable side to him...but I can't."

Jack let out one of his deep booming laughs.

We trudged up to the sanctuary, which was beginning to fill. Pa and Inge sat in a pew, talking softly. I caught the glint of something on her finger; even from halfway across the sanctuary I could tell what that was! *So Pa surprises us again.* I nudged Jack and pointed; he started to giggle. Jack has a giggle that can only be described as *cute.* He has to suppress it when he's with the troops, and can only let it out when he's away from other Marines—poor guy.

We climbed the steps and sat down in the platform chairs, watching the crowd come in. We talked softly.

"How's the leg, Luther?"

"Fine so far. I'll feel it by the end, but it should be OK. I have the *cheater* ready just in case, though."

When I designed the features of this organ, I quietly included a special coupler button. When I pressed it, the pedal division would be coupled to the choir manual (the top of the three), and lock out the usual voices of the choir division. That way I could play the pedals without using my feet, as long as I had a few fingers of one hand free. I wanted that flexibility, just in case my leg started to give trouble while I was playing. Organists do what they have to do!

Carl Christensen and his son came down the aisle and sat where they had that morning. They talked and looked at the programs Pa had insisted we have printed. They came out very nicely, and I was sure they would find their way to people's scrapbooks and waste paper baskets. They were too small to line the bottom of a birdcage.

Pastor Reem came over to us. "Are you gents ready?"

"Ready as we'll ever be, Pastor," I replied.

"OK, we'll start in two minutes."

That gave Jack and I one minute each to pray for the recital.

After he welcomed the nearly full house, and prayed, Pastor told the story of the coming of the new organ, and introduced Pa as the benefactor. He also introduced John Wick, who sat in the audience about halfway back. He introduced Carl Christian Christensen at my request, as he continued to be my teacher and mentor.

"And now, the rules," Pastor concluded. "You may clap if you feel like it after each piece except for the work at the end, where we ask you to hold your applause until Luther puts his hands in his lap when he's done. Rotten vegetables may be thrown at any time, but be prepared to clean up what you throw. Jack wanted me to say that!"

I dissolved in laughter, along with the audience. Jack told me later he conspired with Pastor Reem to help *loosen me up*; he succeeded.

The laughter faded to silence, and Jack and I climbed up to the organ. Jack put out the music for the first piece, and I spread it over the wide music rack. Jack pushed preset one, I cross checked the drawknobs, asked the Lord one more time to help me get through it, and began.

No surprises marred this recital. The choice of music worked well, the pace and contrast of the various pieces came off like I figured they would. I deliberately kept the pieces before the Willan relatively short, so people who weren't used to classical organ recitals wouldn't get too bored. So far as I know, nobody slept through it.

By the time I began the Willan, my leg was definitely reminding me of its existence. I knew I had enough in it to get me through the three sections, but I decided not to risk it with the long fast pedal work of the *fugue*. At the proper time I cut in the 'cheater' coupler and played the right foot part on the choir manual, playing the left foot part with the usual left foot.

Finally, the last grand full-organ blast of the Willan. I cut off the last massive chord, and the sound reverberated through the sanctuary like it was the inside of a violin. A few seconds later I heard a storm of applause I just could not believe.

We stood up, Jack stood back, and I bowed. I have this odd bow I make, partly my Marine training, partly bows I saw while I was in France, partly an effort to make sure I didn't lose my balance and fall on my prosthesis. The audience kept clapping. I was stunned, and very, very grateful.

Eventually I put my hands up and the audience quieted.

"You know, we can just quit now and go downstairs for the refreshments…"

A chorus of howls greeted that comment.

"I suppose that means an encore, right?"

Another round of applause, and even some whistles!

"I'll take that as a yes…."

Laughter and scattered clapping.

"I'll announce this since it's not in the program. I will play 'Prière À Notre-Dame' by Leon Boellmann. It's not long, so we will get to the refreshments shortly!"

To more laughter I climbed back onto the organ. Jack faded out and sat down in front; he hadn't practiced this piece, so he couldn't help me.

I chose this piece for the inevitable encore because it is exquisitely beautiful first of all; also because it showcased the new Vox Humana, the filigree of the reed chorus with the swell doors shut; and because it wasn't too demanding of my tired right leg.

As I played the piece, I found my eyes filling up, and an occasional tear dribbling down my cheek. I had no idea why I was crying, except maybe in response to the tremendous emotions of this remarkable day. Fortunately, I knew the piece by heart and really didn't even have to look at the keys—just as well, I couldn't see them clearly anyway.

The piece ended. I canceled the presets, turned to slide off the bench, and walked to the front of the platform. The applause continued and I bowed a few more times, then pulled out my handkerchief and tried to get the waterworks under control. Finally, as the applause was dying down, I looked out at the assembled group and called out, "That's all folks! Lets go down and eat!"

We gathered in the church basement, and sat on folding chairs set out in rows. This was an odd way to serve refreshments, but I really was too tired to care. I was just glad the whole business was over and done with. My mental fog did not stop me from greeting the members and visitors as they came up to congratulate me. They also wished Jack well, as he was leaving to go back to the battleship *Idaho* the next day.

Eventually a small procession walked to the front of the hall, and sat down in the front row. Pastor Reem led the parade, followed by his wife Deborah, A.K.A. *The Deb* (I was almost afraid to think of his nickname for her, in case she could read minds!). Then my father, with Inge Rasmussen on his arm. Finally, Carl Christian Christensen and his son, whom I still had not been introduced to.

258

Pastor Reem got up and moved to a small lectern in the front of the assembled group.

"Thank you all for coming to the recital today, and this little gathering. I do believe we managed to pull this off without Luther suspecting a thing!"

WHAT?!?

"We'll wait a moment while Luther finishes saying 'WHAT??' in his mind."

Laughter and other odd noises from the group. Through the fog of exhaustion I noted a tingling feeling in my stomach. Pastor Reem continued.

"We have two items of business this afternoon. First, I'd like to introduce Dr. Carl Christian Christensen, an old friend of mine and organist for many years at First Congregational Church in Peoria. He'll explain the first matter. Doctor Christensen."

The group clapped as the tall, bald man I *thought* I knew so well got up and moved to the podium.

"Thank you ladies and gentlemen. I would like to introduce the gentleman with me today. I told Luther my son he was, and trusting soul he is, he believed me!"

More laughter. I looked over at Jack and he was grinning too. *I've been had...*

"Now I have the honor to introduce Doctor Norman Coke-Jephcott, organist and Music Director at the Church of the Messiah in Rhinebeck, New York. He is also Chairman of the Certification Committee of the American Guild of Organists, national organization."

I knew I'd heard that name before! I'd been a member of the American Guild of Organists for years, ever since Dr. Christensen recommended me when I was in High School. *Why is he here?* I wondered through my fog.

Doctor Coke-Jephcott moved to the podium, and opened a folder he carried up with him. He spoke with a distinct British accent.

"Thank you Carl. When we plotted this little deception Carl told Luther I was his son. Of course I'm not his biological son, but I am to a certain extent his *musical* son. When I arrived in the States from England in 1911, Carl took charge of the polishing of my organ playing, helped me assimilate (as much as a Brit can) into American culture, and promoted me on a short recital tour until I found my first Church position. I am forever in his debt. And he decided to call in a bit of that debt with this visit."

259

A smattering of laughter in the assembled group. At least a few of them caught

the understated British sense of humor. I continued to listen through my stupor.

"Carl asked me to come out to visit, and evaluate Mr. Barlow. He told me of his history, and his War service, and his retirement. I wasn't sure what I would find when I went to examine him. I have been, however, very pleasantly surprised!"

I heard several *Amens* from the group in that basement. My exhausted mind finally began to put two and two together. *Uh oh...*

"Carl and I enlisted the services of Pastor Reem and Sergeant Sewell to accomplish this evaluation. I was able to watch and hear from a hidden location in the organ case the last three practices Mr. Barlow performed before today."

I looked over at Jack. "You stinker," I whispered. Jack just grinned.

"I was the one who submitted the request for the improvisation this morning, which Pastor Reem so graciously permitted. Let me say that, as a Master Examiner for the Guild, I've heard close to a thousand improvisations. I can count on one hand the number that have moved me to tears. Yours, Luther, did just that. I don't know how you accomplished it!"

I knew how—*it wasn't me!* I looked over at Carl. He smiled and nodded. He knew.

Dr. Coke-Jephcott continued. "Then the recital this afternoon continued Mr. Barlow's outstanding performances of a variety of difficult pieces. Yes, Luther, I saw the pedal-to-choir coupler you put in there, and how you used it in the Willan fugue. I say *Bravo!* The result was magnificent, and as organists, we do what we have to do to get results."

Whew!

"Dr. Christensen and I have conferred, and we are in agreement. Luther, come up here please."

I stood up and walked over to stand between the two Doctors. Another thought through the fog—*I was in the middle of a paradox!* I'd been hanging around Jack too long...

Dr. Coke-Jephcott pulled a small framed certificate from the folder where it had been hidden.

"Luther Barlow, it gives Dr. Christensen and me great pleasure to confer upon you this certificate, as a Fellow—"

My jaw dropped and my knees buckled involuntarily. That was the highest certificate of proficiency the American Guild of

Organists gave out! Some years nobody in the entire country won that certificate…

Carl put his hand out and held me by the arm.

"We'll wait a moment while Luther's heart starts ticking over again."

More laughter.

"Anyway, you get this certificate, as a Fellow of the American Guild of Organists, to date from today. And let me say congratulations, Luther! You've earned this, and you rate it!"

He handed me the certificate and both men shook my hand. Carl didn't let go of my arm, though; I think he was really afraid I was going to pass out. His fear was not unfounded.

"Let's get him back to the chair before he keels over on us!"

I was helped back to my chair by the two organists. I sat down and just stared off. It took a while to get my bearings back.

Pastor Reem then returned to the lectern.

"That's one item taken care of. Now, about that other item. It is my pleasure to announce the Engagement and impending marriage…*very impending marriage*…of Mrs. Inge Rasmussen of Washington, Illinois, and Mr. Howard Barlow, of this city. Stand up please, Inge and Howard!"

Everyone clapped as Pa and Inge stood up and faced the group. I was glad I had seen that ring appear on her finger before the concert; that at least saved me another surprise.

Right…

"Now it is time for the other matter. We are going to have a quiet little wedding, right here, right now!"

I just turned and stared at the assembled group. They grinned back. Maybe it was exhaustion, maybe just the surprise of the news, but I couldn't move. Jack said I was fun to watch.

Pastor Reem pulled his Bible and the wedding service book out of the lectern where he'd hidden it.

"Luther, if you're able we'd like you to stand up with your Pa. Don't worry, all you have to do is stand there, and sign a name, preferably yours, to the marriage license after we're done. Come on up here!"

In a daze, I walked up to the group. I limped slightly; my stump was not happy.

Pastor looked around; he seemed a little flustered.

"Now to stand up with Inge, I believe that would be The Deb— oops!"

That woke me up. Pastor Reem had just used *The Name Which Must Not Be Spoken!* I looked around for his wife. I spotted her coming out of the kitchen. I half expected her to be wielding a frying pan, but she walked over to Inge, gave her a hug, and turned with Inge to face Pastor. I did see the look she gave her husband; he sobered up quickly.

So it was I found myself an F.A.G.O, and best man at my father's wedding, before four o'clock in the afternoon.

Dinner that evening was a lively affair. Jack recounted the lengths everyone had gone to keep me in the dark about the day's shenanigans. Pa explained how Inge had come to the dealership a few months before to buy a car, and ended up being asked on a date. Her husband had been killed at Chateau Thierry in July, 1918.

"I despaired of ever finding someone again," Inge continued, "until I met this *stocky, balding car dealer* over in Metamora." She reached over and took Pa's hand. "We dated, he courted, and here we are!"

I was very happy for both of them. They seemed totally comfortable in each others' presence, and Pa was happier than I'd seen him in many years.

Jack and I offered to clean up and do the dishes, since we figured they might have other things to do. Pa thanked us, and told us to not wait up for them, as they had the bridal suite in the Jefferson Hotel in Peoria reserved, and they needed to get going before it got dark.

They were packed and had the car loaded already.

*****

Jackie and Don: late afternoon, driving home.

Jackie looked over at Don as he drove. "Are you ready to talk about what happened at lunch?"

"No."

"Good," Jackie replied. "Why did you go down at the restaurant?"

"I said I wasn't ready to talk about it," Don muttered over the sounds of the car.

"Unacceptable response, Boss. You could've really gotten hurt, and I need to know what's going on. Start talking."

Don looked out the windshield as the eastern edge of Kickapoo, Illinois hove into view. His mouth moved, he looked over at Jackie, and sighed.

"All right, but I warn you, it might weird you out."

Jackie snorted. "Listen, *Admiral*—I'm a retired Navy captain, COD pilot, and single mom who decided to travel to another universe eighty some years in the past to crunch numbers for a company bringing *civilization* to said universe, all at the Lord's direction. I think I know *weird* by now. So spill it."

Don slowed for the village. "Odd name for a town—Kickapoo."

"Do I need to report this incident to Pam?"

Don sighed again. "All right, you got me. I used to get woozy when I'd get hit with a major surprise and I hadn't eaten. Some sort of low blood sugar reaction, I think. Hasn't happened since I came out here and visited the Spa. I think I need to go back out to Hoople for a checkup."

Jackie thought a moment, brow furrowed. "OK, Don, I'll buy that. Promise me, promise Pam, you'll get out there this week."

"OK, Jackie, I will. Scout's honor."

Jackie snorted. "You were a Boy Scout? Hard to believe. How high did you get?"

"Second class. I never made first—couldn't swim."

"Figures. But back to today—what shocked you back there? Luther was just introducing folks."

Don paused a moment as he accelerated the big Wills out the other side of the village. He swallowed once, "Luther introduced me to my grandparents."

"Say what?!"

"My grandparents, Jackie. Estelle Meriden is good friends with Agnes, that I knew. I figured I'd meet them eventually, but never *there!*"

Jackie's face softened. "OK, now I understand. You still need to get checked out, but I see how meeting them like that would stop you cold."

"Yeah. Fun to watch them at lunch, though, once I got my wits back."

Jackie laughed. "Fun for you, maybe! No offense, but Charlie's the most self-centered, egotistical *blowhard* I've ever met! He's like a cartoon character."

Now Don chuckled. "No offense taken, Jackie. And you're right! You know that story he told about working at the Rock Island Arsenal during the war?"

"All *ten minutes* of it?"

"Yep! I heard him tell that same story—*word for word*—when I finally got to meet him in the late seventies."

Jackie squinted. "Seventies? That would mean he had to be…"

"In his middle nineties. He finally died at age ninety eight. Took a nap after lunch and didn't wake up—there, anyway."

"So sad," Jackie said, "What of the family?

"I don't know what'll happen here, but Agnes finally divorced him in the forties, after she got enough money to do it. He stopped even visiting them in the early thirties. She raised three kids by running a rooming house. It was really hard in the depression, but she did it. And Marie Heath stayed with them until she died in 1935."

"She's fascinating," Jackie added, "and she kept Charlie in his place!"

"Oh, yes!" Don thought for a moment. "Maybe we'll be able to help all of them this time around."

"But no more fainting!"

Don smiled in the fading light. "No, *Captain*…at least until I meet my *other* grandparents. I love it when a plan comes together."

Jackie rolled her eyes.

Chapter Forty Three

Sylvia: Sunday afternoon, April 9th, 1922, Sylvia's house.

Helen tossed a pocket folder in my direction. "Here, I brought you something."

She was spending Sunday out at my house on the Fremont Road, and we had just finished lunch after attending Sunday morning service.

"What's this?"

"Open it up and see."

In the folder I found two brochures, one for the Chicago Symphony, and one for the 'new' Chicago Civic Opera. I also found two passes.

"What have you been up to?" I asked with mock severity.

"Syl, we need a little variety in our lives. We teach, we grade papers, we settle behaviors. We go home, sleep, and repeat. It's great work, but we need a little *spice!*"

"Spice?"

"Sure! Lucille Rochlus is the elementary music teacher for the Galesburg schools, and a friend of mine. She gets these 'educator pass' offers from the Chicago Symphony all the time. Any teacher can get one. Five dollars for an entire season! It's up in the balconies, but the sound is great everywhere in the Auditorium. This year, they're including a pass for the Chicago Civic Opera, good whenever they manage to put on a performance!"

"They're having problems?"

"Far as I can tell they have one big problem—her name's Mary Garden!"

"I think I've heard of her," I replied, "Didn't she run the Opera before this one?"

"Sure did…right into the ground! But she's worked her contract so they can't get rid of her. And what she puts on is first rate, even if they never break even!"

"A little bit of a *prima-donna?*"

"A little past half *nuts*! She bankrupted the last company, and she's in control of the new one. We'll see if that pass ever gets used—for free, it's at least worth the cost!"

"I like this idea, Helen, and I'm grateful for the opportunity, but how and when are we going to use these things?"

Helen stood up and began to collect the dishes and silverware.

"Got it all worked out! Ma and I went up and *reconnoitered the situation* last weekend. We can take an early Burlington express from Galesburg, get into Union Station, have a nice lunch at any of three decent restaurants, see the Saturday afternoon Matinee performance, then come home on another Burlington express in the early evening! All within walking distance!"

"And you use your *employee pass*, right?"

"You bet! You'll pay for your train fare, but it's not much. And the places we found to eat are inexpensive too. We get a grand day out…and off… at minimal expense! I figure about once a month we can do this. Sound good?"

"Sounds great! But if we do this will it affect your flying jobs?"

"Nope! Don Wain encouraged me when he heard. I guess he's friends with Fredrick Stock, the conductor, and gets up there himself every chance he gets."

I nodded. "I'll need to let the School Board know I'm heading out on these little adventures—they are mighty protective of me, for some reason."

"Yes, they are…but you don't mind, do you?"

"No, not at all. They're like my second family—" I suddenly stopped, and my eyes started to water.

Helen spoke softly. "So they are, Syl. You're blessed to have them watching out for you. In the city my Principal, Lillian Taylor, does that for us to a certain extent,

but it's much more of a professional oversight than a personal one. I like what I'm doing at Ayres, but it was more fun out here."

"But you have other opportunities for fun."

Helen grinned. "Sure do! I flew a Curtiss from Monmouth to Davenport, Iowa yesterday, then a Swallow from Davenport to Chicago, and finally, of all things, a SPAD S-13 from Chicago back to Monmouth!"

"What's a *SPAD*?"

"French fighter from the war. We used 'em too. They're starting to appear on the surplus market, and Jackie Brighthonor bought one of the things!"

"Doesn't she already have a plane?"

"Yep, but she says she wants to tinker on this one a little bit. Put a different engine in it and see what happens. She's a mechanic besides a pilot."

"And accountant. Busy life," I remarked, "Is the SPAD hard to fly?"

"Not bad. Got to watch them every minute; they won't fly *hands off*. But a nice bird."

266

"Why all the strange moves?"

"Horse-trading with aeroplanes. Lee Wright and Don brokered a three way deal, and needed everything delivered. No problems, and I got paid nicely!"

"Doesn't it hinder you that Galesburg doesn't have a real airfield?"

"Oh, yes! It bothers Lee and Don, and their friend Julian Mack too. They've been working on the problem, but since the Caldwell Brothers airfield west of town burned, nobody's wanted to take up the torch—oh, that's a good analogy!"

"I don't remember that. What happened?"

"January 11th, 1921. That was the week I was stuck in Galesburg after the big snowstorm hit, didn't get back out here until that Thursday. This happened on a Tuesday night. I saw the glow in the sky and drove out that way through the snow. They had a large hangar, offices, storage buildings and 7 planes. Everything burned. Never did figure out what caused it, but once it started the wind caught it and everything went. Forty thousand dollars damage, no insurance. Stick a fork in 'em, they're done!"

We both chuckled at that one. Helen came up with some really twisted turns of phrase sometimes. I took another sip of tea, and noticed Helen had gotten quiet, and had a frown on her face. This was unusual. She supplied the answer before I could ask.

"I got a letter from Ruth Law on Friday."

"The woman who gave you your license, and you saved her life?"

"That's her. We've kept in touch the past couple of years. This letter was different."

"It must have been, to change your mood like that."

"Yep. Kind of bittersweet, I guess."

"Do tell."

"Remember when she and I talked after she got out of the hospital, and I witnessed to her? Well, she never forgot what we talked about…and kept the Bible I gave her. Said she read in it from time to time, but said every time she did, she'd find something telling her to repent and trust Christ."

"Imagine that!"

"Heh. She told me she wanted to put it away, or hide it, or drop it out of a plane, but she just couldn't! But that's not all, Syl. While she was reading her Bible and getting convicted, her husband was reading fantasy."

"All right, I'll bite: What's fantasy got to do with getting under conviction?"

"Ah, you see, the author of the fantasies he was reading was George Mac Donald!"

I giggled. Helen and I had been introduced to Mac Donald by our respective Pastor's wives in our early teens. We were enthralled by his fantasies and 'fairy stories', but soon found out he wrote some of the most remarkable books on the Christian life I've ever read. I particularly enjoyed *Unspoken Sermons*—all three volumes!

"I assume Ruth's husband found his *other* books?"

"Oh yes...and one night he surrendered and trusted Christ!"

"That's wonderful! How'd Ruth take it?"

"She was *somewhat annoyed*, to use her words—she has a flair for understatement. Then, she had an accident."

"Oh, my! What happened?"

"She was flying top plane in a plane to plane transfer, like we did when I scrambled Al Wilson."

We both grinned involuntarily. That *was* funny.

"But this time, something happened before the transfer was completed. Air pocket, motor hiccup, she doesn't know—but she dropped twenty feet in a split second, and her wheels hit the top wing of the plane below her. That plane's wings folded right up, and it went in, exploded on impact."

"Oh, my!"

"It gets worse, Syl. Flying that plane was her best friend. Ruth talked her into trying flying, taught her to fly, mentored her for several years. And here she was burned to death—they heard the screams—before her eyes, and she felt she caused it. That got Ruth to thinking..."

"I should think so! How awful!"

"In one of my letters I had told her about the stupid thing I did that brought me to realize I really wasn't good, and couldn't save myself. She re-read that letter many times, and about two weeks after the crash she gave in, and got saved!"

"That's wonderful, Helen! The price was steep, though."

"Sometimes it is. He does what He has to do to get our attention."

"Everyone's different."

"How well I know."

We sat at the kitchen table for a moment, immersed in our own thoughts.

"One more thing..."

"What's that, Helen?"

"The Lord saved Ruth, and gave her His peace as He always does, but then started convicting her about her flying."

"Her flying?"

"Yes. Flying had been the biggest thing in her life for ten years. Everything she did was based on what it would do for her flying career. It was her idol, Syl. She realized it, but she just couldn't pull away from it."

"What happened?"

"She told her husband what she was dealing with. A couple of days later she was reading the paper at the breakfast table, and read that she had retired from flying! Her husband put that information out to the press, and that was that."

"What did she do?"

"After she finished yelling, and crying…she hugged her husband and thanked him for *pushing her off the diving board*!"

"She said that?"

"She did! Once she accepted it, the idol pretty much melted away. She has memories, she says—some good, some not so good. But she doesn't feel the urge to fly anymore. She and her husband own a couple of businesses, and they're involved in a good church. She doesn't know what she's going to do for the rest of her life, but she's trusting the Lord to put her where He wants her."

"I believe I can relate to that."

"She said some in the press were speculating about the reasons she retired, but none of them knew the real story. She wanted me to know, and thanked me again, not only for saving her life, but for pointing her to Christ."

I sat and thought for a moment.

"Wow! Makes me stop and think about the things we say to our students every day, things we hardly give a thought to, but things that can stick with 'em and maybe one day lead to their conversion—or something else."

"Me too. This reminds me—*again*—to watch and make sure the flying doesn't become my idol. So far, it's not."

"I'm glad of that. And thanks for reminding me the Lord's still saving people and busting up idols!"

"My pleasure, Syl!"

Chapter Forty Four

Luther: Monday evening, April 10th, 1922, the Barlow home, Metamora.

"Luther, you've been giggling and snorting at that letter you're reading for the past ten minutes. What's so funny?"

I was sitting at the supper table that evening with Pa and Inge. It was the vacation week before Easter at Bradley, and I decided to take a long weekend at home before going back to study at my room in Peoria.

I probably shouldn't try to read Jack's letters in public, since they always make me laugh, but as this one was particularly hilarious, and had some other news they needed to hear, I had brought it and a few other things to the table.

"It's from Jack, Pa. He's answered a *burning question of the day* I didn't even know I was asking!"

"Inge, whenever Jack writes Luther he says things he knows will make him laugh. Luther does the same thing back. And eventually we get an explanation."

"Now I understand, Howard," Inge said in her soft, lilting *normal* voice.

She then added in her *librarian* voice, "Luther, explain please."

I stifled another giggle, this time at Inge. I'd never been around someone who could change their voice so dramatically and so quickly! She was a wonderful wife for Pa, and we both loved her dearly, but sometimes she could be very direct.

"OK. You've both heard me talk about that odd family I rent my room from in Peoria, the Templemans. Inge, you met them at the recital; Pa knew the husband, Charlie, before I took the room. Remember at the dinner how Charlie dominated the conversation, talked about nothing but himself, and ran roughshod over anyone trying to change the subject—except Marie."

"He's always like that, Dear," Pa said to Inge. "I've never met anyone like him."

"How can you stand living in a house with that man?" Inge asked.

"He's almost never there," I replied, "He has a room over the garage where he works. Agnes and Forrest are fine, and I really enjoy their company. I think you'd like them too. So is Marie Heath. Charlie is the odd one, and I do mean *odd*!"

"So Jack thinks he has Charlie figured out?" Pa asked.

"I think he's got him nailed! He sent me a couple of clippings from the funny pages in the newspaper out there in San Pedro. I'll show them to you in a minute. But here's what he says, quote: *The enclosed comic panels should illustrate the conclusion I've come to concerning you and your college living arrangements. I am convinced you, Luther, are living in Our Boarding House, with none other than Major Hoople!*"

Inge and Pa both had blank looks on their faces. Neither of them read the funny pages; neither did I, until Jack sent me this letter, and I looked through some papers we were ready to throw away.

I passed the clippings over to them.

They each looked at one, brows furrowed for a moment; then first Pa, then Inge, started to chuckle and laugh. They traded clippings and the process repeated.

Without a word I handed them a sheaf of newspaper pages I had pulled from the waste bin.

For the next ten minutes I was treated to the sight of Pa and Inge alternately reading, laughing, crying, whooping, and hugging each other. I thought Inge had a sense of humor, although we didn't see it come out often. Here it was demonstrated, in grand manner! Jack would be gratified.

Finally, they left off hugging each other and wiped their eyes with the napkins from the table. Both took another moment to settle down enough to speak.

"Jack has done it again!" Pa said between gasps.

"Does he always have this kind of an effect on his friends?" Inge asked.

"No, sometimes it's worse."

Another wave of laughter swept the other side of the table.

This time Inge found her voice first. "Oh my!"

"I'm glad we had this laughter now, because the rest of this letter isn't quite so funny."

My father and his bride sobered up rapidly.

"What's happened to him, Luther?" Pa asked.

"Well, he's OK…I guess. Here, let me read the section and you decide. Quote:

Things out in San Pedro got a little exciting about a month ago. I was on Shore Patrol duty again, with the Lieutenant and four other men. We had a tip some sailors were frequenting a speakeasy, so we went to check. When we went in we were met by a lookout, I guess—big fellow in a Navy uniform. We stated our business and he turned around as if to lead us, then turned back

271

with a gun in his hand! He went to shoot the Lieutenant, but I spoiled his aim and he missed. Unfortunately, he got me instead..."

Inge gasped. I continued reading.

"But before I left the party I took care of the situation permanently. A .45 still beats a .38, for the record. Turns out he was a thug in a stolen Navy uniform, and the idea was to lure sailors in and relieve them of their cash...and sometimes their lives. It was pretty messy, the Lieutenant told me later...but I had stepped out for a while. Woke up in the hospital."

Pa held Inge's hand as they listened. "Here we go again! I thought that sort of thing was over when the war ended!"

"Guess not, Pa. Jack finishes up, The docs say I'll be out of here in about another month. Then I get some leave, and a new assignment somewhere else. I was about due to transfer anyway. I can't say what I'll be doing next, but you know what I've always wanted to try my hand at."

"Let me guess—Drill Instructor?"

"Has to be that, Pa! He's always wanted to do that, and maybe he's got an inside track on it somehow. Guess we'll see."

"So he might show up around here, then?" Inge asked.

"Wouldn't be surprised at all. He can sleep on the floor in the parlor."

"Luther!"

*****

Luther: Tuesday, June 6th, 1922, The Nook.

"Well, here we are again!" Jack announced.

Jack had actually taken two months, more or less, to arrive from the west coast. We were sitting in a booth at our pleasant little corner restaurant, waiting for the beef and cabbage to arrive.

"You never told me where you got hit, Jack."

"Just about dead center in the abdomen. A half inch in any direction and we wouldn't be having this conversation. The surgeon sewed up a few stray body parts, cleared out some infection, and here I am!"

"Somehow I suspect it was a bit more involved than that."

Jack took a breath and shifted slightly in his seat. "It was. Actually a lot more complicated. I didn't have the number of holes punched in my person you had, but one was quite enough. The Lord preserved me again. And kept me conscious and functioning long enough to take the other fellow out permanently."

"Did that bother you any?"

"A bit, but it was in defense of my men, and the Lieutenant. I hadn't acted, L-T would have died, and probably others. I couldn't let that happen."

"I understand completely. Sometimes we just have to do what we have to do."

"Whether we remember it afterwards or not," Jack said with a lopsided grin. "This time, I remembered the action, but that was all. And that's fine with me."

Our meals came. I prayed, and we dug in.

"You've been all quiet about where you're headed. You said you were going to a new billet."

Jack grinned. "I got it, Luther!"

"Drill Instructor?"

"Yep! Parris Island. DI school first, then along about September, like the start of school, I get my first group of boots."

"You sound eager."

"I am! I've been waiting for this chance for eight years. I just pray I'm up to it.

"How's your strength and stamina?"

"That's why I was in San Pedro an extra month—they wanted to make sure I was back together and functioning normally. I just started the same routines I used at Walter Reed, and everything came back fine. I know that could change the older I get, but for now I'm good to go!"

"So everything is back to normal?"

Jack said nothing for a moment, then spoke. "Almost everything. OK, I didn't tell you the final act of this little drama. They got me again."

"Another visit from Roosevelt?"

"Not him, no. But haven't you heard? Roosevelt's got polio!"

"What? I hadn't heard about that!"

"Guess he's trying to keep it quiet—as if he can hide a wheelchair! The family was on vacation last year up near Canada, he caught something. Next thing you know he's paralyzed from the waist down! Steve and his people at Johns Hopkins are doing what they can to reverse some of it, but from what I heard they're not able to do much."

"Who told you this?"

"Doctor Raichart was lecturing at the hospital where I was, and he heard I was there. We had lunch together last month. It was a pretty somber lunch, too."

"Why's that?"

"I don't know if you remember, but when we first got to the little unit at Walter Reed, Doctor Raichart made a remark about wondering what would happen if one of those *unfeeling assistant secretaries*, or something like that, had to face what we were going through. Now Roosevelt's in for it, and unlike us, it doesn't look like they can help him much. Bill feels awful about making that remark now, but he can't change what he said."

I thought for a moment. "I remember him saying something like that now. He never had much use for the military bureaucracy. Could you help him?"

"I tried. I reminded him we were all pretty stressed in those days, and occasionally said things we shouldn't have. I also got a chance to witness to him again."

"So something good did come of your little brush with death?"

"Who said—"

"Jack, I know you, and I can read between the lines. You just about bought a ticket to Heaven with this one, didn't you?"

Jack looked down at his plate, uncharacteristically quiet.

"Yeah, I almost bled to death. Just like at Belleau Wood. The docs said another five minutes and I would've been gone."

"Uh huh. And what else? Spill it!"

"I got another Navy Cross."

I wasn't surprised. Jack had been just a little too vague about the incident in his letter, and here at the table.

"Saving the Lieutenant?"

"And my men. I didn't know they gave out NCs in peacetime, but they do."

"Sounds to me like you deserved it, Jack. Congratulations!"

"Thanks, I guess. The first NC didn't bother me so much, but this one does. I think I know better how you felt now."

"At least you remember what you did to get it."

"So I do."

"Now, what about you witnessing to Bill?"

"I explained what I knew about man's nature, and why we say and do the things we do. Then reminded him of the need for a Savior, and suggested One."

"And?"

"He thanked me for a fine meal of hospital food, and said he'd think about it. Got up and left."

"All we can do is pray, Jack."

"All we can do."

274

Chapter Forty Five

Luther: Saturday, December 23rd, 1922, the Templeman boarding house.

Over the years since I trusted Christ, I've looked forward to the Christmas season as a time to reflect upon Our Lord's provision for our sin, and the miracle of that birth so long ago. It's a time to reflect on what He did for us then, and what He's doing with us now. I liked to nestle up with this season like a dog enjoys making a nest in an unmade bed, and then sleeping in it until the humans notice him!

No *nestling* this year, though—I was way too busy.

At least my Christmas shopping was done. Besides the usual small gifts for Pa and Inge, I'd come up with something unique for my landlady. I decided I had had enough of the poor light given off by the ceiling fixture in my room. My eyes were starting to bother me when I studied in the evening. Figuring I didn't need any more physical infirmities, I went down to Block and Kuhl's to look at lamps. I ended up buying a very nice Rainaud slag glass shade, dual bulb table lamp. I thought it would not only provide the light I needed, but also look very nice on the table. In fact, I bought two identical lamps, figuring I'd give one to Agnes for Christmas. They were not cheap, but if they lasted as long as I figured they would, they were a bargain.

My studies were actually in good shape for the Christmas holiday break. Thanks to some planning and the Blick Electric, I had all my class papers typed and turned in for the semester, projects done, and felt good about the final exams the week after New Years'. What had me running were the *other things*.

Dennis Lepper, our music director, had asked me to help organize the Christmas Eve service, which this year was to be various carols and solos, separated by congregational singing and keyboard pieces by Dennis and me. Dennis had worked up a short cantata for them to perform, and asked me to accompany them. Taken individually all these were pleasant tasks; crammed into the time I had available after school and on weekends, the *fun* part dropped dramatically. Dennis always left his kids with his wife's parents, and went into hiding with his wife for the week between Christmas and New Years'; now I understood why!

Plus, this year some stress wafted through the atmosphere at the Templeman house. Agnes was getting near to term with her second

275

child. A birth in winter is always a bit risky, and we boarders were concerned, especially since Charlie continued to keep his very irregular schedule of visits to the house.

When I told Jack back in June of the scheduled arrival of a new Templeman, he had made one of his trademark pithy observations. Every once in a while his acid tongue would get him into trouble; his remark wasn't quite that inappropriate (in fact I agreed with it), but touched the edge of uncharitable. He apologized shortly after…and then we had a good laugh over it!

This Saturday I had driven out to Metamora in the morning for a final run-through of the program, including Dennis' and my instrumentals. Fortunately, the organ continued to perform perfectly, and Dennis was a consummate professional—he was only a *little* bit of an *artiste*! I tried hard to avoid projecting that temperament when I played, and while I worked for John Wick, but sometimes it was hard. Unchecked, that temperament is just another manifestation of the old nature, and must be fought tooth and nail. Only the Grace of God can beat it, of course.

I chuckled as I drove back to Peoria for my afternoon appointments. I started thinking about the performance I had seen in Chicago the previous month. Now there was an *artiste* temperament!

As a college student I was eligible for heavily discounted tickets to the Chicago Symphony Orchestra. I'd heard them off and on for years whenever they played in Peoria or Bloomington, and really liked their conductor, Fredrick Stock. The man wasn't flamboyant like so many conductors (that *artiste* thing again), but his interpretations of the classical repertoire were about the best I've ever heard. He was just plain *solid*.

I had found it was easier for me to get to Chicago than to St. Louis with the train connections available. When I began to work part time for John Wick, I usually arranged to meet him at his branch office up in Des Plaines instead of Highland. Besides being easier to get to, I schemed to combine the trip with a concert whenever I could. The train connections were reliable and frequent, and I found myself going up there about once a month.

For the 1922 season, my package included a pass to the "new" Chicago Civic Opera…more or less. The previous opera company in Chicago had been run by the estimable Mary Garden. My friends across the pond had a particular term which fit her perfectly—*balmy*. She was equally adept at singing lead roles in operas, staging grandiose opera productions, and bankrupting opera companies! She engineered the new company from the wreckage of the old, and was promising her first production *Very Soon Now*. (I should also note my sources told me she'd found time to have an affair with the visiting French conductor Andre Messager, who I'd heard when I was in France. My opinion of his insight and judgment declined accordingly.)

Monday, November 13th, after several false starts, she had finally presented *Aida*. Once I was reasonably sure she was truly going to do it this time, I arranged a couple of days off classes just to attend, and I wasn't disappointed. The performance was truly spectacular—Mary could definitely do opera! I decided that 'free' pass might be useful after all.

I even went out and bought the one book all opera lovers should own—the *Victor Book of the Opera*. I couldn't stand the quality of acoustically recorded phonograph records, but Victor's book almost made up for the lousy records they tried to sell with it! Some day those recordings would be made with electronic recorders; I knew enough of the theory by then to realize it was possible, and frankly I could hardly wait.

I was daydreaming about these pleasant thoughts as I stopped by the Congregational Church to see Carl Christensen. I wanted to hear what he had cooked up for the services the next day, and maybe play him what I had. He wasn't in, but I decided to spend a few minutes and check the old Moller out for him. I also wanted to make sure the new *direct electric* ranks we put into the choir and great divisions that summer were ready to go. Wicks actions were incredibly reliable, but I still had a bit of leftover paranoia from my Old Squeak days.

A half hour of playing and voice checks convinced me everything was good. I wrote him a note to that effect in the log, shut down the organ, and left, carefully locking the door behind me. The place still scared me as it got towards dusk.

I drove out to the Templeman house in the gathering chill of the late afternoon. That Chevrolet was cold, even with the side curtains up. I had an idea for a way to heat the inside of the car using water from the radiator, but I hadn't had time to tinker with it yet. I really should do that sort of thing in the summer, but I didn't need it then!

I was laughing to myself about that little twist as I walked past the front porch to go to my door on the side. Suddenly Forrest burst out of the front door.

"Mister Barlow! Mister Barlow, Come quick! It's Ma!"

I changed course and walked as quickly as the icy walk and my prosthesis would allow up the steps to the porch.

"Let's go inside. Forrest, what's the matter?"

"Ma's in her bedroom with the door locked. She's groaning and moaning, and we can't get in!"

"Let's go!"

We went through the dining room and up the stairs to Agnes's room. I knocked at the door, and got a moan in reply.

Forrest and Marie Heath were standing there with me. All the other boarders had gone home for the holidays; we were the only ones left. We needed to get into the room, and neither one of them could possibly get in. Looked like I was elected.

"You two stand back; I'll break in," I said. They moved back quickly.

I backed up to the other side of the hallway, braced, and charged the door. Jack was much better at this sort of thing than me, but he had taught me the key to success: imagine yourself about a foot beyond the door, and you'll go through it almost every time. That happened here.

The deadbolt gave way, and the door banged off the wall next to the frame.

The three of us went in. Agnes was moaning and moving on the bed; she appeared to be semi-conscious. It was obvious from the condition of the bed that her water had broken, and it looked like birth was immanent. At least, That's what I thought I saw.

I called her name, and shook her shoulder gently. Her eyes opened, but she only whispered three words—
Call...the...midwife—before her eyes closed again.

I turned to Marie. "What midwife? Is there a number?"

Marie's eyes brightened. "I wonder if that's the note I saw by the telephone the other day?"

"Let me go check. You two stay here with her."

I walked quickly down to the telephone. Sure enough, a paper with the word *midwife* and a phone number lay next to the phone. I lifted the receiver, got the operator's attention, placed the call. I got an answer quickly.

"Estelle Meriden."

"Hello, this is Luther Barlow. I am a boarder with Agnes Templeman on Bourland Avenue. She looks like she's gone into labor, and she asked me to call you. Does any of this make sense, ma'am?"

"Of course it does, *Sergeant* Barlow. You people waited almost too long to call me, and now I am expected to come and save the day. Very well. I will be there in ten minutes. Tell Agnes that. MOVE!"

And she disconnected. *This one's bedside manner makes Doctor Raichart sound like Queen of the May...*

I giggled involuntarily at that thought as I turned to go back upstairs.

And how did she know I was a Sergeant?

I was out on the porch in my coat, standing and waiting, when a car drove up precisely ten minutes later. I startled when I saw it looked identical to my Chevrolet, except blue instead of green and sported disc wheels. The car pulled around to the side street and into a driveway, backed up, and parked by the side of the house. It *looked* like my car, but it sounded different somehow, more of a *rumble* than the smooth puttering of mine. Maybe the mufflers were different. The transmission didn't whine when it backed up either. *No time to think about that now.*

I walked up toward the car as a tall, thin, older woman got out. Her hair was gray-white and peeked out from under a floppy hat. She could have been anywhere from sixty to eighty years old, from what I could see. She moved with purpose and speed, and spent no time on introductions. Before I could say a word she thrust a large bag into my hands.

"Take this. Follow me."

I followed.

Up the stairs we went again. The heavy bag I was carrying caused me to shift my balance as I went up, and my stump noted its displeasure.

We trooped into Agnes' room, where Forrest and Marie Heath stood around her bed.

Mrs. Meriden walked up to the bed, and put her hand on Agnes' shoulder. She opened her eyes.

"There, there, Agnes, it's all right. I'm here, and the little one will be arriving shortly. Let me get set up and we'll welcome the little one in."

She spoke to Agnes in a soft, soothing, almost lilting voice. She turned to the three of us.

"Now for you. Forrest, you may go. I will tell you when you may come in and see the baby." Forrest scurried out of the room.

"Ah, Marie, we meet again. I meant to tell you earlier, but Dick and I loved your performance in Peter Pan—the highlight of your career, in my opinion. Now you go find a chair out there and sit down, and keep the Sergeant here from falling apart. Now go."

Marie left the room silently, shaking her head.

Mrs. Meriden now turned to me.

"Very well, Sergeant Barlow. I know you'll do what I tell you for your friend here. I will need the towels from the second shelf in the front hall cabinet. Bring me two blankets from the top shelf. And the galvanized tub in the bottom cabinet. Bring them here now, please."

I scuttled out of the room and walked to the cabinets built into the front wall of the hallway. Everything was as she described-- *how did she know that?* I collected the items and returned to the room.

Mrs. Meriden took the items and set them around her. She wasn't finished with me yet, however.

"There is not enough light in here. I need another lamp to sit there." She pointed to the night stand next to the bed.

"I have just what you need, ma'am. I'll be right back!"

I went down the stairs to my room, waving at Marie as I went by. I unplugged the lamp sitting on my work table, and carefully lifted it. Since it was only a week old, I decided to give it to Agnes instead of the one in the box on the floor; I'd put that one together for me later.

I picked up the lamp with both hands, and marched up the stairs to Agnes' room. Those lamps are heavy, and my center of balance shifted as I climbed; by the time I got to the second floor my leg felt like I had just marched twenty miles with a full pack. There would be a reckoning later, and it wouldn't be pleasant.

"I was going to give Agnes this lamp for Christmas, but it seems we have Christmas coming early," I said as I plugged it in and turned it on.

"You might say that, Sergeant Barlow. This will do; thank you."

"May I ask a question, Mrs. Meriden?"

"You may ask *one*, Sergeant!"

I wasn't expecting that response, and just said the first thing that popped into my head. "OK. I own a Chevrolet Model D just like you do. Yours sounds nothing like mine, not the motor or the transmission noise. And you turned the wheel with one hand when you backed up. How is your car different from mine?"

The tall midwife's mouth dropped open, and her eyes went wide. Three seconds later her mouth snapped shut, and she took a deep breath. She peered at me over her half glasses, and spoke quietly. "My husband Richard works for Wain Engineering Corporation in Galesburg. Donald Wain owns the company—I believe you have met him."

"Yes, I met him at my recital in Metamora last year."

Mrs. Meriden continued to prepare the room for the delivery as she spoke. "So Agnes told me. Anyway, Richard drives home to Peoria every Friday, and returns to Galesburg every Monday. Wain Engineering has developed some experimental equipment for automobiles, and several items have been installed in our car for testing. The details of the installation are most secret; since you own the only other one of those cars in this area, you would be able to tell the difference. That is all I can say."

Another moan from Agnes punctuated her reply.

"Thank you for your candor, ma'am. I will not speak of what you said."

A slight hint of a smile flitted across her wrinkled face. "Thank you, Sergeant, and call me Estelle please. Now you go wait in the hall, or down in the living room, until I call you."

She turned to look at Agnes, but continued speaking to me as I turned to leave. "You may as well try to get hold of Charlie, but I can tell you, you won't. As Agnes said at our last meeting, he's only around for the *consultation*, not the *work!*"

I couldn't help snickering.

"Men!"

Softer, "Now, go keep Marie company. Agnes and I have work to do."

I turned to leave, and shut the door behind me.

Sure enough, I couldn't reach Charlie Templeman. I tried the garage, and a couple of other numbers Mr. Strickfaden gave me, without success. I went back upstairs to sit with Marie. Forrest was down in the parlor working with his radio gear. *there's a practical lad!*

Marie's room was next to Agnes'. Her door was open, and she called out to me, "You might as well come in here and wait, Luther. The chairs are more comfortable, and we can hear with the door open."

I stepped through the door...and for a few seconds I thought I'd stepped through the looking glass.

Marie was seated in a comfortable-looking but worn Morris chair. Next to her chair was her bed, children's height to accommodate her short stature. Around the room were two dressers, a vanity with mirror, and an old washstand—all shorter than normal. A large steamer trunk with the legend *Marie Heath* on the top sat in the corner. Thus the furniture.

On the vanity lay a polished silver brush, comb, and hand mirror set. On the dressers several porcelain dolls dressed in what looked like theatrical costumes were posed sitting on the edge of

281

the top. A large jewelry box nestled in among the dolls on one dresser.

The walls of the room were covered with framed playbills, publicity photographs, and memorabilia from the theater. I was sure each item had a story behind it, and resolved to ask her about them sometime.

She motioned me to sit down in a wooden armchair. As I sat, I decided Marie Heath's room looked just like the living space of someone who had physically aged, but never really grown up. It was very definitely *her room*.

"Remarkable room," I commented.

"It's my little home, the repository of my memories, the mirror of my life. I'm very happy here."

"So I see, Marie."

Despite her words, Marie sat in her chair with a serious look on her face.

"Marie, is there something bothering you?"

The retired actress glanced over at the wall between her room and Agnes'.

"Two things, Luther. First, the birth occurring next door. I was never able to have children, and the closest I've ever come to their birth has been here, first with Forrest and now this one. I love children, but I'll never know how it feels to have one myself. That concerns me, saddens me really, at a time like this."

"I think I understand. I was an only child, and sometimes I think about what it would have been like to watch siblings being born, and help raise them. I've missed out on that."

"I did too, and more. I was orphaned when I was very young. I really don't remember my parents. I was raised in an orphanage, and I was only really close to the other children, not the adults. It's affected how I got along with people later."

I had a hunch, and went with it. "And something else?"

Marie nodded. "Did you hear the compliment Mrs. Meriden gave me about Peter Pan?"

"Yes," I replied.

"That was the last play I did before I retired, in 1906. The critics panned me, the management fired me after two weeks, and suggested it was time I retire. I suppose I did try to milk it longer than I should have—I played young girls and little boys for thirty eight years, after all! But I always thought I really had the character of Peter! As well as any I played, anyway. And Mrs. Meriden saw that play—a two week run, in New York City, in 1906. And she *liked* me?"

I didn't know how to respond, except with the truth. "If this were a play, Marie, I'd come up with some witty line to answer your question and make you feel better, but I really don't know what to say to that."

Marie put her hand on my shoulder. "That's all right, Luther, I know you would if you could. I'm just thankful someone liked what I did back then...and I won't try to figure out how she knew about it."

"She knew right off when I called I was *Sergeant* Barlow. Do you suppose she remembered that newspaper article from so long ago?"

"She might, or Agnes said something. The Meridens are just *odd*—she and Agnes are good friends. Her husband's name is Richard, and he works for some *research and development* firm in Galesburg. I believe he stays there during the week, and comes home on weekends. I don't know how they do it; they're both at least as old as I am!"

"She mentioned her husband and his job when I asked her a question. That lady scares me just a bit."

"I know what you mean, Luther. It doesn't matter if you're a War Hero, ace organist, or retired actress- some people are just scary. I have to admit—I'm 72 years old, and she scares the liver out of me!"

We both laughed at that.

A few moments later we heard a baby cry.

"Thank you Lord," I breathed.

Marie just grinned.

******

Luther: later that afternoon.

"Well, Forrest, that is your new sister. Your mother has named her Dorothy Luella. What do you think of her?"

Forrest peered in for a closer look. "Ma'am, I believe she'll do!"

Mrs. Meriden looked puzzled for a moment, then resumed her commanding persona.

"Very well. Agnes needs to sleep a while longer; she'll be awake to feed the baby in a couple of hours. Luther, you take the tub of soiled linens down to the washer, and I will deal with it after I make supper."

"You're fixing us supper, Estelle?"

283

"Of course I am, Sergeant Barlow! I can't expect *you* to do it, can I?"

Actually, I can cook fairly well, but I decided this was not the time to mention it.

"Marie, if you could stay here and watch Agnes, I'll take Dorothy and go start supper."

"Yes, ma'am."

Marie Heath, retired actress in her seventies, calling Mrs. Meriden *ma'am*? I guess I really wasn't the only one afraid of her!

I followed Mrs. Meriden down the stairs, carrying the laundry pan. *Glad I'll have the cheater coupler on the organ tomorrow*, I thought.

After an excellent supper, prepared only on the top of the gas stove, I started to collect myself to get on the road to Metamora. I had opened my door when Mrs. Meriden stopped me.

"Luther, it is getting cold in this house. I'll go tend to the furnace in a few minutes; your leg has had enough work for one day. But before you go, please open the oven and check the temperature."

I opened the door of the oven and stuck my arm in. "It's warm, but not overly hot. Maybe eighty or ninety degrees."

"Good. Let me put Dorothy in the oven, then. That is the perfect temperature for her right now. Go ahead and get ready to leave, but check with me before you go. And please keep your door open now, so you can hear if she starts to cry."

"Yes, Estelle."

Mrs. Meriden put the basket with little Dorothy in the oven, and propped the door half closed.

As she trudged up the stairs I heard her mutter to herself, "I hope that time in the oven doesn't leave Dorothy like Charlie—*half baked*!"

I chuckled as I went in my room. She does have a sense of humor, after all!

Dorothy was still in the oven when I left a half hour later.

I finally got to Metamora about nine that evening. Pa and Inge were in the parlor,

holding hands on the love seat.

"You're home a bit later than you were figuring. Everything OK in *Our Boarding House*?"

Inge snickered.

"Well, Pa," I replied, "I can honestly say things over there are *half-baked*."

Chapter Forty Six

Sylvia: Saturday April 25th, 1925, the C.B.&Q. Depot, Galesburg.

"One way ticket? Helen, what have you got up your sleeve this time?"

"One arm, a few hairs, some freckles…"

"You know what I mean!"

We were standing in line at the ticket counter of the musty, sprawling C.B.&Q. passenger depot in Galesburg, on a brilliantly clear Spring morning. *Early* morning, as we had to catch the first express train of the day to make it to Chicago in time to have lunch before the matinee performance. The opera was starting early today, so we had to leave earlier to get there.

Helen stood with me, although as usual she would use her *employee pass* to ride.

"I have arranged alternate accommodations for us on the way home. There's no need to waste money on a return ticket."

I could tell she was hiding something—she always got a little *wordier* when she wasn't telling everything she knew.

"All I can say is, I am not flying back from Chicago in one of your open-cockpit biplanes!"

Helen smiled. "I can *absolutely guarantee* you will not fly back from Chicago in an open-cockpit biplane."

I gave Helen my best rendition of *The Look*, but broke up giggling almost immediately when she returned her version, which was way better than mine!

Then I was up to the counter, and I let the matter drop as I purchased my one-way ticket. I'd find out what was up eventually, but I also took Helen at her word, and put the possibility of flying out of my mind.

It wasn't that I was scared to fly, I just didn't trust the airplanes Helen flew, especially after what happened with Ruth Law that day in 1920. I knew Helen was a skilled and careful pilot; I'd seen her logbook with just over three hundred flying hours in it, a remarkable achievement for someone who only flew on the weekends and in the summertime because of her teaching. I knew the Lord had blessed her flying greatly, and that she was beginning to instruct others, teaching them how to fly like she taught her students to read. And she was very, very good at that!

I knew if I ever went up in an airplane, I'd want Helen to be the pilot…*just not today, please!*

The Chicago Civic Opera, and the always entertaining Mary Garden, pulled out all the stops for the first opera of the new season...especially since it was also the last opera of the previous season, a little late.

Giacomo Puccini's *La Boheme* is a collection of interesting stories, threaded together with some incredibly beautiful arias for the main characters. Mary Garden took the lead female role, of course, and crazy as she was about other things, she had a magnificent voice and could act. The male lead was someone I hadn't heard before, a big tenor named Lauritz Melchior. He was very much up to the task, and together they brought the stories to vibrant life. I had an English translation of the Italian, and Helen brought notes culled from her *Victor Book of the Opera*, and we shared them.

I thought the highlight of the performance was Lauritz Melchior singing the aria *Che Gelida Manina* to Mimi, played by Mary Garden. I had to say that was the most beautiful tenor aria I'd ever heard. I almost cried, even though the words weren't that emotive to me. It was just that music!

I know it sounds corny, but we were both humming tunes from the opera as we left the Auditorium Theater to walk back to Union Station. I still didn't know how we were getting home, but Helen knew where she was going.

We went in a different door than usual, and I saw we were going to the commuter gates.

"Where are we going?"

"You'll see."

We walked to the ticket counter for the Chicago and Western Indiana Railroad, and Helen bought two tickets for...someplace or other. That told me exactly nothing, since I didn't know my way around Chicago. We marched to a platform, and in about five minutes a train backed into the station and stopped. We coughed a little at the coal smoke, even though the engine was at the other end of the train.

"You really know where we're going, Helen?"

"Oh, yes, not a problem!"

Easy for her to say, I thought.

We found seats near the exit of the half-full coach. A minute later the train lurched and started out of the station. From the position of the sun I figured we were heading more or less southwest.

After several stops Helen got up. "Next one's ours!"

We got off the train at little more than a roof on posts next to a street. I looked across the street to see a collection of weathered buildings, and a large sign: *Chicago Air Park.*

"And what are you getting me into, Helen Smiley?"

Helen just smiled and started to cross the street. I followed her; fortunately there wasn't much traffic.

"Gil's hired a new mechanic," Helen remarked, "he tells me the fellow is a little uncouth. I haven't met him yet."

"Who's Gil?"

"Gil Foster. You met him the day of my license test. He runs Wain Engineering's operations up here."

"Oh," I said, trying to remember who I met that day. The engine failure and forced landing pretty much wiped the rest of the day from my memory.

We walked over to a small building attached to a hangar, and stepped inside.

My nose and eyes were assaulted by a haze of cigar smoke in the small, overheated office. The source of the smoke was an overweight, middle-aged man in suspenders and a dirty white shirt. A cigar hung from his mouth, and he also appeared to be the source of other odors I detected. Helen stepped over to the desk.

"Good afternoon, I'm here to see Mr. Foster."

The slovenly figure took the cigar out of his mouth and blew a cloud of noxious fumes in our direction.

"Now then, little lady, you would be a-wantin to see the Big Strong Pilot, the Esteemed Gilbert Foster? As if he'd agree to see the likes of you—except in a burlesque show!"

This lout managed to cram more denigration into two sentences than I think I've ever heard in my life. I felt my face reddening, and fancied my chances putting him on the floor in a pile. My Pa had provided for my education in many ways, including training in self-defense the *Marine way.* I knew I could drop him, if I had to.

Helen's expression didn't change. She reached into the pocket of her culottes and pulled out a folding wallet—she almost never carried a purse. She flipped the wallet open and pointed the inside of it at the man.

The man glanced at the open wallet, then looked again. And a third time. He turned pasty white and started to shake!

"Y-Y-Y-Yes, ma'am, right away ma'am!"

With those words he literally scrambled over his overturned chair, and ran out of the office into the hangar as fast as his bloated figure could move.

Helen finally let a small grin change her face. She flipped the wallet shut and brought it up to her lips. She blew on it as if it were a smoking revolver and put it back in her pocket.

Time for a little understatement. "That's one powerful little wallet you got there, Helen."

"Isn't it though! It's like a gun—you never need it unless you need it very, very badly."

"You don't own a gun."

"If I flew the airmail I would."

A younger man about the same size and build as Helen stepped through the door from the hangar.

"Hi Helen!"

He walked quickly over to Helen, and they hugged each other! I began to wonder what she'd been up to on her *flying weekends*.

They released the hug and the man turned to me, face reddening.

"I'm so sorry about that, Sylvia! We just don't see each other very often during the school year, and it's always like meeting a long-lost friend!"

Now I really was confused. "How did you know me?"

"I met you the day Helen got her license—and saved Ruth Law's life!"

"OK, now I understand," I said as I shook the man's hand, "Gil Foster, right?"

"Right," Gil said, and turned to Helen, "Freddy tried to bother you, didn't he?"

"How could you tell?"

Gil chuckled. "I saw him scrambling to get out of the office and put as much space between you and him as he could. He's hiding in the, er, *lavatory* right now."

"Afraid I'll follow him in and flush him?"

"Probably," Gil sputtered and tried to breathe. "He has a terrible mouth around women—did he try to drive you off?"

"He tried, but didn't get too far," Helen replied. "I flashed him my Aero Club license, and between that and my name on it, he crashed and burned nicely. I was watching Syl here sizing him up too—her late Pa was a Marine Gunny, and he taught her their way of self-defense. Were you calculating how many pieces he'd be in when you finished with him?"

I smiled and nodded.

"I've got to ask—how many?" Gil asked me.

"Three."

We laughed some more, then Gil sobered.

"I'm very sorry you had to deal with him. If he wasn't the best engine mechanic I've ever seen, I'd have kicked him out of here the second day!"

"Where'd he come from?" Helen asked.

"Jackie worked with him, er, in a *previous position*. She says he always was brilliant with engines, and kept his personal life together well enough until he retired. He's *gone to seed*, so to speak, now that he doesn't have the discipline of his previous career to order his life."

I wasn't sure what Gil was talking about, but Helen nodded. "OK, that makes sense. Is he a Believer?"

"Claims he is, and Jackie believes he is too. Awfully backslidden, though."

Helen smiled. "He got his comeuppance this time, and I don't think he'll bother me again. I'll put him on my prayer list. Besides," she grinned, "we need all the good mechanics we can get!"

"Ain't that the truth! You're here to pick up the F13, I guess."

"Yep. She ready?"

"Ted and Al are rolling her out now, and doing a preflight. Come on into my office and we'll go over the modifications."

We stepped into Gil's small office and sat down. Gil shut the door. He handed me a form on a clipboard, and a pen.

"Sylvia, this is a nondisclosure form. By signing it you certify that you will not speak of the experimental modifications we have made to the aircraft you will be flying in. These modifications are most secret, and we must keep them that way."

Helen had explained that secrecy was part of the work she performed for Wain Engineering, so I was not surprised. "Of course, Gil," I replied, and signed the form. I then looked at the pen I had been given. "What kind of a pen is this?"

Gil smiled. "Another project the company is involved with. The pen is loaded with a gel-like ink, and the ink flows out past a tiny steel ball. We call it a *ball point pen*. People have been trying to perfect these since the 1880s; we think ours is pretty good."

"Except when one leaked in my pocket," Helen said with a chuckle.

"Pretty good, not perfect," Gil added, "You may keep the pen, Sylvia. Return it to Helen when it runs out of ink and we will see how well it lasted."

"Thank you," I said, and pocketed the pen, "I'll take my chance with it today."

Gil handed Helen a small booklet. "Here are the notes on the modifications we've made to the aircraft. The original Pilot's Notes should give you enough information to fly it home; you can test out the new stuff when you have time."

"Okay," Helen said, and leafed through the booklet. "So we're calling the engine an *IO-720*?"

"Right," Gil replied, "The specifications are what we estimated. Fit on the aircraft like it was designed for it!"

"Good—no more of those awful war surplus engines. Even the BMWs are just failures-in-waiting. How's the cockpit?"

Gil grinned. "Fine. Windshield fit perfectly. Cut the door to the cabin, installed the new instruments. Still no radio—I think Sammy is planning to install it in Galesburg."

"It'll be so nice to have some communication in the ships," Helen remarked, "Anything to watch out for?"

Gil nodded. "Yeah, the brakes. Pretty touchy, still trying to get 'em to modulate with pedal force. Watch out. Flaps are fine by the way."

"Thanks for the heads up, *brother*. Shall we take Syl out and show her our ride home?"

"Are you OK if we run into Freddy again?" Gil asked.

"I'll give him *the look*—maybe he'll soil himself!"

I gasped. "Really?"

Helen smiled as we got up to leave. "Naah, I won't do that—it's too cruel. However, if he does make a social indiscretion…

We laughed as we stepped out of the office.

Chapter Forty Seven

Sylvia: Chicago Air Park.

We walked out the door and over to the side of the hangar. Outside the open hangar sat the strangest aeroplane I had ever seen. It was larger than what I had seen Helen fly before, and where the others were made of wood and fabric, this one was obviously made of metal—*corrugated* metal! It reminded me of one of the Johnson's corn cribs with wings!

I noticed other details. It only had a lower set of wings—I think they called that a monoplane. It had two windows and a door on the side, and in front what seemed like a large glass bubble over two slanted oval holes. At least the engine and propeller looked normal—except the propeller had three blades instead of the usual two.

On the tail I noticed a strange logo- a triangle with some sort of three-pronged figure in the middle, and above it the name *Junkers*. I had a wild thought—the only junkers I knew of were cars like Helen drove! I couldn't help giggling.

"This is funny?"

"No, Helen, I just had a crazy thought."

"Trust me, a *junker* it is not!"

I laughed again, but stopped short when I realized this contraption was going to be my ride home.

I tagged along as Helen and Gil walked slowly around the craft, checking this and that, and discussing the plane's features.

Helen turned to Gil, "How about the gyrocompass?"

"I checked it on the compass rose, and it's accurate. That gyroscopic turn and bank indicator works well too."

"Good enough. Well, Gil, Guess we'd better hit the road."

"There ought to be a different way of saying that," Gilbert hugged Helen again.

"Be careful, sis. I'll call Jackie and tell her when you're off. She's going to Monmouth to pick you up. And nice seeing you again, Sylvia! Hope you come up here again."

"Thanks, Gil. It's been a surprise, and a pleasure!"

"Maybe dinner next time, Gil?"

"Count on it, Sis!"

Helen led the way to the side of the plane and climbed up on the wing. She opened the door and motioned me in. Helen climbed in behind me and shut the door.

Four seats filled the small passenger compartment. Helen opened a door in the front wall and we clambered into the cockpit. I sat on the right, Helen on the left.

This cockpit was nothing like the ones in the planes Helen usually flew. First, it was warm in there—the sun shone through the glass bubble over our heads. Then, everywhere I looked there was metal, except for two squares down by our knees which were windows about a foot square in the side of the plane. I looked out and could see the front of the right tire.

"Another change we made," Helen remarked. Otherwise it's hard to see out of this thing."

We settled into the comfortable cushioned seats, and fastened the wide seat belts.

Helen handed me a paper. "Here, Syl, read this to me please, line by line, starting at the top."

"What is this?"

"Checklist. This plane's complicated enough I want something to remind me what I'm doing, and keep me from forgetting something. You read a line, I'll respond. Then read me the next line."

"Sure."

So I started at the top, and read off the checklist. Helen flipped switches and turned valves, and replied to me before I read the next line.

Shortly I got to the end. "That's it."

"Checklist is complete," Helen replied. She slid open a small window set in the larger bubble. I saw Gilbert standing in front of the plane.

"Clear!" Helen yelled.

"Clear!" replied Gilbert.

"OK, Syl, here goes!" She grasped a lever with one hand and pushed the button labeled 'starter' with the other.

I heard a whining sound, and the propeller turned. It made about two turns and Helen moved the lever forward. Suddenly, the engine caught and started to run.

Helen looked at the instruments closely. A moment later she made a motion with her hands out the window. Through my lower window I saw a hand pull the wheel blocks from my wheel.

Out in front, Gilbert drew himself up to attention, snapped a salute, then blew her a kiss.

Helen laughed as she returned the salute. "That last part's not in the checklist!"

Helen increased power and the plane started to move forward. We both kept a watch out the windshield as she taxied toward the end of the single runway.

"This could get confusing if they add another couple of runways," Helen said. "I've heard that's in the wind. This field's too small to serve such a big city."

As we moved toward the end of the runway, Helen said, "Better try the brakes, I guess."

She placed her feet on two small pedals below two larger ones, and pushed the pedals with her feet.

"Whoa!"

The plane seemed to stop dead in its tracks as the tail started to come up and the propeller headed down toward the ground!

Helen released the levers and the back of the plane returned to the ground with a thump.

"Got brakes."

"Scared yourself, didn't you?" Helen always got quiet after a scare.

"You got it. I've never seen brakes work that well. Gil was right—and I'm sure he's back there laughing his head off!"

"He probably did that himself. He did warn you, after all."

"So he did," Helen said with a grin.

We got to the end of the cinder-covered runway, and turned down the long path towards the other end of the field.

Now we wait for—there it is," Helen said. She pointed to the green light shining from the top of one of the buildings. "That's our signal to go. See any other planes?"

I craned my neck around the glass bubble. "Nope, looks clear."

"Then we're outta here!"

With that Helen pushed the throttle forward, and the tick of the engine became a roar. We started to roll down the cindered path, constantly picking up speed.

After a bit the tail rose in the air, and we were level. Another moment and the tinking of the cinders slung against the bottom of the plane stopped.

So this is flying!

Helen constantly looked out the windshield, down at the instruments, and out the small window at her knee. Her head never quit moving. She turned the plane to the left—I think it's called a bank—and we headed more or less west.

I could see Helen was completely absorbed in her job, so I just sat there and *experienced.* The engine was loud, but not nearly as loud as I expected. I had imagined what the land would look like from above, but I seriously underestimated the beauty of it, even the city parts I was seeing. With a windshield in front of us I only had a vague sensation of air rushing past us, and not that much sensation of speed. I could feel vibration through my seat—the engine I guessed. Overall, the experience was pleasant, but not addictive.

"Well, whaddya think?"

We had to raise our voices to be heard, but no more than we did during a behavior in the classroom.

"This is nice. Not something I'd want to do every day, but then I'm not you!"

"Nope. I will say this is the most *civilized* aeroplane I've ever flown! They keep building planes like this, maybe more people will fly."

"Where'd this one come from?"

"Germany. The Junkers Company, pronounced *yunkers,* have been making these things since 1919. Sold quite a few. Fellow named John Larsen imports 'em here, and Gil distributes them in the Midwest. This one has the Wain Engineering modifications, of course."

I changed the subject slightly. "So, Helen, How many times have you flown one of these?"

Helen turned to me with a grin. "One, actually. Today, in fact!"

"How can you fly something like this first time around? Aren't you afraid you'll forget something?"

"I sure could, Syl! That's why I memorized the Pilot's Notes. They're like an instruction manual for flying, each plane has one. Then I made up those checklists. There'll be one for landing, too, so don't lose 'em!"

"I've got them right here, not to worry."

The built-up area around Chicago passed behind us and we headed over farmland and small towns.

"How high are we?" I asked.

"We're cruising at five thousand feet. Speed's pretty good— thanks to the new engine and that windshield. We're making a hundred thirty miles an hour at cruise power. Be to Monmouth in just about an hour and twenty minutes from now, the way I'm taking."

"That sun is starting to glare through the windshield."

"So it is. That reminds me—see that sack between the seats? Open it up. That's two pair of sunglasses—Don had Gil leave 'em for us. We keep 'em."

"That's nice of him. How'd he know you were bringing me along?"

"I mentioned this would be a good time to get you up in the air, since we'd be up here at the opera anyway. He agreed."

I handed Helen a small case, and opened mine up. I took the sunglasses out of the case, and put them on. They really cut down the glare! I looked at my reflection in the windshield—they looked good on me too.

Helen put her pair on, and grinned. "I like these! With these, he'd almost not have to pay me! *Almost*, that is."

An hour later we passed over a large city straddling a river.

Helen pointed down. "Peoria."

"Not much longer, then?"

"Twenty five minutes, more or less."

A few minutes later Helen spoke. "Uh oh."

I looked out the windshield. The sun was fairly low on the horizon, but was close to being obscured by what appeared to be the curvature of the Earth. However, the sun wasn't supposed to set for another hour this time of the year.

"Is that a storm front?" I asked.

"Yep. Bad one."

Helen moved the throttle forward, and the sound of the engine changed.

"Looks like we're racing that storm."

"'Fraid so," Helen replied through clenched teeth, "and it's gonna be close. Wish we had the radio hooked up—I need to know what's going on in Monmouth."

"Can we fly through one of those?"

"No way! We might last a couple more minutes in this ship than what I usually fly—one good gust and they're down. This bird's very strong, but not that strong. We either get into Monmouth field, or find someplace else to land in a hurry."

"But where?"

"Don't have an answer for you. Keep looking out for Galesburg. We should see it in about five minutes."

"Right."

The sun disappeared behind the storm front. We took off our sunglasses and I put them back in their cases.

I looked out in the distance. Just to the left of our nose I saw some smoke trails near the ground, then the tall gasworks smokestack.

"Galesburg just off to the left."

"Got it."

Helen slipped into her *all business* mode. Things were getting serious indeed.

"Praying?" she asked.

"Constantly."

"Good. In a little bit I'll ask you to tell me the airspeed every five seconds or so. You can read it off that dial there," she pointed to one in the center of the panel. "It's reading one forty right now. See it?"

"Yes. Every five seconds when you say so."

"OK. For now, keep an eye out the front. Watch for a green light shining at us. Sing out when you see it!"

"Right."

Helen pointed the nose of the airplane slightly down, and the wind noise increased. We slipped over Galesburg and headed west. The storm front now reached halfway up the sky in front of us, and we could begin to see lightning shooting through the front of the wall. Like that evening in 1919, this stretched from horizon to horizon.

The air was very calm, and we slid through it without a bump. That would change shortly, I knew.

Chapter Forty Eight

Sylvia: in the air, near Monmouth, Illinois.

"What's our speed?"

"One hundred fifty five, if I'm reading it right."

"You are. The field in about one minute, I think."

That was the longest minute I can ever remember.

I saw it! "Green light, straight ahead!"

"Got it. Start calling speed when I start maneuvering."

"Right."

We flashed over the middle of the field at about fifty feet, Helen said later. We were headed right for the black wall of the storm.

Helen hauled back on the wheel and yelled, "Speed!"

"One thirty...one twenty...one ten..."

We soared into the air and curved to the left, out over the gravel road into Monmouth.

"Ninety...eighty...seventy five..."

Helen snapped the plane over in a hard bank to the left. I could see us lining up with the runway, but we were way too high!

"Hang on!"

Helen moved the controls, and the plane seemed to fall out of the sky onto its left wing. A side-slip, like I saw that day with Ruth Law, but much quicker, and harder. A gust of wind caught the wing as she leveled out—we almost went over the other way, but she caught it.

We crossed the gravel road below the trees, and Helen pulled back on the control wheel. All three tires hit the grass at the same time, with a thud.

"Thank you Lord!" We both said it at the same time.

As we rolled down the field Helen began making small movements with the brake pedals, gradually slowing us down and aiming us toward a medium sized hangar about two-thirds down the field. The door was open, and a green light flashed from within.

"There's our safety. We were going to taxi right in anyway, and now we really need to!"

The rain began to spatter on the metal skin of the plane as we headed toward the open hangar. The wind started to move the wings up and down as we taxied, but Helen kept firm control.

We bounced onto the concrete pad in front of the hangar and pulled straight in. It was large enough to take us, and some others too. I saw a smaller biplane parked in one corner, and on the other side of us a Model T and two larger cars.

With a squeak of brakes we stopped on the concrete floor of the hangar. Helen cut the switch and with one last pop the engine stopped. Behind us the hangar doors started to roll shut as the rain began to pour, and the wind eddied around the half-closed door.

The cabin door opened, and I heard Lee Wright.

"Helen, Sylvia, come quickly! There's tornadoes and large hail in the area, and we have to get to the shelter!"

Helen had been flipping switches and turning valves. "Get moving Syl, I'm right behind you."

She was still all business. I unbuckled and propelled myself out the cockpit door and out of the plane. Helen was indeed right behind me.

The hangar doors shut completely. I couldn't hear anything above the sound of the wind and rain on the metal shell of the hangar.

We followed Lee as he walked quickly into a small office in one corner of the hangar, then down a flight of concrete stairs at the back of the office. He opened a door, and motioned us in. He took one last look around, and followed.

The room was well lit, but a bit chilly. Several nondescript chairs and a battered dining room table competed with a threadbare Victorian couch and love seat for the limited space. The room seemed new, but the furniture definitely was *not*.

A small group of people stood in the center of the room. I recognized Lee Wright and Jackie Brighthonor. Two other men I did not recognize; one of those, a shorter, dark-haired man spoke up..

"Sorry this isn't any better furnished, folks, but we only finished it a month ago and it's just caught whatever furniture we could scrounge."

Lee chuckled. "Don't worry about it, John. I kind of like the décor—*early bunker?*"

"We need it tonight, that's for sure!," the man Lee called *John* replied, "I suppose we should introduce around; we all just *collected* here as you two ladies landed."

A crash from outside punctuated John's statement.

"Lee, how about you start, then I'll introduce our unexpected guest."

"Sure, John. Folks, the tongue tied gentleman to my right is John Livingston—pilot, instructor, operator of this airport for Mid-West Airways, Inc. We seem to find ourselves tangled up in business deals from time to time, including the one just arrived! To my immediate left is Jacqueline Brighthonor, Aero Club pilot and the accountant for Wain Engineering Corporation, the new owners of that Junkers."

Another massive crash shook the ground a bit. Lee continued, louder because of the increasing noise outside.

"And our two last arrivals. On the left is Sylvia Trimble, an old friend. Her late husband worked for me before the war, and she teaches school out by Appleton. And finally, the star of that air show we just witnessed, Helen Smiley. Helen teaches elementary school in Galesburg during the week, but weekends and summers she flies for Don Wain and me. She's begun instructing this year too—and you just saw a demonstration of why she's the one I call when I have a tough flying job to get done! We'll all do that handshaking thing in a minute—"

At that point the lights went out.

Lee spoke again. "Anybody got a flashlight, just in case—"

The lights came back on.

"Hmmm…I guess that generator with the automatic start works after all!"

"Less than five seconds, Lee," John Livingston said. "That's amazing!"

"Something Wain Engineering cooked up—he said it was experimental."

"Must have some real wizards in that company. Anyway, may I finish the introductions now?"

"Be my guest, John!"

"Thanks, Lee. We were up there with the light waiting for Helen and Sylvia to come in, watching the storm to the west, and wondering which would get here first. We heard an airplane, flying low. It seemed to be looking for a place to land. We finally saw it, and I pointed the green light at him. He saw it, and came in; that's his OX-5 Standard upstairs."

So far the other person in the room just sat quietly listening. Now John motioned for him to stand up. He was tall, thin, and had an expression on his face I had seen before, but couldn't place.

"You never know who'll blow in on a night like this. Folks, I'd like you to meet an old friend of mine, a fellow who flies like he wants to grow old, never mind what they say about him—the one, the only—"

The surprise guest interrupted John. He spoke quietly.

"Aw, stick a sock in it, John! Folks, I'm Charles Lindbergh, but you can call me 'Slim', if you want."

I'd never heard the name before, but Helen's face showed she had.

We began shaking hands all around. I started with Helen, of course, and we all were laughing as we continued.

When Slim got to Helen, he stopped.

"Helen, I've been hoping I'd get to meet you, and I guess this is the best time to do that. What you did up there a few minutes ago was the only maneuver you could have possibly done to bleed off the speed and put that Junkers on the field safely before the storm hit. How many hours do you have in that type?"

Helen turned red. She looked at her watch. "Uh…just shy of two hours, Slim."

Slim's mouth dropped open. "One flight? Any checkout?"

"Nope. I memorized the Pilot's Notes, and wrote up checklists to make sure I didn't forget anything—didn't get to use the landing one. Syl, show him please."

I held out the checklists, and Slim took them. He read them for a moment, then handed them back.

Slim scratched his head, as the rest of the group watched.

"Helen, I've heard about you. I talked with Ruth Law last year, and she told me how you saved her life in 1920. Said she's very proud of you. She'll be gratified to hear about tonight. What I want to know, is how do you keep your cool in situations like that one with Ruth, or what happened tonight?"

I silently started to pray. *Lord, You just gave Helen a barn door sized opening. Please give Helen the words to say to this young man!*

"Well, Slim, I do all the usual things—study, practice, learn all I can. That's all good—got to do that stuff to survive. But it's not enough. A long time ago I realized I couldn't do anything in my own strength except mess up. It wasn't just me—it's the human condition. We really are lost, all of us."

Slim stared at Helen, but nodded his head.

"It's true, sad to say. All the religions you can name, their purpose is to get us to Heaven on our own. Not gonna happen. *Not.* Someone's got to save us—and Someone did."

Jackie and I nodded. Oddly enough, John Livingston nodded too. Helen continued.

"I admitted I was a rebel, couldn't do anything about it, and asked Jesus to save me. And he did! Now everything I do, everything I am, is to do what He wants me to do. I teach, I fly, I *live*—according to His purpose. It's the only way I can face this

300

crazy world—and it *is* crazy! And Jesus has done all the work; only have to trust Him. That's how I do what I do."

"Amen," Jackie and I whispered. John Livingston nodded his head again. Lee was quiet. Only Slim spoke.

"Thank you for that statement, Helen. I don't see it that way. If you'll excuse me, I need to go up to check my airplane."

Slim turned and left the room, heading up the stairs.

John Livingston came over to Helen. He spoke quietly, even though the hail was now battering the hangar.

"Please don't feel offended by Slim, Helen. He's a very serious young man, and has had to grow up mighty young when his father died last year. He also has that Swedish stubborn streak, which he hides by keeping quiet. I believe he'll think about what you said tonight. I know I will."

"Thanks, John. I'm not offended. I'm asked to give a reason for the Faith that is in me, I give it. He asked; I told him. All I'm supposed to do—except pray, of course."

"Let's talk about this some time, OK Helen?"

"Sure, John. Anytime."

Suddenly I remembered where I'd seen the look on Slim's face before. Young John Bohan, starting the day we lost Ma. Every time I'd seen him since I'd seen the same look—intense, focused, as if he could just put his head down and break through a brick wall! Slim Lindbergh had that look.

The hail finally stopped. Slim stuck his head in the stairwell, and called down to us, "The storm's past, folks, but you should see the ground outside!"

We all trooped up the stairs and opened the back door of the hangar. It looked like at least an inch of ice balls, anywhere from a pea to a quarter in diameter, covered the ground. If we walked out there we'd have to watch out to keep from slipping and falling!

We trooped to the front door and opened it. The same scene greeted us. We looked over to the other hangars; bits and pieces were fluttering in the wind, but they were intact. Jackie stuck her head out the door and looked across the field. "Good—my hangar's still there," she remarked, and walked back toward the office.

We found out later a tornado had passed within a half mile of the field, continuing on to dissipate just west of Galesburg. It was close, but the Lord preserved us again.

Jackie came out of the office. "Phone line to Galesburg still works," she said, "Don's relieved you got in safely, and we made it through the storm."

She turned to our tall guest. "Don welcomes you, Slim. He says you're always welcome to visit and fly from this field. John," she turned to the field manager, "Don says to check over Slim's plane, and top it off with gas and oil, on us."

"Sure, Jackie, will do," John replied.

"Please tell Don thank you for me, Jackie."

"Sure thing, Slim. And Helen, Don said to give you this."

Jackie pulled a small envelope from her dress pocket and handed it to Helen. "That does say number '2' on it, doesn't it?"

Helen looked. "It says '3'…"

Jackie looked surprised. Helen gave her *The Look* for two seconds, then giggled, "Gotcha!"

"So you did," Jackie laughed, "Come on, lets get outta here before Helen and Syl fall asleep on their feet!"

Jackie called that one right, as I was starting to wobble.

Jackie drove us back to Galesburg in a large sedan with a very comfortable back seat. Slim was staying overnight with John Livingston; I suspected he didn't want to ask Helen another question! The roads were wet and dark, but once we left the area of the field there was no hail on the ground.

Helen and Jackie were talking softly and I curled up on the back seat. I heard them talking as I dozed; I might have dreamed what they said—I don't know.

Helen spoke. "So that's Slim Lindbergh."

"Yep. Pretty much as the biographies say."

"You suppose he'll be any different here?"

"He might," Jackie said softly, "and we can't be sure if he'll succeed in the flight this time around. He'll try it though, I think."

"Definitely lost."

"For sure. His father was a freethinker, he's been exposed to all sorts of odd religions already. He only gets more confused after the flight, if the script holds. You gave him the Gospel square on tonight, though."

"Thanks, Jackie, I only told him what I know."

"The Lord knows how he'll turn out here; we don't. We'll keep praying of course. And I have a feeling we're being set up to have more contact with him."

"I think you're right," Helen said, "That was no coincidence tonight."

"Nope."

The next thing I knew we were stopped in the depot parking lot.

I was too tired to drive home, so Helen invited me to stay the night, and I gladly accepted.

Bessie was concerned when we got in so late, but grateful the Lord had spared us. We ate sandwiches, and after Bessie went to bed we sat in the living room, each cradling a cup of coffee. We were tired, but not quite ready to sleep yet (or again).

"What about John Livingston?" I asked, "When you were giving Slim Lindbergh the Gospel he seemed to agree with what you were saying."

Helen took a sip. "I'm not surprised. I get the feeling he's a really backslidden Christian who's gotten himself in so deep he can't see how to get out. I've been praying the Lord gets hold of him again. He told me a while back the Lord got his attention a couple years ago, when he got drunk one night and made his first parachute jump...in the dark."

I smirked. "What's so wrong with that?"

Helen giggled. "It's never too late in the evening for a little understatement. He and his buddies in the Al Wilson Flying Circus..."

"Not him again!"

"Oh, yes. He hasn't killed himself yet—far as I know. Anyway, Al and his buddies strap a 'chute on John, stick him in a JN-4—at night—, take him up to around ten thousand, and roll the aircraft. Since he's too drunk to fasten his seatbelt, out he goes! He's also too drunk to pull the ripcord."

"What happened? I see he's still alive."

"They tied the ripcord to the side of the plane. As soon as he cleared the aircraft, the 'chute opened. Since it was ten thousand feet, he had quite a while to cool down and think up there. He said he woke up floating, freezing, and completely disoriented. He got right with the Lord in the time between wakeup and landing—in a tree, of course. Had to cut him out of the tree; no real injuries. Since then, though, he's been the classic *double-minded man*, unstable in all his ways. We'll see what he and Slim talk about tonight."

"Did you see the look on Slim's face tonight? I've seen that look on young John Bohan's face several times, starting when he came out with his pa to tell me about Ma."

"I saw that too, and I think it's the same drive, intensity, I guess I'd call it *focus*, I see in both of 'em. And they both need the Lord."

"Amen, Helen...Hey, did you open the envelope yet?"

"No, I forgot. Let's see," Helen pulled the envelope from her pocket and opened it. She gasped a little.

"It's a check for one hundred dollars!"

"That's high, isn't it?"

"High? That's on the *Moon*! I can't say what I get for my ferry jobs, but this is way, way more than I've ever gotten. Maybe my joke about 'envelope 3' wasn't so far off after all!"

"What will you do with all that money?"

"Save it, of course. The help Ma and Pa out if something happens fund, the replace the car when it dies fund, the buy Helen an airplane fund..."

"Do you want your own plane?"

"Sure...someday. It's not my first wish, and I know if the Lord sees I need one He'll send it along. Besides, I haven't found a plane I really want yet, although that F-13 comes close."

"And then you might find a man..."

"Not yet, Syl. I thought Gil might be the one, but he really isn't. He knows it too. We're too much alike—we'd drive each other crazy."

"Someday, Helen."

"Goes for you too, Syl."

"Right. And it's midnight. Guess we'd better turn in."

Chapter Forty Nine

Luther: Saturday July 5th, 1924, Galva Baptist Church, Galva, Illinois.

"You know, John, this gag is getting a little old."

"You'll notice none of us are laughing, Luther."

The trademark room-filling flatulence of a failed tubular pneumatic organ filled the sanctuary of the church. I had come to think of it as a most depressing sound.

"This one didn't even give us ciphers before it passed out," I commented as I flipped the blower switch.

"And keeps passing," added John Wick.

The flaccid buzz finally faded out.

I slid off the organ bench and turned to our embarrassed host.

"Pastor, can you show us the access door to the organ mechanism?"

"Of course, come this way please," Pastor Robert Eshleman led the way back to the organ case. He was short, stocky, with short black hair streaked with gray. He had been Pastor of Galva Baptist Church for fifteen years, he told us, and this instrument had been unplayable for fourteen of them. His wife Kathleen (he called her Kathi) was an Associate in the AGO, and performed frequent recitals—on other organs.

After one organ repairer looked at the instrument and pronounced it beyond repair, it had just reposed in the sanctuary, gathering dust and other things. Pastor Eshleman (his congregation called him *Pastor Bob*) said they never seemed to have enough money to tackle the organ. Since Kathi could also play the piano, they were still able to play the music of the church.

A benefactor had now stepped up to finance the rebuilding of the organ. Kathi had dragged her husband to that recital in Metamora in 1921 (He claimed he had a 'tin ear', and after hearing him sing I concurred), and her appreciation of the Direct Electric action had only grown since then. So she naturally insisted Wicks Organ, and me personally, get the call for this one.

Pastor opened an undersized door in the hallway behind the organ case, and John and I shone our flashlights in the case. I spotted the broken wind line right away, and noted it was within reach. This was promising.

"Two things, Pastor. One, are there electric lights in there?"

"There might be—I've never gotten up the nerve to explore in there, to tell you the truth."

"I can relate to that. Two, do you mind if I get in there and try to stick that wind line together well enough so maybe we can hear the pipes?"

"Go right ahead! What have we got to lose?"

I could flip the wrong switch and burn the church down, I thought, *but perhaps I shouldn't mention that here.*

"The Flatulence Repair Kit?" John asked.

"Yep. Be back in a minute."

I walked through the church and out to my car. I had finally gotten smart, and carried a special box with me when we went to check out a tubular pneumatic. I'd put rubber sheets, pre-cut sheet metal, and big hose clamps in it, and a set of wrenches and screwdrivers to fit. I thought about including a crying towel and earplugs, but decided that was carrying the joke a bit far.

I walked back into the church with the box, and rejoined the little party in the front.

"Let me squeeze in here and see what I can do. John, keep your light on me please."

"Sure thing. Be careful!"

I selected a patch and a few tools, got on my back and slid into the case. Fortunately I could reach the offending pipe without going completely in. Since you never know what you'll find in an old organ case, I had a *shtick* I'd set up with John.

"If I yell, grab my leg and pull me out. Remember, only the left leg!"

"Right, Luther."

"No, Left!"

"Right."

Organists have a strange sense of humor.

"Why just the left leg?" I heard Pastor Eshleman ask.

Though I couldn't see him, I knew John pointed down to my right leg, where the pant leg had ridden up, exposing the metal of the prosthesis.

"Belleau Wood" John whispered.

"Oh."

He'd had to explain the prosthesis before.

After clearing the thick cobwebs from the area I managed to get one of my repair patches fitted around the broken pipe, and start the hose clamps. I tightened them down, and felt around for other breaks. I couldn't feel any. If this got the thing running, even for a few minutes, it was worth the effort. We really needed to hear the

306

organ pipes sounding in the sanctuary to know what we needed to keep and what needed changing.

I slid back out of the case, stood up, and brushed myself off. This was why I wore denim coveralls instead of a suit to these parties.

"You have mice," I observed.

"I know," Pastor Eshleman replied. "We do the best we can, but they get in there and we can't get to them. I'm sorry for whatever you found."

"That's OK, Pastor. We're used to it. When we design the new chests, we'll make sure you have better access to the apparatus. With the electric actions, there'll be a lot more room to work with in there."

We moved back to the organ console. I sat on the bench and reviewed the available stops.

"Pastor, what we're going to do is turn this beast on, and start pulling stops and testing the pipes as fast as we can before the thing fails again, assuming it'll sound at all. I think it might, but we'll see."

"I understand, Luther—oh, here comes Kathi now!"

We were joined at the organ by a blonde woman of medium height. I had met Kathi Eshleman at various AGO chapter meetings and recitals. I admired her mastery of the classical literature, especially while having to keep in practice using someone else's instruments. I introduced her to John Wick, and explained what we were about to do.

"Sounds like we're going to have some fun here! Can I help?"

"Sure. Get ready to pull the drawknobs on that side, and listen to the voices, or whatever we get. John's got a list of the ranks there, and he'll scribble notes beside the voices, whatever we say. If this thing is still running when we get through the stops, I'll hop off and you can have the honor of playing something on it."

"I won't hold my breath for that."

"Neither will I. These beasts usually progress rapidly to the *end stage*, and when we hear *the end*, we're done."

Kathi giggled. "Let's go for it!"

"Everyone ready?"

The others nodded. John stood poised with a clipboard and pencil.

"Go ahead, Kathi."

"Geronimo!" She flipped the switch.

I heard the clicks of the motor relays and rising whine of the blower from the basement, and some hissing came from the organ case…but no flatulence. I pulled a stop in the choir division, and touched a key.

"Lo, a sound!"

I began the rapid-fire drill of stop and pipe testing. I didn't worry about every pipe in each stop, but only enough to give us an idea of the rank's overall sound. About a quarter of the drawknobs we pulled gave us nothing, or a flat hiss; I figured one wind chest was compromised somehow. Since the ranks of pipes were divided among several wind chests, I shifted up or down on the keyboards until I found notes that would sound.

After a few minutes I nodded to Kathi, and she began pulling stops on her side of the organ. We had ciphers appear, but were able to hear enough from each stop to tell us what we needed to know. Every so often Kathi or I would remark 'Nice voice', or 'that's a dud', and John would make the appropriate note.

At the end of our testing the organ was still running—wheezing, ciphering, and terribly out of tune, but running.

"You're on!" I called to Kathi as I slid off the organ bench to the left.

Kathi slid onto the bench, pulled a few stops, and started to play. She turned to me and grinned—she started with 'Let the Lower Lights Be Burning'. She managed three more hymns—one of them in the reed chorus, she didn't chance moving the swell doors—before the ciphers became so bad we could hardly hear what she was playing.

She canceled the presets and slid over to pull the power switch. "Praise the Lord, we got through that without—"

At that moment, the main wind line broke again.

"Another example of perfect *Estey Timing*!" John said as the blower…and the buzz…slowly wound down.

The Eshlemans invited us to stay for supper. We were sitting in their parlor before the meal when someone knocked at the door. Pastor went to the door.

"Hey, Paul, come on in! Our *organ experts* are here, and I'd like you to meet them."

I had another stray thought about the more appropriate definition of expert—*drip under pressure*.

"Drip under pressure."

"Mind reader!" I whispered back to John as I giggled. I was still giggling when Pastor and his guest entered the room.

"Gentlemen, I'd like to introduce—Luther, what's the matter?"

John spoke up. "I whispered to him the alternate definition of *expert*."

"Drip under pressure?" The newcomer spoke.

John and I erupted in fresh giggling

"Or little squirt away from home?" Pastor added.

I looked up to see Kathi Eshleman standing in the dining room doorway, rolling her eyes. *That makes three formidable Pastor's wives—must be a requirement.*

When we finally settled down Pastor Eshleman continued. "Gentlemen, I'd like you to meet Paul Sherwood. He's one of our members, and General Manager of the Little John Coal Company. He's the one who is graciously funding the organ rebuild."

We introduced ourselves.

"You don't remember me, do you, Luther?"

I looked closer at Mr. Sherwood. I never was any good at remembering faces.

"You look vaguely familiar, but to be honest, I just can't place you."

"I was a captain in the army during the war. I was wounded in August, and ended up in the little unit at Walter Reed."

Light dawns on Marble Head. "I am so sorry, Paul! I remember you now. That's been a long time now—six years already!"

"Sometimes it seems like a lifetime. But it's a happier lifetime, I'll say that. Sit down, gentlemen, Kathi, and I'll explain."

We all sat back down, Pastor Bob and Kathi on the love seat. Paul continued.

"Pastor here knows the story, but not the rest of you. I had never given much thought to spiritual things. I figured when we were done here, we were done, that's all. A lot of people think that. Then I got wounded, and nearly bled to death. But I didn't, and eventually ended up on a transport back to the states. Then the influenza blew through that ship. Two hundred soldiers out of two thousand on board died...and the Army pretended it didn't happen! I got sick...but I got over it. I had no idea why."

"Then I landed in this little ward—more like a house than a ward—and met you and your associates, Jack and Gary. I was bored, still getting used to *this*," He tapped his left lower leg, and we heard the *tonk* of a prosthesis.

"I'm not too interested in life by that time. Like I said, I was bored, and depressed, so I started attending the Sunday morning services you gents started up. I began to wonder about my beliefs...and why I was still alive when so many of my friends were dead. April 27th—before the brass showed up—Jack Sewell sat up one night and showed me what the Bible really said about humans...and me. I repented and trusted Christ that night."

309

"Praise the Lord!" was all I could say.

"You saw the awards ceremony the Army gave us, the week after yours. I ended up with the DSC…and my retirement papers. I came back to Illinois, and Uncle Lex gave me a job in one of our mines down by Herrin. Eventually, I moved up, and they sent me up here to scope out the land for a new venture in Eastern Knox County. I turn up in Galva, and decide to visit a church. And here I am!"

"Wow!" Kathi Eshleman pronounced.

Over supper we talked about many things. Somehow the conversation worked around to my college career and my double major. When he heard I had a Geology major, Paul sat back and appeared thoughtful.

"Luther, next time you're in town stop by my office. I have an idea I need to pray about, and bounce off you."

"We're coming back next Saturday to present our proposal. Would that be a good time to visit?"

"That would be fine. I suggest you keep praying about what the Lord wants you to do in the meantime."

"Of course, Paul."

*****

Luther: the next week, Little John Coal Company office, Galva.

I was seated in Paul's spartan office on the square in Galva. Paul leaned back in his elderly wooden office chair and spoke.

"First, I think your estimate on the organ is fine in all particulars. I accept the estimate, and I'm sure Pastor Bob will too. The congregation has already approved the project; that was easy since I'm paying for it!"

"Thank you for your confidence in us, Sir."

"Paul. Forget that *sir* business!"

"All right, Paul. And I'm Luther, of course."

"And I won't call you Shirley!"

We both laughed at that old chestnut.

"Luther, I've been praying about something, and the Lord's given me peace about the matter. I want to bring it up to you, and see if it is something you'd like to do, and if it might be in the Lord's will for your life. Interested?"

"I am. I know the Lord has something more for me to do besides the organ work, although I really enjoy it."

"Even the flatulence? I heard about your experiences with that."

310

"It's cat-crazed funny the first time or two, but drops off after that."

Paul chuckled. "I can imagine. Well, here's the idea. How much do you know about coal mining, particularly open-seam mining?"

"We looked at that some in my geology classes. I wrote a short paper on coal seams in Illinois. I didn't go too deep into the subject, no pun intended."

Paul snorted. "Right. Well, our company intends to set up an open seam mining operation in eastern Knox county. Two seams run through that area, and we need to know just where they are, so we can plan to purchase land over them. What we do is drill test holes at predetermined spots, and try to gauge the size and spread of the seams so we know which land to buy. We don't want to buy any more land than we have to, to save money. We also don't want to disrupt the other land we don't buy, so the farmers can keep farming untroubled. My branch of the family, at least, really wants to minimize the impact on the surrounding neighbors."

"That's unusual, Paul. Usually a company comes in, buys the land, destroys it, and hightails it out of town."

"Unfortunately, you're right…Some of my relatives think that is the way to succeed—we really don't want to do that. We want to give the land back in some useful form when we're through with it."

I had a thought. "Are you going to strip off all the topsoil and store it someplace before you start digging deeper? That way you can put it back in some places when you're done, and the vegetation will grow back."

Paul's eyes widened. "You know, Luther, I've never thought of that! Now that I hear it, it makes so much sense! If we can possibly do that, we will. Could you do a little checking and see how we could economically do that?"

"Sure…but does this mean I'm working for you?"

"Oh! Cart before the horse, I guess. Anyway, we need someone to decide where to drill the test holes, manage the crews who drill them (and put the dirt back where they found it!), and advise us what land to buy. That position would officially be 'Staff Geologist', but it could work into something different, or bigger, as we go along. Luther, I've been praying about this, and I think you're who we need. You would need to live here in Galva, to be close to the work. You would pretty much set your own hours, and I can tell you this, you'll probably have more responsibilities than this sent your way as we go along. What do you think? And what sort of salary do you require?"

311

I bowed my head for a moment. *Lord, is this the answer I've been asking for?*

A thought popped into my mind. *Yes, for now, this is where I want you. Go.*

All that took about ten seconds. I looked up at Paul. "This looks like where the Lord wants me for now. I have some things I need to do for my Pa, and for John Wick, before I can come aboard full time. Is that OK?"

"Oh, yes, Luther! Once we get into the drilling cycle you'll be pretty busy, but often in this first year, especially in the winter, this job will actually be part time. Is that a problem?"

"Not in the least! I'd like to continue part time for Wicks..."

"And you certainly should! I don't want my investment here to end up in a pile!"

I laughed. "I guarantee that won't happen! That poor Estey has great potential, but we have to wreck it to get to the point of rebuilding it."

"Not unlike us, eh?"

"Now that you mention it, just like He does with us. His purpose, always His purpose..."

"Amen"

In the ensuing discussion we almost forgot to set my salary. I wasn't too worried about it, and in the end the salary turned out quite satisfactorily too. So I now had a job—two jobs, actually—and I would get to move to a new town, happily with a good church.

I stayed over at Paul's house that Saturday night, caught him up on the lives of our mutual friends, and he gave me the sad news from Baltimore. Doctor Raichart had passed from a stroke just after my visit in the Spring, then three weeks later Steve and Francine Mason had been killed in an automobile accident. Paul had his appointment in early June, and spoke with their replacements— Doctor Jennifer Setterdahl and her husband Keith. I had met both of them over the years, and was glad to hear they were both believers.

Chapter Fifty

Luther: Thursday, April 23rd, 1925, Wright-Allensworth Motor Company and elsewhere.

In the middle of the busiest year of my life, I found I needed another car, finally. The Model D was running well, but I could tell I was gradually pounding it into scrap on the bad roads I had to travel. I didn't want to see that happen, and I also didn't want to get stranded on the road!

I did my research, and found what I wanted—a Chrysler Six of some sort. They were new on the market, but Walter Chrysler had been building cars for other makers for many years, and he had figured out what new technology to use to make a truly good car. He had bought the old Maxwell company, and after unloading a bunch of unsold *not so good* Maxwells, had designed and built his own car. I thought it was just what I needed for my travels, so I asked Pa to put the word out like he did the last time. We figured someone would tire of their new toy, and trade one in. Pa's advice to me (but not his customers!) had always been, *Why buy new when used will do?*

Pa's dealer grapevine came through again—and with the same dealer! Lee Wright in Galesburg had a customer trade in a 1925 Chrysler touring car with less than 500 miles on it. Seems his wife didn't like the color—canary yellow. Lee immediately called Pa.

And Lee had more good news. He said he had a customer who kept a list of cars he wanted to buy if they became available, for a museum of some sort, and at the top of the list was a Chevrolet model D! Lee said this gentleman had a history of paying more than the going rate for the right car, and he also thought I might like to meet him. Lee said he was an unusual fellow, but one of the most honorable men he'd ever met. All this sounded interesting, so I had Pa call him back to set up a visit.

So it was on this Thursday I drove over to Galesburg to see Lee Wright. I stopped in front of the building on Simmons Street, and walked in. A stocky fellow with an eyeshade introduced himself as Rol Allensworth, Lee's business partner.

"I'm very glad to meet you, Mr. Barlow! I remember when you got that Model D—1919 I think. That was a busy week around here, and oddly enough that also involved the *estimable* Don Wain. He's the gentleman who wants the Model D."

"Thanks, Mr. Allensworth—and it's Luther. I met Don at an organ recital in Metamora in 1921. I think one of his employees has a model D too."

"And I'm Rol. That other D belongs to Dick Meriden, Don's *executive officer* as he calls him. We never see it in the shop here— they've packed it full of *experimental equipment* and work on it themselves. Let's go back into the shop and see Lee and Don; he's just doing a final check on the Chrysler. Clare, you got the phone!"

"Right, Rol," replied the man behind the parts counter at the side of the showroom.

We stepped through a spring-loaded door set in a larger door in the back wall, and walked through the service area. The area was small, but clean—as clean as an automotive repair shop ever is. In the back, Lee was standing next to a canary-yellow Chrysler touring car. He was talking to a middle aged man with thinning hair and a slight stoop. The man wore a suit, but the jacket seemed to fit a bit loosely. *Don hasn't changed any*, I thought.

Lee turned as we approached. "Hello, Luther! Let me introduce Don Wain to you. He's the one interested in your Model D."

"No need, Lee, we've already met." Don said as he shook my hand, "I wondered if you were the one with the D, *Sergeant*."

Uh oh. Another one with a long memory.

Don turned to Lee. "Hey, Lee, how would you like to go about this?"

"How about you and Luther go for a drive and see how you like the D. Then Luther, you and one of us can take the Chrysler out for a run. If you like the cars we'll hammer out a deal."

"That OK with you, Luther?" Don asked.

"Sure. I'm parked out front. Back shortly, Lee!"

"Be sure you're back by lunchtime—I know someplace I want to try, and I'm buying."

"Thanks, Lee," Don replied, "Whaddya know, there is such a thing as a free lunch!"

I laughed as we walked back to the showroom.

We walked out to the Chevrolet. I opened the hood so Don could look in.

"Purolator?"

"Yep. I had it put in when I had it overhauled last year. About time they invented something logical like an oil filter."

"Sure is," Don replied, "All my vehicles with oil pumps have one, plus a couple other types we're testing. You say you overhauled this?"

314

"Yes. Pa's mechanics at the dealership did it. So far everything's fine. They said it was a change from working on Cadillac V-8s though."

Don spoke louder as he stuck his head close to the engine under the hood. "It would be, especially with Cadillac's new block design—I think they improved that one, in my humble opinion."

Don closed one side of the hood while I closed the other. We got into the car.

"I've driven one of these before—Dick Meriden, my Administrative Assistant has one. It's had some serious modifications, though, so how about I name off the controls and stop me if I get one wrong?"

"Sure, go ahead."

Don identified each of the controls within his reach.

"You got 'em, Don. Go ahead and start up."

"OK."

Don slowly went through the starting routine, and engaged the starter. The car started normally, but ran a bit rough.

"Spark needs advanced a bit," I said.

"Oops! Most of our vehicles have automatic spark control—it's one of the things we work on I can actually mention." He moved the lever on the steering wheel hub, and the engine smoothed.

We pulled out of the parking place and drove west toward Prairie Street.

"Very nice, Luther! How many miles does it have on it?"

"The odometer's gone around once, otherwise that's accurate."

"I'm amazed! 122,480 miles! I'm sure it's not a record, but that's a lot for something from this era. You've kept it up wonderfully!"

"I do try. I don't want to trust it with the miles I have to put on a car this year, though."

"Running every which way?" Don asked.

"You might say that. I'm starting full time with Little John Coal out of Galva, I'm still working with John Wick of Wicks Organ, plus I keep my room in Peoria while I finish a couple of courses to prepare for the coal work."

"Wow! You're meeting yourself coming and going! You're working for John Wick? Engineering or performance?"

"Both, actually. You were at my recital in Metamora a few years ago. I kind of backed into the construction side of the organ business after I helped with that installation."

Don's mouth quirked as we crossed Cherry Street and passed the Post Office.

"Hmmm…You know, I think we can cut this test drive short. I want the car, and I'm sure we'll work out a deal with Lee. If you don't mind, let me take you by the theater I bought last month. I want you to see the wreck of an organ we inherited, and tell me how much of the remains we should save. I've already contacted John, since I know we want Direct Electric action for the basic organ we're going to install. Maybe having you look at the poor thing will give us a jump on the process."

"I'd be happy to look at it." I replied.

Don turned right at Broad Street, and we passed the big Congregational Church on our left before he spoke again.

"I'll warn you, Luther, the organ in there now is truly awful! It will not turn on at all; in fact, the one time we had it close to working, it all of a sudden developed the worst case of flatulence you ever did hear!"

"I believe I'm acquainted with that sound," I said.

I waited until Don shut off the car in the parking lot by the side of the Galesburg Armory, across the street from the Auditorium Theater, before I told him about Old Squeak. Don started snorting and laughing so hard he began to cry.

"Whew! I'm glad you waited before you told me that! I never caught that at the recital. Oh, my!" He pulled out a handkerchief and dabbed at his eyes.

He was still chuckling as we got out of the car and walked towards the Auditorium. My stump decided it did not like the rough surface of the lot, and I involuntarily limped a bit.

"What's wrong, Luther? Oh, I see, never mind. That happen much?"

"Not really. I just have to watch uneven surfaces. I'll be fine."

"Ok. Hold up—here comes Dick in his model D now."

The same blue Chevrolet Model D I saw back when Dorothy Templeman was born pulled into the lot and the parking space next to ours. It still sounded different from mine. I also noticed the driver was turning the steering wheel with one hand as he parked. Either the man was very strong, or something was *really* different under the hood.

The driver moved a lever on the dash, the engine tone changed, and a noise somewhere between a whine and a whistle began, ending when he shut off the engine.

A tall, elderly, bald man got out of the car and walked over to us.

"Luther, I'd like you to meet Dick Meriden, my Administrative Assistant. Dick, this is Luther Barlow, He owns that other Model

D, which I hope to buy, and also works for John Wick of Wicks Organ."

We shook hands. His handshake was much stronger than his elderly appearance would indicate. *Maybe he really could turn the wheel with one hand,* I thought.

"I've never met you, Dick, but I think I met your wife in Peoria in December, 1922. Is she a midwife?"

"Estelle? Oh yes. You must have seen her when she went someplace to make a delivery. Who was the mother?"

"Agnes Templeman, and she brought in little Dorothy."

"Sure, I know that family! Do you know them well?"

"I've roomed with them since the fall of 1919. Looks like I'll finally move out this summer."

Dick grinned and squinted one eye. "Estelle and I just think the world of Agnes and the kids. Charlie thinks the world of himself."

Dick and I both laughed at that remark. Don rolled his eyes at us.

Dick headed off toward the Wain offices on the square as Don and I walked into the Auditorium. We stepped through the lobby doors, and into the largest wreck of a building I'd ever seen. All the seats, the fancy curtains, the gilded wallpaper of a typical Victorian public auditorium were gone. Workers wearing masks were chewing away at the lath and plaster in the hall proper, creating piles of debris which were then carted off by others with wheelbarrows. Several large fans sucked in the plaster dust and dirt, and blew the dust through huge bags, which caught most of it. The air was breathable, but not pleasant.

I turned to Don. "Not saving much, are you?"

"Not up here," Don spoke up to be heard over the destruction. "We knew it was bad going in, and haven't been surprised. The basic building is solid, it's the right size, and close to our offices on the square. Since it'll be a testing place for some of our projects as well as an entertainment venue for the community, I decided to go for the *big project*."

Don grinned. "Besides, it was really cheap!"

"Good thing. So you're doing a total rebuild?"

"Absolutely! This place'll shine when we get through with it."

"What will you present here?" I asked.

"Mostly serious music—symphonies, chamber groups, some opera if they'll fit on the stage. I doubt if Mary Garden will drop in!"

I laughed. "I'm hoping to get up to Chicago to see her do *La Boheme* this Saturday. She barely fits up there!"

317

Don chuckled. "I wanted to get up to see that, but I've got an airplane being delivered that afternoon, and I need to be in the shop, as it were."

"Airplane?"

"Yep. Need it for some research, and to get to our other facilities if it works out. We'll base at the Monmouth airport, at least until Lee and Julian Mack can talk the city fathers here into letting us put in a permanent airport."

A woman of medium height and indeterminate age wearing a mask over her nose and mouth walked up to us.

"Hey, Jackie, what's up? I think you two met at the recital in Metamora a few years ago."

"I remember that. Hello, Luther, I'm Jackie Brighthonor, the company accountant—the one who tries to figure out where the money to finish this *monstrosity* will come from!"

"Now, Jackie, you approved this project without a murmur."

"That's because I fainted dead away when you told me, buster!" Jackie shot back, her wide grin not quite hidden by her mask.

Don snorted. "As I recall, I'm the one who keeled over last time we met Luther."

"You were, but that's not important right now," Jackie replied, then turned to me. "John Wick tells me you're the one we want to look over the junkpile in the second balcony, and design our new organ. He says you're the best."

I blushed. "Thanks, Jackie, I just do what I can. Don brought me over to see it this morning."

Don interrupted. "Jackie, when did John tell you that?"

"At the meeting last week while you were camped out in the *head, Admiral*. We thought you'd fallen in."

I snorted, then a voice called out, "Hey Jackie, I need to see you a minute!"

"Ah, duty calls. Nice to see you, Luther, I'm sure we'll be working closely as this pile of bricks gets transformed."

"Nice to see you again, Jackie," I said, and she hustled off across the hall.

"If Jackie wasn't here minding the finances I don't know what I'd do," Don took out his handkerchief and wiped his eyes. "Too much dust," he said, "If you're up for a climb let's go up and see the organ remains."

"I can manage it," I replied, hoping I could. We walked out of the hall and toward the stairs.

318

We trudged up several flights of increasingly rickety stairs and came out to a small lobby leading to the second balcony. Boards, plaster chunks, and other detritus littered the space.

Don looked around, frowned, and walked over to a battered sign lying on the floor.

"I asked the foreman to get rid of this," he said as he picked it up. The sign read:

Colored Seating Only.

"Even in Galesburg," Don muttered, then sent the sign spinning to crash against the bare bricks of the front wall. "Never again in this hall, by God's Grace. Never again!"

Don turned back to where I was standing, the veins in his neck bulging and his face red. He took three deep breaths, and his color returned to normal.

"I'm sorry, Luther, I didn't mean to blow up like that in front of you."

"That's OK, Don—don't give it a thought. And, for the record, I agree completely with your sentiment, and your action."

Don smiled. "Thanks, Luther, you didn't have to say that, but I really appreciate it. We have some cardinal principles we operate under in this company, and that's one of them. We're hoping the Auditorium, and what we present here, will help give opportunity to everyone—and I do mean *everyone*!"

We walked over to the hole in the wall where the doors to the balcony had been removed. I looked over the bare rafters of the roof close by. "You've really stripped this building down to its bones."

"Yeah," Don replied, "Didn't have to do much to get rid of the old ceiling. Couple days after we closed on the building, about half of it just came down like hard rain! We persuaded the rest to follow."

"What a mess!"

"Fortunately, we already had the seats out. I'm having them rebuilt—since they fit the hall, no sense buying new ones."

We walked into the old second balcony. Don stopped and pointed. "Well, there it is."

I thought I had seen the worst a pipe organ could be in my six years of crawling through every variation of deteriorated organ cases. I was very wrong.

The case was gone, and what remained was the sorriest assortment of corroded metal pipes and rotting wood I had ever seen. Obviously the roof had been leaking into it for many years. The console faced the mess, and was not much better. I could find

319

no builder's plate on it; given its appearance, I figured nobody wanted to put their name on it.

I dodged the piles of plaster on the floor and walked over to the assemblage. The pipes were all metal, and showed signs of heavy corrosion. I had to think for a moment what they reminded me of; then I had it.

"Former calliope?"

Don laughed. "Got it in one, Luther! Whoever put this monstrosity together did so out of, best we can tell, *three* retired steam calliopes! They cobbled together a tubular pneumatic action, built a console out of junk parts and packing crates, and called it done!"

"You actually tried to turn this thing on?"

"Once. We had fire extinguishers ready just in case, and we used 'em. Then we brought in a portable blower and a long extension cord, and cut it in at the main feed. Still nothing but hiss and social indiscretion."

"Is there anything worth salvaging from this mess?"

"Believe it or not, I think there is. Look closer."

I looked, then in the back of the pile I saw a rank of gleaming metal pipes, sitting on a wind chest like sentinels!

I walked over and looked closer. Engraved in the usual spot was *Vox Celeste, MP Moller, 1909.*

I turned to Don. "Save that rank, for sure! How did they get in this wreck?"

Don grinned. "I wondered that too, so I did a little research. Have a seat, Luther, we both need to rest before going down those steps anyway."

We sat down on a couple of folding chairs nailed to the floor and looked out at the expanse of the empty hall.

"I had these nailed in temporarily. It's a long way down."

"I'd rather not think about that, Don. I've got this problem with bridges…"

"My problem is with heights like this. Bridges I can manage."

"We can go on down—"

"Naah, that's why I had these chairs nailed in. Anyway, here's the story. You've heard of the Marx Brothers, I assume?"

I nodded.

"They used to play this theater a lot on the circuit. There's a story the boys got their nicknames during a poker game backstage here, but I haven't been able to confirm that. I know a lot of people, but not them."

320

"Maybe you could get them to come back after you rebuild the place."

Don put his finger to his temple. "Now there's an idea! Thanks, Luther."

I nodded, and Don continued his story.

"Anyway, one night in 1909 they're playing here, and Leonard—they call him Chico now—becomes annoyed at the organ, which he says sounds like a calliope."

"Imagine that!"

"Yeah," Don snorted, "That organ really bothers him, because even though the act is all comedy, he's a pretty good piano and organ player. It's after the last show, and he's had something more than his quota of spirits. He decides to go up to that organ and set the thing to rights, or figure out why it sounds so bad. Somehow he staggers up those steps, gets to the organ case, and forces open a little door in the side of it, right where you were standing. He leans in...and falls in!"

"Didn't he get skewered by the pipes?"

"Nope. They were just pot metal, and so loose in the wind chest, when he fell in he sent one whole rank over like dominoes, and crushed them with his body. Good thing they crushed; they broke his fall. His brothers fished him out, and they all thought it was very funny. The management thought otherwise."

I couldn't resist. "Terrible carnage—a whopping fifty eight cents damage."

Don's laugh boomed over the sounds of destruction below.

"However, the very next day a fire started in the Methodist church downtown here. I wasn't around then, but they say the firemen could do nothing to save it, and it took a long time to go down. At one point, the updrafts in the burning sanctuary made the organ pipes sound the eeriest death knell you ever did hear! Several people I've talked to said it gave them nightmares for weeks."

"As it happened, the organ case in that church was open, and the organ was prepared to receive another rank someone had donated the money for. MP Moller was the contractor, and the new Vox Celeste had just arrived in town that morning, but was still sitting in the Q freight house waiting to be picked up. So Moller was out a job, and a nicely packed Vox Celeste was sitting there orphaned. The manager of the theater at the time heard about it, and cut a deal to take the rank off their hands and have it installed in this thing to replace what Chico crushed. I've verified this from several sources; I couldn't make this stuff up!"

321

I shook my head. "Don, that's a great story! I think we can save that Vox Celeste, and junk the rest. Are your folks going to do the tear-out?"

"Oh, yes. We'll also take good care of that rank. We have some preliminary ideas for the replacement organ, but that can wait till you and John are here one of these days soon. Let's get back downstairs; I think lunch, and a car deal, are calling us!"

We drove back to the dealership, and sat down in Lee's office. I decided I didn't even have to drive the Chrysler; I could see it was virtually new, and Lee assured me it drove like it.

The negotiations were nothing at all like the usual car buying experience. Lee and I both had access to a dealer's collection of pricing guides, updated monthly; it was obvious Don had that information too. We all wrote down what we thought the retail and wholesale value of both cars were, and compared figures; we were within ten dollars on all figures.

Don then proposed a trade-in value for the model D half again what the retail value of the car was! Lee had seen him do this sort of thing before; I was stunned. Don grinned and said the Lord had blessed him abundantly, and he knew when to be a cheapskate, and when not to. The Auditorium, he said, was of the former; this car was of the latter.

There wasn't much else to say. We shook hands all around, and left Rol to sort out the paperwork while we went to lunch. Lee led us to Main Street, and across Kellogg Street past the Bank of Galesburg. We had a very nice meal at the American Beauty Restaurant, and I filed the place away in my mind for further investigation. When we returned, Rol had the documents all ready, and grumped about the cheese sandwich he had to eat while we went to the restaurant!

So, I left my faithful Chevrolet in Don's care, and headed back to Peoria (I almost took the road to Galva, but remembered just in time!) in my Chrysler. It performed like I expected, and I praised the Lord for the opportunity to get it—and get acquainted with Don. Looked like I had another organ project in my increasingly crowded future!

Chapter Fifty One

Sylvia: Saturday, August 15th, 1925, the Smiley house.

"So, what is this meeting you're so secretive about? I think it's about time I hear the story, so spill it, Helen Smiley!"

Helen and I were sitting on the front porch of the house on West South Street, sipping our iced tea and waiting for time to go to a confidential meeting. Helen hadn't told me what the meeting was about, and I was beginning to wonder what she was up to.

"All right, Syl, it's time to explain," Helen replied, "In twenty minutes we walk west on this street for three houses, and visit Jackie and Evelyn Brighthonor. They will have another guest visiting them—Jeffrey Potter."

"Jeff? I've known him ever since I met—" I stopped short and gulped. Jeff's late brother Ken was the best friend of my late husband, Hal. Jeff had many challenges in his life, and had never attended school.

Helen looked at me. "I'm sorry Syl—you just remembered, didn't you?"

"Yes," I said, then took a breath. "I'm OK now. What's going on with them?"

Helen set her teacup on the table beside her chair. "You know Evelyn Brighthonor is really close to Jeff, right?"

"Yes, I've seen them together several times over the years."

"Well, it seems Ev has a real liking for Jeff—she understands him and somehow communicates without him saying a word!"

"What? How could she do that?" I asked.

"Can't tell you, Syl, but I've seen them do it!"

I sat back in my chair and took a good swig of tea.

"I'm confused—why are you involved with Ev and Jeff?"

Helen picked up her teacup. "Because Ev is student teaching in my classroom this year—and Jeff will be there too!"

I sat back and took a moment to think through what my friend had said.

"So, he's ready for school, and Ev's the one who prepared him?" I asked.

"Right. She's been working with him since they met, and she's taught him to read and write using a typewriter. I've seen him in action. And you will too—today."

"OK, so you want me to be another pair of eyes, to make sure he can communicate with someone other than Ev and you?"

"Right, Syl. He knows you, but as a friend, not as a teacher. We figure if he can communicate with you without freezing up or running away, he'll make it in the classroom. Does that make sense?"

I thought fast. "OK, I see what you want, and I'll do the best I can."

"Thanks, Syl. I know this'll work, and so do Ev and Jackie."

I took another swig of tea. "And you've gotten this by the School Board and everything?"

Helen nodded. "Yep, but it wasn't easy. Lillian Taylor, my principal, really went to bat for Jeff. And Jackie pitched in too. But one board member is just hateful—said Jeff belonged in a state school for *morons and idiots*, as he called them. Said this in front of Jeff and his parents—all of us—in a board meeting!"

"That's just vile!" I clenched my fists without thinking. "What happened?"

"Don Wain—the man who bought your car when it blew up— asked for the floor. He's a retired Vice Admiral in the Navy Supply Corps. Anyway, he stood up and calmly, logically, took that board member and his hateful ideas apart piece by piece! Took him about five minutes—and the vote was eight to one to let Jeff in!"

"Praise the Lord!" I said, and pulled out my handkerchief. "and he's the one you fly for, right?"

"You said it!" Helen replied, pulling out her own handkerchief, "Don and his wife Pam, and Jackie and Ev—all of them—are wonderful to work for. I've never met anyone like them." She blew her nose, "And now it's time to go visiting.

We walked the half block to the one-story brick house with green shutters. Jackie met us at the door. "Come on in, we're in the living room," she said, and we stepped inside.

The living room—a room with comfortable chairs and a couch instead of the old formal parlor furniture—was larger than I expected. In one corner Jeff sat in a wooden rocking chair. He rocked slowly today; I had seen him rock a chair, and rock his body at the same time, when he was really anxious. Next to him Evelyn sat in a straight chair; they did not touch, but looked at each other every few seconds.

A portable typewriter with a sheet of paper in it sat on a table next to the rocker. "We found Jeff communicates best using the typewriter," Evelyn said.

I started the conversation. "Ev, Helen tells me you'll be practice teaching in her room at Ayers this fall."

"Right, Syl," the thin teen-ager replied, "I'm training to teach elementary grades, and specialize in reading and writing. I'll teach all subjects, of course."

"You'll have to in my classroom," Helen added with a smile, "I was impressed with your work in Mrs. Hunt's class last year, and I'm pleased to have you with me this year. And your *associate* there," she nodded toward Jeff, who gave a small smile as he rocked.

"Right, Helen. Jeff, do you have any questions for us?"

Jeff stopped rocking, a serious look on his face. He then reached toward the typewriter and tapped keys for a moment. Helen got up and went over to read.

"*Where bathroom in school?* Jeff, it is just outside my classroom, about ten feet down the hall. You'll want the door with the word 'boys' on it."

Jeff gave a little grin and nodded once.

"Any other questions?" Helen asked.

Some more tapping on the typewriter.

"*Take typewriter?* You won't have to; I have one just like it in the classroom. You'll have it next to your desk. Will that work for you?"

A grin and two nods.

"Anything else?"

Jeff shook his head no.

"Any questions Jackie? Sylvia?" Helen asked.

I spoke up. "I have a couple I'd like to ask you, Jeff, if you don't mind. May I?"

Jeff turned to look directly at me. He nodded once, and stopped rocking.

"Thanks, Jeff. I see you are communicating with us using the typewriter. I'm very glad that is working for you. As you've been learning to type thoughts and sentences, what has been the most difficult thing for you to learn?"

I figured I would just ask what I wanted to know straight out, and see how he handled the language. Jeff sat motionless for about twenty seconds, then turned to the typewriter and started pecking away. He typed faster than I could, that's for sure!

He typed for maybe two minutes, then stopped, pulled out the paper, and handed it to Evelyn. She in turn handed it to me. I read it silently, then out loud.

"Jeff says, quote, Articles do not make sense to me. I do not need to see a, and, the, to understand what I read. Other people need them to keep their place when they read, so I work to put them where people expect to see them. Spelling of words is strange too. Illogical rules explain inconsistent spelling. Very happy I do not have to learn rules, only see words and remember them. When I added words to thoughts and pictures in my mind reading became easy. Unquote."

Helen, Jackie and Evelyn grinned and nodded at Jeff, who also nodded. I stared at the words on the paper, struggling to reconcile everything I *thought* I knew about how children learn with the amazing statements this young man—*genius, for sure*—had just made.

A question came to me, and I had to ask it. "How do you remember what you read?"

Again, Jeff stayed motionless for about fifteen seconds; then, two more minutes of typing. He handed the sheet to me, and I read.

"Quote, I see the words, I see the page, I remember it. I combine pictures of words into sentences, and understand meaning. Evelyn and Helen ask me questions about what I read to see if I understand it. They tell me not only do I understand what I read, but I possess eidetic memory. I praise Lord I have been given this ability, and thank Evelyn and Jacqueline and Helen for helping me find and use it. Unquote."

I paused, staring at the paper. "What is *eidetic memory*?"

Before anyone else could reply, Jeff began typing again. He gave the next paper to me, and I read.

"Quote, Eidetic memory—ability to vividly recall images from memory after only one or a few times I look, with high precision. Some people remember images for short time; Jacqueline and Evelyn tell me far as they can tell I never forget. Good for me, because if I read something I do not understand, I remember it later and compare it with other things I read, and understand. I have read of others with this ability. Un...quote."

Now I sat down in the nearest chair, still staring at the paper. Eventually I looked up, and saw the ladies smiling and dabbing at their eyes with handkerchiefs. Jeff stared at me, serious expression on his face, waiting for me to say something.

I looked at Jeff. "I...I am completely amazed! I'm so happy for you!"

We were all getting a bit emotional right then...all except Jeff. He just sat motionless, looking intently at us as we fought back the tears.

I had one more question. "Jeff, Evelyn tells me you read many books. Is that correct?"

326

Jeff smiled and nodded, and looked over at Evelyn, who smiled through her tears.

"What are the names of the last three books you read?"

Jeff turned to the typewriter, and pecked for a few seconds. Ev looked over at what he had written. "Which order? He has to have an order to place them in," she added.

I nodded. "Third from the latest first, please.

Jeff turned back to the typewriter. A moment later he pulled the sheet out of the machine and handed it to me.

I read slowly, "*Mathematical Principles of Natural Philosophy by Sir Isaac Newton, Behind The Front Panel: The Design & Development of 1920's Radio by David Rutland and Richard Watts, Thinking in Pictures: Autism and Visual Thought by Doctor Temple Grandin.*"

What a combination! I thought. "May I see that last book, please?" I asked.

Jackie, Evelyn, and Helen all turned beet red and looked at each other. *What kind of response is this? I only want to look at a book.*

"Do we know where that book is?" Jackie asked in a serious voice.

"It's on the shelf in the den, Mom," Evelyn replied.

"Syl, I'd love for you to see it, but—I *can't!*" Helen looked like she'd swallowed a bug!

Through the cacophony Jeff was typing quickly. He ripped the paper out of the typewriter, and thrust it in Evelyn's hands. She looked at the paper and spoke, trembling, "Jeff says, *Jacqueline and Evelyn, time to tell Sylvia who you really are. Has need to know. Still small voice.*"

The three stopped and looked at Jeff. He gave a small smile and nodded.

Jackie wiped her brow with a handkerchief, and spoke. "Okay."

*****

Sylvia: later that afternoon.

I decided to stop at the school before going to my house. I had some cleaning to finish, and in the quiet of the small deserted building I could continue to try to process the incredible story I'd been told.

As I worked in the familiar surroundings I pondered the friends I *thought* I had known. *The future? So advanced, but yet just like us? Here to help?* I would have called it insanity if I hadn't seen some of their amazing equipment in the room Jackie called *the den*. And then she played that motion picture—she called it a *video*—of her previous career, *then*... I could do without the *so-called music* of the show, but what it depicted—incredible! I guess the words of the raucous song made sense—*take me higher*—but instead of higher, they are *here*!

And Helen's known about them for five years! She certainly can keep a secret—*well, so can I.*

I occasionally glanced over at the paperback book on my desk. *Thinking in Pictures*...the photo of the middle aged woman in Western clothing sitting in a feed lot among cattle—the author. *Written seventy years in the future—but I get to read it. I hope I can stay awake in church tomorrow, because I'm going to be awake all night reading!*

I finished up in my classroom by doing a little dusting. Being close to a gravel road, the dust accumulated in the classroom quickly. I didn't want my students (or me!) sneezing from the dust. It would be nice to have a Delco Light and vacuum cleaner in the school to take care of the dust, but we didn't have the money for that. I made do with dust mops and dampened rags.

I worked my way around the classroom...and came to the insignia and star behind my desk. As I dusted the polished wood, my eyes started to well up, and not from the dust.

Lord, it was many years ago. It still affects me. Please heal me from the grief and hurt, in Your time, Your way.

I had no idea how my wonderful Lord was preparing the healing, even as I prayed.

Chapter Fifty Two

Monday, August 24th, 1925, the Templeman boarding house.

"You know, this isn't bad."

"See? You should listen to your elders once in a while!"

"Right, Marie," I laughed.

Marie Heath and I were sitting in the cozy kitchen of the Templeman house that August evening. The Templeman family had left the previous day for the annual pilgrimage to their ancestral home of West Liberty, Iowa. Charlie always insisted they go see his mother and sister during the last month before school started, but this year's trip had been delayed a week while Dorothy was recuperating from the measles. The rest of us had already suffered through them years ago, so we were able to continue about our business while Agnes and Dorothy stayed in Agnes' bedroom.

Now they had gone, on what Charlie called *a pilgrimage*, and Agnes called *torment week*.

Agnes had said, and Marie confirmed, that Charlie's mother was three times worse than he was, a veritable ogre in black cloth. I'd seen pictures, and was inclined to agree. Charlie's younger sister Irene was her mother's caretaker—*slave*, according to Agnes. She'd had every opportunity to marry thwarted by the black-robed Visage, and now approached middle age with her life pretty much confined to caring for her mother, who though confined to a wheelchair showed every sign of living to a hundred.

I had committed to minding the house for this last week of August while they were gone, as a final gift to the lady who had put up with so much from me the past six years of my *four year* college education. When they returned I would finally vacate my room off the kitchen permanently. It was time to get to Galva and begin work full time for the coal company. I had already moved most of my belongings, and cleaned up the room. The Templeman family was sorry to see me go, and I was too for that matter, but it was time to move on.

Since school wouldn't start for another week and a half, Marie and I were the only ones in the house. The first thing I had done after the family left was check Forrest's electronic gadgetry in the parlor, to make sure he hadn't left something connected to power. His radio apparatus now used alternating current, and unpleasant things happened if a rectifying power supply was left on too long unattended!

This evening I was at loose ends about what to cook for two such different appetites as mine and Marie's. She suggested we fall back on something she ate often when she was on the road touring. At her direction, I took two slices of bread and put peanut butter on them. I then fried an egg so the yolk was mostly hard, and gently laid the egg on one of the slices of bread. I put the other piece of bread on top, cut it, and we had one peanut butter and fried egg sandwich!

At her request, I made one sandwich for Marie, and two for me. I knew she was watching me as I silently prayed over the food as I always did; perhaps she thought this time I was praying I could get the sandwich down without gagging! Then I tried it, and found it actually pretty good.

"So you ate these while you were on the road?" I asked.

"Yes, Luther. We were always short on time, and usually short of money. This was filling, quick, and pretty cheap. It was easy to carry a small jar of peanut butter in my valise, and we could usually get bread and eggs somewhere."

"Did you haul that trunk in your room around with you?"

Marie smiled. "Oh, yes! I lived out of that trunk. It contained my 'street' clothes, and a selection of costumes for my various roles—we were responsible for our own costumes in those days. We had porters to carry the trunks for us…usually. Sometimes we just had to do it ourselves."

"But you're so small! How could you even move that thing, much less take it someplace?"

"We girls would help each other, and sometimes one of the gentlemen would help us, particularly if he were interested in getting to *know* one of us."

I detected the change of inflection in her voice, but replied before the meaning of her statement fully sunk in.

"I would think those of you in the troupe would get to know each other pretty well while you were touring."

Marie sat and looked at me for a moment. Her face froze, and she seemed to be looking through the back door of the house toward something far beyond.

"Wait here, Luther; I'll be right back," she said, and headed upstairs.

As I sat there finishing my second sandwich, the alternate meaning of *to know* suddenly occurred to me. I didn't know whether to apologize for taking her statement the wrong way, or not say anything. I decided to say nothing unless she mentioned it.

Marie came back downstairs and sat in her chair. It really was *her* chair, the seat built up so she could sit at the table with the proper height. She had three old mounted photographs in her hand, and she handed them to me.

"Luther, I've known you for six years now, and I believe I can trust you. I need to talk about something, and I think you're the one I can talk to. Do you mind?"

"Not at all, Marie. What is it?"

"Take a look at these photographs, Luther. Those two similar ones were taken in 1906, when I was deciding what to do after I was fired from Peter Pan. They show me as a serious, middle-aged lady, someone who could play that kind of role. What they don't show is my size! I was so small I couldn't play that kind of adult role believably."

"I can see where that could be a problem" I wondered where this was heading.

"Worse than a problem, Luther. It meant I couldn't be an actress any more. Look at the third picture now. That's me in costume for one of my favorite roles. I look just like a little girl, don't I? That photo had some retouching done to it of course, but I did look like that. That photograph was made in 1885, when I was thirty five years old! My entire career I played young girls and adolescent boys. I was that size, my voice always sounded young, and I always had my lines and movements down precisely. I was in great demand to play those parts."

"So you had a successful career?"

"Yes, I guess you could say that. I'm poor now, but I made pretty good money in those days. But…well, I lived the *actress life* too."

Now it was my turn to look directly at Marie. "I'm almost afraid to ask you this, but I really don't know what you're driving at. What is the *actress life*?"

Marie folded her hands and rested her elbows on the table. She took a deep breath and frowned.

"For a long time acting and the people who perform had a reputation as a group. We were thought of as, oh, wanton, libertine, of negotiable virtue, given to various addictions, and just not accepted in *Polite Society*. Although that reputation has lessened since I started acting, it still exists. And once I left home and started with the troupe, I found those sorts of activities held a certain amount of interest."

Marie was speaking very softly, and choosing her words carefully, but I started to understand what she was getting at. *Lord, this sounds like an opportunity to tell this lady about You! Please give me the words to say as I try to introduce her to You, and bless my feeble efforts, please!*

Marie continued.

"I found I enjoyed the attention of the gentlemen in the troupe, my fellow actors. This led to...*assignations*, to put it discretely. I never did anything like that for money, mind! But if I was attracted to a gentleman...things tended to happen. I was careful with my choices, and never contracted any social diseases...but I certainly could have."

I listened silently as Marie Heath, retired actress in her seventies, recounted her past life. Mercifully, she gave no details.

"And when I found that the same condition which accounted for my small size also precluded me from having children, I engaged in the aforesaid behavior with considerable vigor."

I thought of another explanation for her popularity with the gentlemen, but I banished it immediately, and prayed she wouldn't stumble on it.

"I should tell you the title of *Mrs. Heath* was given to me by Agnes when I moved in, so the children would not ask embarrassing questions. I never married."

She looked down at the table for a moment, then back up at me.

"Children have always liked me, because they think of me as one of them. That result of my condition has been a joy for many years...but there was the other side to my life, which I could never speak of, and really feared to think of after a time."

Up to this point Marie had recounted her life dispassionately, directly. She now started to sniffle.

"And I've never told anyone this, but I'm telling you, Luther, because it is driving me mad—lately I've had this terrible thought that at least some of the men I had...*assignations*...with were not interested in me as a woman, but as a surrogate for a child!" Marie began to sob.

Oh, my. She did come up with the thought I'd had...and it is tearing her apart! Lord, what do I say? I need Your Grace right now!

"Luther, I've been so awful! I can't go back and change my life, and I can't bear to think of what I've done! I'm lost! What shall I do?"

Marie Heath, retired actress in her seventies, had just come apart before my eyes.

Time, now.

"Just a minute, Marie; I'll be right back!"

332

I got up, took two steps to my room door, and stepped in. I grabbed my Bible, and another Bible I had stashed in case it was needed, and went back into the kitchen. Marie, tears streaming down her face, looked up at me as I sat down.

"Marie, I am honored and sobered that you've told me this. Before I say another word let me promise you your secret is safe with me. Nobody but the Lord hears this from me, and He knows all about it already."

Marie, tears streaming, looked up at me as I continued.

"You're right, you can't change your past life, just like I couldn't change mine. You say you were awful; I'd like to tell you that no, you weren't, but I'd be lying. I will tell you that I was awful, for many years. My sins, some of them, were different from yours, but they're all the same before God. And we can't change it. But I can introduce you to Someone who can. And I will right now, if I may."

Marie continued to sniffle, but nodded.

"Let me show you the cases of two women told about in the Bible, and what happened to them." I flipped to John chapter 8.

"Marie, start reading at the first verse of that chapter, and if you will read to verse 11, I think. Or I'll read it if you wish—"

"I'll read it," she said, and in a melodious voice, punctuated a few times by catches and sniffles, she read the passage.

"Thank you, Marie. What did Jesus remind the scribes and Pharisees of in this episode?"

Marie hesitated, and then replied, "That all of them had sinned too?"

"Yes, Marie, that's right. That's why they all left. Only Jesus was left. Her, and Him. What have you heard about Jesus?"

This wasn't the question I figured I'd be asking, but it just came out.

Marie seemed to be looking out the back door again, then smiled a little. "I remember now! I went to Sunday School for a few months when I was a child; the orphanage moved and I didn't find another church. I remember hearing that Jesus never sinned."

"That's right, Marie. The only One in the 'form of a man' who never sinned. So could He have cast that first stone?"

"Yes."

"What did he say to her?"

"Neither do I condemn you."

She still had a good memory.

"And what else?"

"Go and sin no more."

333

"What do you think He did, that He told her He didn't condemn her?"

Marie got a funny look on her face. "He forgave what she'd done!"

"Exactly. And what did the woman call Jesus?"

"Lord."

"If He forgave her sins, she had reason to call Him that."

From there we moved to the story of the woman at the well in John 4. Marie readily identified with that woman, and found Jesus' answers to the woman also answered questions she had. From there we moved to several passages in the book of Romans.

In a few minutes Marie Heath, retired actress in her seventies, bowed her head and trusted Jesus to save her. Her prayer that evening seemed very childlike—in its faith, not its verbiage.

We talked until close to midnight. I think we went through three pots of coffee...and several trips upstairs each. I told her more fully of what had happened to me since that day in 1918, and answered her questions as best I could. I gave her the spare Bible, of course; during the next week she spent about twelve hours a day reading it, often by the light of the Rainaud lamp on the dining room table.

Over the years I'd noticed Marie didn't go out very much, saying this or that hurt, or she didn't feel well. That next Saturday, though, I needed to travel to Metamora to take care of a few things, and substitute for Dennis Lepper in the Sunday services. To my amazement, Marie invited herself along! She left a note on the kitchen table so Agnes would know where she was in case they came home early, and we took off.

Marie had met Pa and Inge at the recital in 1921. She was thrilled to see them again, and the three of them talked for most of the weekend. She came to church with us on Sunday, and loved the services. She went down front at the invitation on her own initiative, to testify of what Jesus had done for her. Pastor Reem, and *The Deb*, had us all over for Sunday dinner. Marie was baptized after the evening service.

As a result of that weekend, Pa and Inge asked Marie to move in with them—and Marie agreed! I was amazed she would do that after so many years with the Templemans, and said so.

"I've had a great time with the Templeman family," Marie replied, "but now I need to spend time with people who know Christ, to learn from them while I still have time to grow in the Faith. As nice as Agnes and the children are, I won't get that living with them."

So there, I thought.

For the next week I found myself borrowing the service car to make multiple trips from Peoria to Metamora, and from either place to Galva.

To my great relief, Inge took a week off from her job at the Washington Library to ride over to Peoria with me, carefully pack Marie's room, and help her unpack and decorate her new room in Metamora. Her new room was actually my old room; Pa and Inge suggested I finally give it up, and I couldn't imagine a better reason to do so! When I visited I'd stay in the small guest bedroom.

Agnes was surprised, to say the least, but accepted Marie's explanation better than I expected. It helped that I quietly paid the regular room and board rate for Marie's room, which she hadn't been able to pay in years, through the end of the year, with no refund if she rented her room, which I knew she would. Agnes was a businesswoman first, last, and always.

So I now had an adopted grandmother, who was also my sister, in the Lord. I commented to the Lord that all this was quite enough excitement for one year, thank You very much!

Heh.

About the Author

Donald Bowers served as a Naval officer and teacher before spending over thirty years as a Case Manager for adults with intellectual disabilities. He finally got around to writing in his late fifties. He lives in Galesburg, Illinois with his wife, Ellen Anne Eddy Bowers, two cats and a greyhound.

Want to Learn More?

With Patience Wait, and all the other *According to His Purpose* novels are inspired by actual historical people, places, inventions, and times. Learn more at Don's web site,
www.acordingtohispurposeweb.wordpress.com
Also check there for information on upcoming books by Don.